Losing Hope
&
Finding
Cinderella

Also by Colleen Hoover

Losing Hope
&
Finding Cinderella

Colleen Hoover

SIMON &
SCHUSTER

London · New York · Amsterdam/Antwerp · Sydney/Melbourne · Toronto · New Delhi

First published as a bind-up edition in Great Britain by Simon & Schuster UK Ltd, 2025

Losing Hope first published in Great Britain by Simon & Schuster UK Ltd, 2013. Originally published in the United States by Atria Paperback, an imprint of Simon & Schuster, LLC, 2013

Finding Cinderella first published in Great Britain by Simon & Schuster UK Ltd, 2014. Originally published in the United States by Atria Paperback, an imprint of Simon & Schuster, LLC, 2014

3 5 7 9 10 8 6 4 2

Simon & Schuster UK Ltd, 1st Floor
222 Gray's Inn Road, London WC1X 8HB

Simon & Schuster Australia, Sydney
Simon & Schuster India, New Delhi

www.simonandschuster.co.uk
www.simonandschuster.com.au
www.simonandschuster.co.in

The authorised representative in the EEA is Simon & Schuster Netherlands BV, Herculesplein 96, 3584 AA Utrecht, Netherlands. info@simonandschuster.nl

Simon & Schuster strongly believes in freedom of expression and stands against censorship in all its forms. For more information, visit BooksBelong.com

A CIP catalogue record for this book
is available from the British Library

Paperback ISBN: 978-1-3985-4920-3
eBook ISBN: 978-1-3985-4921-0

Printed and Bound in the UK using 100% Renewable Electricity
at CPI Group (UK) Ltd

MIX
Paper | Supporting
responsible forestry
FSC
www.fsc.org   FSC® C013604

This book is dedicated to my husband and sons,
for their endless, selfless support.

Losing Hope

Chapter One

My heart rate is signaling for me to just walk away. Les has reminded me more than once that it's not my business. She's never been a brother before, though. She has no idea how hard it is to sit back and *not* let it be my business. That's why, right now, this son-of-a-bitch is my number-one priority.

I slide my hands into the back pockets of my jeans and hope to hell I can keep them there. I'm standing behind the couch, looking down at him. I don't know how long it'll take him to notice I'm here. Considering the grip he has on the chick straddling his lap, I doubt he'll notice for a while. I remain behind them for several minutes while the party continues around us, everyone completely unaware that I'm a fraction away from losing my mind. I would take out my phone so that I'd have evidence, but I couldn't do that to Les. She doesn't need a visual.

"Hey," I finally say, unable to contain my silence a second longer. If I have to watch him palm this chick's breast one more time without a single ounce of respect for his relationship with Les, I'll rip his fucking hand off.

Grayson tears his mouth away from hers and tilts his head back, looking up at me with glossed-over eyes. I can see the fear settle in when it clicks—when he finally realizes that the last person he thought would be here tonight actually showed up.

"Holder," he says, pushing the girl off his lap. He struggles to his feet but can hardly stand up straight. He looks at me pleadingly, pointing at the girl, who's now adjusting her barely-there skirt. "This isn't . . . it's not what it looks like."

I slide my hands out of my back pockets and fold my arms across my chest. My fist is closer to him now and I have to clench it, knowing how good it would feel to punch his face in.

I look down to the floor and inhale a breath. Then another. And one more just for show, since I'm really enjoying watching him squirm. I shake my head and raise my eyes back to his. "Give me your phone."

The confusion on his face would be comical if I weren't so pissed. He laughs and attempts to back up a step, but bumps into the coffee table. He catches himself by pressing his hand onto the glass and straightens back up. "Get your own fucking phone," he mumbles. He doesn't look back at me as he maneuvers his way around the coffee table. I calmly walk around the couch and intercept him, holding out my hand.

"Give me your phone, Grayson. *Now*."

I'm not really at an advantage sizewise, since we're about the same build. However, I'm definitely at an advantage if you take my anger into consideration, and Grayson can clearly see that. He takes a step back, which probably isn't a very smart move considering he's backing himself straight into the corner of the living room. He fumbles with his pocket and finally pulls out his phone.

"What the hell do you want my phone for?" he says. I grab it out of his hands and dial Les's number without hitting send. I hand it back to him.

"Call her. Tell her what a bastard you are and end it."

Grayson looks down at his phone, then back up at me. "Go fuck yourself," he spits.

I inhale a calming breath, then roll my neck and pop my jaw. When that doesn't help ease my urge to make him bleed, I reach forward, grab the collar of his shirt and shove him hard against the wall, pinning his neck with my forearm. I remind myself that if I kick his ass before he makes the call, my remaining calm for the past ten minutes will have been pointless.

My teeth are clenched, my jaw is tight, and my pulse is pounding in my head. I've never hated anyone more than in this moment. The intensity of what I wish I could do to him right now is even scaring *me*.

I look him hard in the eyes and let him know how the next few minutes are about to play out. "Grayson," I say through clenched teeth. "Unless you want me to do what I really want to do to you right now, you will put the phone to your ear, you will call my sister, and you will end it. Then you're going to hang up the phone and never speak to her again." I press my arm harder against his neck, taking note of the fact that his face is now redder than his shirt, due to lack of oxygen.

"Fine," he grumbles, attempting to free himself from the hold I have on him. I wait until he looks down at the phone and hits send before I release my arm and let go of his shirt. He puts the phone to his ear and never stops looking at me as we both stand still and wait for Les to answer.

I know what this will do to her, but she has no idea what he does behind her back. No matter how many times she hears it from other people, he's somehow able to weasel his way back into her life every time.

Not this time. Not if I have any control over it. I won't sit back and let him do this to my sister anymore.

"Hey," he says into the phone. He tries to turn away from me to speak to her, but I shove his shoulder back against the wall. He winces.

"No, babe," he says nervously. "I'm at Jaxon's house." There's a long pause while he listens to her speak. "I know that's what I said, but I lied. That's why I'm calling. Les, I . . . I think we need some space."

I shake my head, letting him know that he needs to make it an absolute break-up. I'm not looking for him to give her space. I'm looking for him to give my sister permanent freedom.

He rolls his eyes and flips me off with his free hand. "I'm breaking up with you," he says flatly. He allows her to talk while he remains silent. The fact that he's showing no remorse whatsoever proves what a heartless dick he is. My hands are shaking and my chest tightens, knowing exactly what this is doing to Les right now. I hate myself for forcing this to happen, but Les deserves better, even if she doesn't think she does.

"I'm hanging up now," he says into the phone.

I shove his head back against the wall and force him to look at me. "Apologize to her," I say quietly, not wanting her to hear me in the background. He closes his eyes and sighs, then ducks his head.

"I'm sorry, Lesslie. I didn't want to do this." He pulls the phone from his ear and abruptly ends the call. He stares at the screen for several seconds. "I hope you're happy," he says, looking back up at me. "Because you just broke your sister's heart."

That's the last thing Grayson says to me. My fist meets his jaw twice before he hits the floor. I shake out my hand, back away from him, and make my way to the exit. Before I even reach my car, my phone is buzzing in my back pocket. I pull it out and don't even look at the screen before answering it.

"Hey," I say, attempting to control the trembling anger in my voice when I hear her crying on the other end. "I'm on my way, Les. It'll be okay, I'm on my way."

It's been an entire day since Grayson made the call, but I still feel guilty, so I tack on an extra two miles to my evening run for self-inflicted punishment. Seeing Les torn up like she was last night wasn't something I had expected. I realize now that having him call her like I did probably wasn't the best way of handling things, but there's no way I could just sit back and allow him to dick around on her like he was.

The most unexpected thing about Les's reaction was that her anger wasn't solely placed on Grayson. It was as if she was pissed at the entire male population. She kept referring to men as "sick bastards," pacing her bedroom floor back and forth, while I just sat there and watched her vent. She finally broke down, crawled into bed, and cried herself to sleep. I lay awake, knowing I had a hand in her heartache. I stayed in her room the whole night, partly to make sure she was okay, but mostly because I didn't want her picking up the phone and calling Grayson in a moment of desperation.

She's stronger than I give her credit for, though. She didn't attempt to call him last night and she's made no attempt to call him today. She didn't get much sleep last night, so she went to her room before lunch to nap. However, I've been pausing outside her bedroom door throughout the day just to make sure I couldn't hear her on the phone, so I know she hasn't made any attempts to call him. At least while I've been home. In fact, I'm pretty sure the heartless phone call from him last night was exactly what she needed to finally see him for who he really is.

I kick my shoes off at the door and walk to the kitchen to refill my water. It's Saturday night and I would normally be heading out with Daniel, but I already texted him to let him know I was staying in tonight. Les made me promise I would stay in with her because she didn't want to go out and chance running into Grayson yet. She's lucky she's cool, because I don't know many seventeen-year-old guys who would give up a Saturday night to watch chick flicks with his heartbroken sister. But then again, most siblings don't have what Les and I have. I don't know if our close relationship has anything to do with the fact that we're twins. She's my only sibling, so I don't have anything to compare us to. She might argue that I'm too protective of her, and there may be some truth to that argument, but I don't plan on changing anytime soon. Or ever.

I run up the stairs, pull my shirt off, and push open the bathroom door. I turn the water on, then walk across the hall and knock on her bedroom door. "I'm taking a quick shower, will you order the pizza?"

I brace my hand against her door and reach down to pull my socks off. I turn around and toss them into the bathroom, then beat on her door again. "Les!"

When she doesn't respond, I sigh and look up at the ceiling. If she's on the phone with him, I'll be pissed. But if she's on the phone with him, it probably means he's telling her the break-up was all my fault and *she'll* be the one who's pissed. I wipe my palms on my shorts and open the door to her bedroom, preparing for another heated lecture on how I need to mind my own business.

I see Les on her bed after I walk into her room, and I'm immediately taken back to when I was a little boy. Back to the moment that changed me. Everything about me. Everything about the world *around* me. My whole world turned from a place full of vibrant colors to a dull, lifeless gray. The sky, the grass, the trees . . . all the things that were once beautiful were stripped of their magnificence the moment I realized I was responsible for our best friend Hope's disappearance.

I never looked at people the same way. I never looked at nature the same way. I never looked at my future the same way. Everything went from having a meaning, a purpose, and a reason, to simply being a second-rate version of what life was *supposed* to be like. My once effervescent world was suddenly a blurred, gray, colorless photocopy.

Just like Les's eyes.

They aren't hers. They're open. They're looking right at me from her position on the bed.

But they aren't hers.

The color in her eyes is gone. This girl is a gray, colorless photocopy of my sister.

My Les.

I can't move. I wait for her to blink, to laugh, to revel in the twisted aftermath of the sick, fucking joke she's playing right now. I wait for my heart to start beating again, for my lungs to start working again. I wait for control of my body to return to me because I don't know who has control of it right now. *I* sure as hell don't. I wait and I wait and I wonder how long she can keep this up. How long can people keep their eyes open like that? How long can people not breathe before their body jerks for that desperately needed gasp of air?

How fucking long before I do something to *help* her?

My hands are touching her face, grabbing her arm, shaking her whole body until she's in my arms and I'm pulling her onto my lap. The empty pill bottle falls out of her hand and lands on the floor but I refuse to look at it. Her eyes are still lifeless and she's no longer looking at me as the head between my hands falls backward every time I try to lift it up.

She doesn't flinch when I scream her name, and she doesn't wince when I slap her, and she doesn't react when I start to cry.

She doesn't do a goddamned thing.

She doesn't even tell me it'll be okay when every single ounce of whatever was left inside my chest is propelled out of me the moment I realize that the very best part of me is dead.

Chapter Two

"Will you look for her pink top and the black pleated pants?" my mother asks. She keeps her eyes trained on the paperwork laid out in front of her. The man from the funeral home reaches across the table and points to a spot on the form.

"Just a few more pages, Beth," he says. My mother mechanically signs the forms without question. She's trying to keep it together until they leave, but I know as soon as they walk out the front door she'll break down again. It's only been forty-eight hours, but I can tell just by looking at her that she's about to experience it all over again.

You would think a person could only die once. You would think you would only find your sister's lifeless body once. You would think you would only have to watch your mother's reaction once after finding out her only daughter is dead.

Once is so far from accurate.

It happens repeatedly.

Every single time I close my eyes I see Les's eyes. Every time my mother looks at me, she's watching me tell her that her daughter is dead for the second time. For the third time. For the thousandth time. Every time I take a breath or blink or speak, I experience her death all over again. I don't sit here and wonder if the fact that she's dead will ever sink in. I sit here and wonder when I'll stop having to watch her die.

"Holder, they need an outfit for her," my mother repeats again after noticing I haven't moved. "Go to her room and get the pink shirt with the long sleeves. It's her favorite one, she'd want to wear it."

She knows I don't want to go into Les's bedroom any more than she does. I push my chair away from the table and head upstairs. "Les is dead," I mutter to myself. "She doesn't give a shit what she's wearing."

I pause outside her door, knowing I'll have to watch her die all over again the moment I open it. I haven't been in here since I found her and I really had no intention of *ever* coming back in here.

I walk inside and shut the door behind me, then make my way to her closet. I do my best not to think about it.

Pink shirt.

Don't think about her.

Long sleeves.

Don't think about how you would do anything to go back to Saturday night.

Pleated black pants.

Don't think about how much you fucking hate yourself right now for letting her down.

But I do. I think about it and I become hurt and angry all over again. I grab a fistful of shirts hanging in the closet and rip them as hard as I can off their hangers until they fall to the closet floor. I grip the frame on top of the door and squeeze my eyes shut, listening to the sound of the now empty hangers swinging back and forth. I try to focus on the fact that I'm in here to grab two things and leave, but I can't move. I can't stop replaying the moment that I walked into this bedroom and found her.

I fall to my knees on the floor, look over at her bed, and watch her die one more time.

I sit back against the closet door and close my eyes, remaining in this position for however long it takes me to realize that I don't want to be in here. I turn around and rummage through the shirts that are now on the closet floor until I find the long-sleeved pink one. I look up at the pants hanging from their hangers and I grab a pair of black pleated ones. I toss them to the side and begin to push up from the floor, but immediately sit back down when I see a thick, leather-bound notebook on the bottom shelf of her closet.

I grab it and pull it onto my lap, then lean back against the wall and stare at the cover. I've seen this notebook before. It was a gift to her from Dad about three years ago, but Les told me she'd never use it because she knew the notebook was just a request made by her therapist. Les hated therapy, and I was never sure why Mom encouraged her to go. We both went for a while after Mom and Dad split up, but I stopped attending the sessions once they started interfering with junior high football practice. Mom didn't seem to mind that I didn't go, but Les continued with the weekly sessions up until two days ago . . . when her actions made it clear the therapy wasn't exactly helping.

I flip the notebook open to the first page and it doesn't surprise me that it's blank. I wonder, if she had used the notebook like the therapist suggested, would it have made a difference?

I doubt it. I don't know what could have saved Les from herself. Certainly not a pen and paper.

I pull the pen out of the spiral binding, then press the tip of the pen to the paper and begin to write her a letter. I don't even know why I'm writing her. I don't know if she's in a place where she can see me right now, or if she's even in a place at *all*, but in case she can see this . . . I want her to know how her selfish decision affected me. How hopeless she left me. *Literally* hopeless. And completely alone. And so, so incredibly sorry.

Chapter Two-and-a-half

Les,

You left your jeans in the middle of your bedroom floor. It looks like you just stepped out of them. It's weird. Why would you leave your jeans on the floor if you knew what you were about to do? Wouldn't you at least throw them in the hamper? Did you not think about what would happen after I found you and how someone would eventually have to pick your jeans up and do something with them? Well, I'm not picking them up. And I'm not hanging all your shirts back up, either.

Anyway. I'm in your closet. On the floor. I just don't really know what I want to say to you right now, or what I want to ask you. Of course the only question on everyone else's mind right now is "Why did she do it?" But I'm not going to ask you why you did it for two reasons.

1) You can't answer me. You're dead.
2) I don't know if I really care why you did it. There isn't anything about your life that would give you a good enough reason to do what you did. And you probably already know that if you can see Mom right now. She's completely devastated.

You know, I never really knew what it meant to actually be devastated. I thought we were devastated after we lost Hope. What happened to her was definitely tragic for us, but the way we felt was nothing compared to how you've made Mom feel. She's so incredibly devastated; she gives the word a whole new meaning. I wish the use of the word could be restricted to situations like this. It's absurd that people are allowed to use it to describe anything other than how a mother feels when she loses her child. Because that's the only situation in this entire world worthy of the term.

Dammit, I miss you so much. I'm so sorry I let you down. I'm sorry I wasn't able to see what was really going on behind your eyes every time you told me you were fine.

So, yeah. Why, Les? Why did you do it?

H

Chapter Two-and-three-quarters

Les,

Well, congratulations. You're pretty popular. Not only did you fill the parking lot of the funeral home with cars, but you also filled the lot next door and both churches down the street. That's a lot of cars.

I held it together, though; mostly for Mom's sake. Dad looked almost as bad as Mom. The whole funeral was really weird. It made me wonder, had you died in a car wreck or from something more mainstream, would people's reactions have been different? If you hadn't purposely overdosed (that's the term Mom prefers), then I think people might have been a little less weird. It was like they were scared of us, or maybe they thought purposely overdosing was contagious. They discussed it like we weren't even in the same room. So many stares and whispers and pitiful smiles. I just wanted to grab Mom and pull her out of there and protect her from the fact that I knew she was reliving your death with every hug and every tear and every smile.

Of course I couldn't help but think everyone was acting like they were because they blamed us in a way. I could tell what they were thinking.

How could a family not know this would happen?

How could they not see the signs?

What kind of mother is she?

What kind of brother doesn't notice how depressed his own twin sister is?

Luckily, once your funeral began, everyone's focus was momentarily taken off us and placed on the slideshow. There were a lot of pictures of you and me. You were happy in all of them. There were a lot of pictures of you and your friends, and you were happy in all of those, too. Pictures of you with Mom and Dad before the divorce; pictures of you with Mom and Brian after she remarried; pictures of you with Dad and Pamela after he remarried.

But it wasn't until the very last picture came up on the screen that it hit me. It was the picture of you and me in front of our old house. The one that was taken about six months after Hope went missing? You still had the bracelet on that matched the one you gave her the day she was taken. I noticed you stopped wearing it a couple of years ago, but I've never asked about it. I know you don't really like to talk about her.

Anyway, back to the picture. I had my arm around your neck and we were both laughing and smiling at the camera. It's the same smile you flashed in all the other pictures. It got me to thinking about how every picture I've ever seen of you; you have that same exact, identical smile. There isn't a single picture of you with a frown on your face. Or a scowl. Or a blank expression. It's like you spent your whole life trying to keep up this false appearance. For whom, I don't know. Maybe you were scared that a camera would permanently capture an honest feeling of yours. Because let's face it, you weren't happy all the time. All those nights you cried yourself to sleep? All those nights you needed me to hold you while you cried, but you refused to tell me what was wrong? No one with a genuine smile would cry to themselves like that. And I realize you had issues, Les. I knew our life and the things that happened to us affected you differently than they did me. But how was I supposed to know that they were as serious as they were if you never let it show? If you never told me?

Maybe... and I hate to think this. But maybe I didn't know you. I thought I did, but I didn't. I don't think I knew you at all. I knew the girl who cried at night. I knew the girl who smiled in the pictures. But I didn't know the girl that linked that smile with those tears. I have no idea why you flashed fake smiles, but cried real tears. When a guy loves a girl, especially his sister, he's supposed to know what makes her smile and what makes her cry.

But I didn't. And I don't. So I'm sorry, Les. I'm so sorry I let you go on pretending that you were okay when obviously you were so far from it.

H

Chapter Three

"Beth, why don't you go to bed?" Brian says to my mother. "You're exhausted. Go get some sleep."

My mother shakes her head and continues stirring, despite the pleas from my stepdad for her to take a break. We've got enough food in the refrigerator to feed an army, yet she insists on cooking for everyone just so we don't have to eat the *sympathy food*, as she refers to it. I'm so sick of fried chicken. It seems to be the go-to meal for anyone dropping food off at the house. I've had fried chicken for every meal since the morning after Les died, and that was four days ago.

I walk to the stove and take the spoon out of her hands, then rub her shoulder with my free hand while I stir. She leans against me and sighs. It's not a good sigh, either. It's a sigh that all but says, "I'm done."

"Please, go sit on the couch. I can finish this," I say to her. She nods and walks aimlessly into the living room. I watch from the kitchen as she takes a seat and leans her head back into the couch, looking up to the ceiling. Brian takes a seat next to her and pulls her to him. I don't even have to hear her to know she's crying again. I can see it in the way she slumps against him and grabs hold of his shirt.

I look away.

"Maybe you should come stay with us, Dean," my father says, leaning against the counter. "Just for a little while. It might do you some good to get away."

He's the only one who still calls me Dean. I've been going by Holder since I was eight, but the fact that I was named after him may be why he never took to calling me anything other than Dean. I only see him a couple of times a year, so it doesn't bother me too much that he still calls me Dean. I still hate the name, though.

I look at him, then back to my mother still holding on to Brian in the living room. "I can't, Dad. I'm not leaving her. Especially now."

He's been trying to get me to move to Austin with him since they divorced. The truth is, I like it here. I haven't liked visiting my old hometown since I moved away. Too many things remind me of Hope when I'm there.

But I guess too many things are going to start reminding me of Les, here.

"Well, my offer doesn't expire," he says. "You know that."

I nod and switch off the burner. "It's ready," I say.

Brian comes back to the kitchen with Pam and we all take seats at the table, but my mother remains in the living room, softly crying into the couch throughout dinner.

I'm waving good-bye to my father and Pam when Amy pulls up in front of our house. She waits for my father's car to clear, then she pulls into our driveway. I walk to the driver's side door and open it for her.

She smiles half-heartedly and flips the visor down, wiping the mascara from underneath the frame of her sunglasses. It's been dark for over an hour now, yet she's still wearing sunglasses. That can only mean she's been crying.

I haven't really talked to her much in the past four days, but I don't have to ask her how she's holding up. She and Les have been best friends for seven years. If there's anyone that feels like I do right now, it's her. And I'm not even sure if *I'm* holding up all that well.

"Where's Thomas?" I ask when she steps out of the car.

She pushes her blonde hair away from her face with her sunglasses, adjusting them on top of her head. "He's at his house. He had to go help his dad with some yard stuff after school."

I don't know how long the two of them have been dating, but they were together before Les and I even moved here. And we moved here in the fourth grade, so it's been a while.

"How's your mom?" she asks. As soon as she says it, she shakes her head apologetically. "I'm sorry, Holder. That was a really stupid question. I promised myself I wouldn't be one of those people."

"Believe me, you're not," I assure her. I motion behind me. "You coming inside?"

She nods and glances at the house, then to me. "Do you mind if I go up to her room? It's fine if you don't want me up there yet. It's just that she had a few pictures I'd really like to have."

"No, it's fine." Based on the relationship she had with Les, Amy has just as much right to be in Les's bedroom as I do. I know Les would want Amy to take whatever it is she wants.

She follows me into the house and up the stairs. I notice my mother isn't on the couch anymore. Brian must have finally coaxed her into going to bed. I walk to the top of the stairs with Amy, but have no desire to go into Les's room with her. I nudge my head toward my bedroom. "I'll be in my room if you need me."

She inhales a deep, nervous breath and nods while releasing it. "Thanks," she says, eyeing Les's door warily. She takes a reluctant step toward the bedroom, so I turn away and head to my room. I shut the door behind me and take a seat on the bed, picking up Les's notebook while I lean back against my headboard. I've already written her today, but I grab a pen because I've got nothing better to do than write to her again. Or at least there's nothing else I *want* to do because it all leads back to thoughts of her anyway.

Chapter Three-and-a-half

Les,

Amy's here. She's in your room, going through your shit.

I wonder if she had any clue as to what you were about to do? I know sometimes girls share stuff with their girlfriends that they wouldn't share with anyone else—even twin brothers. Did you ever tell her how you really felt? Did you give her any hints at all? I'm really hoping you didn't, because that would mean she probably feels pretty damn guilty right about now. She doesn't deserve to feel guilty over what you did, Les. She's been your best friend for seven years now, so I hope to hell you thought about that before you made such a selfish decision.

I feel guilty for what you did, but I deserve to feel guilty. There's a responsibility that comes along with being a brother that doesn't necessarily come along with being a best friend. It was my job to protect you, not Amy's. So she doesn't deserve to feel guilty.

Maybe that was my problem. Maybe I spent so much time trying to protect you from Grayson that I never thought who I really needed to be protecting you from was yourself.

H

*   *   *

There's a light tap on my bedroom door, so I close the notebook and set it on the nightstand. Amy pushes open the door and I sit up on the bed. I motion for her to come in so she eases through the door and shuts it behind her. She walks over to my dresser and sets the pictures she collected down, running her finger over the top one. Tears are silently streaming down her cheeks.

"Come here," I say, holding a hand out to her. She walks closer to me and takes my hand, then completely breaks down the second she makes eye contact with me. I continue to pull her forward until she's on the bed and I wrap my arms around her. She curls up against my chest, sobbing uncontrollably. She's shaking so hard and it's almost a devastated cry, but like I said before, *devastated* should be reserved for mothers.

I close my eyes tightly and try not to let it all hit me like it's hitting Amy right now, but it's hard. I can hold it in for my mother because she needs me to be strong for her. Amy doesn't, though. If Amy feels anything like I do, then she just needs to know there's someone else out there just as blindsided and heartbroken as she is.

"Shh," I say, stroking her hair. I know she doesn't want me to console her with empty, overused words. She just needs someone to understand how she feels and I may be the only one she knows who truly does. I don't tell her to try to stop crying, because I know it's impossible. I press my cheek against her head, hating the fact that I'm now crying, too. I've done a pretty damn good job of keeping it in, but I can't anymore. I continue to hold her and she continues to hold on to me because it's nice to be able to find solace in such an ugly, lonely situation.

Listening to Amy cry reminds me of all the nights I used to be in this same position with Les. She wouldn't want me to talk to her or help her stop crying. Les just needed me to hold her and let her cry, even if I had no idea why she needed it. Just being able to be here for Amy in this same small way gives me that familiar sense of being needed like I used to feel with Les. I haven't felt needed since Les decided she didn't need *anyone*.

"I'm so sorry," Amy says, her voice muffled by my shirt.

"For what?"

She catches her breath and attempts to stop crying, but her effort is wasted with the new tears that follow. "I should have known, Holder. I had no idea. I was her best friend and I feel like everyone blames me and . . . I don't know. Maybe they should. I don't know. Maybe I've been so wrapped up in my relationship with Thomas that I missed something she was trying to tell me."

I continue stroking her hair, empathizing with every word coming out of her mouth. "You and me both," I sigh. I wipe the moisture away from my eyes with the back of my hand. "You know, I keep trying to pinpoint moments that might have changed the outcome. Things I might have said to her or things she might have said to me. But even if I was able to go back and change something about the past, I'm not sure that it would have changed the outcome. You don't know that, either. Les is the only one who knows for sure why she went through with it and unfortunately she's the only one not here to enlighten us."

Amy lets out a small laugh, although I'm not sure why. She pulls back slightly and looks at me with a solemn expression. "She better be glad she's not here, because I'm so mad at her, Holder." Her somberness gives way to another sob and she brings a hand to her eyes. "I'm so, so mad at her for not confiding in me and I feel like I can't say that to anyone but you," she whispers.

I move her hand away from her face and look her in the eyes because I don't want her to feel like I'm judging her for that comment. "Don't feel guilty, Amy. Okay?"

She nods and smiles a sympathetic smile, then looks down at our hands resting on the pillow between us. I lay my hand on top of hers and smooth reassuring strokes across the top of it with my fingers. I know how she feels and she knows how I feel and it's good to have that, even if only for a moment.

I want to tell her thank you for being there for Les all these years, but it seems so inappropriate to thank her for being there when she's feeling the exact opposite right now. Instead, I remain quiet and bring my hand up to her face. I don't know if it's the magnitude of the moment or the fact that she made me feel somewhat needed again or if it's simply because my head and my heart have been numb for so many days. Whatever it is, it's here and I don't want it to go away yet. I just let it completely take over while I slowly lean forward and press my mouth to hers.

I didn't intend to kiss her. In fact, I expect myself to pull away any second, but I don't. I expect her to push me away, but she doesn't. The moment my mouth meets hers, she parts her lips and sighs as if this is exactly what she needs from me. Oddly enough, that makes me want to kiss her even more. I kiss her, knowing she's my sister's best friend. I kiss her, knowing she has a boyfriend. I kiss her, knowing this isn't something I would do with her under any circumstance other than in this moment.

She slides her hand up my arm and slips her fingers inside the sleeve of my shirt, lightly tracing the contours of the muscles in my arm. I pull her closer to the middle of the bed with me and deepen our kiss. The more we kiss, the more we both recognize the fact that desire and need might just be the only thing that can minimize grief. We simultaneously grow more impatient, doing whatever we can to rid ourselves of the grief completely. Every stroke of her hand against my skin pulls me farther out of my own mind and more into the moment with her, so I kiss her more desperately, needing her to take my mind *completely* away from my life right now. My hand makes its way up her shirt and the second I cup her breast, she moans and digs her nails into my forearm, arching her back.

That's a nonverbal cue for *yes* if I've ever seen one.

I've only got two things remaining on my mind as she begins to pull off my shirt and my hands are eagerly fumbling with the zipper on her jeans.

1. *I need to get these clothes off her.*
2. *Thomas.*

I normally don't make a habit of thinking about other guys while I'm making out with girls, but I normally don't make a habit of making out with other guys' *girls*. Amy isn't mine to kiss, but here I am doing it anyway. Her clothes aren't mine to be helping her out of, but here I am doing it anyway. Her panties aren't something I should be slipping my hand inside of, but here I am doing it anyway.

I pull away from her mouth when I touch her and watch as she moans and presses her head back against my pillow. I keep doing what I'm doing to her with one hand while I lean across the bed and pull a condom out of the drawer with my other hand. I tear it open with my teeth, watching her intently the whole time. I know that neither of us is in the right frame of mind right now or this wouldn't be happening. Regardless if we're in the right frame of mind or not, at least we're in the *same* frame of mind. I'm hoping we are, anyway.

I know how incredibly and completely wrong it is to ask a girl about her boyfriend when she's thirty seconds away from completely forgetting all about him, but I have to. I don't want her regretting this any more than she already will. Than we *both* will.

"Amy?" I whisper. "What about Thomas?"

She whimpers slightly and keeps her eyes closed, bringing her palms up to my chest. "He's at his house," she mutters, giving no hint that the mention of his name is making her want to stop what we're doing. "He had to go help his dad with some yard stuff after school."

Her exact repetition of the answer she gave me when I asked about him in the driveway makes me laugh. She opens her eyes and looks up at me, probably confused about why I would laugh at a time like this. She just smiles, though. I'm thankful she smiled, because I'm really sick of everyone's tears. I'm so damn sick of all the tears.

And *shit*. If she doesn't feel guilty right this second, then I'm *sure* as hell not about to feel guilty. We can regret this all we need to later.

I lower my mouth to hers at the exact moment she gasps, then moans loudly—completely and wholeheartedly forgetting all about her boyfriend. Every last bit of her attention is one hundred percent focused on the movement of my hand, and every last bit of my attention is one hundred percent focused on getting this condom on before she starts thinking about her boyfriend again.

I ease myself on top of her, ease my mouth back to hers, ease myself inside her, and completely take advantage of the situation, knowing how much I'll regret it later. Knowing how much I *already* regret it.

But here I am, doing it anyway.

She's dressed and sitting on the edge of my bed, putting on her shoes. I've already got my jeans on and I'm walking to the bedroom door, not sure what to say. I have no idea how or why any of that just happened, and based on the look on her face, neither does she. She stands up and walks toward the door, picking up the pictures she grabbed from Les's room as she passes by my dresser. I hold the door open, unsure if I should follow her out or kiss her good-bye or tell her I'll call her.

What the hell did I just do?

She walks into the hallway and pauses, then turns around to face me. She doesn't make eye contact, though. She just stares at the pictures in her hands. "I just came for pictures, right?" she asks cautiously. A worried frown consumes her face and I realize she's afraid I might think what just happened between us was more than it actually was.

I want to reassure her that I'm not going to say anything. I lift her chin so that she's looking me in the eyes and I smile at her. "You came for pictures. That's it, Amy. And Thomas is at home, helping his dad with the yard work."

She laughs, if you can even call it that, then she looks at me appreciatively. There's an awkward silence for a moment before she finally laughs again. "What the hell *was* that, anyway?" she says, waving her hand in the direction of my bedroom. "That's not us, Holder. We're not that type of people."

We're *not* that type of people. I agree with that. I lean my head against the doorframe and already feel the regret seeping in. I don't know what came over me or why the fact that she's not remotely mine for the taking didn't stop me in my tracks. The only excuse I can come up with is that whatever happened between us just now is a direct product of our grief. And our grief is a direct product of Les's selfish decision.

"Let's blame it on Les," I say, only half-teasing. "It wouldn't have happened if she had been here."

Amy smiles. "Yeah," she says, squinting playfully. "What a bitch, making us do something despicable like that. How dare she."

I laugh. "Right?"

She holds up the pictures in her hand. "Thanks for . . ." she looks at the pictures and pauses for a moment, then brings her eyes back to mine. "Just . . . thank you, Holder. For listening."

I acknowledge her thanks with a single nod and watch as she turns to head down the stairs. I close the door and walk back to my bed, picking up the notebook on the way over. I open it up to the letter where I left off before Amy walked into my room an hour earlier.

Chapter Three-and-three-quarters

Les,

What happened with Amy just now was all your fault.
Just so we're clear.

   H

Chapter Four

Les,

Happy two-week deathiversary. Harsh? Maybe so, but I'm not apologizing. I have to go back to school Monday and I'm not looking forward to it at all. Daniel has been keeping me up to date on all the rumors, despite the fact that I keep telling him I don't give a shit. Of course everyone thinks you killed yourself because of Grayson, but I know that isn't true. You were pretending to be alive long before you ever met Grayson.

And then there's the whole incident that I still haven't told you about. The one that involved me forcing Grayson to break up with you? It's a complicated story, but because of that night, everyone is now saying that I was indirectly responsible for your suicide. Daniel says people are even sympathizing with Grayson and the asshole is eating it up.

The best part about this particular rumor is that apparently my immense guilt over the hand I played in your suicide is causing me to be suicidal. And if that's what the masses are saying, then it must be true, right?

To be honest, I'm way too scared to kill myself. Don't tell anyone that. (Not that you could now, even if you

wanted to.) But it's true. I'm a pussy when it comes to
the fact that I have no idea what to expect after this
life. What if the afterlife is worse than the life you're
running from? Willingly taking a dive headfirst into the
unknown takes some serious courage. I have to hand it
to you Les, you're way braver than I am.

Okay, I'm signing off. I'm not used to writing so
much. Texting would be way more convenient, but you
like to do everything the hard way, don't you?

If I see Grayson at school on Monday, I'll rip
his balls off and mail them to you. What's your new
address?

H

* * *

Daniel is waiting for me by his car when I pull into the parking lot.

"What's the game plan?" he says as soon as I open my door.

I'm racking my brain for anything I might have missed. I don't
remember anything significant about today that would require a
game plan.

"Game plan for what?" I ask.

"The game plan for today, dipshit." He points his clicker toward
his car and locks his doors, then begins walking toward the school
with me. "I know how much you didn't want to come back, so maybe
we need a game plan to counteract all the attention. Do you want me
to be all sad and mopey with you so people won't want to confront
us? I doubt it," he answers himself. "That might encourage people
to approach you with words of encouragement that resemble condo-
lences and I know you're sick of that shit. If you want, I can be super
excitable and take all the attention off you. As much as you don't

want to admit it, you're all everyone's been talking about for two weeks. I'm so fucking sick of it," he says.

I hate that people don't have anything better to talk about, but I like that it bothers Daniel as much as it bothers me.

"Or we could just be normal and hope people have better things to talk about than what happened with Les. Ooh! Ooh!" he says giddily, turning to face me while he walks backward. "I could act all pissed off and walk in front of you like a bodyguard, even though you're bigger than me. And if anyone tries to approach you I'll punch them in the face. Please? Will you play the part of pissed-off, grieving brother? For me? Please?"

I laugh. "I think we'll be just fine without a game plan."

He frowns at my unwillingness to participate. "You underestimate the enjoyment other people gain from gossip and speculation. Just stay quiet and if anything needs to be said today, I'll be the one to say it. I've been dying to yell at these people for two weeks now."

I appreciate his concern, but I really anticipate today being just like any other day. If anything, I think it would be too awkward for people to mention it when I'm actually in their presence. They'll be too uncomfortable to say anything to me at all, which is exactly how I prefer it.

The bell for first period hasn't rung yet, so everyone's still standing outside. It's the first time I'm walking into the school without Les by my side. Just the thought of her takes me right back to that moment when I walked into her bedroom and found her. I don't want to relive that moment again. Not right now. I pull my phone out of my pocket and pretend to be interested in it for the sake of just taking my mind off the fact that Daniel could be right. Everyone around us is way too quiet and I hope to hell it's back to normal soon.

Daniel and I don't have class together until third period so when we make it inside the building he waves me off and heads in the opposite direction. I open the door to my homeroom and almost immediately, a sudden hush falls over the classroom. Every single pair of eyes is staring back at me, quietly watching me walk to my desk.

I keep my phone out and continue to pretend I'm engaged in it, but I'm acutely aware of everyone around me. It keeps me from having to make eye contact with anyone, though. If I don't make eye contact, they'll be less likely to approach me. I wonder if I'm just imagining a difference in the way people are acting today as opposed to before Les killed herself. Maybe it's just me. I don't want to think it's just me, though. If that's the case, then how long does this last? How long will I have to go through every second of the day thinking about her death and how it affects every aspect of my life?

I compare losing Les to losing Hope all those years ago. It seemed back then that everything that happened for months after Hope was taken somehow led to thoughts of her. I would wake up in the morning and wonder where *she* was waking up. I would brush my teeth and wonder if whoever took her thought to buy her a new toothbrush, since she didn't get to take anything with her. I would eat breakfast and wonder if whoever took her knew that Hope didn't like orange juice and whether or not they were letting her have white milk, because that was her favorite. I would go to bed at night and look out my bedroom window that used to face hers, and I would wonder if she even had a bedroom window where she was.

I try to think of when the thoughts finally stopped, but I'm not so sure they have. I still think about her more than I should. It's been years now, but every time I look up at the sky I think about her. Every time someone calls me Dean instead of Holder, I think about her and how I used to laugh at the way she said my name when we were kids. Every time I see a bracelet on a girl I think about the bracelet Les gave her just minutes before she was taken from us.

So many things remind me of her and I hate knowing that it's just going to be worse now that Les is gone, too. Every single thing I think or see or do or say reminds me of Les. Then every single time I'm reminded of Les, it leads to thoughts of Hope. Then every single time I think about Hope, I'm reminded of how I let them down. I failed them both. It's as if the day I gave them their nickname, I was somehow nicknaming myself the same. Because I sure as hell feel pretty fucking hopeless right now.

I've somehow made it through two classes without a single person speaking to me. Not that they aren't discussing it, though. It's like they think I'm not even here, the way they whisper and stare and speculate about what's going on in my head.

I take a seat next to Daniel once I arrive in Mr. Mulligan's class-room. Daniel silently asks how I'm doing with just a look. Over the past few years we seem to have formed some sort of nonverbal communication between us. I shrug, letting him know that it's going. Of course it sucks and I'd rather not be here at all right now, but what can I do? Suck it up. That's what.

"I heard Holder's not speaking to anyone," the girl in front of me whispers to the girl seated in front of her. "Like, *at all*. Not since he found her."

It's obvious by the volume at which she's speaking that she has no idea I'm sitting right behind her. Daniel lifts his head to look at them and I can see the disgust on his face, knowing I can hear their conversation.

"Maybe he's taking a vow of silence," the other girl speculates.

"Yeah, maybe. It wouldn't have hurt Lesslie to take a vow of silence every now and then. Her laugh was so freaking annoying."

I instantly see red. I clench my fists and find myself wishing for the first time in my life that it wasn't wrong for a guy to hit a girl. I'm not angry that they're talking about her behind her back, I expected as much. I'm not even angry that they're talking about her beyond the grave. I'm angry because the *one thing* I loved the most about Les was her laugh. If they're going to say anything about her, they better not mention her fucking laugh again.

Daniel grips the edges of his desk and lifts his leg, then kicks the girl's desk as hard as he can, scooting her a good twelve inches across the floor. She squeals and immediately turns in her seat to face him.

"What the hell is wrong with you, Daniel?"

"What's *wrong* with me?" he asks, raising his voice. He leans forward in his chair and glares at her. "I'll tell you what's wrong with me. I'm pissed that you're a girl because if you had a dick, I'd be punching you in your disrespectful, fat mouth right now."

Her mouth drops open and it's obvious she's confused why he's targeted her. Her confusion is instantly cleared up the second she notices that I'm right behind her, though. Her eyes grow wide and I smile at her, lifting my hand in a half-hearted wave.

I don't say anything, though. I don't really feel the need to add to anything Daniel just said and apparently I'm taking a vow of silence, so I just keep my mouth shut. Besides, Daniel said he's been dying to yell at these people for two weeks now. Today might be his only chance, so I just let him do his thing. The girl immediately turns and faces the front without even offering up the slightest hint of an apology.

The classroom door opens and Mr. Mulligan enters, breaking up the tension and naturally replacing it with his own. Les and I did everything we could to avoid having him at all this year, but we weren't very lucky. Well, *I'm* not, anyway. Les doesn't have to worry about sitting through his tedious, hour-long lectures anymore.

"Dean Holder," he says as soon as he reaches his desk. "I'm still waiting for your research paper that was due last week. I hope you have it with you, because we're presenting today."

Shit. I haven't even thought about what I might have had due over the past two weeks.

"No, I don't have it with me."

He looks up from whatever it is he's looking at on his desk and eyes me. "See me after class, then."

I nod and maybe even roll my eyes a little. Eye rolling is inevitable in his class. He's a douchebag who gets off on the control he thinks he has over a classroom. It's obvious he was bullied as a kid and anyone not wearing a pocket-protector is the recipient of his misguided revenge.

I ignore the presentations during the rest of the period and try to make a list of what assignments I might have due. Les was the organized one of the two of us. She always let me know what was due and when it was due and which class it was due in.

After what seems like hours, the bell finally rings. I remain seated until the class clears out so that Mr. Mulligan can practice his retaliation on me. Once the classroom is occupied by just the two of us, he walks to the front of his desk and leans against it, folding his arms over his chest.

"I know your family has been through quite the ordeal and I'm sorry for your loss." *Here we go.* "I just hope you understand that unfortunate things like this are going to happen throughout your life, but that doesn't give you the excuse to not live up to what's expected of you."

Jesus Christ. It's a fucking *research* paper. It's not like I'm rewriting the Constitution. I know I should just nod and agree with him, but he picked the wrong day to play preacher.

"Mr. Mulligan, Les was the only sibling I had, so I actually *don't* foresee this happening again. As much as it seems like it happens repeatedly, she can only kill herself once."

The way his eyebrows crease together and his lips tighten into a firm line make it apparent that he doesn't find me amusing at all. Which is good, because I wasn't trying to be amusing.

"Some situations should remain off-limits to your sarcasm," he says flatly. "I would hope you would have a little more respect for your sister than that."

As much as I hate that I can't hit girls today, I hate the fact that I can't punch teachers even more. I immediately stand up and walk swiftly to where he's standing, stopping just inches from him, my fists down at my sides. My proximity causes his body to go rigid and I can't help but feel a sense of satisfaction knowing I've scared him. I look him directly in the eyes, clench my teeth, and lower my voice.

"I don't give a shit if you're a teacher, a student, or a goddamned priest. Don't you ever mention my sister again." I stare at him for several more seconds, seething, waiting on his reaction. When he fails to say anything, I turn around and grab my backpack. "You'll get your report tomorrow," I say, exiting the classroom.

I've been convinced I was minutes away from being expelled. However, Mr. Mulligan apparently chose not to report our little interaction, because nothing has been said or done and it's now lunch break.

Moving along.

"Holder," someone says from behind me in the hallway. I turn around to find Amy catching up to me.

"Hey, Amy." I wish her presence gave me even the slightest hint of comfort, but it doesn't. Seeing her standing here just reminds me of two weeks ago, then that reminds me of the pictures she was at my house for, then that reminds me of Les, then that reminds me of Hope. Then of course I'm consumed with guilt again.

"How are you?" she asks hesitantly. "I haven't heard from you since . . ." Her voice trails off, so I answer her quickly, not wanting her to feel she has to go into more detail.

"I'm okay," I reply, feeling guilty that she seems disappointed I didn't call her. I thought she was pretty clear with what happened between us. I hope she is, anyway. "Did you um . . ." I look down at my feet and sigh, unsure how to bring it up without sounding like a complete asshole. I shift my weight from one foot to the other and look back up at her. "Did you *want* me to call you? Because I thought what happened . . ."

"No," she says quickly. "No. You thought right. I just . . . I don't know." She shrugs and looks as though she already regrets this conversation. "Holder, I just wanted to make sure you were okay. I've been hearing rumors and I'd be lying if I didn't say they have me worried. I felt like I made that day at your house all about me, and I never even thought to ask you how you were holding up at all."

She looks guilty for even bringing up the rumors, but she shouldn't feel that way. She's the only person all day to actually make an active effort to ensure the rumors aren't true. "I'm okay," I assure her. "Rumors are rumors, Amy."

She smiles, but doesn't seem to believe the words coming out of my mouth. The last thing I want her to do is worry about me. I wrap my arms around her and whisper in her ear. "I promise, Amy. You don't need to worry about me, okay?"

She nods, then pulls away from me, looking nervously down the hall to her left, then to her right. "Thomas," she whispers, excusing the fact that she pulled away from me. I smile at her reassuringly.

"Thomas," I say, nodding. "Not at home helping his dad with yard stuff, I guess?"

She purses her lips together and shakes her head. "Take care, Holder," she says, turning to walk away.

I put my things in my locker, then head to the cafeteria. I walk in several minutes after the cafeteria has filled up with people, and at first it's like any other day at lunch. But once people begin to spot me as I make my way to the table where Daniel is seated, the voices drop entire octaves and eyes can't seem to mind their own business.

The amount of drama I've witnessed today is comical, really. Everyone I pass, even people I've been friends with for years, all seem to think if they don't quietly watch my every move, they might miss the moment that I completely break down and lose it. I hate to disappoint them, but I've got a pretty good handle on things today. Nobody's going to be losing it, so they might as well go back to their regular routine.

By the time I actually reach the table, the entire sound of the lunchroom has dropped to a dull murmur. All eyes are on me and I seriously wish I could tell everyone to go fuck themselves. But that would be giving them exactly the meltdown they want, so instead I keep my mouth shut.

The one thing I don't do, though, is tell Daniel *he* can't say what I'm wishing I could say. I look him straight in the eyes as I approach the table and we have one of our quick, nonverbal conversations. A nonverbal conversation in which I give him the go-ahead to release any pent-up frustration he might still be harboring.

He grins mischievously and loudly slaps his palms down on the table. "Holy motherfucking shit!" he yells, climbing up onto his chair. He gestures wildly toward me. "Look, everybody! It's Dean Holder!" He proceeds to climb on top of the lunchroom table, pulling all the attention away from me and placing it on himself.

"Why is everyone staring at *me*?" he yells, motioning with huge, exaggerated gestures toward me. "We have *the* Dean Holder here! The one and only!" When only a few people look away from him toward me, he throws his hands up in the air like he's disappointed in them. "Come on, guys! We've been anticipating this moment for two *weeks* now! Now that he's finally here, you all decide to shut the hell up? What's up with that?" He looks down at me and frowns, slumping his shoulders in defeat. "I'm sorry, Holder. I thought today would be a little more interesting for you. I was hoping for a Q&A session to kind of clear the air, but I didn't realize every single person in this school is a spineless dipshit." He begins to climb down from the table but then shoots his arm up into the air and holds up a finger. "Wait!" he says, spinning to face the entire crowd. "That's actually a very good idea!"

I look around and expect one of the cafeteria monitors to be making their way over to him to put a stop to his spectacle, but the only monitor in the cafeteria right now is just watching him like everyone else, waiting to see what he's up to.

Daniel jumps from our table to the table next to us, stepping on a few trays in the process. He spills chocolate milk all over the table and almost slips, but presses his hand onto the top of a guy's head and straightens himself back up. The entire spectacle is pretty damn entertaining, so I take a seat at our table and watch him like I'm not even the reason behind his whole outburst.

He looks down at a girl seated at the table beneath his feet and he extends his arm, pointing his finger down at her. "What about you, Natalie? Now that we have Dean Holder here and live in person, would you like to ask him if your theory about why Les killed herself is correct?"

Natalie's face reddens and she stands up. "You're an asshole, Daniel!" She grabs her tray and walks away from the table. Daniel remains standing on top of the table, but his extended index finger follows her across the cafeteria.

"Wait, Natalie! What if Lesslie *did* kill herself because Grayson dumped her the same week he took her virginity? Don't you want to know if you're right? Don't you want to know what you've won?"

Natalie exits the cafeteria, so he immediately turns his attention to Thomas, who is seated next to Amy a few tables down. She's got her hand over her mouth and she's looking at Daniel in shock like the rest of the cafeteria. He points to Thomas, then hops across three cafeteria tables to get to him. "Thomas!" Daniel yells excitably. "What about you? Would you like to participate in the Q&A? I heard your theory this morning during first period and it was a doozy."

Thomas stands up and grabs his tray just like Natalie did. "Daniel, you're being a jerk." He nods toward me. "He doesn't need this right now."

I don't say anything, but I actually hope Thomas gets away unscathed. I don't know what rumor he started, but even so. I'm pretty sure what I did with Amy was retaliation enough, even though he'll likely never know about it.

"Oh?" Daniel says, pulling his hand up to his mouth in false shock. He looks over at me. "Holder? Do you not need this right now? Are you like, in *mourning* or something? Should we be respecting that?"

I try not to smile, but Daniel's doing a damn good job of turning this shitty day upside down. He steps from one table to the next, moving back toward our table.

"Do you not want to participate in the Q&A, Holder? I thought maybe you would want to set the record straight." He spins around and addresses the entire cafeteria again without waiting on an answer from me. Several students begin picking their trays up and exiting the cafeteria in fear that they'll be pointed out next. "Where's everyone going? None of you seem to mind discussing it any other time. Why not right now when we can actually get some honest answers? Maybe Holder could tell us all why Les really did it. Or better yet, *how* she did it. Maybe we could even find out the truth behind the speculation that he's suicidal, too!" Daniel looks at me again and props his hands on his hips. "Holder? Are the rumors true? Do you actually have the date set for when you plan to kill yourself?"

Now all eyes are definitely on me. Before I can answer, and not that I was going to, Daniel holds up his arms and faces his palms out toward me. "Wait! Don't answer that, Holder." He spins around to address the quickly dwindling crowd again. "I think we should open it up for bets! Somebody find me a pen and paper! I've got dibs on next Thursday," he says, pulling his wallet out of his pocket.

Apparently the cafeteria monitor draws the line at illegal betting, because she's now walking determinedly toward Daniel. He notices the monitor stalking toward him, so he shoves his wallet back into his pocket. "We'll take bets after school, then," he says quickly, jumping off the table.

I turn and head toward the doors to the cafeteria and he follows behind me. As soon as the doors swing shut behind us, the murmur of the cafeteria returns, but much louder this time. Once we're both back in the hallway near our lockers, I turn to face him.

I can't decide whether I want to punch him for what he just did or bow down to him. "You're messed up, man." I laugh.

He runs his palms down his face and falls against the lockers with a big sigh. "Yeah. I didn't really mean for it to go on like that. I just couldn't take another second of this shit. I don't know how you're doing it."

"Me either," I say. I open my locker and grab my car keys. "I think I'm just gonna call it a day. I really don't want to stick around right now."

Daniel opens his mouth to respond, but he's interrupted by someone clearing his throat behind me. I turn around to find Principal Joiner eyeing Daniel angrily. I turn back to Daniel and he lifts his shoulders innocently. "I guess I'll see you tomorrow then. Looks like me and Principal Joiner have a lunch date."

"More like a detention date," Principal Joiner says firmly from behind me. Daniel rolls his eyes and follows the principal toward the office.

I grab the book I need to finish Mr. Mulligan's research paper and shut my locker, then walk down the hall toward the exit. Before I round the hallway, I hear someone say Les's name and it causes me to stop in my tracks. I peer around the corner and there is a small group of four people leaning up against their lockers. One of the guys is holding a cell phone and they're all leaning over him, watching the video he's playing. Daniel's voice is coming from the speaker. Apparently someone recorded his display during lunch just now and it's already circulating. *Great.* Even more fuel for the gossip.

"I don't understand why Daniel made such a big deal out of it," the guy holding the phone says. "Does he really expect us *not* to talk about it? If someone is pathetic enough to kill themselves, we're obviously going to talk about it. If you ask me, Les should have tried to stick it out rather than take the easy—"

I don't wait for him to finish his sentence. His phone shatters when I throw it against the locker, but the sound doesn't even come close to the sound my fist makes when it meets his jaw for the first time. I don't know if the punches get louder after that, though, because everything around me is instantly tuned out. He's on his back on the floor of the hallway now and I'm on top of him, hitting him hard enough that I hope he's never able to open his fucking mouth again. People are pulling on my shoulders and my shirt and my arms, but I continue hitting him. I put my rage on repeat and watch as my fist grows redder and redder from the blood that smears my hand every time I swing at him.

I guess they're getting their wish after all. I'm breaking down.

I'm losing it.

And I don't really give a fuck.

Chapter Five

Les,

Happy five-week deathiversary.

   Sorry I haven't kept you up to speed lately, but a lot has happened. You're going to love this. I, Dean Holder, got arrested.

   I got into a fight at school defending your honor two weeks ago. Well, I guess I can't really call it a fight, per se. I think two people have to be involved to constitute a fight and this incident was definitely one-sided.

   Anyway, I was taken into custody. I was barely there for three hours before Mom bailed me out, though, so it sounds more badass than it actually was. I will admit, it was the first time I've ever been thankful she's a lawyer.

   I'm a little more than upset right now and I don't really know what to do about it. Mom has been struggling a lot lately and my little incident at school really didn't help matters. She thinks she failed us. You killing yourself left her completely doubting her abilities as a mother, which is really hard for me to watch. Now that I went and fucked up, too, she's doubting herself even more. So much so that she's forcing me to go stay with Dad for a while.

I think it's all too much for her. After I beat that asshole up at school, she admitted to me that she thinks I need more help than she's able to give me right now. I did everything I could to change her mind, but after my court hearing this morning, it seems the judge agrees with her. Dad is on his way here right now to pick me up. Five more hours and I'll be heading back to our hometown.

Back to where the downhill slope began.

Do you remember how things used to be when we were kids? Before I let Hope climb into that car?

Things were good. Really good. Mom and Dad were happy. We were happy. We loved our neighborhood, our house, our cat that kept jumping in that damn well in the backyard. I don't even remember that cat's name, but I remember him being the stupidest damn cat I've ever encountered.

It wasn't until the day I walked away from Hope, leaving her crying in the front yard, that our lives began going downhill. After that day everything changed. The reporters showed up, the stress intensified, and our innocent trust in other people completely disappeared.

Mom wanted to move out of town and Dad didn't want to leave his job. She didn't like the fact that we still lived next door to where it happened. Remember how she wouldn't let us go outside alone for years after Hope was kidnapped? She was so scared the same thing would happen to us.

They tried to not let the stress affect their marriage, but it eventually ended up being too much. I remember the day they told us they were divorcing and selling the house, and that Mom was moving us here to be closer to her family. I'll never forget it because, aside from Hope being taken, it was the worst day of my life.

But it seemed like your best.

You were so excited to move. Why, Les? I wish I had thought to ask you while you were alive. I want to know what it was you hated about living there so much, because I really don't want to go back to Austin. I don't want to have to leave Mom. I don't want to have to stay with Dad and pretend that I'm okay with him giving up on his family all those years ago. I don't want to go back to a town where every time I turn a corner, I'm looking for Hope.

I miss you so damn much, Les, but it's different from the way I miss Hope. With you, I know it's not a possibility that I'll ever see you again. I know you're gone and you're not suffering anymore. But I don't have that sense of closure with Hope. Because I don't know that she's not suffering anymore. I don't know if she's dead or alive. My mind does this awful thing where it imagines the worst possible scenarios for her, and I hate it.

What are the chances that the only two girls in my life I've ever loved... I've lost? It's killing me piece by piece every single day. I know I should probably find a way to try to get over it... to let go of the blame. But to be honest, I don't want to get over it. I don't want to forget that my inability to protect either of you is why I'm the only one of us left. I deserve to be reminded every second that I'm alive that I let both of you down, so that I can be conscious not to let myself ever do this again to anyone else.

Yeah, I definitely need a reminder. Maybe I should get a tattoo.

Chapter Five-and-a-half

Les,

What a year. I almost forgot about this notebook. Must have left it behind in my haste to pack last September. It was still sitting on my dresser, and judging by the layer of dust on it, I'm guessing Mom hasn't been snooping in it. If Mom reacted to my moving in with Dad for the past year in the same way she reacted to your death, I'm sure she hasn't set foot in my bedroom since the day I left. It seems easier for her to just close the doors and not think about the stillness of the rooms behind them.

I'm pretty sure the plan was for me to stay in Austin until I graduated, but I thwarted that plan with my magical ability to turn eighteen. Dad couldn't really hold me there against my will anymore. And speaking of turning eighteen... it was weird not having to share a birthday with you. But it was nice because Dad bought me a new car. I'm pretty sure if you were alive he would have made us share the car, but you aren't alive so I get to keep it all to myself. And he didn't make me leave it in Austin when I came back home a few days ago, so that's a plus.

I missed Mom, which is the primary reason I came back. And as much as I hate to admit it, I've missed

Daniel. In fact, I'm about to leave with him in a few minutes. Got to go catch up with the old crowd. It's Saturday night, so I'm sure we'll find somewhere for me to show up and give people something else to talk about.

Daniel says there have been some pretty far-out rumors related to where I've been for the past year. He said he didn't waste time dispelling any of them. He's the only one who knows where I really took off to, so I appreciate that he didn't feel the need to set anyone straight. I think he likes the fact that he's the only one who knows the truth.

One more tiny thing could be responsible for my coming back. My huge fight with Dad. Remind me to tell you all about it later.

Oh, wait. I guess you can't remind me. Fine, I'll remind myself.

Holder, don't forget to tell Les about your fight with Dad.

H

Chapter Six

I can't believe he talked me into any form of social gathering my first week back. I swore I wouldn't be around these people again, but it has been a whole year. I've had a while to adjust, so maybe they have, too.

I walk up to the unfamiliar house a few feet ahead of Daniel, but stop just short of passing through the front door. Of all the people from school I haven't seen for the past year, the last person I expect to run into is Grayson. But of course the last thing I expect is always the first to happen.

I haven't seen him since the night before Les died, when I left him bleeding on the living room floor of his best friend's house. He's walking out as I'm walking in and for a few seconds, we're face to face, staring each other down. I haven't really thought about him much since I left, but seeing him now brings every ounce of hatred I had for him right back to the surface like it never even left.

I can tell by the look in his eyes that he has absolutely no idea what to say to me. I'm blocking his exit and he's blocking my entrance and neither of us seems to want to be the one to step aside. Both of my hands are clenched into defensive fists, preparing for whatever he has to say. He could yell at me, he could spit at me, he could even apologize to me. Whatever words come out of his mouth, it won't matter. The urge I'm having right now isn't to listen to him speak; it's to shut him up.

Daniel walks in shortly after me and notices the silent standoff occurring between us. He slips around me, then stands facing me, blocking my view of Grayson. He slaps my cheeks with both hands until my eyes meet his. "No time for jerk-offs!" He yells over the music. "We have beer that needs consuming!" He grabs my shoulders, still blocking my view from Grayson, and pulls me to the right. I continue to resist, not wanting to be the first to back down from our visual standoff.

Jaxon walks up and places his hand on Grayson's arm, pulling him in the opposite direction. "Let's go see what Six and Sky are up to!" he yells to him.

Grayson nods, watching me sternly as he backs away. "Yeah," he answers Jaxon. "This party just got lame."

If this were last year, he'd be on the floor with my knee resting comfortably on his throat. But this isn't last year, and his throat isn't worth it. I simply smile at him while I continue to allow Daniel to pull me away and toward the kitchen. Once Jaxon and Grayson have exited the front door, I release a pent-up breath. I'm relieved at their decision to leave the party in search of whatever girls are pathetic enough to entertain them.

I grimace with that last thought, knowing I inadvertently lumped Les into that category of girls. But fortunately, I don't have to worry about the chicks Grayson hooks up with anymore. Les isn't here to be deceived by him, so as far as I'm concerned, Grayson can hook up with whoever is desperate enough to have him.

"Press mouth to rim, tilt head back, down your shot, and get happy," Daniel says, handing me a shot of something. I don't ask what it is, I just do what he says and down it.

One more shot, two beers, and half an hour later, Daniel and I have made our way into the living room. I'm on the couch with my feet propped up on the coffee table and Daniel is next to me, running through the list of people we're friends with and telling me all about what they've been up to for the past year. I forgot how talkative alcohol makes him and I'm finding it hard to keep up. I bring my fingers to the bridge of my nose, squeezing the headache away. I don't really know anyone at this party. Daniel says most of them are friends of the kid who lives here, but I don't even know who lives here. I ask Daniel why we're even here if he doesn't know anyone and the question miraculously shuts him up. He looks past me into the kitchen and nods in that direction. "Her," he says.

I look behind me at a couple of girls leaning against the bar. One of them is staring straight at Daniel, stirring her drink flirtatiously.

"If she's the reason we're here, why aren't you over there?"

Daniel turns around and faces forward, folding his arms across his chest. "No fucking way, man. We haven't talked since we broke up two weeks ago. If she wants to apologize to me she can walk her pretty little ass over here."

I glance back at the girl again and notice that maybe she's not looking at him flirtatiously like I first thought. Because flirtatious grins and evil grins are divided by a very faint line and I'm not sure which side of the line she's standing on, now that I'm witnessing her glare.

"How long did you date her?"

"A few months. Long enough to find out she's fucking crazy," he says with a huge roll of his eyes. "And long enough to realize that the *reason* why I love her is because she's fucking crazy." He sees me staring at her and he narrows his eyes. "Stop looking at her, man. She'll know we're talking about her."

I laugh and look away, but not fast enough to avoid witnessing the duo making their way back through the front door. Grayson is following behind Jaxon and they're both headed toward the kitchen. I rest my head into the couch and wish I had downed a few more shots. I really don't want to be preoccupied with Grayson for the rest of the night.

Daniel begins talking incessantly again. I tune him out after he tells me about his new tires for the second time tonight, and I'm doing a pretty good job of staying inside my own head until Jaxon and Grayson move closer to the living room. They have no idea I'm seated on the couch and I'd really like to keep it that way. Now if Daniel would just shut up long enough for me to tell him I'm ready to leave.

"I'm so fucking sick of it," I overhear Grayson saying. "Every Saturday night it's the same thing. I swear to God if she doesn't give it up next weekend I'm done."

Jaxon laughs. "I'm pretty sure all Sky needs is a good dose of rejection. Girls like rejection."

I'm not sure who Sky is, but I like that she's refusing to give it up to Grayson. Smart girl.

"I doubt that would work with her," Grayson says, laughing. "She's pretty damn stubborn."

"Yeah she is," Jaxon agrees. "You would think with everything we've heard about her that she'd be a little less difficult. That girl has got to be the sluttiest *virgin* I've ever met."

Grayson laughs at Jaxon's comment, and I have to try extra hard in my attempt to tune them out. Hearing the way they're talking about this girl infuriates me, because I know Grayson more than likely talked about Les this same way when he dated her.

Grayson continues talking shit about her, and the more I sit here and listen to it, the more I have to hear that pathetic laugh come out of his mouth. All it makes me want to do is shut him up.

I pull my feet off the coffee table and begin to turn around in order to tell them to fuck off, but Daniel puts a hand on my shoulder and shakes his head. "Allow me," he says with a mischievous grin. He pulls his legs up onto the couch and spins around, facing Grayson and Jaxon.

"Excuse me," he says, holding his hand up in the air like he's in class. He's always so animated, even when he knows he's about to get his ass kicked. I may be able to hold my own against Grayson, but Daniel knows he can't, yet that doesn't seem to stop him.

Both Grayson and Jaxon turn to him, but Grayson's eyes stop short once they collide with mine. I hold his obnoxious stare while Daniel hugs the pillow on the back of the couch and continues speaking to them. "I couldn't help but overhear your conversation just now. As much as I'd like to agree that Sky is the sluttiest virgin either of you have ever met, I feel the need to point out that this observation is completely inaccurate. You see, after I spent last night with her, she can't really be considered a virgin anymore. So, maybe it's not her *virginity* she's attempting to hold on to by refusing to sleep with you, Grayson. It's more than likely her dignity."

Grayson is over the back of the couch and has Daniel pinned to the floor in a matter of seconds. I, being of somewhat sound mind, give Daniel the ten seconds he needs to reverse the situation before I interrupt. However, I'm disappointed in my lack of faith in Daniel because he has Grayson flipped over and on his back in less than five. He must have been working out while I was away.

I slowly stand up when I see Jaxon make his way to the front of the couch to assist Grayson. He grabs Daniel by the shoulder to pull him off Grayson, but I grab the back of Jaxon's shirt and yank him until he's seated on the couch. I step closer, just as Grayson delivers a punch to Daniel's jaw. Daniel is about to return the swing, but I grab his arm and pull him up before he has the chance.

Over the years this has become a game to Daniel. He urges people on and counts on me to step in and put a stop to his fights before he gets fucked up. Unfortunately, since I always seem to be in the background during these incidents, my name has become associated with all of the fights and his quick temper. In reality, I've only actually ever hit three people.

1) *The asshole who talked shit about Les.*
2) *Grayson.*
3) *My father.*

And I only regret the last one.

People are rushing through the front door to get a glimpse of the action, but they'll be disappointed, because I'm pushing Daniel out of the house before he can do or say anything else. The last thing I need right now is an excuse to fight Grayson. I've been back less than a week. I sure as hell don't want to give my mother another reason to force me back to Austin.

Daniel is wiping blood from his lip and I've still got hold of his arm when we reach his car. He yanks his arm free and grabs the bottom of his shirt, pulling it up to his mouth. "Dammit," he says, pulling back the shirt to look at the blood. "Why do I keep instigating shit that risks fucking up this beautiful face of mine?" He grins and wipes the blood from his mouth for a second time.

"I wouldn't worry about it," I say, laughing at how worried he always is about his looks. "You're still prettier than me."

Daniel grins. "Thanks, babe," he says teasingly.

Someone is walking up behind Daniel and for a second my fists clench, thinking it might be Grayson. I relax when I see it's just the girl Daniel was referring to who was staring at him from the kitchen earlier. I don't know why I relax, though, because this girl has a definite murderous look about her. Daniel is still wiping the blood from his mouth when she walks up beside him.

"Who the hell is *Sky*?"

Daniel snaps his head in her direction and his eyes grow wide with surprise. "*Who?* What the hell are you talking about, Val?"

She rolls her eyes and lifts her hand, pointing toward the house. "I heard you in there telling Grayson you screwed her last night!"

Daniel glances at the house, then back to Val, and it suddenly hits him. "No, Val!" Daniel says, walking forward and grabbing her hands. "No, no, no! He was talking shit and I was just trying to piss him off. I don't even know the girl he was talking about. I swear—"

She's walking away from him and he's following after her, pleading with her to listen to him. I decide now is a good time to head home. I caught a ride here with Daniel, but it looks like he'll be pre-occupied for a while. I'm only four miles from my house so I text him and tell him I'm headed home, then start in that direction.

This entire night has reminded me of all the things I don't want to be around. Drama. Testosterone. Grayson. Everything about high school in general, really. I'm supposed to fill out my transfer paper-work on Monday, but I honestly don't know that I really want to go back. I know there are ways I can test out. There's just no way in hell my mother would allow that to happen.

Chapter Six-and-a-half

Les,

Okay, so here goes.

Last week, our dear stepmother Pamela walked in on me and a girl. She wasn't just any girl. Her name was Makenna and I'd been out with her a few times. She was cool but it was nothing serious and that's all I'm going to say about that. But anyway, Pamela got home early and Makenna and I were sort of in a compromising position on the living room sofa. You remember the sofa that Pamela kept the plastic on for three years because she was too scared anyone would get stains on it?

Yeah. It wasn't pretty.

Especially since Makenna and I had made our way into the living room after leaving a trail of clothing from the pool, down the hallway, and to the couch. So, not only were we both completely naked, but I had to walk down the hall and back outside to find my shorts and Makenna's clothes. Pamela was screaming at me the entire way outside and the entire way back into the house and the entire way to Makenna's car.

It embarrassed the hell out of Makenna and she kind of called things off with me after that. But that's fine, because I have this cool tattoo now that says Hopeless (remember the nickname I gave you and Hope?) and it reminds me not to get too close to anyone, so I hadn't allowed myself to develop any real feelings for her yet. It was really just about the sex.

I can't believe I just said that to my own sister. Sorry.

Anyway, as you can guess, Dad was furious when he got home. He has one rule and one rule only in his house.

Don't piss off Pamela.

I broke the rule. I broke it hard.

He actually tried to ground me, and I might have laughed a tiny bit when he said it. I wasn't trying to be disrespectful, because you know that, as much as he disappointed me throughout the years, I still wouldn't do something to outright disrespect him. But the fact that he tried to ground me four days after I turned eighteen just really struck a funny chord and dammit... I laughed.

He didn't find it amusing at all and he was pissed. He started yelling at me, calling me disrespectful and ungrateful, and it pissed me off because I mean shit, Les. I'm eighteen! I'm a guy! Guys do shit like have sex with girls in their parents' houses when they're eighteen. But Christ if he didn't act like I'd murdered someone! So, yeah. He pissed me off and I might have lost my temper.

But that's not the bad part. The bad part happened after I yelled at him in return and he bowed up to me. He actually had the balls to bow up to me. Not that he's bigger than me, but still. I'm his son and he bowed up to me like he wanted to fight me.

So what did I do?

I hit him.

I didn't hit him very hard, but it was hard enough that it hurt him in the most sensitive spot possible. His pride.

He didn't hit me back. He didn't even yell at me. He just pulled his hand up to his jaw and he looked at me like he was disappointed, then he turned around and walked away. I left an hour later and drove back home. We haven't spoken since.

I know I should probably call him and apologize, but didn't he start it by bowing up to me? Just a little bit? What kind of dad does that to his own son?

But then again, what kind of son hits his own dad?

God, Les. I feel like shit. I never should have done it. I know I need to call him, but... I don't know. Shit.

To my knowledge, he never even told Mom what happened because she hasn't mentioned it at all. She was surprised to see me back when I walked through the front door a few days ago. Happy, but surprised. She didn't ask what prompted my return, so I didn't volunteer the information. She seems different now. I can still see the heartache in her eyes, but it's not as prominent as it was when I left last year. She actually smiles now, which is good.

Her happiness will be short-lived, though. It's Monday and school started today. The first day of senior year. She left for work before I woke up. I actually had my alarm set and everything ready. I made it to school and did my morning workout, but all I could think about while I was running the track was how much I didn't want to be there.

I don't want to be there without you. I don't want to face everything I hate about that school and the majority of the people in it.

So what did I do when I finished my run? I walked back to the parking lot, got into my car, drove home, and went back to sleep. Now it's almost three o'clock in the afternoon and Mom will be home in a couple of hours. I'm about to head to the grocery store for a few things because I'll be cooking her dinner tonight. I plan to break the news to her about my dropping out of school. I know she won't be happy about my testing out, rather than getting a traditional diploma, so I put cookies on the grocery list, too. Women love cookies, right?

I can't believe I'm not going back to school. I just never thought it would come to that. I'm blaming you for that one, too.

H

Chapter Seven

"Will that be all for you today?" the cashier asks.

I mentally run through the items on my list, ending with cookies. "Yep," I say as I pull my wallet from my pocket to pay the cashier. I'm just relieved I got in and out without seeing anyone I know.

"Hey, Holder."

Spoke too soon.

I glance up to see the cashier operating the line next to me, staring me down. She's practically offering herself up on a platter with the way she's looking at me. Whoever this girl is, her expression is begging for attention. I feel sort of bad for her, especially with the way her voice climbed into that annoying, high-pitched, *why-do-girls-think-baby-talk-is-sexy* range. I glance down at her nametag, because I honestly can't place her face for the life of me.

"Hey . . . *Shayla*." I give her a quick nod, then look back at my cashier, hoping my guarded response is enough to let her know that I'm not in the mood to feed her ego.

"It's *Shayna*," she snaps.

Oops.

I glance at her nametag again, disappointed that I'm giving her even more reason to keep talking. However, her nametag clearly reads *Shayla*. I want to laugh, but feel even more sympathy for her now. "Sorry. But you do realize your nametag says Shayla, right?"

She immediately flips the nametag up on her smock and frowns. I'm hoping this is embarrassing enough that she doesn't look up at me again, but it doesn't even faze her.

"When did you get back?" she asks.

I have no idea who this chick is, but she somehow knows me. Not only does she know me, but she knows I had to *leave* in order to come *back*. I sigh, disappointed that I still underestimate everyone's penchant for gossip.

"Last week," I say, offering up no further explanation.

"So are they gonna let you come back to school?" she asks.

What's with the "*let you*" part of her question? Since when was I not allowed back at school? That has to be attached to some sort of rumor.

"Doesn't matter. Not going back."

I haven't really decided whether or not I'll be enrolling tomorrow, since I failed to do it today. It really all depends on my conversation with my mother tonight, but it seems easier just to give the people what they want, which is more fuel for their gossip. Besides, if I dispel every single thing everyone has said about me for the past year, I'll be leaving everyone with no one to spread rumors about.

"You suck, man," my cashier says quietly as he removes the debit card from my hand. "We had bets on how long it would take her to realize her nametag was misspelled. She's been wearing it for two months now and I had dibs on three. You just lost me twenty bucks."

I laugh. He hands me back the debit card and I place it in my wallet. "My bad," I say. I pull out a twenty-dollar bill and hold it out to him. "Take this, because I'm pretty sure you would have won."

He shakes his head, refusing to take the twenty.

I'm placing the money back into my wallet when I notice out of the corner of my eye someone in the next checkout line. The girl has completely turned around and is staring at me, more than likely trying to get my attention in the same way that Shayna/Shayla tried. I just hope this chick doesn't start up with that same baby-talk voice.

I glance up at her to get a quick look. I really wanted to avoid glancing at her, but when people are staring you down it's hard not to make eye contact, if even for a second. But the second I actually do make eye contact with her, I freeze.

I can't look away now, even though I'm trying like hell to shake the image standing in front of me.

My heart stops.

Time stops.

The whole *world* stops.

My quick glance turns into a full-on, unintentional stare.

I recognize those eyes.

Those are *Hope's* eyes.

It's her nose, her mouth, her lips, her hair. Everything about this girl is Hope. Out of all the times in the past I thought I'd spotted her when glancing at girls my age, I've never been more sure than I am right now. I'm so sure about it that it completely inhibits my ability to speak. I don't think I could say her name even if she begged me to.

So many emotions are coursing through me right now and I can't tell if I'm angry or elated or freaked the hell out.

Does she recognize me, too?

We're still staring at each other and I can't stop wondering if I look familiar to her. She doesn't smile. I wish she would smile because I would recognize Hope's smile anywhere.

She tucks in her chin, darts her eyes away, and quickly turns around to face her cashier again. She's obviously flustered and it's not in the same way that I tend to leave girls like Shayna/Shayla flustered. It's a completely different reaction, which only makes me all the more curious if she just remembered me.

"Hey." The word rushes loudly out of my mouth involuntarily and I notice her flinch when I speak. She's hurrying her cashier at this point, grabbing her sacks in a frenzy. It's almost as if she's trying to get away from me.

Why is she trying to run from me? If she didn't just recognize me . . . why would she be this disturbed? And if she *did* recognize me, why wouldn't she be happy?

She exits the store in a rush, so I grab my sacks and leave the receipt with the cashier. I have to get outside before she drives away. I can't just let her go again. I head directly through the exit and scroll over the parking lot until I spot her. Luckily, she's still loading her groceries into her backseat. I pause before walking up behind her, hoping I don't come off as crazy, because that's exactly how I feel right now.

She's about to shut her door, so I take a few steps closer.

I don't think I've ever been this scared to speak.

What do I say? What the hell do I say?

I've imagined this moment for thirteen years and I have no fucking idea how to approach her.

"Hey."

Hey? Jesus, Holder. Nice. Real nice.

She freezes midmovement. I can tell by the way her shoulders rise and fall that she's taking a calming breath. Does she need calming because of me? My heart is racing at warp speed and thirteen years' worth of pent-up adrenaline is making its way through my body.

Thirteen years. I've been looking for her for thirteen years and I very well may have just found her. *Alive.* And in the same *town* as me. I should be elated, but I can't stop thinking about Les and how I know she prayed every single day for this moment. Les spent her whole life wishing we would find Hope and now I've found her and Les is dead. If this girl really is Hope, I'll be devastated that she showed up thirteen months too late.

Well, maybe not *devastated.* I forgot that word is on reserve. But I'll be pretty damn pissed.

She's facing me now. She's looking right at me and it's killing me because I want to grab her and hug her and tell her how sorry I am for ruining her life, but I can't do any of these things because she's looking at me like she has no clue who I am. I just want to scream, "Hope! It's me! It's Dean!"

I grip the back of my neck and try to process this whole situation. This isn't how I pictured finding her. Maybe I fictionalized it and played it up all these years but I thought her recovery would be way more climactic. I thought she would have way more tears and way more emotion and not appear to be nearly as . . . *inconvenienced*?

The look on her face right now doesn't register as recognition in the least. She looks terrified. Maybe she *doesn't* recognize me. Maybe she appeared flustered inside because of the idiotic way I was staring at her. Maybe she appears terrified now because I practically chased her down and I'm giving her absolutely no explanation. I'm just standing here like a creepy stalker and I have no idea how to even ask her if she's the girl I lost all those years ago.

She eyes me warily up and down. I hold out my hand, hoping to ease some of her fear with an introduction. "I'm Holder."

She drops her gaze to my extended hand and, rather than accept the handshake, she actually takes a step away from me.

"What do you want?" she says sharply, cautiously peering back up to my face.

Definitely not the reaction I expected.

"Um," I say, not really meaning to appear taken aback. But honestly, this isn't going in the direction I was hoping it would go. I don't even know what direction that was at this point. I'm starting to doubt my own sanity. I glance across the parking lot at my car and wish I had just kept walking, but I know if I did, I'd regret not confronting her.

"This might sound lame," I warn, looking back at her, "but you look really familiar. Do you mind if I ask what your name is?"

She releases a breath and rolls her eyes, then reaches behind her to grab the doorknob of her car. "I've got a boyfriend," she says. She turns and opens the door, then quickly climbs into the car. She starts to pull the door shut, but I catch it with my hand.

I can't let her leave until I'm positive she's not Hope. I've never been so sure about anything in my life and I'm not about to let thirteen years of guilt and obsessing and analyzing her disappearance go to waste just because I'm afraid I might piss her off.

"Your name. That's all I want."

She stares at my hand holding open her door. "Do you mind?" she says through clenched teeth. Her eyes fall to the tattoo on my arm and my adrenaline kicks up a notch when she reads it, hoping it'll spark some recognition on her part. If she can't remember my face, I'm almost positive she'll remember the nickname I gave her and Les.

Not even the slightest jar of emotion flashes in her eyes.

She attempts to pull the door shut again but I refuse to release it until I get what I need from her.

"Your name. *Please.*"

When I say *please* this time, her expression eases slightly and she looks back up at me. It isn't until she looks at me this way, without all the anger, that I realize why I'm so flustered. It's because I care more for this girl than any other girl in the world who isn't Les. I loved Hope like a sister when we were kids and seeing her again has brought back all those same feelings. It's causing my hands to shake and my heart to pound and my chest to ache because all I want to do is wrap my arms around her and hold her and thank God we finally found each other.

But all those feelings come to a screeching halt when the wrong answer comes out of her mouth. "Sky," she says quietly.

"Sky," I say aloud, trying to make sense of it. Because she's *not* Sky. She's Hope. She can't not be my Hope.

Sky.

Sky, Sky, Sky.

She's not saying she's Hope, but the name *Sky* is still eerily familiar. What's so significant about that name?

Then it hits me.

Sky.

This is the girl Grayson was referring to Saturday night.

"Are you sure?" I ask her, hoping for a miracle that she's as dense as Shayna and just gave me the wrong name. If she really isn't Hope, then I completely understand her reaction to my seemingly erratic behavior.

She sighs and pulls her ID from her back pocket. "Pretty sure I know my own name," she says, flashing her driver's license in front of me.

I take it from her.

Linden Sky Davis.

A wave of disappointment crashes around me, swallowing me up. *Drowning* me. I feel like I'm losing her all over again.

"Sorry," I say, backing away from her car. "My mistake."

She watches me as I back up even farther so she can shut her door. In a way, she looks disappointed. I don't even want to think about what kind of expression she's seeing on my face right now. I'm sure it's a mixture of anger, disappointment, embarrassment . . . but most of all, *fear*. I watch as she drives away and I feel like I just let Hope go all over again.

I know she's not Hope. She proved she wasn't Hope.

So why is my gut instinct telling me to stop her?

"Shit," I groan, threading my hand through my hair. I'm seriously messed up. I can't get over Hope. I can't get over Les. It's getting so bad it's to the point that I'm chasing random girls down in the damn grocery store parking lot?

I turn away and slam my fist down on the hood of the car next to me, pissed at myself for thinking I finally had it all together. I don't have it together. Not in the least.

I'm not even completely out of my car before I have Facebook pulled up on my phone. I enter Sky's name and no results come up. I swing open the front door and head straight up the stairs to get my laptop.

I can't let this rest. If I don't convince myself that she isn't Hope, I'll drive myself crazy. I open my laptop and enter her information again but come up empty. I search every site I can think of for over half an hour, but her name doesn't return any results. I try searching by her birthday, but come up empty again.

I type in Hope's information and immediately have a screen full of news articles and returns. But I don't need to look at them. I've spent the last several years reading every article and every lead that's reported about Hope's disappearance. I know them by heart. I slam the computer shut.

I need to run.

Chapter Eight

She has no distinct features that I can remember. No birthmarks. The fact that I saw a girl with brown hair and brown eyes and felt she was the same brown-haired, brown-eyed girl from thirteen years ago is quite possibly borderline obsessive.

Am I obsessed? Do I somehow feel as though I won't be able to move past Les's death if I don't rectify at least one of the things I've fucked up in my life?

I'm being ridiculous. I've got to let it go. I've got to let go of the fact that I'll never have Les back and I'll never find Hope.

I have these same thoughts for the entire two miles of my run. The weight in my chest lightens little by little with each step I take. I remind myself with each step that Sky is Sky and Hope is Hope and Les is dead and I'm the only one left and I've got to get my shit together.

The run begins to help ease some of the tension built up from the incident at the grocery store. I've convinced myself that Sky isn't Hope, but for some reason even though I'm almost positive she's not Hope, I still find myself thinking about Sky. I can't get the thought of her out of my head and I wonder if that's Grayson's fault. If I hadn't heard him talking about her at the party the other night, I probably would have moved on from the grocery store incident fairly quickly and I wouldn't be thinking about her at all.

But I can't stop this growing urge to protect her. I know how Grayson is and somehow, just seeing this girl for even a few minutes, I know she doesn't deserve what he's likely going to put her through.

There isn't a single girl in this world who deserves the type of guy Grayson is.

Sky said she had a boyfriend at the store and the possibility that she might consider Grayson her boyfriend gets under my skin. I don't know why, but it does. Just thinking she was Hope for even a few minutes already has me feeling extremely territorial about her.

Especially now as I round the corner and see her standing in front of my house.

She's here. *Why the hell is she here?*

I stop running and drop my hands to my knees, keeping my eyes trained on her back while I catch my breath. *Why the hell is she standing in front of my house?*

She's at the edge of my driveway, propped up against my mailbox. She's drained the last of her water bottle and she's shaking it above her mouth, attempting to get more water out of it, but it's completely empty. When she realizes this, her shoulders slump and she tilts her face toward the sky.

It's obvious she's a runner with those legs.

Holy shit, I can't breathe.

I try to recall everything on her driver's license and what all Grayson said about her Saturday night because I suddenly want to know everything there is to know about her. And not because I thought she was Hope, but because whoever she is . . . she's fucking beautiful. I don't know that I even noticed how attractive she was at the store, because my mind wasn't going there. But right now, seeing her in front of me? My mind is *all over* that.

She takes a deep breath, then begins walking. I immediately kick into gear and ease up behind her.

"Hey, you."

She pauses at the sound of my voice and her shoulders immediately tense. She turns around slowly and I can't help but smile at the wary expression strewn across her face.

"Hey," she says back, shocked to see me standing in front of her. She actually seems more at ease this time. Not as terrified of me as she was in the parking lot, which is good. Her eyes slowly drop down to my chest, then to my shorts. She looks back up at me momentarily, then diverts her gaze to her feet.

I casually lean against the mailbox and pretend to ignore the fact that she totally just checked me out. I'll ignore it to save her embarrassment, but I'm definitely not going to forget it. In fact, I'll probably be thinking about the way her eyes scrolled down my body for the rest of the damn day.

"You run?" I ask. It's probably the most obvious question in the world right now, but I'm completely out of material.

She nods, still breathing heavily from the effect of her workout. "Usually in the mornings," she confirms. "I forgot how hot it is in the afternoons." She lifts her hand to her eyes to shield them from the sun while she looks at me. Her skin is flush and her lips are dry. I hold out my water bottle and she flinches again. I try not to laugh, but I feel pretty damn pathetic that I freaked her out so much at the store that she's afraid I might actually do something to *harm* her.

"Drink this." I nudge my water bottle toward her. "You look exhausted."

She grabs the water without hesitation and presses her lips to the rim, downing several gulps. "Thanks," she says, handing it back to me. She wipes the water off her top lip with the back of her hand and glances behind her. "Well, I've got another mile and a half return, so I better get started."

"Closer to two and a half," I say. I'm trying not to stare, but it's so hard when she's wearing next to nothing and every single curve of her mouth and neck and shoulders and chest and stomach seems like it was made just for me. If I could preorder the perfect girl, I wouldn't even come close to the version standing in front of me right now.

I press the bottle of water to my mouth, knowing it's more than likely the closest I'll ever get to her lips. I can't even take my eyes off her long enough to take a drink.

"Huh?" she says, shaking her head. She seems flustered. God, *please* let her be flustered.

"I said it's more like two and a half. You live over on Conroe, that's over two miles away. That's almost a five-mile run round trip." I don't know many girls who run, let alone a five-mile stretch. Impressive."

Her eyes narrow and she pulls her arms up, folding them across her stomach. "You know what street I live on?"

"Yeah."

Her gaze remains tepid and focused on mine and she's quiet. Her eyes eventually narrow slightly and it looks like she's growing annoyed with my continued silence.

"Linden Sky Davis, born September 29; 1455 Conroe Street. Five feet three inches. Donor."

As soon as the word "donor" leaves my mouth, she immediately steps back, her look of annoyance turning into a mixture of shock and horror. "Your ID," I say quickly, explaining why I know so much about her. "You showed me your ID earlier. At the store."

"You looked at it for two seconds," she says defensively.

I shrug. "I have a good memory."

"You stalk."

I laugh. "*I* stalk? You're the one standing in front of my house." I point to my house behind me, then tap my fingers against the mailbox to show her that she's the one encroaching. Not me.

Her eyes grow wide in embarrassment as she takes in the house behind me. Her face grows redder with the realization of how it must look for her to be randomly hanging out in front of my house. "Well, thanks for the water," she says quickly. She waves at me and turns around, breaking into a stride.

"Wait a sec," I yell after her. I run past her and turn around, trying to think up an excuse for her not to leave just yet. "Let me refill your water." I reach down and grab her water bottle. "I'll be right back." I take off toward the house, hoping to buy myself some more time with her. I've obviously got a lot to make up for in the first-impressions department.

"Who's the girl?" my mother asks once I reach the kitchen. I run Sky's bottle of water under the tap until it's full, then I turn around to face her. "Her name is Sky," I say, smiling. "Met her at the grocery store earlier."

My mother glances out the window at her, then looks back at me and cocks her head. "And you already brought her to our house? Moving a little quickly, don't you think?"

I hold up the water bottle. "She just happened to be running by and now she's out of water." I walk toward the door and turn back to my mother and wink. "Lucky for me, we just happen to have water."

She laughs. The smile on my mother's face is nice because they've been so few and far between. "Well, good luck, Casanova," she calls after me.

I run the water back out to Sky and she immediately takes another drink. I attempt to find a way to rectify her first impression of me.

"So . . . earlier?" I say hesitantly. "At the store? If I made you uneasy, I'm sorry."

She looks me straight in the eyes. "You didn't make me uneasy."

She's lying. I *absolutely* made her uneasy. Terrified her, even. But she's looking at me now with such confidence.

She's confusing. *Really* confusing.

I watch her for a minute, trying my best to read her, but I have no clue. If I was to hit on her right now, I don't know if she'd punch me or kiss me. At this point, I'm pretty sure I'd be more than okay with either.

"I wasn't trying to hit on you, either," I say, wanting to get some sort of reaction from her. "I just thought you were someone else."

"It's fine," she says softly. Her smile is tight-lipped and the disappointment in her voice is clear. It makes me smile, knowing that disappointed her a little bit.

"Not that I *wouldn't* hit on you," I clarify. "I just wasn't doing it at that particular moment."

She smiles. It's the first time I actually get a genuine smile from her and it feels like I just won a triathlon.

"Want me to run with you?" I ask, pointing toward her path home.

"No, it's fine."

I nod, but don't like her answer. "Well, I was going that way anyway. I run twice a day and I've still got a couple . . ."

I take a step closer to her when I notice the fresh, prominent bruise under her eye. I grab her chin and tilt her head back to get a better look at it. My previous thoughts are sidetracked and I'm suddenly overwhelmed with a need to kick the ass of whoever touched her.

"Who did this to you? Your eye wasn't like this earlier."

She backs away from my grasp. "It was an accident. Never interrupt a teenage girl's nap." She tries to laugh it off, but I know better. I've seen enough unexplained bruises on Les in the past to know that girls can hide this kind of shit better than anyone wants to admit.

I run my thumb over her bruise, calming the anger coursing through me. "You would tell someone, right? If someone did this to you?"

She just stares up at me. No response. No, *"Yes, of course I would tell."* Not even a, *"Maybe."* Her lack of acknowledgment takes me right back to these situations with Les. She never admitted to Grayson physically hurting her, but the bruises I saw on her arm the week before I made him break up with her almost ended in murder. If I find out he's the one who did this to Sky, he'll no longer have a hand left to lay on her.

"I'm running with you," I say. I place my hands firmly on her shoulders and turn her around without giving her the opportunity to object.

She doesn't even try to object, though. She begins running, so I fall into a steady stride with her. I'm fuming the entire run back to the house. Pissed that I never got to the bottom of what happened with Les and pissed that Sky might be dealing with the same shit.

We don't speak the entire run back to her house until she turns and waves good-bye at the edge of her driveway. "I guess I'll see you later?" she says, walking backward toward her house.

"Absolutely," I say, knowing full well I'll be seeing her again. Especially now that I know where she lives.

She smiles and turns toward her house and it isn't until she's halfway up her driveway that I realize I don't even have a way to contact her. She doesn't have a Facebook, so I can't contact her that way. I don't know her phone number. I can't really just show up at her house unannounced.

I don't want her to walk away until I know for sure I'll talk to her again.

I immediately twist the lid off my water bottle and pour the contents of it onto the grass. I put the lid back on it.

"Sky, wait," I yell. She pauses and turns back around. "Do me a favor?"

"Yeah?"

I toss her the conveniently empty bottle of water. She catches it, then nods and runs inside to refill it. I pull my cell phone from my pocket and immediately text Daniel.

Sky Davis. Girl Grayson was talking about Saturday night? Does she have a boyfriend?

Sky opens her front door and begins to make her way back outside when he responds.

She has several from what I hear.

I'm still staring at the text when she reaches me with the water. I take it from her and down a drink, not sure why it's hard for me to find truth in Daniel's text. As much as she's still an enigma to me, I can tell by the way she's so guarded that she doesn't let people in that easily. Based on my interaction with her, she just doesn't fit the description that's being painted of her by everyone else.

I put the lid back on the water bottle and do my best to keep my eyes focused on hers, but dammit if that sports bra isn't a magnet right now. "Do you run track?" I ask her, attempting to stay focused.

She covers her stomach with her arms and her movement makes me want to punch myself for being so obvious about checking her out. The last thing I want to do is make her uncomfortable.

"No," she says. "I'm thinking about trying out, though."

"You should. You're barely out of breath and you just ran close to five miles. Are you a senior?"

She smiles. That's twice she's smiled at me like that, and it's really beginning to mess with my head.

"Shouldn't you already know if I'm a senior?" she says, still grinning. "You're slacking on your stalking skills."

I laugh. "Well, you make it sort of difficult to stalk you. I couldn't even find you on Facebook."

She smiles again. I hate that I'm keeping count. *Three.*

"I'm not on Facebook," she says. "I don't have internet access."

I can't tell if she's lying to let me off easily, or if she's actually being honest about not having internet access. I don't know which one is harder to believe. "What about your phone? You can't get internet on your phone?"

She lifts her arms to tighten her ponytail and I feel like *I'm* the one out of breath right now. "No phone. My mother isn't a fan of modern technology. No TV, either."

I wait for her to laugh, but it's obvious in just a few short seconds that she's completely serious. This isn't good. How the hell am I supposed to get in touch with her? Not that I need to. I just have a pretty good feeling I'll *want* to. "Shit." I laugh. "You're serious? What do you do for fun?"

She shrugs. "I run."

Yes, she certainly does. And if I have anything to do with it, she won't be running alone, anymore.

"Well in that case," I say, leaning toward her, "you wouldn't happen to know what time a certain someone gets up for her morning runs, would you?"

She sucks in a quick breath, then attempts to control it with a smile. *Three and a half.*

"I don't know if you'd want to get up that early," she says.

If she only knew I would go so far as to never sleep *again* if she would just agree to run with me. I lean in a little closer and lower my voice. "You have no *idea* how bad I want to get up that early."

As soon as her fourth smile appears, she *disappears*. It happens so fast, I don't even have time to react. The sound she makes when she smacks the pavement makes me wince. I immediately kneel down and roll her over.

"Sky?" I say, shaking her. She's out cold. I look toward her house, then scoop her up and rush her to the door. I don't bother knocking, since I have no extra hands. I lift my foot and kick at the front door, hoping someone is home to let me in.

Within seconds, the front door swings open and a woman appears. She looks at me in utter confusion until she recognizes Sky in my arms.

"Oh, my God!" She immediately opens the door to let me in.

"She passed out in the driveway," I say. "I think she's dehydrated."

The woman immediately runs to the kitchen while I lower Sky onto the living room sofa. As soon as her head meets the arm of the couch, she moans and her eyelids flutter open. I breathe a sigh of relief, then step aside when her mother reappears.

"Sky, drink some water," she says. She helps her take a sip, then she sets the glass of water down. "I'll get you a cold rag," she says, walking toward the hallway.

Sky looks up at me and winces. I kneel next to her, feeling awful that I just let her fall like that. It happened so fast, though. One second she was standing in front of me; the next second she wasn't. "You sure you're okay?" I ask after her mother has left the room. "That was a pretty nasty fall."

There's gravel and dirt stuck to her cheek, so I wipe most of it away. She squeezes her eyes shut and throws her arm over her face.

"Oh, God," she groans. "I'm so sorry. This is so embarrassing."

I take her wrist and pull it away from her face. The last thing I want her to feel is embarrassed. I'm just thankful she's okay. And even more thankful it gave me an excuse to carry her inside. Now I'm inside her house with an excuse to come back and check on her this week. Things couldn't have worked out better for me.

"Shh," I whisper. "I'm sort of enjoying it."

Her mouth curls up into a smile. *Five.*

"Here's a rag, sweetie. Do you want something for the pain? Are you nauseous?" Her mother hands me the rag and walks to the kitchen. "I might have some calendula or burdock root."

Sky rolls her eyes. "I'm fine, Mom. Nothing hurts."

I wipe the rest of the dirt off her cheek with the rag. "You might not be sore now, but you will be," I say quietly. She didn't see how hard she hit the ground. She'll definitely feel it tomorrow. "You should take something, just in case."

She nods and attempts to sit up, so I assist her. Her mother walks back into the room with a small glass of juice and hands it to Sky.

"I'm sorry," she says, extending her hand out to me. "I'm Karen Davis."

I stand up and return the handshake. "Dean Holder," I say, taking a quick glance at Sky. "My friends call me Holder."

Karen smiles. "How do you and Sky know each other?"

"We don't, actually," I say. "Just in the right place at the right time, I guess."

"Well, thank you for helping her. I don't know why she fainted. She's never fainted." She turns her attention to Sky. "Did you eat anything today?"

"A bite of chicken for lunch," Sky says. "Cafeteria food sucks ass."

Cafeteria food. So she goes to public school. I might just be rethinking my educational decision after all.

Karen rolls her eyes and throws her hands up in the air. "Why were you running without eating first?"

"I forgot," Sky says defensively. "I don't usually run in the evenings."

Karen walks back to the kitchen with the glass and sighs heavily. "I don't want you running anymore, Sky. What would have happened if you had been by yourself? You run too much, anyway."

The look on Sky's face is priceless. Apparently running is as vital to her as breathing.

"Listen," I say, finding an opportunity to appease all parties involved, especially myself. "I live right over on Ricker and I run by here every day on my afternoon runs. If you'd feel more comfortable, I'd be happy to run with her for the next week or so in the mornings. I usually run the track at school, but it's not a big deal. You know, just to make sure this doesn't happen again."

Karen returns to the living room and eyes both of us. "I'm okay with that," she says. She turns her attention to Sky. "If Sky thinks it's a good idea."

Please think it's a good idea.

"It's fine," Sky says with a shrug.

I was hoping for a "*Hell yes,*" but "*fine*" will suffice.

She attempts to stand up again, but she sways to the left. I immediately reach out and grab her arm to ease her back down onto the sofa.

"Easy," I say to her. I look at Karen. "Do you have any crackers she can eat? That might help."

Karen walks away to the kitchen and I give Sky my full attention again. "You sure you're okay?" I run my thumb over her cheek for no reason at all other than the simple fact that I wanted to touch her cheek again. As soon as my fingers graze her skin, chills rush down her arms. She tightens her arms over her chest and rubs the chills away. I can't help but grin, knowing it was my hand on her skin that did that to her. Best. Feeling. Ever.

I glance at Karen to make sure she's not making her way back into the living room, then I lean in toward Sky. "What time should I come stalk you tomorrow?"

"Six-thirty?" she says breathlessly.

"Six-thirty sounds good." *Six-thirty is my new favorite time of day.*

"Holder, you don't have to do this." She looks me directly in the eyes as if she wants to give me the opportunity to back out. Why the hell would I want to back out?

"I know I don't have to do this, Sky. I do what I want." I lean even closer, hoping to see the chills run down her arms again. "And I want to run with you."

I pull away just as Karen is walking back into the living room. Sky keeps her eyes focused hard on mine and it makes me wish more than anything that it was tomorrow morning already.

"Eat," Karen says, placing crackers in Sky's hand.

I stand up and tell Karen good-bye. "Take care of yourself," I say to Sky as I back my way toward the front door. "I'll see you in the morning?"

She nods and it's all the confirmation I need. I pull the door shut behind me as I leave, pleased that I somehow managed to redeem myself. As soon as I'm out of her driveway and back on the sidewalk, I pull my phone from my pocket and call Daniel.

"Hey, Hopeless," he says when he answers.

"I said stop calling me that, Jackass."

"Shoulda thought about that before you got the tattoo," he quips back. "What's up?"

"Sky Davis," I say quickly. "Who is she, where's she from, does she go to school here, and is she dating Grayson?"

Daniel laughs. "Whoa, buddy. Slow down. First of all, I've never met her. Second of all, if that's the same Sky that I claimed to have deflowered in front of Val at that party the other night, there's no way I'm asking around about her. I'm still trying to convince Val I never really slept with the chick. Asking people about her will only make it worse for me, man."

I groan. "Daniel, please. I need to know and you're better with this shit than I am."

There's a long pause on his end. "Fine," he says. "But on one condition."

I knew there'd be a condition. There's always a condition when it comes to Daniel. "What condition?"

"You come to school tomorrow. Just one day. Enroll tomorrow and try it for one day and if you absolutely hate it you can officially drop out with my blessing."

"Deal," I say immediately. I can do one day. Especially if Sky will be there.

Chapter Eight-and-a-half

Les,

Holy shit, Les. HOLY. SHIT.

It feels like forever since I wrote to you but it was just this morning. So much has happened, my hands are shaking and I can barely write.

I still haven't talked to Mom about dropping out yet, but only because I'm not so sure I want to drop out anymore. We'll see after tomorrow.

Are you sitting down for this? Sit your ass down, Les.

I.

Found.

Hope.

But I didn't.

Well, I'm still not so sure I didn't, but I'm more sure that she isn't Hope than sure that she is. Does that even make sense? I mean, the second I saw her I was positive it was her. But when I realized she didn't recognize me, I thought maybe I was wrong or she was pretending or... I don't know. I just started doubting myself. Then I acted sort of stalkerish and crazy so she showed me her ID, which was really dumb of her if you consider how stalkerish I was acting. But her ID proved she wasn't Hope, which crushed me, but only for a couple of hours. Because when I went running I ran into her again thanks to fate or coincidence or divine intervention or maybe you had something to do with it. Whatever or whoever made it happen, she was there, standing in front of our house, looking all beautiful and shit. Jesus, she looked good, Les.

I'm sure you want to hear that, right?

Anyway, so I'm convinced now that if she really is Hope, she would have remembered me. Especially after I told her mother that my name was Dean Holder. I glanced down at Sky to see if my first name rang a bell but based on her lack of reaction, it didn't ring a bell at all, so there's no way she could be the same girl.

Do you want to know the strangest part, Les? The part of this entire day that has thrown me for the biggest loop?

I don't even want her to be Hope.

If she's Hope, all of the drama and the stress and the media attention would surround us again and I don't want that for her. This girl seems happy and healthy and not at all how I expected our Hope to be if we ever found her. So I'm glad Sky isn't Hope and Hope isn't Sky.

I had Daniel do some investigating and I learned a little bit about her. She's lived in this area for years and has been homeschooled by her mom, who seems really nice, by the way.

Daniel also said she's not officially dating Grayson, so that's a plus. I'm still not sure how she's connected to him, because according to Daniel she's definitely connected to him in some way. I'm hoping to stop that before it becomes anything significant, though.

Sorry I'm rambling. It's just been the type of day you don't expect at all when you wake up for it. I'll let you know how tomorrow goes. I owe Daniel a day of school.

P.S. Sky had a black eye today. She never said what actually happened, but you know how paranoid I am about anything remotely connected to Grayson. I'll never forget that day you came home with those bruises on your arm, Les. You begged me not to kill him because I swear to you, I would have if you hadn't sworn that he didn't do it.

I don't know if you were telling the truth when you said it happened during your athletics class. I don't know if Grayson is capable of doing something like that. But seeing Sky with that bruise under her eye had me just as worked up as when I thought Grayson had hurt you. And you aren't here for me to protect anymore, so I feel this unrelenting need to protect Sky and I don't even know her.

Don't tell Daniel this, not that you could, but I would have shown up to school tomorrow whether he made it a condition or not. I need to see how Sky and Grayson interact with my own two eyes so I can determine whether I actually need to kill him this time.

H

Chapter Nine

I'm ten minutes early when I reach her house, so I take a seat on the curb and stretch. After leaving here yesterday, I felt like me offering to run with her might have been a little forward. It is out of my way and I don't usually run this much in a day, but I didn't know how else I would see her again.

I hear her walking up behind me, so I spin around and stand up. "Hey, you."

I expect her to smile or return a greeting of some sort, but instead she eyes me up and down with an uncomfortable frown. I shrug it off, hoping she's just not a morning person.

"You need to stretch first?" I ask her.

She shakes her head. "Already did."

I'm curious if the solemn attitude is because she's sore from her fall yesterday. Her black eye is still prominently displayed, but her cheek doesn't look as bad as I thought it would. I reach out and run my thumb over the scrape on her face. "Doesn't look so bad. You sore?" She shakes her head no. "Good. You ready?"

She nods. "Yeah."

Three words is all the conversation I get from her? She turns and we both begin running in silence. I've never run with a girl before but I expected there to be a little more back and forth. I can't tell from the guarded greeting we just had in her front yard if she's uncomfortable around me, or if the quietness is actually a *sign* of comfort. It could go either way.

The tension lessens once I fall into step behind her. It's easier to get away with not speaking when I'm not running side by side with her. I just have no idea what to say. I'm not much of a talker to begin with, but being in her presence suppresses the conversational side of me even more. I guess if I really want to get anywhere with her, I need to suck it up. I speed up and step back into stride with her.

"You better try out for track," I say. "You've got more stamina than most of the guys from the team last year."

She shakes her head and continues to focus on the sidewalk in front of us. "I don't know if I want to," she says. "I don't really know anyone at school. I planned on trying out, but so far most of the people at school are sort of . . . mean. I don't really want to be subjected to them for longer periods of time under the guise of a team."

I hate that she's been in school for a day and she already knows how mean everyone is. I wonder what the hell they did to make her first day so bad?

"You've only been in public school for a day. Give it time. You can't expect to be homeschooled your whole life, then walk in the first day with a ton of new friends."

I feel bad telling her the exact opposite of what I really feel. If I was being completely honest, I'd tell her to go back to homeschooling, because she had it made before she entered public school. I turn to look at her but she's not running next to me. I spin around and she is stopped several feet behind me with her hands on her hips. I rush to her.

"Are you okay? Are you dizzy?" I hold her shoulders in case she feels faint again. I'd feel like the ultimate jackass if I just let her bust the pavement like I did yesterday.

She shakes her head no, then pushes my hands off her shoulders. "I'm fine," she says.

She's pissed about something. I try to think of what I might have said, but nothing seemed offensive. "Did I say something wrong?"

She drops her eyes to the pavement and starts walking again, so I follow her. "A little," she says with a miffed tone. "I was halfway joking about the stalking yesterday, but you admitted to looking me up on Facebook right after meeting me. Then you insist on running with me, even though it's out of your way. Now you somehow know how long I've been in public school? And that I was homeschooled? I'm not gonna lie, it's a little unnerving."

Shit. What the hell is wrong with me? How do I admit that I learned most of what I know about her based on overhearing Grayson at a party and through speculative rumors from Daniel? She doesn't need to know that. I don't *want* her to know that.

I sigh and continue walking toward her house with her. "I asked around," I say. "I've lived here since I was ten, so I have a lot of friends. I was curious about you."

She focuses on me as if she's trying to figure out how I know so much about her. I'm not about to admit the things I overheard Grayson say, because I don't want to hurt her. But I also don't want to admit that I begged Daniel for more information, because I don't want to scare her off. But based on the skeptical look spread across her face, she's already formed a good amount of distrust in me.

I take her by the elbow and she stops walking. I turn her so that she's facing me.

"Sky. I think we got off on the wrong foot at the store yesterday. And the talk about stalking, I swear, it was a joke. I don't want you to feel uncomfortable around me. Would it make you feel better if you knew more about me? Ask me something and I'll tell you. Anything."

"If I ask you something, will you be honest?"

I look her hard in the eyes. "That's all I'll ever be," I say. And I intend to be completely honest with her, unless I think it'll hurt her.

"Why did you drop out of school?"

I sigh, wishing she had asked me something a little less complicated. I should have known things wouldn't be simple with her, though.

I start walking again. "Technically, I haven't dropped out yet."

"Well you obviously haven't been in over a year. I'd say that's dropping out."

That comment makes me curious if she's heard the rumors about *me*. Of course I've been to school in the past year, it just wasn't *this* one. But she didn't ask about the rumored stint in juvi, so I'm not going to offer up unnecessary information.

"I just moved back home a few days ago," I say. "My mother and I had a pretty shitty year last year, so I moved in with my dad in Austin for a while. I've been going to school there, but felt like it was time to come back home. So here I am."

She squints like she's trying to scowl at me, but the expression she makes is too adorable to find intimidating. I keep my smile in check, though, because I can tell she's taking this school thing seriously. "None of that explains why you decided to drop out, rather than just transfer back."

She's right, but only because I really don't know the answer to her question.

"I don't know. To be honest, I'm still trying to decide what I want to do. It's been a pretty fucked-up year. Not to mention I hate this school. I'm tired of the bullshit and sometimes I think it would be easier to just test out."

She stops dead in her tracks again and glares at me. "That's a crap excuse."

"It's crap that I hate high school?"

"No. It's crap that you're letting one bad year determine your fate for the rest of your life. You're nine months away from graduation, so you drop out? It's just . . . it's stupid."

She's really taking this seriously. I laugh, even though I'm trying really hard not to. "Well, when you put it so eloquently."

She crosses her arms and huffs. "Laugh all you want. You quitting school is just giving in. You're proving everyone that's ever doubted you right."

Her eyes drop to the tattoo on my arm. I've never wanted to hide it until this moment, but something about her reading it seems like an invasion of privacy in a way. Maybe because I was so certain yesterday that she was half the reason for the tattoo on my arm. But now that I know she's not, I really don't want her asking about it. "You're gonna drop out and show the world just how hopeless you really are? Way to stick it to 'em."

I look down at the tattoo. She has no idea what the meaning is behind it and I realize that. But her assumption that it means anything other than what it means sort of pisses me off. I don't want to explain it to her and I certainly don't want to be judged by someone who seems to be receiving her own fair share of judgments. Rather than stick around and allow her to decipher me even more, I nudge my head toward her house. "You're here," I say flatly. I turn around and head toward home without looking back at her. No need to get too detailed with her, anyway, until I find out more about her relationship with Grayson. And in order to do that, I need to hurry up and get back to my house so I can shower and change in time for my first and possibly *only* day of senior year.

This is a large school, which is why I didn't expect to actually have a class with her, much less the first one. And with Mr. Mulligan, to top it off.

She didn't seem too happy to see me, either. And the fact that she just practically ran past me to get out of the classroom doesn't seem to bode well. I pick up my textbook and make my way out of the classroom. Rather than search for my next class, I head straight to find her, instead.

She's facing her locker, switching books. I walk up behind her but pause for a moment before speaking to her. I want to give her a chance to get what she needs from her locker, because I'm hoping I'll be walking her to her next class.

"Hey, you," I say optimistically. There's a pause.

"You came," she says, her voice cool and composed. She turns around to face me and just seeing her eyes again makes me smile. I lean against the locker next to hers and tilt my head against the cold metal. I eye her outfit for a second, taking in the fact that she somehow looks even better after a shower.

"You clean up nice. Although, the sweaty version of you isn't so bad, either," I say, smiling at her. I'm trying to ease some of the tension rolling off her, but nothing seems to be working in my favor.

"Are you here stalking me or did you actually re-enroll?" she asks.

A joke. She made a joke.

"Both," I say, tapping my fingers against the metal. I'm still smiling at her but she won't maintain eye contact with me for more than two seconds. She shifts her feet and looks nervously around us.

"Well, I need to get to class," she says, her voice monotone. "Welcome back."

She's being weird. "You're being weird."

She rolls her eyes and turns back to her locker. "I'm just surprised to see you here," she says unconvincingly.

"Nope," I say. "It's something else. What's wrong?"

My persistence seems to be paying off because she sighs and presses her back against the locker and looks up at me. "You want me to be honest?"

"That's all I ever want you to be."

She purses her lips together. "Fine," she says. "I don't want to give you the wrong idea. You flirt and say things like you have intentions with me that I'm not willing to reciprocate. And you're . . ."

She doesn't want to give me the wrong idea? Who is this and what the hell did she do with the girl who was blatantly flirting with me last night? I narrow my eyes at her. "I'm *what*?" I say, challenging her to finish her thought.

"You're . . . *intense*. Too intense. And moody. And a little bit scary. And there's the other thing . . . I just don't want you getting the wrong idea."

And *there it is*. She's been fed the lies and now I'm left to have to defend myself to the one person I incorrectly assumed might empathize with me.

"*What* other thing?"

"You know," she says, darting her eyes to the floor.

I take a step toward her and place my hand against the locker beside her head. "I *don't* know, because you're skirting around whatever issue it is you have with me like you're too afraid to say it. Just say it."

Her eyes grow wide and I immediately feel guilty for being so harsh with her. It just frustrates me no end that she would feed into their bullshit. The *same* bullshit that surrounds *her*.

"I heard about what you did," she blurts out. "I know about the guy you beat up. I know about you being sent to juvi. I know that in the two days I've known you, you've scared the shit out of me at least three times. And since we're being honest, I also know that if you've been asking around about me, then you've probably heard about my reputation, which is more than likely the only reason you're even making an effort with me. I hate to disappoint you, but I'm not screwing you. I don't want you thinking anything will happen between us besides what's already happening. We run together. That's it."

Wow.

I was expecting her to hear the rumors about me, but I wasn't expecting her to think I believe the rumors about her. So that's why her guard is up? Because she thinks I heard the rumors and now I'm just trying to *screw* her?

I mean, don't get me wrong. I'm not saying the thought hasn't crossed my mind. But *Jesus*, not like *that*. The fact that she even feels this way only makes me want to hug her. The thought of anyone intentionally trying to get close to her for that sole reason pisses me off. It doesn't help matters that Grayson is standing next to her now.

Where the hell did he come from? And why the hell does he have his arm around her like he owns her?

"Holder," Grayson says. "Didn't know you were coming back."

They're the first words he's spoken directly to me since the night before Les died. I'm afraid if I look at him I'll lose it, so I keep my eyes trained hard on Sky's. Unfortunately, my eyes can't seem to stop looking at the hand that's still gripping her waist. The hand that Sky hasn't slapped away. The hand that has obviously been around that same waist before. The same hand that used to be around Les.

This entire situation is too ironic. So much so, I crack a smile. *Just my luck.*

I straighten up and keep my eyes locked on the hand around Sky's waist. "Well, I'm back," I say. I can't watch this for another second. That familiar feeling of wanting to rip his fucking hand off has returned tenfold.

I walk away and make it a few feet down the hall before I turn around and face Sky again. "Track tryouts are Thursday after school. Go."

I don't wait for her response. I walk to my locker and exchange books, then head to my next class. I don't know why, though. I'm pretty sure I won't be coming back tomorrow.

*   *   *

"Hey, dickweed. What's this sudden infatuation with Sky?" Daniel asks as we make our way toward the cafeteria.

"It's nothing," I say, attempting to brush it off. "I met her yesterday and was just curious about her. But apparently she's with Grayson, so . . . whatever."

Daniel raises an eyebrow, but says nothing about the Grayson comment. He pushes through the cafeteria doors and we walk to our table. I take a seat and scan the crowd, searching for her.

"You gonna eat today?" he asks.

I shake my head. "Nah. I don't really feel like it." I lost my appetite this morning as soon as Grayson's arm went around Sky's waist.

Daniel shrugs and walks away to get himself food. I search the cafeteria a while longer and finally spot her a few tables down, sitting with a guy. He's not Grayson, though. I scan the crowd for Grayson and find him seated at a table on the opposite end of the cafeteria. They're not sitting together. Why wouldn't they sit together if they're dating? And if they're not dating, why would he be touching her like he was?

"I got you a water," Daniel says, sliding it across the table to me. "Thanks."

He sets his tray down and takes a seat across from me. "Why are you being such a cunt nugget?"

Water spews out of my mouth and I drop my arms onto the table and laugh, wiping my mouth. "*Cunt nugget?*"

He nods and pops the lid on his soda. "Something's off with you. You stared at that girl the entire time I was in line for food. You won't tell me anything about her. You've been on edge since you got here this morning and it has nothing to do with the fact that it's your first day back at school since . . . well . . . since your *last* day at school. And you haven't even commented about how no one seems to give a shit that you're even here today. Aren't you a little excited everyone has stopped with the gossip?"

I would be excited if I was convinced the gossip had stopped. But it hasn't stopped, it's just been shifted in a different direction. I heard Sky's name mentioned in every single class I've had today. Not to mention the shit I've seen slapped on her locker in the form of sticky-notes.

"They didn't stop with the gossip, Daniel. They just found someone new to target."

Daniel starts to reply, but he's cut off by several trays dropping down onto the table. Guys slide into seats and several of them welcome me back, going on about how I made it right in time for football season. That leads into a conversation about practices and Coach Riley, but none of it can hold my attention like she does. I ignore everyone around me and watch her, still trying to figure her out.

I honestly don't want to impede if she's dating Grayson. If she's happy with him, then fine. Good for them. But I'll be damned if I don't get to the bottom of what happened to her eye. I need a straight explanation from her before I can let it go. Otherwise, I'll be going to Grayson to find out what happened to her eye, and I know how that'll end.

The guy she's sitting with nods in my direction when he sees me staring at them. I make it a point not to turn away, because I actually want to get her attention. When she looks at me, I nudge my head toward the cafeteria doors, then stand up and walk toward them.

I walk out into the hallway, hoping she'll follow me. I know it's not my business, but if I expect to make it through the rest of the day without murdering Grayson, I have to know the truth. I walk around the corner for more privacy and lean back against the row of lockers. She walks around the corner and spots me, then comes to a stop.

"Are you dating Grayson?" I ask. I keep it short and sweet. She doesn't seem to like having conversations with me, so I don't want to force her to do something she doesn't want to do. I just want the truth so I can justify my next move.

She rolls her eyes and walks to the lockers across from me, leaning against them to face me. "Does it matter?"

Hmm. It shouldn't matter, but it does. I have no idea what kind of person she is, but Grayson doesn't deserve her. So yes, it does matter.

"He's an asshole," I say.

"Sometimes you are, too," she bites back.

"He's not good for you."

She laughs and rolls her eyes toward the ceiling, shaking her head. "And you *are*?"

I groan. She's missing my point completely. I turn around to face the lockers and hit one of them with an open palm, releasing some of the frustration she's causing me with her stubbornness. When the sound echoes through the hallway I cringe. That came off a little harsher than I meant for it to.

But I am angry and I hate that I'm angry because I shouldn't even give a shit. Les isn't around for Grayson to fuck over, so why *do* I care?

Because I don't want her with him. That's why.

I turn around and face her again. "Don't factor me into this. I'm talking about Grayson, not me. You shouldn't be with him. You have no idea what kind of person he is."

She rolls her head back against the locker, fed up with me. "Two days, Holder. I've known you all of two days," she says. She kicks off the lockers and walks toward me, eyeing me angrily. "In those two days, I've seen five different sides of you, and only one of them has been appealing. The fact that you think you have any right to even voice an opinion about me or my decisions is absurd. It's ridiculous."

I inhale through my nose and exhale through my clenched teeth, because I'm pissed. Pissed that she's *right*. She's seen me go from hot to cold more than once over these past two days and I haven't given her a single explanation. She deserves an explanation for my oddly overprotective behavior, so I attempt to give her one.

I take a step toward her. "I don't like him. And when I see things like this?" I bring my fingers up to trace the bruise underneath her eye. "And then see him with his arm around you? Forgive me if I get a little *ridiculous*."

The moment my fingers finish tracing the bruise, I fail to remove them from her cheek. Her breath hitches and her eyes grow wider and I can't help but notice the obvious reaction she has to my touch. I have an overwhelming urge to run my hand through her hair and pull her mouth to mine, but she pulls away from me and takes a step back.

"You think I should stay away from Grayson because you're afraid he has a temper?" She narrows her eyes and tilts her head. "A bit hypocritical, don't you think?"

I keep my eyes locked on hers as I process her comment. She's comparing me to *Grayson*?

I have to turn away from her so she doesn't see the disappointment on my face. I grip the back of my neck with both hands, then slowly turn back around to face her, but I keep my eyes trained on the floor.

"Did he hit you," I say with a defeated sigh. I look back up at her and directly into her eyes. "Has he *ever* hit you?"

She doesn't flinch or look away. She just shakes her head. "No," she says softly. "And no. I told you . . . it was an accident."

I can tell by her reaction that she's telling the truth. He didn't hit her. He never hit her, and I'm more than relieved. But still confused. If she's not dating him and he really didn't hit her, then what's her connection to him? Does she *want* to date him? Because I sure as hell don't want her to.

The bell rings right when I open my mouth to ask her what her relationship is with Grayson. The hallway fills with students and she breaks eye contact with me, then walks back toward the cafeteria.

I haven't seen Daniel again. I also didn't have another class with Sky, which disappoints me. I don't know why, though. We can't seem to have a conversation without it ending in an argument, but that doesn't stop me from wanting to have another conversation with her.

I leave my books in my locker, still not sure if I'll be back tomorrow. I grab my keys and walk toward the parking lot. I'm several feet from my car when I look up and see Grayson leaning against it. I stop and assess the situation. He's eyeing me coldly, but he's alone. Not sure what he wants or why he's touching my car.

"Grayson, whatever it is, I'm not interested. Just let it go." I'm not in the mood for him right now and he really needs to get the hell off my car.

"You know," he says, pushing off the car with his foot. He folds his arms across his chest and walks toward me. "I really wish I *could* just let it go, Holder. But for some reason you seem so focused on my business, you really make it impossible for me to let it go."

He's within reach of my fist now, which isn't very smart of him. I keep my eyes locked on his, but watch his hands out of my peripheral vision.

"You've been back less than a day and you're already at it again," he says, stupidly walking even closer to me. "Sky is off-limits to you, Holder. Don't talk to her. Don't look at her." *I can't believe I'm still allowing him to speak.* "Don't go fucking *near* her. The last thing I need is for another one of my girlfriends to kill herself because of you."

I'm in that moment.

The moment when rational thought is drowned out by anger.

The moment when a person's conscience is stifled by rage.

The moment when the vision of releasing every pent-up feeling I've had for thirteen months surfaces, and it actually feels *good*. His face would feel so good against my fist right now and the thought of it makes me smile as I clench my fists and inhale a breath.

But Grayson quickly becomes an afterthought when I look over his shoulder and see Sky across the parking lot, climbing into her car. She doesn't even glance around the parking lot to look for Grayson. She just climbs into her car, shuts her door, and leaves.

It's in that moment that I realize he's full of shit.

They weren't sitting together at lunch.

She wasn't at the party with him Saturday night.

She's not waiting for him after school.

She's not even looking for him in the parking lot right now.

Everything falls into place as Grayson takes a step back, gauging my reaction, waiting for me to take his bait. Sky doesn't care about him. That's why he's so pissed that I was talking to her in the hallway. She doesn't give a shit about him and he doesn't want me to know that.

He's not worth it, I repeat to myself.

I watch as Sky pulls out of the parking lot, then I slowly refocus my gaze on Grayson. I'm oddly calm after coming to this new realization, but his jaw is clenched tighter than his fists. He wants me to fight him. He wants me to get kicked out of school.

He doesn't deserve to get a single damn thing he wants.

I raise my arm. His eyes dart to my hand and he puts his own hands up in defense. I point the clicker toward my car and press the button, unlocking my doors. I silently walk around him and climb into my car, then pull out of the parking lot without giving him the reaction he was hoping for.

Fuck him. He's not worth it.

Chapter Ten

I open the refrigerator door because I'm starving, but I haven't had anything to eat in over thirteen months. I haven't taken a single bite of food since Les died and it's weird that I'm still alive after all this time.

It takes the refrigerator light a second to kick on, even after I have the door open. As soon as the contents of the refrigerator are illuminated, I'm immediately disappointed. Every single shelf is stuffed with Les's jeans. They're all folded neatly on the shelves of the refrigerator and it pisses me off because this is where the food should be and I'm fucking hungry.

I open one of the crisper drawers, hoping the food is hidden in there, but there's no food. Just another pair of neatly folded jeans. I shut it and open the other crisper drawer and her jeans are in there, too.

How many fucking pairs of jeans does she *need*? And why are they in the refrigerator where the food is supposed to be?

I close the refrigerator door and open the freezer, but I'm met with the same thing, only this time the jeans are frozen. They're all in freezer bags labeled "Les's jeans." I slam the freezer door shut, irritated, and turn toward the pantry, hoping to find something to eat in there.

I walk around the kitchen island and look down.

I see her.

I squeeze my eyes shut and open them again, but she's still there.

Les is huddled in a fetal position on the kitchen floor, her back pressed up against the pantry door.

This makes no sense.

How is she here?

She's been dead for thirteen months.

I'm hungry.

"Dean," she whispers.

Her eyes flick open and I immediately have to reach my hand out in order to steady myself against the island. My body suddenly becomes too heavy to hold up and I take a small step back, right before my legs give out and I fall to my knees in front of her.

Her eyes are open wide now and they're completely gray. No pupil, no irises. Just glossed-over gray eyes that are searching for me, unable to find me.

"Dean," she says again in a hoarse whisper. She blindly reaches her arm out toward me and her fingers feel around in front of her.

I want to help her. I want to reach out and grab her hand but I'm too weak to move. Or my body weighs too much. I don't know what it is that's stopping me, but I'm only two feet in front of her and I'm doing everything I can to lift my arm and take her hand but it won't fucking move. The more I struggle to regain control over my movements, the harder it becomes to breathe. She's crying now, saying my name. My chest tightens and my throat begins to close up and now I can't even calm her down with words because nothing will come out. I work the muscles in my jaw, but my teeth are clenched tight and my mouth won't open.

She's pulling herself up on her elbow, slowly scooting closer to me. She's trying to reach out for me but her lifeless eyes can't find me. She's crying even harder now.

"Help me, Dean," she says.

She hasn't called me Dean since we were kids and I don't know why she's calling me Dean now. I don't like it.

I squeeze my eyes shut and try to focus on getting my voice to work or my arms to move, but all the concentration in the world can't help me right now.

"Dean, *please*," she cries, only this time it's not her voice. It's the voice of a child. "Don't go," the child begs.

I open my eyes and Les is no longer there, but someone else has taken her place. A little girl is sitting with her back pressed against the pantry door and her head is buried in her arms that are wrapped tightly around her legs.

Hope.

I still can't move or speak or breathe and my chest is growing tighter and tighter with each sob that racks the little girl's body. All I can do is sit and watch her cry, because I'm physically unable to even turn my head or close my eyes.

"Dean," she says, her voice muffled by her arms and her tears. It's the first time I've heard her say my name since the day she was taken and it knocks out what little breath I had left in me. She slowly lifts her head away from her arms and widens her eyes. They're solid gray, identical to Les's. She leans her head back against the pantry door and wipes away a tear with the back of her hand.

"You found me," she whispers.

Only this time, it's not the voice of the little girl anymore. It's not even Les's voice.

It's Sky's.

Chapter Eleven

I open my eyes and I'm no longer on the kitchen floor.

    I'm in my bed.

    I'm covered in sweat.

    I'm gasping for air.

Chapter Twelve

I couldn't go back to sleep last night after the nightmare. I've been awake since two in the morning and it's now after six.

I drop down onto the sidewalk when I reach her house. I stretch my legs out in front of me and lean forward, grabbing my shoes while I stretch the muscles in my back. I've been tense for days and nothing I do seems to help.

Before I went to sleep last night I had no intention of running with her again today. But I've been sitting alone for over four hours, wide awake, and the only thing that even remotely appealed to me was the thought of seeing Sky again.

I also had no intention of going back to school today but it seems way more appealing than staying home all day. It's like I've been living minute to minute since the moment I got back from Austin last week. I'm not sure from one moment to the next what I'm doing or where I'll be or even what frame of mind I'll be in.

I don't like this instability.

I also don't like that I'm at her house again today, waiting on her to come outside for her morning run. I don't like that I still feel the need to be around her. I don't like the fact that I don't want her to believe the rumors about me. I don't give a shit when anyone else believes them. Why do I give a shit if *she* believes them?

I shouldn't. I should just go back home and leave her to believe whatever she wants to believe.

I stand up in an attempt to talk myself into leaving, but I just stand here, waiting on her. I know I need to leave and I know I don't want to be involved with anyone even remotely interested in Grayson, but I can't do it. I can't leave because I want to see her again a whole lot more than I want to leave.

A noise comes from the side of her house, so I take a few steps to get a look. She's climbing headfirst out of her window.

Just seeing her again, even from a distance, reminds me of why I crave to be around her so much. It's only been a few days, but since the moment I met her, no matter where I am, I'm constantly wondering about her. My attention is constantly homed in on her like I'm a compass and she's my North.

Once she's outside, she pauses and looks up toward the sky, inhaling a deep breath. I take a few hesitant steps toward her. "Do you always climb out your window or were you just hoping to avoid me?"

She spins around, wide-eyed. I try not to let my eyes dip below her neck, but the things I've seen her run in are hard not to stare at.

Keep looking at her face, Holder. You can do it.

She glances at me, but doesn't make eye contact. Her eyes lock on my stomach and I'm curious if it's because she likes that I'm not wearing a shirt or if it's because she can't stand me to the point that it's hard for her to look me in the eyes. "If I was trying to avoid you I would have just stayed in bed." She walks past me and lowers herself onto the sidewalk.

I hate that her voice does things to my body that no other voice could ever do. But I also love it and want her to keep talking, even if she *is* rude most of the time.

I watch as she pushes her legs out in front of her and begins to stretch. She seems fairly calm today, despite the fact that I showed up. I sort of expected her to tell me to go the hell away after how we left things in the hallway yesterday.

"I wasn't sure if you'd show up," I say, taking a seat on the sidewalk in front of her.

She lifts her head and looks me in the eyes this time. "Why

wouldn't I? I'm not the one with the issues. Besides, neither of us owns the road."

Issues?

She thinks I have *issues?*

I'm not the one feeding into the rumors like she is. I'm also not the one leaving notes on her locker, nor am I one of the many people at school who have treated her like shit. If anything, I've been one of the few people to be nice to her.

But she thinks *I'm* the one with the issues?

"Give me your hands," I say, mirroring her position. "I need to stretch, too."

She shoots me a curious look, but takes my hands and leans back, pulling me forward.

"For the record," I say, "I wasn't the one with the issue yesterday."

I can feel her lean back farther, tightening her grip on my wrists. "Are you insinuating *I'm* the one with the issue?" she asks.

"Aren't you?"

"Clarify," she says. "I don't like vague."

She doesn't like vague.

Funny, because I don't either. I like truth and that's exactly the point I'm trying to make to this girl. "Sky, if there's one thing you should know about me, it's that I don't do vague. I told you I'll only ever be honest with you, and to me, vague is the same thing as dishonesty." I switch positions and pull her forward as I lean back.

"That's a pretty vague answer you just gave me," she says.

"I was never asked a question. I've told you before, if you want to know something, just ask. You seem to think you know me, yet you've never actually asked me anything yourself."

"I *don't* know you," she snaps.

I laugh, because she's absolutely right. She doesn't know me at all, but it certainly seems like she's a quick one to judge.

I don't know why I'm even bothering with her. She obviously doesn't *want* me to bother with her. I should just leave and let her think whatever the hell she wants to think.

I drop her hands and stand up. "Forget it," I mutter, turning to walk away. As much as I like being around her, there's only so much I'm willing to put up with.

"Wait," she says, following after me.

I honestly expected her to just let me walk away. Hearing the word "wait" come out of her mouth and knowing she's following behind me does this thing to my chest that makes it feel alive again and it pisses me off because I don't want her to have that effect on me. "What did I say?" she asks, catching up to me. "I *don't* know you. Why are you getting all pissy with me again?"

Pissy?

Her word-choice makes me want to smile, but the fact that she doesn't recognize that she's the one who has been *pissy* for two days irritates the hell out of me. I stop walking and turn to face her, taking two steps toward her.

"I guess after spending time with you over the last few days, I thought I'd get a slightly different reaction from you at school. I've given you plenty of opportunity to ask me whatever you want to ask me, but for some reason you want to believe everything you hear, despite the fact that you never heard any of it from *me*. And coming from someone with her own share of rumors, I figured you'd be a little less judgmental."

Her eyes narrow and she puts her hands on her hips. "So that's what this is about? You thought the slutty new girl would be sympathetic to the gay-bashing asshole?"

I groan out of frustration. I hate hearing her refer to herself like that. "Don't do that, Sky."

She takes a step toward me. "Don't do what? Call you a gay-bashing asshole? Okay. Let's practice this honesty policy of yours. Did you or did you not beat up that student last year so badly that you spent a year in juvenile detention?"

I want to grab her by the shoulders and shake her out of sheer frustration. Why can't she see that she's behaving just like everyone else? I know she's not like them, so I don't understand her attitude at all. Anyone that can brush off rumors about themselves isn't the type of person who would spread them. So why the hell is she *believing* them?

I look her hard in the eyes. "When I said *don't do that*, I wasn't referring to you insulting me. I was referring to you insulting *yourself*." I close the gap between us and when I do, she takes in a small rush of air and closes her mouth. I lower my voice and confirm the only part of the rumors that are true. "And yes. I beat his ass to within an inch of his life, and if the bastard was standing in front of me right now, I'd do it again."

We stare at each other in silence. She's looking at me with a mixture of anger and fear, and I hate that she's feeling either of those things. She takes a slow step back, putting space between us, but doesn't break her firm stare.

"I don't want to run with you today," she says flatly.

"I don't really feel like running with you, either."

I turn around at the same time she does and immediately feel nothing but regret. I didn't accomplish anything by coming here today. If anything, I just made things worse with her. I shouldn't have to come out and tell her that the majority of what she thinks she knows about me is false. I shouldn't have to explain myself to anyone and neither should she.

But I regret that I *didn't* explain myself, because I need her to know that I'm not that guy.

I just don't know why I need her to know that.

Chapter Twelve-and-a-half

Les,

Remember when we were fourteen and I had a crush on Ava? You hardly knew her but I forced you to become friends with her so she could come to the house and spend the night with you. She was the first girl I ever kissed and we lasted all of two weeks before she started to get on my everlasting nerve. Unfortunately, by the time we broke up, you really did like her. Then I was forced to see her on a recurring basis for an entire year after that until she moved.

I know you were sad when she moved, but I was so relieved. It was way too awkward having to interact with her on a regular basis after that.

I also know it was cruel of me to force you to be her friend just so she would come stay the night at our house. I thought I learned my lesson and I never asked you to do it again.

Well, I didn't learn my lesson. Today I've been wishing you were still here, purely for selfish reasons, because I would give anything for you to be friends with Sky. After running with her this morning, I can see clearly that she's irritating and irrational and stubborn and gorgeous as hell and I want so bad to stop thinking about her, but I can't. If you were here,

I could ask you to be her friend so she would have a reason to come over to our house, even though we're eighteen now and not fourteen. But I want an excuse to talk to her again. I want to give her one more chance to hear me out, but I don't know how to go about doing that. I don't want to do it at school and we aren't running together anymore. Short of walking up to her house and knocking on her front door, I can't figure out a way to get her to talk to me.

Wait. That's actually not a bad idea.

Thanks, Les.

H

Chapter Thirteen

"We going out tonight?" I ask Daniel as we make our way toward the parking lot. We usually do something on Friday nights, but tonight I'm actually hoping he says no. I decided a few days ago that I wanted to go to Sky's house tonight to try to talk to her. I don't know if it's a good idea, but I know if I don't at least try, I'll drive myself crazy wondering if it would have made a difference.

"Can't," Daniel says. "I'm taking Val out. We could do something tomorrow night, though. I'll call you."

I nod and he turns to head toward his car. I open my door, but pause when I see Sky's car out of the corner of my eye. She's leaning against it, talking to Grayson.

From the looks of it, they might be doing more than just talking.

I'd be lying if I didn't admit that seeing his hands on her makes every muscle in my body clench tight. I prop my arm on my door and watch them for some stupid, self-torturous reason.

From here, she doesn't look happy. She pushes him away from her and takes a step away from him. She's watching him while he talks, then he moves in and wraps his arms around her again. I take a step away from my car, prepared to walk across the parking lot and pull his ignorant ass off her. She clearly doesn't want him touching her, but I stop and take a step back when it looks like she relents and gives in to him. As soon as he leans in to kiss her, I have to look away.

It's physically impossible to watch. I don't understand her. I don't understand what she sees in him and I really don't understand why she can't seem to stand me, when he's the actual asshole.

Maybe I'm wrong about her. Maybe she really *is* just like everyone else. Maybe I've just been hoping she was different for my own sake.

Or maybe *not*.

I'm looking at them again, seeing her reaction to what he's doing to her. His arms are still around her and it looks like he's still kissing her neck or shoulder or wherever the fuck his mouth is. But I could have sworn she just rolled her eyes.

Now she's looking at her watch, not responding to him at all. She drops her arm and rests her hands at her sides and she's just standing there, looking more inconvenienced by him than interested.

I continue to watch them and continue to grow more and more confused by her lack of interest. Her expression is almost lifeless, until the second she locks eyes with mine. Her whole body tenses and her eyes grow wide. She immediately looks away and pushes Grayson off her. She turns her back to him and gets into her car. I'm too far away to hear what she says to him, but the fact that she's driving away and he's flipping her off with both hands tells me that whatever she said to him wasn't at all what he wanted to hear.

I smile.

I'm still confused, I'm still angry, I'm still intrigued and I'm still planning on showing up on her doorstep tonight. Especially after witnessing whatever that was I just witnessed.

I ring the doorbell and wait.

I'm a ball of nerves right now, but only because I don't have a clue how she'll react to seeing me on her doorstep. I also don't know what the hell I'm going to say to her once she does finally open the door.

I ring the doorbell again after waiting several moments. I'm sure I'm the last person she'll expect to see here on a Friday night.

Shit. It's Friday night. She's probably not even home.

I hear footsteps making their way toward the door and it opens. She's standing in front of me a frazzled mess. Her hair is loosely pulled back, but strands have fallen all around her face. She's got white powder dusted across her nose and cheek and even has some in the loose strands of hair framing her face. She looks adorable. And shocked.

Several seconds pass with us just standing there and I realize that I should probably be the one speaking right now, since I'm the one who showed up at her house.

God, why does every single thing about her throw me off like this?

"Hey," she says.

Her calm voice is like a breath of fresh air. She doesn't seem pissed that I'm here unannounced. "Hi," I say, returning her greeting.

Another round of awkward silence ensues and she tilts her head to the side. "Um . . ." She squints and crinkles up her nose and I can tell she's not sure what to do or say next.

"You busy?" I ask her, knowing just by the disarray of her appearance that whatever she was doing, she was working hard at it.

She turns and glances back into her house, then faces me again. "Sort of."

Sort of.

I take her reply for what it is. She's obviously trying not to be rude, but I can see that this stupid idea of mine to just show up unannounced was just that . . . a stupid idea.

I glance at my car behind me, gauging how far the walk of shame I'm about to take will be. "Yeah," I say, pointing over my shoulder at my car. "I guess I'll . . . go." I take a step down and begin to turn toward my car, wishing I was anywhere but in this awkward predicament.

"No," she says quickly. She takes a step back and opens the door for me. "You can come in, but you might be put to work."

Instant relief overcomes me and I nod, walking inside. A quick glance around the living room makes it appear that she might be the only one home right now. I hope she is, because it would make things a lot easier if it were just the two of us.

She walks around me and into the kitchen. She picks up a measuring cup and resumes whatever it was she was doing before I showed up on her doorstep. Her back is to me and she's quiet. I slowly make my way into the kitchen and eye the baked goods lining her bar.

"You prepping for a bake sale?" I ask, making my way around the bar so that her back isn't completely to me.

"My mom's out of town for the weekend," she says, glancing up at me. "She's antisugar, so I kind of go crazy when she's not here."

Her mom's out of town, so she bakes? I really can't figure this girl out. I reach over to the plate of cookies between us on the bar and pick one up, looking to her for permission to try it.

"Help yourself," she says. "But be warned, just because I like to bake doesn't mean I'm good at it." She refocuses her attention to the bowl in front of her.

"So you get the house to yourself and you spend Friday night baking? Typical teenager," I tease. I take a bite of the cookie and *ohmygod*. She can bake. I like her even more.

"What can I say?" she says with a shrug. "I'm a rebel."

I smile, then eye the plate of cookies again. There have to be a dozen there and I plan on eating at least half of them before she kicks me out of her house. I'm gonna need milk.

She's still intensely focused on the bowl in front of her, so I take it upon myself to find my own glass. "Got any milk?" I ask, making my way to the refrigerator. She doesn't answer my question, so I open the refrigerator and remove the milk, then pour myself a glass. I finish the rest of the cookie, then take a drink. I wince, because whatever the hell this is, it's not real milk. Or it's rotten. I glance at the label before shutting the refrigerator and see that it's almond milk. I don't want to be rude, so I take another drink and turn around.

She's looking straight at me with an arched eyebrow. I smile. "You shouldn't offer cookies without milk, you know. You're a pretty pathetic hostess." I swipe another cookie and take a seat at the bar.

She grins right before she turns around to face the counter again. "I try to save my hospitality for *invited* guests."

I laugh. "Ouch."

The sarcasm in her voice is nice, though, because it helps ease my tension. She powers on the mixer and keeps her focus on the bowl in front of her. I love that she hasn't asked why I'm here. I know she's wondering what I'm doing here, but I also know from previous interaction with her that she's incredibly stubborn and more than likely won't ask what I'm doing here, no matter how much she wants to know.

She turns off the mixer and pulls the mixing blades loose, then brings one to her mouth and licks it.

Holy shit.

I gulp.

"Want one?" she says, holding one up for me to take. "It's German chocolate."

"How hospitable of you."

"Shut up and lick it or I'm keeping it for myself," she says teasingly. She smiles and walks to the cabinet, then fills a glass with water. "You want some water or do you want to continue pretending you can stomach that vegan shit?"

I laugh, then immediately push my cup toward her. "I was trying to be nice, but I can't take another sip of whatever the hell this is. Yes, water. *Please.*"

She laughs and fills my cup with water, then takes a seat across from me. She picks up a brownie and takes a bite, holding eye contact with me. She doesn't speak but I know she's curious why I'm here. The fact that she still hasn't asked, though, makes me admire her stubbornness.

I know I should offer up my reason for showing up out of the blue, but I'm a little stubborn myself and feel like dragging this thing out with her a little longer. I'm kind of enjoying it.

We silently watch each other until she's almost finished with her brownie. The way she's semismiling at me while she eats is making my pulse race and if I don't look away from her, I'm afraid I'll blurt out everything I want to say to her all at once.

In order to avoid that, I stand up and walk into the living room to take a look around. I can't watch her eat for another second and I need to refocus my attention on why I'm here, because *I'm* even starting to forget.

There are several pictures hanging on her walls, so I walk closer to them to take a look. There aren't any pictures of her that are more than a few years old, but the ones where she's younger than she is now are jarring to look at. She really does look just like Hope.

It's surreal, looking into those big brown eyes of the little girl in the picture. If it weren't for the fact that she's in several pictures with her mother, I'd be convinced she really was Hope.

But she can't be Hope, because Hope's mother passed away when she was just a little girl. Unless Karen isn't Sky's mom.

I hate that my mind is still going there. "Your mom seems really young," I say, noticing the noticeable small age difference between them.

"She *is* young."

"You don't look like her. Do you look like your dad?"

She shrugs. "I don't know. I don't remember what he looks like."

She looks sad when she says it, but I'm curious why she doesn't remember what he looks like.

"Is your dad dead?"

She sighs. I can tell she's uncomfortable talking about it. "I don't know. Haven't seen him since I was three." It's clear she doesn't feel like elaborating. I walk back to the kitchen and reclaim my seat.

"That's all I get? No story?"

"Oh, there's a story. I just don't want to tell it."

I can see I'm not getting any more information out of her right now, so I change the subject. "Your cookies were good. You shouldn't downplay your baking abilities."

She smiles, but her smile fades as soon as the phone on the counter between us sounds off, indicating a text. I look down at it just as she jumps up and rushes to the oven. She swings it open to eye the cake and I realize she thinks the sound came from the oven, rather than the phone.

I pick up the phone just as she shuts the oven and turns to face me. "You got a text." I laugh. "Your cake is fine."

She rolls her eyes and throws the oven mitt on the counter, then walks back to her seat. I'm curious about the cell phone, especially since she told me earlier this week that she didn't have one.

"I thought you weren't allowed to have a phone," I say, glancing at all the texts as I scroll my finger down the screen. "Or was that a really pathetic excuse to avoid giving me your number?"

"I'm *not* allowed," she says. "My best friend gave it to me the other day. It can't do anything but text."

I turn the phone around to face her. "What the hell kind of texts *are* these?" I read one out loud.

"Sky, you are beautiful. You are possibly the most exquisite creature in the universe and if anyone tells you otherwise, I'll cut the bitch." I glance at her, the texts making me even more curious about her than I was

before. "Oh, God," I say. "They're all like this. Please tell me you don't text these to yourself for daily motivation."

She laughs and snatches the phone out of my hand. "Stop. You're ruining the fun of it."

"Oh, my God, you do? Those are all from you?"

"No!" she says defensively. "They're from Six. She's my best friend and she's halfway around the world and she misses me. She wants me to not be sad, so she sends me nice texts every day. I think it's sweet."

"Oh, you do not," I say. "You think it's annoying and you probably don't even read them."

"She means well," she says, folding her arms defensively across her chest.

"They'll ruin you," I tease. "Those texts will inflate your ego so much, you'll explode." I scroll through the settings on her phone and punch the number into my phone. There's no way I'm leaving here without her number, and this is the perfect excuse to get it. "We need to rectify this situation before you start suffering from delusions of grandeur." I give her back her phone and text her.

Your cookies suck ass. And you're really not that pretty.

"Better?" I ask after she reads it. "Did the ego deflate enough?"

She laughs and places the phone facedown on the counter. "You know just the right things to say to a girl." She walks into the living room and spins around to face me. "Want a tour of the house?"

I don't hesitate. Of course I want a tour of her house. I follow her through the house and listen as she speaks. I pretend to be interested in everything she's pointing out, but in reality I can only concentrate on the sound of her voice. She could talk to me all night and I'd never get tired of listening to her.

"My room," she says, swinging open the door to her bedroom. "Feel free to look around, but being as though there aren't any people eighteen or older here, stay off the bed. I'm not allowed to get pregnant this weekend."

I pause as I'm passing through her door and eye her. "Only *this* weekend?" I ask, matching her wit. "You plan on getting knocked up next weekend, instead?"

She smiles and I continue making my way into her room. "Nah," she says. "I'll probably wait a few more weeks."

I shouldn't be here. Every minute I spend with her makes me like her more and more. Now I'm in her room and there's no one in the house other than her and me, not to mention the fact that there's this bed between us that she told me to stay off of.

I shouldn't be here.

I came here to show her I'm the good guy, not the bad guy. So why am I looking at her bed and not having good thoughts right now?

"I'm eighteen," I say, unable to stop imagining what she looks like when she lies in this bed.

"Yay for you?" she says, confused.

I smile at her, then nod toward her bed as explanation. "You said to stay off your bed because I'm not eighteen. I'm just pointing out that I am."

Her shoulders tense and she inhales a quick breath. "Oh," she says, slightly flustered. "Well then, I meant nineteen."

I like her reaction a little too much, so I try to refocus and concentrate on why I'm here.

Why *am* I here? Because all that's running through my mind right now is *bed, bed, bed.*

I'm here to make a point. A much-needed, valid point. I walk as far away from the bed as I can get and end up at the window.

The same window I've heard so much about over the course of the past week at school. It's amazing the things you can learn if you just shut up and listen.

I lean my head out of it and look around, then pull back inside. I don't like that she keeps it open. It's not safe.

"So this is the infamous window, huh?"

If that comment doesn't direct the conversation in the direction I'm hoping, I don't know what will.

"What do you want, Holder?" she snaps.

I turn to face her and she's eyeing me fiercely. "Did I say something wrong, Sky? Or untrue? Unfounded, maybe?"

She immediately walks to her door and holds it open. "You know exactly what you said and you got the reaction you wanted. Happy? You can go now."

I hate that I'm pissing her off, but I ignore her request for me to leave. I look away and walk to the side of her bed and pick up a book. I pretend to flip through it while I contemplate how to start the conversation.

"Holder, I'm asking you as nicely as I'm going to ask you. Please leave."

I set the book down and take a seat on her bed, despite the fact that she told me not to. She's already pissed at me. What's one more thing?

She stomps over to the bed and actually grabs my legs, attempting to physically pull me off the bed. She then reaches up and yanks on my wrists in an attempt to pull me up, but I pull her down to the bed and flip her onto her back, holding her arms to the mattress.

Now that I've got her good and riled up, it would be a good time to tell her what I came here to tell her. That I'm *not* that guy. That I wasn't in juvi for a year. That I didn't beat that kid up because he was gay.

But here I am holding her down to the mattress and I have no idea how we even got to this point, but I'll be damned if I can form a coherent thought. She's not struggling to get out from under me at all and we're both staring at each other like we're daring the other one to be the first to make a move.

My heart is pounding against my chest and if I don't back away from her right now I'll do something to those lips of hers that will for sure end up with me getting slapped.

Or kissed back.

The thought is tempting, but I don't risk it. I let go of her arms and wipe my thumb across the end of her nose. "Flour. It's been bugging me," I say. I back away and rest my back against her headboard.

She doesn't move. She's breathing heavily and staring up at the ceiling. I'm not sure what she's thinking, but she's not trying to kick me out of her room anymore, so that's good.

"I didn't know he was gay," I say.

She turns her head in my direction and she's still flat on her back. She doesn't say anything, so I use the opportunity to explain in more detail while I've got her full attention.

"I beat him up because he was an asshole. I had no idea he was gay."

She eyes me, expressionless, then slowly turns her head back toward the ceiling. I give her a moment to ponder what I just said. She'll either believe me and feel guilty or she *won't* believe me and she'll still be pissed. Either way, I don't want her to feel guilty *or* pissed. But we're not left with any other choices of emotions in this situation.

I remain quiet, wanting her to respond to me with *something*, at least.

A sound comes from the kitchen and it actually resembles an oven timer rather than her phone. "Cake!" she yells. She's off the bed and out the bedroom door and I find myself alone in her room on her bed. I close my eyes and lean my head against the headboard.

I want her to believe me. I want her to trust me and I want her to know the truth about my past. There's something about her that tells me she's not like all the other people I've encountered who disappoint me. I just hope I'm not wrong about her, because I like being around her. She actually makes me feel like I have a purpose. I haven't felt like I had a purpose in over thirteen months.

I glance up when she walks back into the room and she smiles sheepishly. She has a cookie in her mouth and another in her hand. She holds it out to me and drops down next to me on the bed. Her head lands against her pillow and she sighs.

"I guess the gay-bashing asshole remark was really judgmental on my part then, huh? You aren't really an ignorant homophobe who spent the last year in juvenile detention?"

Mission accomplished.

And it was so much easier than I thought it would be.

I smile and scoot down until I'm flat on the bed next to her. "Nope," I say, looking up at the stars plastered across her ceiling. "Not at all. I spent the entire last year living with my father in Austin. I don't even know where the story about me being sent to juvi came into the picture."

"Why don't you defend yourself against the rumors if they aren't true?"

What an odd question, coming from someone who hasn't defended herself at all this entire week. I glance in her direction. "Why don't *you*?"

She quietly nods. "Touché."

We both look back up to her ceiling. I like that she was so easy to come around. I like that she didn't argue about it, especially knowing how stubborn she is.

I like that I was right about her.

"The window comment from earlier?" she says. "You were just making a point about rumors? You really weren't trying to be mean?"

I hate that she actually thought I was just being cruel, even if it was only for a minute. I don't want her to ever think that about me. "I'm not mean, Sky."

"You're intense. I'm right about that, at least."

"I may be intense, but I'm not mean."

"Well, I'm not a slut."

"I'm not a gay-bashing asshole."

"So we're all clear?"

I laugh. "Yeah, I guess so."

It's quiet for another moment until she inhales a long, deep breath. "I'm sorry, Holder."

"I know, Sky," I say. I didn't come here for an apology. I don't want her to feel guilty about her misconception. "I know."

She doesn't say anything else and we both continue to look up at the stars. I'm conflicted right now because we're both on her bed and as much as I try to ignore my attraction for her, it's sort of hard when I'm inches from her.

I'm curious if she finds *me* attractive at all. I'm almost positive she does based on the tiny things she does when I'm around her that she tries to hide. Like the times I've caught her staring at my chest when I ran with her. Or the way she sucks in a breath when I lean in to speak to her. Or how she always seems to be struggling not to smile when she's trying so hard to be mad at me.

I'm not positive what she thinks about me or how she feels, but I know one thing . . . she definitely doesn't act indifferent toward me like she does toward Grayson.

Thinking about that incident and how just a few hours ago she was kissing him makes me grimace. It may not be appropriate to ask her about it, but I sure as hell can't stop thinking about how much I hate the thought of her kissing anyone, *especially* Grayson. And if there's ever a chance that I'll be the one kissing her, I need to know that she won't be kissing him again.

Ever.

"I need to ask you something," I say. I prepare myself to bring it up, knowing she more than likely doesn't want to talk about it. But I have to know how she feels about him. I inhale a deep breath and roll over to face her. "Why were you letting Grayson do what he was doing to you in the parking lot?"

She winces and shakes her head ever so slightly. "I already told you. He's not my boyfriend and he's not the one who gave me the black eye."

"I'm not asking because of any of that," I say, even though I really am. "I'm asking because I saw how you reacted. You were irritated with him. You even looked a little bored. I just want to know why you allow him to do those things if you clearly don't want him touching you."

She's quiet for a second. "My lack of interest was that obvious?"

"Yep. And from fifty yards away. I'm just surprised he didn't take the hint."

She immediately flips onto her side and props up on her elbow. "I know, right? I can't tell you how many times I've turned him down but he just doesn't stop. It's really pathetic. And unattractive."

I can't even describe how good it feels to hear her say that.

"Then why do you let him do it?"

She keeps her eyes locked on mine, but she doesn't answer me. We're inches apart. On her bed. Her mouth is right here.

So close.

We both flip onto our backs almost simultaneously.

"It's complicated," she says. Her voice sounds sad and I definitely didn't come here to make her feel sad.

"You don't have to explain. I was just curious. It's really not my business."

She pulls her arms up behind her head and rests her head on her hands. "Have you ever had a serious girlfriend?"

I have no idea where she's going with this, but at least she's talking, so I go with it. "Yep," I say. "But I hope you aren't about to ask for details, because I don't go there."

"That's not why I'm asking," she says, shaking her head. "When you kissed her, what did you feel?"

I *definitely* don't know where she's going with this. But still, I indulge her. It's the least I can do for showing up unannounced, then practically insulting her reputation before getting my point across.

"You want honesty, right?"

"That's all I ever want," she says, mimicking my own words.

I grin. "All right, then. I guess I felt . . . horny."

When I say the word horny, I swear she sucks in a breath. She's quick to recover, though. "So you get the butterflies and the sweaty palms and the rapid heartbeat and all that?" she asks.

"Yeah. Not with every girl I've been with, but most of them."

She tilts her head toward me and arches an eyebrow, which makes me grin. "There weren't *that* many," I say. At least I don't *think* there were that many. I'm not sure what number constitutes a lot at this point and even then, people measure things on different scales. "What's your point?" I ask, relieved she isn't asking me to clarify exactly how many there have been.

"My point is that I *don't*. I don't feel any of that. When I make out with guys, I don't feel anything at all. Just numbness. So sometimes I let Grayson do what he does to me, not because I enjoy it, but because I like not feeling anything at all."

I was absolutely not expecting that answer. I'm not sure that I *like* that answer. I mean, I like that she doesn't actually feel anything for

Grayson, but I hate that it hasn't stopped her from letting him try to get what he wants.

I also don't like that she admitted to never feeling anything, because I can honestly say when I'm around her, I've never felt so *much*.

"I know it doesn't make sense, and no, I'm not a lesbian," she says defensively. "I've just never been attracted to anyone before you and I don't know why."

I quickly turn and look at her, not sure that I heard her correctly. But based on her reaction and the way her arm comes up and immediately covers her face, I know for a fact I heard her correctly.

She's attracted to me.

And she didn't intend to admit that out loud.

And I'm pretty sure that accidental admission just made my entire year.

I reach over and slide my fingers around her wrist, pulling her arm away from her face. I know she's embarrassed right now, but there's no way in hell I'm letting this go.

"You're attracted to me?"

"Oh, God," she groans. "That's the last thing you need for your ego."

"That's probably true," I admit, laughing. "Better hurry up and insult me before my ego gets as big as yours."

"You need a haircut," she blurts out. "Really bad. It gets in your eyes and you squint and you're constantly moving it out of the way like you're Justin Bieber and it's really distracting."

I know she doesn't have access to technology, so I let it slide that Justin Bieber cut his hair off a long time ago. I'm disappointed that I even know that. I tug at my hair with my fingers and fall back against my pillow. "Man. That really hurt. It seems like you've thought that one out for a while."

"Just since Monday," she says.

"You *met* me on Monday. So technically, you've been thinking about how much you hate my hair since the moment we met?"

"Not *every* moment."

I laugh. I wonder if it's possible for people to fall in love with a person one characteristic at a time, or if you fall for the entire person at once. Because I think I just fell in love with her wit. And her bluntness. And maybe even her mouth, but I won't allow myself to stare at it long enough to confirm.

Shit. That's already three characteristics and I've only been here an hour.

"I can't believe you think I'm hot," I say, breaking the silence.

"Shut up."

"You probably faked passing out the other day, just so you could be carried in my hot, sweaty, manly arms."

"Shut up," she says again.

"I'll bet you fantasize about me at night, right here in this bed."

"Shut up, Holder."

"You probably even . . ."

She slaps her hand over my mouth. "You're way hotter when you aren't speaking."

I shut up, but only because I want to revel in the fact that this night has already turned out better than I ever anticipated. Every second I'm with her I like her more and more. I like her sense of humor and I like that she gets *my* sense of humor. She's the first girl besides Les to ever actually give me a run for my money and I can't seem to get enough of it.

"I'm bored," I say, hoping she'll suggest an interesting make-out session in lieu of staring at her ceiling. Although, if my options are limited to staring at her ceiling all night or going home, I'll gladly stare at her ceiling.

"So go home."

"I don't want to," I say resolutely. I'm having way too much fun to go home. "What do you do when you're bored? You don't have internet or TV. Do you just sit around all day and think about how hot I am?"

"I read," she says. "A lot. Sometimes I bake. Sometimes I run."

"Read, bake, and run. And fantasize about me. What a riveting life you lead."

"I like my life."

"I sort of like it, too," I say. And I *do* like it. We already have the running in common. And she may not realize it, but we also have the fantasizing in common. I don't bake, but I do like *her* baking.

That leaves reading. I read when I need to, which isn't a lot. But I suddenly want to know everything about everything that interests her and if reading interests her, it interests me too. I reach over and pick up the book from her nightstand. "Here, read this."

"You want me to read it out loud? You're that bored?"

"Pretty damn bored."

"It's a romance." She says it like it's a warning.

"Like I said. Pretty damn bored. Read."

She shrugs and adjusts her pillow, then begins reading.

"*I was almost three days old before the hospital forced them to decide. They agreed to take the first three letters of both names and compromised on Layken . . .*"

She continues to read and I continue to let her. After several chapters, I can't tell if my rapid-fire pulse is a result of listening to her voice for so long or if it's from the sexual tension in the book. Maybe both of them coupled together is what's doing it. Sky should really think about a career in voiceovers or audiobooks or some shit like that because her voice is . . .

"*He glides across the room . . .*"

Her voice is trailing off.

". . . and bends down, snatching up the . . ."

And . . . she's out. The book falls against her chest and I laugh quietly, but I don't get up. because the fact that she fell asleep doesn't mean I'm ready to leave.

I lie with her for about half an hour, confirming the fact that yes, I'm definitely in love with her mouth. I watch her sleep until my phone chimes. I scoot her away from me and onto her back, then pull my phone out of my pocket.

> **Dude. It's Daniel, me. Val is f'ng crazy n I think I'm at that Burker Ging and come get me I can't drive. I drank and I hate her.**

I text him back immediately.

> **Good idea. Stay put. Be there in thirty.**

I slide the phone back in my pocket, but it sounds off again with an incoming text.

> **Holder?**

I shake my head and shoot a text back that says, *Yeah?* He replies immediately.

> **Oh, good. Just mak'n sure it was u, man.**

Jeez. He's more than just *drunk.*

I stand up and take the book out of her hands, then set it on the nightstand and mark the page she stopped at so I'll have an excuse to come back over here tomorrow. I walk to the kitchen and spend the next ten minutes cleaning up her mess. I swear you would think she harbored resentment toward flour considering the amount I have to wipe up. After all the food is wrapped in Saran Wrap (minus the few cookies I might have swiped), I walk back to her bedroom, then sit down on the edge of her bed.

She's snoring.

I love it.

Shit. That's four things already.

I really need to leave.

Before standing up to leave, I slowly lean forward, hesitating, not wanting to wake her. But I can't leave here without a little preview. I continue inching toward her until my mouth grazes her lips, and I kiss her.

Chapter Thirteen-and-a-half

Les,

Sky, Sky, Sky, Sky, Sky, Sky, Sky, Sky, Sky.

There. Get used to it, because I have a feeling she's all I'm going to be talking about for a while. Oh, my God, Les. I can't even explain to you how perfect this girl is. And when I say perfect, I mean imperfect, because there's just so much wrong with her. But everything wrong with her is everything that draws me in and makes her perfect.

She's flat-out rude to me and I love it. She's stubborn and I love it. She's a smartass and she's sarcastic and every witty thing that comes out of her mouth is like music to my ears because that's exactly what I want. She's what I need and I don't want her to change at all. There's not a single thing about her I would change.

There is one thing about her that worries me, though, and that's the fact that she seems to be a little emotionally detached. And as noticeable as it was when I saw her with Grayson, I don't see that at all when she's with me. I'm almost convinced she feels different about me, but I would be lying if I said I wasn't worried that she wouldn't feel anything if I kissed her. Because dammit, Les, I want to kiss her so fucking bad but I'm too scared. I'm scared if I kiss her too soon, it'll feel like every other kiss she's ever received. She'll feel nothing.

I don't want her to feel nothing when I kiss her. I want her to feel everything.

H

Chapter Fourteen

What you want to do tonight?

I read Daniel's text and respond.

Sorry. Plans.

WTF, puss flap!? No! Me. You. Plans.

Can't. Pretty sure I have a date.

Sky?

Yep.

Can I come?

Nope.

Can I be your date next Saturday, then?

Sure, babe.

Can't wait, sugar.

I laugh at Daniel's text, then clear the screen and find Sky's number.

I haven't heard from her since she fell asleep on me last night, so I'm not even sure if she wants me at her house tonight.

> **What time can I come over? Not that I'm looking forward to it or anything. You're really, really boring.**

After I hit send, I get another incoming text from a number I don't recognize.

> **If you're dating my girl, get your own prepaid minutes and quit wasting mine, Jackass.**

The only person I know with prepaid minutes is Sky. And she said her best friend bought her the phone, so I'm seriously hoping this text is from her friend and not someone else. I immediately text back, hoping to find out more.

> **How do I get more minutes?**

As soon as I hit send on that text, Sky's response comes through.

> **Be here at seven. And bring me something to eat. I'm not cooking for you.**

Rude.

I love it.

She texted me again while I was at the grocery store, asking me to hurry. I really, seriously like that she wanted me here sooner. I like it a lot. I like *her* a lot. I like this whole *weekend* a lot.

Her front door swings open just moments after I ring the doorbell. She's smiling as soon as she sees me and I curse under my breath because that's just one more thing about her that I just fell in love with. She looks down at the sacks of groceries in my hands and arches an eyebrow.

I shrug. "One of us has to be the hospitable one." I walk up the steps and ease past her, then make my way into her kitchen. "I hope you like spaghetti and meatballs, because that's what you're getting."

"You're cooking dinner for me?" she asks skeptically from behind me.

"Actually, I'm cooking for *me*, but you're welcome to eat some if you want." I glance back at her and smile so she'll know I'm teasing.

"Are you always so sarcastic?"

I shrug. "Are *you*?"

"Do you always answer questions with questions?"

"Do *you*?"

She grabs a towel off the bar and throws it at me but I dodge it. "You want something to drink?" I ask her.

"You're offering to make me something to drink in my own house?"

I walk to the refrigerator and scan the shelves, but my options are limited. "Do you want milk that tastes like ass or do you want soda?"

"Do we even have soda?"

I peer around the refrigerator door and grin at her. "Can either of us say anything that isn't a question?"

"I don't know, can we?"

"How long do you think we can keep this up?" I ask, taking the last soda from the fridge. "You want ice?"

"Are *you* having ice?"

Dammit, she's cute. "Do you think I should have ice?"

"Do you *like* ice?"

She's quick. I'm impressed. "Is your ice any good?"

"Well, do you prefer crushed ice or cubed ice?"

I almost answer by saying cubed, but realize that wouldn't be a question. I narrow my eyes and glare at her. "No ice for you."

"Ha! I win," she gloats.

"I let you win because I feel sorry for you," I say, making my way back to the stove. "Anyone that snores as bad as you do deserves a break every now and then."

"You know, the insults are really only funny when they're in text form," she says.

She stands up and walks to the freezer at the same time I turn around to walk to the refrigerator for the minced garlic. Her back is to me and she's filling her cup with ice. She turns around when I reach the refrigerator. She looks up at me with those big brown eyes and those pouty lips and I take a step closer to her, hoping I make her flustered again. I love making her flustered.

I lift my arm and press my palm flat against the refrigerator and look her in the eyes. "You know I'm kidding, right?"

She immediately sucks in a rush of air and nods. I grin and move in even closer. "Good. Because you *don't* snore. In fact, you're pretty damn adorable when you sleep." I don't know why I told her she didn't snore. Maybe I don't want her to know just how long I actually stayed in her bed watching her after she fell asleep last night.

She tugs on her bottom lip, looking up at me hopefully. Her chest is heaving and her arms are dusted in chills and I wish more than anything I could just grab her face and kiss her. I want to kiss her more than I want air.

But I already told myself I wouldn't, so I'm not.

That doesn't mean I can't have a little fun with her, though. I move my lips until they're almost touching her ear. "Sky. I *need* you . . ." I pause for a second and wait for her to catch her breath. ". . . to move. I need in the fridge." I pull back and watch for her reaction. Her palms are flat against the refrigerator behind her like she's struggling to hold herself upright.

Seeing her physical reaction to my proximity makes me smile. When I smile and she sees I was purposely teasing her, she narrows her eyes and I laugh.

She pushes against my chest and shoves me back. "You're such an ass!" she says, walking to the bar.

"I'm sorry, but damn. You're so blatantly attracted to me, it's hard not to tease you." I'm still laughing when I walk back to the stove with the garlic. I pour some into the pan and glance at her. She's covering her face with her hands from embarrassment and I immediately feel guilty. I don't want her thinking I'm not into her, because I'm positive I'm into her way more than she's into me. I guess I haven't made that very clear to her, though, which is a little unfair.

"Want to know something?" I ask.

She looks up at me and shakes her head. "Probably not."

"It might make you feel better," I say.

"I doubt it."

I look at her and she's not smiling and I hate it. I meant for this to be lighthearted; I didn't mean to hurt her feelings. "I might be a little bit attracted to you, too," I admit, hoping it'll help her realize that I didn't mean to embarrass her.

"Just a little bit?" she asks, teasingly.

No. Not just a little bit. A whole helluva lot.

I continue to prepare the food and I'm doing everything I can to get it all started so I can sit and talk with her while it cooks. She just sits silently at the bar, watching me work my way around her kitchen. I love that she's not modest when it comes to the way she watches me. She stares at me like she doesn't want to look at anything else and I like it.

"What does *lol* mean?"

"Seriously?"

"Yes, seriously. You typed it in your text earlier."

"It means laugh out loud. You use it when you think something is funny."

"Huh," she says. "That's dumb."

"Yeah, it is pretty dumb. It's just habit, though, and the abbreviated texts make it a lot faster to type once you get the hang of it. Sort of like OMG and WTF and IDK and . . ."

"Oh, God, stop," she says quickly. "You speaking in abbreviated text form is really unattractive."

I wink at her. "I'll never do it again, then." I walk to the counter and pull the vegetables out of the sack. I run them under the water and move the cutting board to the bar in front of her. "Do you like chunky or smooth spaghetti sauce," I ask, placing the tomato in front of me. She's looking past me, lost in thought. I wait to see if she'll answer me when she catches back up, but she just keeps staring off into space.

"You okay?" I ask her, waving my hand once in front of her eyes. She finally snaps out of it and looks up at me. "Where'd you go? You checked out for a while there."

She shakes it off. "I'm fine."

I don't like her tone of voice. She doesn't seem fine.

"Where'd you go, Sky?" I ask her again. I want to know what she was thinking. Or maybe I don't want to know, because if she was thinking about how she wants me to leave then I hope she continues to pretend she's fine.

"Promise you won't laugh?" she asks.

Relief rushes through me because I don't think she'd ask me that if she was hoping I would leave. But I'm not about to promise her I won't laugh, so I shake my head in disagreement. "I told you that I'll only ever be honest with you, so no. I can't promise I won't laugh because you're kind of funny and that's only setting myself up for failure."

"Are you always so difficult?"

I grin, but don't respond. I love it when she gets irritated with me, so I don't give her a response on purpose.

She straightens up in her chair and says, "Okay, fine." She inhales a deep breath like she's preparing for a long speech.

I'm nervous.

"I'm really not any good at this whole dating thing, and I don't even know if this *is* a date, but I know that whatever it is, it's a little more than just two friends hanging out, and knowing that makes me think about later tonight when it's time for you to leave and whether or not you plan to kiss me and I'm the type of person who hates surprises so I can't stop feeling awkward about it because I *do* want you to kiss me and this may be presumptuous of me, but I sort of think you want to kiss me, too, and so I was thinking how much easier it would be if we just went ahead and kissed already so you can go back to cooking dinner and I can stop trying to mentally map out how our night's about to play out."

I'm pretty sure it's too soon to love her, but *shit*. She's got to stop doing and saying these unexpected things that make me want to fast-forward whatever's going on between us. Because I want to kiss her and make love to her and marry her and make her have my babies and I want it all to happen *tonight*.

But then we'll be out of firsts, and the firsts are the best part. Good thing I'm patient.

I set the knife down on the cutting board and look her in the eyes. "That," I say, "was the longest run-on sentence I've ever heard."

She doesn't like my comment. She huffs and falls back against her seat in a pout.

"Relax." I laugh. I take a second to finish the sauce and start the pasta and do everything I need to do to get to a point where I can actually talk to her while I'm not trying to cook at the same time. When I finally get the pasta going, I wipe my hands on the dishtowel and place it on the counter. I walk around the bar to where she's seated.

"Stand up," I tell her.

She slowly stands up and I place my hands on her shoulders, then look around the room for a good spot to break the news to her that I'm not going to kiss her tonight. As much as I want to and as much as I now know she wants me to, I still want to wait.

And I know I told her I'm not mean, but I never said I wasn't cruel. And I'm just having too much fun watching her when she's flustered and I really want to make her flustered again. "Hmm," I say, still pretending I'm looking for the perfect spot to kiss her. I glance into the kitchen, then take her by the wrists and pull her with me. "I sort of liked the fridge backdrop." I push her against the fridge and she lets me. She hasn't stopped watching me intently the whole time and I love it. I lift my arms to the sides of her head and begin to lean in toward her. She closes her eyes.

I keep mine open.

I look at her lips for a moment. Thanks to the peck I stole while she was sleeping last night, I kind of have an idea what they feel like. But now I can't help but wonder what they taste like. I'm so tempted to lean in a few more inches and see for myself, but I don't.

I've got this.

They're just lips.

I watch her for a few more seconds until her eyes flick open when I fail to kiss her. Her whole body jumps when she sees how close I am and it makes me laugh.

Why do I enjoy teasing her so much?

"Sky?" I say, looking down at her. "I'm not trying to torture you or anything, but I already made up my mind before I came over here. I'm not kissing you tonight."

The hope in her expression dwindles almost immediately.

"Why not?" she says. Her eyes are full of rejection and I absolutely hate it, but I'm still not kissing her. But I do want her to know how much I *want* to kiss her.

I bring my hand up to her face and trace a line down her cheek. The feel of her skin beneath my fingertips is like silk. I keep trailing down her jaw, then her neck. My whole body is tense because I'm not sure if she feels all of this the way I do. I can't imagine someone like Grayson could be lucky enough to touch her face or taste her mouth and that he wouldn't care if she was even enjoying it or not.

When my hand reaches her shoulder, I stop and look her in the eyes. "I want to kiss you," I say. "Believe me, I do."

So, so bad.

I remove my hand from her shoulder and bring it up to her cheek. She leans into my hand and looks up at me, her eyes full of disappointment. "But if you really want to, then why don't you?"

Ugh. I hate that look. If she keeps looking at me like that I'll lose every shred of willpower I have left. Which isn't much.

I tilt her face up to mine. "Because," I whisper. "I'm afraid you won't feel it."

The look on her face when I say it is a mixture of realization and regret. She knows I'm referring to her lack of response to other guys and I'm not sure she knows how to respond. She's silent, but I just want her to argue with me. I want her to tell me how wrong I am. I want her to tell me she already feels like I do, but instead she just nods and covers my hand with hers.

I close my eyes, wishing she had responded any other way. But the fact that she didn't just proves that not kissing her tonight is exactly what needs to happen. I don't understand why she's so closed off, but I'll wait however long I have to. There's no way I could walk away from this girl now.

I pull her away from the refrigerator and wrap my arms around her. She slowly returns the embrace by clasping her arms around my waist and conforming to my chest. She willingly leans into me and just feeling her want me to hold her is better than anything I've felt this entire year. All she did was hug me back, but little does she know she just knocked a whole lot of life back into me. I press my lips into her hair and inhale. I could stay like this all night.

But the damn oven timer dings, reminding me that I'm cooking her dinner. If it means having to let her go, I'd rather starve. But I promised to cook for her, so I release my hold from around her and take a step back.

The embarrassed and almost heartbroken look on her face is the last thing I expect to see. She drops her gaze down at the floor and I realize that I just disappointed her. A lot. All I'm trying to do is go at a pace that's best for her. I can't have her thinking that I'm going slow because it's my choice. Because if she didn't have whatever issue it is she has with guys, we wouldn't be standing in this kitchen right now. We'd be back on her bed just like we were last night, only this time she wouldn't be reading to me.

I grab both of her hands and interlock our fingers. "Look at me." She hesitantly lifts her face and looks at me. "Sky, I'm not kissing you tonight but believe me when I tell you, I've never wanted to kiss a girl more. So stop thinking I'm not attracted to you because you have no idea just how much I am. You can hold my hand, you can run your fingers through my hair, you can straddle me while I feed you spaghetti, but you are not getting kissed tonight. And probably not tomorrow, either. I need this. I need to know for sure that you're feeling every single thing that I'm feeling the moment my lips touch yours. Because I want your first kiss to be the best first kiss in the history of first kisses."

The sadness is gone from her eyes now and she's actually smiling at me. I lift her hand and kiss it. "Now stop sulking and help me finish the meatballs. Okay?" I ask, wanting reassurance from her that she believes me. "Is that enough to get you through a couple more dates?"

She nods, still smiling. "Yep. But you're wrong about one thing."

"What's that?"

"You said you want my first kiss to be the best first kiss, but this won't be my first kiss. You know that."

I don't know how to break it to her, but she hasn't been kissed before. Not like she deserves, anyway. I hate that she doesn't realize this, so I take it upon myself to show her exactly what a real kiss feels like.

I let go of her hands and cup her face, walking her back against the refrigerator. I lean in until I can feel her breath on my lips and she gasps. I love the helpless, hungry look in her eyes right now, but it doesn't compare to what it does to me when she bites her lip.

"Let me inform you of something," I say, lowering my voice. "The moment my lips touch yours, it *will* be your first kiss. Because if you've never felt anything when someone's kissed you, then no one's ever really kissed you. Not the way *I* plan on kissing you."

She exhales a pent-up breath and her arms are covered in chills again.

She felt *that*.

I grin victoriously and back away from her, then turn my attention to the stove. I can hear her sliding down the refrigerator. I turn around and she's sitting on the floor, looking up at me in shock. I laugh.

"You okay?" I say with a wink.

She smiles up at me from the floor and pulls her legs up to her chest with a shrug. "My legs stopped working." She laughs. "Must be because I'm *so* attracted to you," she says sarcastically.

I look around the kitchen. "You think your mother has a tincture for people who are too attracted to me?"

"My mother has a tincture for everything," she says.

I walk over and take her hand, then pull her up. I press my hand against the small of her back and pull her against me. She looks up at me with hooded eyes and a small gasp parts her lips. I lower my mouth to her ear and whisper, "Well, whatever you do . . . make sure you never take that tincture."

Her chest rises against mine and she's looking into my eyes like everything I've said tonight meant nothing. She wants me to kiss her and she doesn't care that I'm doing everything in my power *not* to.

I slide my hand down her back and slap her on the ass. "Focus, girl. We have food to cook."

"Okay, I have one," she says, placing her cup down on the table.

We're playing a game she suggested called Dinner Quest, where no question is off limits and eating and drinking isn't allowed until the question has been answered. I've never heard of it, but I like the thought of being able to ask her anything I want to ask her.

"Why did you follow me to my car at the grocery store?" she asks.

I shrug. "Like I said, I thought you were someone else."

"I know," she says. "But who?"

Maybe I don't want to play this game. I'm not ready to tell her about Hope. I'm definitely not ready to tell her about Les, but there's no way around it because my answer just dug me into a hole. I shift in my seat and reach for my drink, but she snatches it out of my hands.

"No drinks. Answer the question first." She sets my drink back down on the table and waits for my explanation. I really don't want to go into my screwed up past, so I try to keep my answer simple.

"I wasn't sure who you reminded me of," I lie. "You just reminded me of someone. I didn't realize until later that you reminded me of my sister."

She makes a face and says, "I remind you of your sister? That's kind of gross, Holder."

Oh, *shit*. That's not at *all* what I meant. "No, not like that. Not like that at all, you don't even look anything like she did. There was just something about seeing you that made me think of her. And I don't even know why I followed you. It was all so surreal. The whole situation was a little bizarre, and then running into you in front of my house later . . ."

Should I really tell her how that made me feel? How I thought for sure Les had something to do with it or that it was divine intervention or a freaking miracle? Because I honestly feel like it was too perfect to be chalked up to coincidence.

"It was like it was meant to happen," I finally say.

She inhales a deep breath and I look up at her, afraid of how forward that might have been. She smiles at me and points to my drink. "You can drink now," she says. "Your turn to ask me a question."

"Oh, this one's easy. I want to know whose toes I'm stepping on. I received a mysterious inbox message from someone today. All it said was, 'If you're dating my girl, get your own prepaid minutes and quit wasting mine, jackass.'"

"That would be Six," she says, smiling. "The bearer of my daily doses of positive affirmation."

Thank God.

"I was hoping you'd say that. Because I'm pretty competitive, and if it came from a guy, my response would not have been as nice."

"You responded? What'd you say?"

"Is that your question? Because if it isn't, I'm taking another bite."

"Hold your horses and answer the question," she says.

"Yes, I responded to her text. I said, 'How do I buy more minutes?'"

Her cheeks redden and she grins. "I was only joking, that wasn't my question. It's still my turn."

I drop my fork onto my plate and sigh at her stubbornness. "My food's getting cold."

She ignores my feigned irritation and she leans forward, looking me directly in the eyes. "I want to know about your sister. And why you referred to her in the past tense."

Ah, shit. Did I refer to her in the past tense? I look up at the ceiling and sigh. "Ugh. You really ask the deep questions, huh?"

"That's how the game is played. I didn't make up the rules."

I guess there's no getting out of this explanation. But honestly, I don't mind telling her. There are certain things about my past I'd rather not discuss, but Les doesn't really feel like my past. She still feels very much a part of my present.

"Remember when I told you my family had a pretty fucked-up year last year?"

She nods, and I hate that I'm about to put a damper on our conversation. But she doesn't like vague, so . . . "She died thirteen months ago. She killed herself, even though my mother would rather we use the term 'purposely overdosed.'"

I keep my eyes locked on hers, waiting for the "I'm so sorry," or the "It was meant to happen," to come out of her mouth like it comes out of everyone else's mouth.

"What was her name?" she asks. The fact that she even asks like she's genuinely interested is unexpected.

"Lesslie. I called her Les."

"Was she older than you?"

Only by three minutes. "We were twins," I say, right before I take a bite.

Her eyes widen slightly and she reaches for her drink. I intercept her this time.

"My turn," I say. Now that I know nothing is off limits, I ask her about the one thing she didn't really want to talk about yesterday. "I want to know the story about your dad."

She groans, but plays along. She knows she can't refuse to answer that question, because I just completely opened up to her about Les.

"Like I said, I haven't seen him since I was three. I don't have any memories of him. At least, I don't think I do. I don't even know what he looks like."

"Your mom doesn't have any pictures of him?"

She cocks her head slightly, then leans back in her seat. "You remember when you said my mom looked really young? Well, it's because she is. She adopted me."

I drop my fork.

Adopted.

The genuine possibility that she could be Hope bombards my thoughts. It wouldn't make sense that she was three when she was adopted, though, because Hope was five when she was taken. Unless she's been lied to.

But what are the chances? And what are the chances that someone like Karen would be capable of stealing a child?

"*What?*" she asks. "You've never met anyone who was adopted?"

I realize the shock I'm feeling in my head and my heart is also registering in my expression. I clear my throat and try to regroup, but a million more questions are forming in my mind. "You were adopted when you were three? By Karen?"

She shakes her head. "I was put into foster care when I was three, after my biological mother died. My dad couldn't raise me on his own. Or he didn't *want* to raise me on his own. Either way, I'm fine with it. I lucked out with Karen and I have no urge whatsoever to go figure it all out. If he wanted to know where I was, he'd come find me."

Her mother is dead? Hope's mother is dead.

But Hope was never put into foster care and Hope's dad didn't put her up for adoption. It all makes absolutely no sense, but at the same time I can't rule out the possibility. She's either been fed complete lies about her past, or I'm going insane.

The latter is more likely.

"What does your tattoo mean?" she asks, pointing at it with her fork.

I look down at my arm and touch the letters that make up Hope's name.

If she was Hope, she would remember the name. That's the only thing that stops me from believing in the possibility that she could be Hope.

Hope would remember.

"It's a reminder," I say. "I got it after Les died."

"A reminder for what?"

And this is the only answer she'll get that's vague, because I'm definitely not about to explain. "It's a reminder of the people I've let down in my life."

Her expression grows sympathetic. "This game's not very fun, is it?"

"It's really not." I laugh. "It sort of sucks ass. But we need to keep going because I still have questions. Do you remember anything from before you were adopted?"

"Not really. Bits and pieces, but it comes to a point that, when you don't have anyone to validate your memories, you just lose them all. The only thing I have from before Karen adopted me is some jewelry, and I have no idea who it came from. I can't distinguish now between what was reality, dreams, or what I saw on TV."

"Do you remember your mother?"

She pauses for a moment. "Karen is my mother," she says flatly. I can tell she doesn't want to talk about it and I don't want to push her. "My turn. Last question, then we eat dessert."

"Do you think we even have enough dessert?" I say, trying to lighten the mood.

"Why did you beat him up?" she says, darkening the mood completely.

I don't want to get into that one. I push my bowl away. I'll just let her win this round. "You don't want to know the answer to that, Sky. I'll take the punishment."

"But I do want to know."

Just thinking about that day already has me worked up again. I pop my jaw to ease the tension. "Like I told you before, I beat him up because he was an asshole."

"That's vague," she says, narrowing her eyes. "You don't do vague."

I know that I like her stubbornness, but I only like it when she's not pushing me to bring up the past. But I also have no clue what she's been told about the whole situation. I've made it a point to get her to open up to me and ask me questions so she can hear the truth from me. If I refuse to answer her, then she'll stop opening up.

"It was my first week back at school since Les died," I say. "She went to school there, too, so everyone knew what happened. I overheard the guy saying something about Les when I was passing him in the hallway. I disagreed with it, and I let him know. I took it too far and it came to a point when I was on top of him that I just didn't care.

I was hitting him, over and over, and I didn't even care. The really fucked-up part is that the kid will more than likely be deaf out of his left ear for the rest of his life, and I *still* don't care."

My fist is clenched on the table. Just thinking about the way everyone acted after she died has me pissed off all over again.

"What did he say about her?"

I lean back in my chair and my eyes drop to the table between us. I don't really feel like looking her in the eyes when I'm only thinking about stuff that infuriates me. "I heard him laughing, telling his friend that Les took the selfish, easy way out. He said if she wasn't such a coward, she would have toughed it out."

"Toughed what out?"

"Life."

"You don't think she took the easy way out." She doesn't say it like it's a question. She says it like she's truly trying to understand me. That's all I've wanted from her all week. I just want her to understand me. To believe *me* and not everyone else.

And no. I *don't* think she took the easy way out. I don't think that at all.

I reach across the table and pull her hand between both of mine. "Les was the bravest fucking person I've ever known," I say. "It takes a lot of guts to do what she did. To just end it, not knowing what's next? Not knowing if there's *anything* next? It's easier to go on living a life without any life left in it than it is to just say 'fuck it' and leave. She was one of the few that just said, 'fuck it.' And I'll commend her every day I'm still alive, too scared to do the same thing."

I look at her after I'm finished speaking and her eyes are wide. Her hand is shaking, so I clasp my hands around hers. We look at each other for several seconds and I can tell she has no idea what to say to me. I attempt to lighten the mood and change the subject. She said that was the last question, then we get dessert.

I lean forward and kiss the top of her head, then walk into the kitchen. "You want brownies or cookies?" I watch her from the kitchen as I grab the desserts and she's staring at me, wide-eyed.

I freaked her out.

I just completely freaked her out.

I walk back to where she's seated and I kneel down in front of her. "Hey. I didn't mean to scare you," I tell her, taking her face in my hands. "I'm not suicidal if that's what's freaking you out. I'm not fucked up in the head. I'm not deranged. I'm not suffering from post-traumatic stress disorder. I'm just a brother who loved his sister more than life itself, so I get a little intense when I think about her. And if I cope better by telling myself that what she did was noble, even though it wasn't, then that's all I'm doing. I'm just coping." I allow her time to let my words sink in, then finish my explanation. "I fucking loved that girl, Sky. I need to believe that what she did was the only answer she had left, because if I don't, then I'll never forgive myself for not helping her find a different one." I press my forehead to hers, looking her firmly in the eyes. "Okay?"

I need her to understand that I'm trying. I might not have it together and I might not know how to move past Les's death, but I'm trying.

She presses her lips together and nods, then pulls my hands away. "I need to use the bathroom," she says, quickly slipping around me. She rushes to the bathroom and shuts the door behind her.

Jesus Christ, why did I even go there? I walk to the hallway, prepared to knock on the door and apologize, but decide to give her a few minutes first. I know that was really heavy. Maybe she just needs a minute.

I wait across the hallway until the bathroom door opens up again. It doesn't look like she's been crying.

"We good?" I ask her, taking a step closer to her.

She smiles up at me and exhales a shaky breath. "I told you I think you're intense. This just proves my point."

She's already herself again. I love that about her.

I smile and wrap my arms around her, then rest my chin on top of her head while we make our way to her bedroom. "Are you allowed to get pregnant yet?"

She laughs. "Nope. Not this weekend. Besides, you have to kiss a girl before you can knock her up."

"Did someone not have sex education when she was home-schooled? Because I could totally knock you up without ever kissing you. Want me to show you?"

She falls onto the bed and picks up the book that she read to me last night. "I'll take your word for it," she says. "Besides, I'm hoping we're about to get a hefty dose of sex education before we make it to the last page."

I lie down beside her and pull her to me. She rests her head on my chest and begins reading to me.

I ball my hand up into a tight fist and keep it at my side, doing everything in my power not to touch her mouth. I've just never seen anything so perfect before.

She's been reading for well over half an hour now and I haven't heard a damn word she's said. Last night it was so much easier to pay attention to the actual story because I wasn't looking directly at her. Tonight it's taking every ounce of willpower I have not to claim her mouth with mine. She's propped against me with her head on my chest, using me as her pillow. I'm hoping she can't feel my heart pounding right now because every time she glances up at me when she flips a page, I squeeze my fists even tighter and try to keep my hands to myself but my resistance resonates in my pulse. And it's not that I don't *want* to touch her. I want to touch her and kiss her so bad it physically hurts.

I just don't want it to be insignificant to her. When I touch her . . . I want her to feel it. I want every single thing I say to her and every single thing I do to her to have significance.

Last night when she told me she's never felt anything when she was kissed, my heart did this crazy thing where it felt bound, like it was being constricted, just like the lungs in my chest. I've dated a lot of girls, even though I might have downplayed that to her. With every single girl I've been with, my heart has never reacted like it reacts to her. And I'm not referring to my heart's *feelings* for her, because let's be honest, I barely know her. I'm referring to my heart's literal, *physical* reaction to her. Every time she speaks or smiles or, God forbid, *laughs* . . . my heart reacts like it's been sucker-punched. I hate it and like it and somehow have become addicted to it. Every time she speaks, the sucker-punch in my chest reminds me that there's still something there.

A huge internal part of me was lost when I lost Hope, and I was convinced Les took the very last contents of my chest with her when she died last year. After being with Sky these last two days, I'm not so sure about that, anymore. I don't think my chest has been empty this whole time like I thought. Whatever is left inside me has just been asleep, and she's somehow slowly waking it up.

With every word she speaks and every glance she sends my way, she's unknowingly pulling me out of this thirteen-year-long nightmare I've been trapped in, and I want to continue to allow her to pull me.

Fuck it.

I unclench my fist and bring it up to her hair that's spilled across my chest. I pick up a loose strand and curl it around my finger, keeping my eyes trained on her mouth while she reads to me. I find myself still comparing her to Hope every now and then, despite my efforts not to. I'm trying to recall exactly what Hope's eyes looked like or if she had the same four freckles across the bridge of her nose that Sky has. Every time I start to compare them, I force myself to stop. It doesn't matter anymore and I need to let it go. Sky has proved that she can't be Hope and I have to accept it. The odds of the girl I lost being right here, pressed against my chest, her strand of hair between my fingertips . . . it's impossible. I need to separate the two of them in my head before I screw up and do something stupid, like refer to Sky by the wrong name.

That would suck.

I notice her lips are pressed into a tight, thin line and she isn't speaking anymore. It's a damn shame because her mouth is fucking hypnotizing.

"Why'd you stop talking?" I ask her, without looking at her eyes. I keep my gaze trained on her lips, hoping they start moving again.

"Talking?" she says, her top lip curling up in a grin. "Holder, I'm *reading*. There's a difference. And from the looks of it, you haven't been paying a lick of attention."

The feistiness in her reply makes me smile. "Oh, I've been paying attention," I say, lifting up onto my elbows. "To your mouth. Maybe not to the words coming out of it, but definitely to your mouth." I slide out from under her until she's on her back, then I scoot down until I'm beside her. I pull her against me and take her hair between my fingertips again. The fact that she doesn't resist in the slightest only means I'll be at war with myself the rest of the damn night. She's already made it clear she wants me to kiss her, and I'll be damned if backing away from having her pressed up against the refrigerator wasn't the hardest thing I've ever had to do.

Shit. Just thinking about it is almost as intense as when it was actually happening.

I drop the strand of hair and watch as my fingers fall straight to her lips. I don't know how the last five seconds just occurred, but I'm looking down at my hand as it grazes over her mouth like I have no control over my limbs anymore. My hand has a mind of its own but I really don't care . . . nor do I want to stop it.

I feel her breath against my fingertips and I have to bite the inside of my cheek to center my focus on something other than what I want. Because it's not my wants that are important right now—it's hers. And I highly doubt she wants to taste my mouth as much as I need to taste hers right now.

"You have a nice mouth," I say, still slowly tracing it with the tips of my fingers. "I can't stop looking at it."

"You should taste it," she says. "It's quite lovely."

Holy shit.

I squeeze my eyes shut and drop my head to her neck, forcing my focus away from those lips. "Stop it, you evil wench."

She laughs. "No way. This is your stupid rule; why should I be the one to enforce it?"

Oh, Jesus. It's a game to her. This whole *not kissing* thing is a game to her and she's going to tease the hell out of me. I can't do this. If I give in and kiss her before she's ready I know I won't be able to stop. And I don't know what the hell is going on inside my chest right now but I really like the way it feels when I'm around her. If I can drag whatever this is out to make sure she feels the same way, then that's exactly what I'll do. Even if it takes me weeks to ensure she gets to that point, then I guess I'll wait weeks. In the meantime, I'll do whatever I can to make sure her next first is anything but insignificant.

"Because you know I'm right," I say, explaining exactly why she needs to help me enforce this rule. "I can't kiss you tonight because kissing leads to the next thing, which leads to the next thing, and at the rate we're going we'll be all out of firsts by next weekend. Don't you want to drag our firsts out a little longer?" I pull away from her neck and look down at her, very aware that there is less space between our mouths right now than between our bodies.

"Firsts?" she says, looking up at me curiously. "How many firsts are there?"

"There aren't that many, which is why we need to drag them out. We've already passed too many since we met."

She tilts her head and her expression grows attractively serious. "What firsts have we already passed?"

"The easy ones," I say. "First hug, first date, first fight, first time we slept together, although I wasn't the one sleeping. Now we barely have any left. First kiss. First time to sleep together when we're both actually *awake*. First marriage. First kid. We're done after that. Our lives will become mundane and boring and I'll have to divorce you and marry a wife who's twenty years younger than me so I can have a lot more firsts and you'll be stuck raising the kids." I bring my hand to her cheek and smile at her. "So you see, babe? I'm only doing this for your benefit. The longer I wait to kiss you, the longer it'll be before I'm forced to leave you high and dry."

She laughs and the sound is so toxic I'm forced to swallow the huge lump in my throat so I can make room to breathe again.

"Your logic terrifies me," she says. "I sort of don't find you attractive anymore."

Challenge accepted.

I slowly slide on top of her, careful to hold my weight up with my hands. If my body were to touch any part of hers right now, we'd already be moving on to seconds and thirds. "You *sort of* don't find me attractive?" I say, staring straight down into her eyes. "That can also mean you sort of *do* find me attractive."

Her eyes grow dark and she shakes her head. I can see the dip in the base of her throat barely move as she gulps before speaking. "I don't find you attractive at all. You repulse me. In fact, you better not kiss me because I'm pretty sure I just threw up in my mouth."

I laugh, then drop onto my elbow so I can move closer to her ear, still careful not to touch any other part of her.

"You're a liar," I whisper. "You're a whole *lot* attracted to me and I'm about to prove it."

I had every intention of pulling away, but as soon as the scent of her hits me, I can't pull back. My lips are pressed against her neck before I even have a chance to weigh the decision. But right now it feels a hell of a lot more like a *necessity* to taste her rather than just a *decision*. She gasps when I pull back and I can't help but hope that her gasp was genuine. The thought of her actually feeling what I felt when my lips touched her neck makes me feel ridiculously victorious. It's too bad I like a challenge, because that gasp just made me want to up my game. I drop my mouth back to her ear and whisper, "Did you feel that?"

Her eyes are closed and she's shaking her head no, breathing heavily. I look down at her chest, heaving dangerously close to mine.

"You want me to do it again?" I whisper.

I want her to *beg* me to do it again, but she shakes her head no. She's breathing twice as fast as she was sixty seconds ago, so I know I'm getting to her. I laugh that she's so adamantly shaking her head no, while at the same time clenching the sheet next to her with her fist. I move closer to her mouth because I suddenly have an over-whelming need to take in some of the breaths she's wasting. It feels like I need them more than she does right now, so I inhale at the same time my lips meet her cheek. I don't stop there, though. I *can't* stop there. I continue to trail kisses from her cheek, down to her ear. I pause and catch my breath enough to speak in a steady voice. "How about that?"

Again, she stubbornly shakes her head, but tilts it back and slightly to the left, allowing me better access. I lift my hand from the bed and bring it to her waist, keeping my eyes trained on her as I slip my hand under her shirt, just far enough to graze her stomach with my thumb. I watch for any kind of reaction from her, but she's got a stern, tight-lipped expression on her face now, like she's trying to hold her breath. I don't want her to hold her breath. I need to hear her breathe.

When I drop my mouth and nose to her jawline, she releases her pent-up breaths just like I was hoping she would. I trail my nose across her jaw, inhaling the scent of her, then move down, listening intently to every single gasp that escapes her lips as if they're the last sounds I'll ever hear. When I reach her ear, four of my senses are in overdrive and one is seriously lacking—*taste*. I know I can't taste her mouth tonight, but I have got to taste at least one part of her. I press my lips to her ear and she immediately brings her hand up to my neck, pulling me in deeper. Feeling her need my mouth against her skin rips my chest wide open and I completely give in, wanting to feel that need from her even more. I immediately part my lips and glide my tongue across her skin, taking in the sweetness of her and locking it in my memory. I've never tasted anything that rivaled perfection like she does.

Then she moans and *holy hell*. Everything I thought I previously knew about my desires or wants or needs becomes lost in that sound. From this point forward, my new and only goal in life is to find a way to get her to make that exact same sound again.

I bring my hand to the side of her head and completely let loose, kissing and teasing every inch of her neck, trying to find that exact spot that got to her a few seconds ago. She drops her head against her pillow and I take the opportunity to explore more of her neck. As soon as my lips begin to trail toward the rise in her chest, I force myself north again, not wanting to push it to the point that she asks me to stop. Because I absolutely don't want to stop whatever this is we're doing.

Her eyes are still closed and I drop my mouth to her lips, kissing her softly near the corner of her mouth.

And there it is. The softest, most delicate sound escapes her throat again. I can't ignore the fact that another part of me wakes up with that sound. I continue kissing a full circle around the edges of her lips, impressed that I'm somehow able to find strength to pull back.

I have to stop for a moment because if I don't, I'll for sure break my one and only rule tonight—which is absolutely no mouth contact. I know if I kiss her right now it'll be great. But I don't want her to have great. I want her to have incredible. Looking at her lips right now, I know for a fact it'll be incredible for me.

"They're so perfect," I say. "Like hearts. I could literally stare at your lips for days and never get bored."

She opens her eyes and smiles. "No. Don't do that. If all you do is stare, then *I'll* be the bored one."

Damn that smile. It's painful having to watch that mouth smile and frown and pout and laugh and speak when all I want to watch it do is kiss me.

But then she licks her lips and everything I thought I just knew about pain actually starts to feel good compared to the way my heart is gouged out of my chest with that small tease. *Jesus Christ*, this girl.

I groan and press my forehead to hers. Having her mouth this close to mine sucks the self-control right out of me. I drop myself on top of her and it's as if a rush of warm air swarms the room and encircles us. We both feel everything simultaneously and we moan together, move together, and breathe together.

Then we completely give in together. All four of our hands are frantically pulling off my shirt as if two hands can't do it fast enough. As soon as it's off, her legs lock around my waist and she pulls me tightly against her. I drop my forehead back to hers and move against her, finding a new way to force those tiny sounds from her mouth that have quickly become my new favorite song. We continue to move together and the more she gasps and quietly moans, the closer my lips move to hers, wanting to experience those sounds first-hand. I just need a tiny sample of what her kiss will feel like. A little preview, that's all. I allow my lips to brush against hers and we both suck in a breath.

She feels it. She actually fucking feels this right now and I think I'm drowning in satisfaction. I don't want to speed things up and I definitely don't want to slow things down. I just want to keep things exactly as they are right now because it's perfect.

I bring my hand to the side of her head and keep my forehead pressed against hers, my lips resting against hers. I love the feel of our mouths sliding together, so I pull back and lick my lips to create smoother traction. I straighten my legs out, taking some of my weight off my knees, not expecting the small shift to do what it does to her. She arches her back and whispers, "*Oh, God.*"

I feel like I should answer her, because it sure as hell seems like she's referring to me right now with the way she throws her arms around my neck and tucks her head against me. Her arms are trembling and her legs are clenching my waist and I realize that not only is she *feeling* this right now, she's doing everything in her power to fight it.

"Holder," she whispers, clenching my back. I'm not sure if she's wanting me to answer her or not, but I forgot how to speak so it doesn't matter. I can barely even remember how to breathe right now.

"Holder."

She says my name with more urgency this time so I kiss the side of her head and slow my movements against her. She hasn't asked me to stop or slow down yet, but I'm pretty sure that's what she's about to do. I do whatever I can to intercept her plea because she feels incredible and I absolutely don't want to stop.

"Sky, if you're asking me to stop, I will. But I'm hoping you're not, because I really don't want to stop, so please." I lift up and look down at her, still barely moving against her. She still hasn't asked me to stop yet and honestly, I'm afraid to. I'm afraid if I stop, then whatever she's feeling right now will disappear. That scares me because I know that with me, I'll be feeling her for days after this. I love knowing that what I'm doing to her right now is having enough of an effect that she feels she needs me to stop before she passes an unexpected first tonight.

I reach to her cheek and stroke it with the back of my hand, wanting . . . no, *needing* for her to pass this first tonight. "We won't go any further than this, I promise," I say to her. "But please don't ask me to stop where we already are. I need to watch you and I need to hear you because the fact that I know you're actually feeling this right now is so fucking amazing. You feel incredible and this feels incredible and *please*. Just . . . *please*."

I drop my mouth to hers and kiss her softly, immediately pulling back before that amazing connection turns into more than just a peck. Her lips feel so inconceivably perfect; I have to lift off her completely in order to regain my bearings. Otherwise, I won't be able to hold myself at bay for another second. I look down at her and she's looking back up at me, searching my eyes for an answer to a question she can only answer for herself. I wait patiently for her to decide where we go from here.

Her head begins to shake back and forth and she places her hands on my chest.

"Don't. Whatever you do, don't stop."

I remain still for a few seconds, repeating what she just said in my head several times until I'm absolutely certain she just told me *not* to stop. I slip my hand behind her neck and pull her forehead to mine. "*Thank* you," I say breathlessly. I ease myself back down on top of her until we recapture our rhythm. She feels so incredible pressed against me, I don't know that I'll ever be the same again. This girl just raised the bar so far above all other girls' heads, no one could ever come close.

I kiss her everywhere my lips have already touched her tonight, picking up pace with the timing of her gasps and moans. When I feel her body tensing around mine I pull away from her neck and look down at her. She digs her nails deeper into my skin, then tilts her head back and closes her eyes. She looks absolutely beautiful like this, but I need her eyes on mine. I need to watch her feel this.

"Open your eyes," I tell her. She winces, but doesn't look up at me. "*Please.*"

Her eyes immediately open beneath me when I say please. Her eyebrows crease together and she loses all rhythm to her breathing pattern. She's fighting to breathe now as her body begins to tremble beneath me, all the while keeping our gaze locked together. All I can do is hold my breath and watch the most incredible thing I've ever seen unfold beneath me. When the loudest of her moans has escaped her lips, she can no longer keep her eyes open. As soon as she closes them, I drop my lips back to hers, needing to feel them against mine again. When she's finally calm, I move my lips down to her neck and kiss it like I wish I could be kissing her mouth right now.

But seeing how much she needs me to kiss her mouth right now is making the wait even more important for me. Considering what just happened between us, it almost seems absurd to keep up the assurance of not kissing her. But I'm stubborn and I like knowing that the next time we're together like this, we'll be able to experience another first that's likely to drive me even more insane than tonight has.

I press my lips to her shoulder and push up on my arm. I trail my fingers down her hairline and wipe away the loose strands from her face. She looks absolutely content and it's the most beautiful, satisfying thing I've ever felt.

"You're incredible," I say, knowing that word is a severe understatement for what she actually is. She smiles at me and inhales a deep breath at the same time I do. I collapse beside her on the bed, needing to get off her immediately. My chest is completely alive right now and the only thing that I know could satisfy me is to be pressed against her again with my mouth on hers. I force the image of it out of my mind and attempt to cool myself off by matching my breathing pattern with hers.

After silently finding a stable enough point to touch her again, I move my hand closer to hers on the bed and wrap my pinky around hers. The sensation of her pinky in mine feels way too familiar. Way too right. Way too long overdue. I squeeze my eyes shut and attempt to deny my conscience the satisfaction of being right.

She's Sky. That's who she is. I only doubt this because of how she feels so familiar. Familiarity is hardly enough to convince me otherwise.

I hope my instincts are wrong, because if I'm right, the truth will destroy her.

Please, just let her be Sky.

My fear of being right keeps pushing through and I sit up on the bed, needing to separate myself from her. I need to clear my head of all this craziness. "I have to go," I say, looking down at her. "I can't be on this bed with you for another second."

I'm being honest. I *can't* be on this bed with her for another second, although I'm sure she thinks it's for other reasons. Not for the reason I really need to separate myself from her—the fact that I'm terrified my intuition is finally right for once.

I stand and pull my shirt over my head and notice that she's looking at me like I'm rejecting her. I know she probably thought I'd end up kissing her tonight, but she's got a lot to learn when it comes to doubting my word.

I lean in close to her and smile reassuringly. "When I said you weren't getting kissed tonight, I meant it. But *dammit*, Sky. I had no idea how fucking difficult you would make it." I slip my hand behind her neck and lean in to kiss her cheek. When she gasps, it takes everything I have to release my hold and climb off the bed. I watch her as I walk toward the window and pull my phone from my pocket. I send her a quick text, then wink at her, right before I climb outside. I pull the window shut and back a few steps away. As soon as the window is shut, she jumps off her bed and runs out of her bedroom, more than likely to go grab her phone and check her text. Normally, her excitement would more than likely make me laugh. Instead I find myself staring blankly through her bedroom window. My heart feels heavy and my mind even heavier as the pieces of the puzzle slowly begin to fit together, right down to her name.

"The sky is always beautiful . . ."

The memory causes me to flinch. I brace my hand against the brick wall and inhale a deep breath. It's almost laughable, really—the fact that I can sit here and entertain the possibility that this could actually happen after thirteen years. If it were true . . . if she really were her . . . it would ruin her. Which is exactly why I refuse to accept it without tangible proof—something I can actually touch that would confirm it. Without tangible proof, she'll remain Sky to me.

I just want her to be Sky.

Chapter Fifteen

Les,

Remember when we were kids and I made everyone stop calling me Dean? I have never told anyone the truth about why I go by Holder, not even you.

We were eight years old and it was the first and only time we ever went to Disneyland. We were waiting in line for one of the roller-coasters and you and Dad were in front of me because you couldn't ride it by yourself. I was a few inches taller than you and it pissed you off that I was able to ride most of the rides alone and you weren't.

When we made it to the front of the line, they put you and Dad on first and I had to wait for the next car to pull in. I was standing there alone, patiently waiting. I turned around to find Mom and she was about a hundred yards away at the exit to the ride, waiting for all of us to finish. I waved at her and she waved back at me. I turned back around when the next car pulled up.

That's when I heard her.

I heard Hope yelling my name. I spun around and stood on my tiptoes, facing the sound of her voice.

"Dean!" she yelled. She sounded really far away, but I knew it was her because she said it with that accent of hers. She always dragged out the middle of my name and made it longer than one syllable. I always liked how she said my name, so hearing her yell it, I knew it was her. She must have spotted me and now she was trying to call for me to come help her.

"Dean," she yelled again, only this time she sounded farther away. I could hear the panic in her voice. I began to panic myself, because I knew I'd get in trouble if I lost my place in line. Mom and Dad spent the entire week before we left reminding us to stay by one of them at all times.

I glanced over at Mom but she wasn't looking at me, she was watching you and Dad on the ride. I didn't know what to do, because she wouldn't know where I was if I left the line. But as soon as Hope screamed my name again I didn't care. I had to find her.

I started running toward the back of the line—toward the sound of her voice. I was yelling her name, hoping she would hear me and walk toward the sound of my voice.

God, Les. I was so excited. I was terrified and excited and knew that all our prayers had been answered, but it was up to me to hurry up and find her and I was scared I wouldn't be able to. She was here and I couldn't get to her fast enough.

I had it all planned out in my head. As soon as I found her, I would hug the hell out of her first, then I was going to grab her hands and pull her back to where Mom was standing. We were going to wait by the exit to the ride so when you walked off, she would be the first thing you would see.

I knew how happy you were going to be when you saw her. Neither of us had been truly happy in the two years since she was taken and this was our chance. After all, Disneyland is the happiest place on earth, and for the first time, I was starting to believe it.

"Hope!" I yelled, cupping my hands around my mouth. I had been running for several minutes, still trying to listen for the sound of her voice. She would yell my name, then I would yell her name, and this went on for what felt like forever until someone grabbed my arm and yanked it, stopping me in my tracks. Mom threw her arms around me and hugged me, but I was trying to get out of her grasp.

"Dean, you can't run off like that!" she said. She was kneeling down, shaking my shoulders, looking me frantically in the eyes. "I thought I lost you."

I pulled away from her and tried to keep running toward Hope, but Mom wouldn't let go of my shoulders. "Stop it!" she said, confused why I was trying to get away from her.

I looked back at her in a panic and shook my head vigorously, trying to catch my breath and find the words. "It's..." I pointed toward the direction I wanted to run. "It's Hope, Mom! I found Hope! We have to go to her before I lose her again."

Sadness instantly reached her eyes and I knew she didn't believe me. "Dean," she whispered, shaking her head sympathetically. "Sweetie."

She felt sorry for me. She didn't believe me, because this wasn't the first time I thought I'd found her. But I knew I was right this time. I knew it.

"Dean!" Hope cried again. "Where are you?" She was much closer this time and I could tell by the sound of her voice that she was crying now. Mom's eyes darted toward the voice and I knew she heard her calling for me, too.

"We have to find her, Mom," I pleaded. "It's her. That's Hope."

Mom looked me in the eyes and I could see the fear in them. She nodded, then grabbed my hand.

"Hope?" she yelled, scanning over the crowd. We were both calling her name now and I remember looking up at Mom at one point, watching her while she helped me search. I loved her more than I ever had in that moment, because she actually believed me.

We heard my name called again and it was so much closer this time. Mom looked down at me and her eyes were wide. We both broke out into a run toward the sound of Hope's voice. We pushed through the crowd and... that's when I saw her. Her back was to us and she was standing all by herself.

"Dean!" she yelled again.

Mom and I were both frozen. We couldn't believe it. She was standing right in front of us, looking for me. After two years of not knowing who took her or where she was, we had finally found her. I started to walk forward, but I was suddenly shoved aside by a teenage boy rushing toward her. When he reached her, he grabbed her by the arm and spun her around.

"Ashley! Thank God!" he said, pulling her to him.

"Dean," she said to the boy, wrapping her arms around his neck. "I got lost."

He picked her up. "I know, sis. I'm so sorry. You're okay now."

She pulled her tear-streaked face away from his chest and she glanced in our direction.

She wasn't Hope.

She wasn't Hope at all.

And I wasn't the Dean she was looking for.

Mom squeezed my hand and knelt down in front of me. "I'm so sorry, Dean," she said. "I thought it was her, too."

A sob broke free from my chest and I cried. I cried so damn hard, Les. Mom wrapped her arms around me and she started crying, too, because I don't think she knew that an eight-year-old could have his heart crushed like that.

But I was crushed. My heart broke all over again that day.

And I never wanted to hear the name Dean again.

H

Chapter Sixteen

I practically skip down the stairs and into the kitchen. It's the second Monday of school and just thinking about my attitude when I woke up last week as opposed to this morning makes me laugh. I never in a million years imagined I'd be so consumed with the thought of a girl as I have been. Since the second I left her house Saturday night, I've done nothing but eat, breathe, and sleep with her on my mind.

"So how are you liking Sky?" my mom asks. She's seated at the kitchen table eating her breakfast and reading the paper. I'm surprised she remembers her name. I only mentioned her once. I shut the refrigerator door and walk to the bar.

"She's great," I say. "I like her a lot."

My mom puts down the paper and cocks her head. "*She?*" she says with an arched eyebrow. I don't understand her confusion. I just stare at her until she shakes her head and laughs. "Oh, Jesus," she says. "You've got it bad."

Still confused. "What do you mean? You asked how I liked Sky and I answered you."

She's laughing even harder now. "I said *school*, Holder. I asked how you were liking *school.*"

Oh.

Maybe I *do* have it bad.

"Shut up." I laugh, embarrassed.

She stops laughing and picks the newspaper up, holding it out in front of her. I grab my drink and my backpack and head toward the door. "Well?" she asks. "How do you like *school*?"

I roll my eyes at her. "It's fine," I say, backing out of the kitchen. "But I like Sky more."

I walk to the car and shove my backpack inside. I wish I had thought to offer to pick her up today, but after spending most of Sunday texting back and forth, we agreed that we would take things slow. We decided not to run together in the mornings. She said it would be too much, too soon, and I definitely want to keep it at her pace, so I agreed. However, I can't deny the fact that I was a little disappointed that she wants to run alone. I want to be around her every second of the day, but I also know she's right. We spent one weekend together and it already feels like I've connected with her on a much deeper level than with any other girl I've dated. It's a good feeling, but it also scares the hell out of me.

Before I back out of the driveway, I pull my phone out and text her.

> I don't know if your ego needs deflating today. I'll judge for myself when I finally get to see you in fifteen minutes.

I set my phone down and back out of the driveway. When I make it to the first stop sign, I pick my phone back up and text her again.

> Fourteen minutes.

I keep the phone in my hand and text her again when another minute has passed.

> Thirteen minutes.

I do this every minute until I pull into the school parking lot and all the minutes have passed.

When I reach the classroom I peek through the window of the door. She's seated in the back of the room next to a conveniently empty desk. My pulse kicks up a notch just from seeing her again. I open the door and walk inside and her face immediately lights up with a smile as soon as she sees me.

I reach the back of the room and begin to lay my backpack down on the empty desk at the same time some dude tries to set his drinks down. I look at him and he looks at me, then we both look at Sky, because I don't want to shove him away until she gives me permission.

"Looks like we have quite the predicament here, boys," she says with an adorable grin. She looks at the coffee being held in the hands of the guy standing next to me. "I see the Mormon brought the queen her offering of coffee. Very impressive." She looks at me and arches an eyebrow. "Do you wish to reveal your offering, hopeless boy, so that I may decide who shall accompany me at the classroom throne today?"

She's teasing me. I love it. And now that I think about it, this must be the guy she's been sitting with at lunch all week. One look at his hot pink shoes and matching pants relieves me of any worry that he's about to become my competition.

I pick up my backpack and let him have the seat. "Looks like someone's in need of an ego-shattering text today." I take an empty seat in the row in front of her.

"Congratulations, squire," she says to the guy with the coffee. "You are the queen's chosen one today. Sit. It's been quite the weekend."

He takes a seat, but he's eyeing her curiously. It's clear by the look on his face that he has no idea what happened between Sky and me this weekend. "Breckin, this is Holder," Sky says, introducing me to him. "Holder is not my boyfriend, but if I catch him trying to break the record for best first kiss with another girl, then he'll soon be my *not breathing* nonboyfriend."

Oh, don't worry, babe. I'm not about to try and break that record with anyone but you.

I smile at her. "Likewise."

"Holder, this is Breckin," she says, gesturing her hand toward him. "Breckin is my new very bestest friend ever in the whole wide world."

If he's Sky's best friend, then I'm pretty sure he's about to become my second-best friend. I reach my hand out to him. Breckin is cautious as he returns the handshake, then he turns to Sky and lowers his voice. "Does *not-your-boyfriend* realize I'm Mormon?"

Sky smiles and nods. "It turns out, Holder doesn't have an issue with Mormons at all. He just has an issue with assholes."

Breckin laughs and I'm still trying to process if Mormon really means Mormon in this case, because it sure sounds like code for something else entirely.

"Well, in that case, welcome to the alliance," Breckin says to me.

I look down at the coffee cup on his desk. If Mormon means Mormon, that better be decaf. "I thought Mormons weren't allowed to have caffeine," I say to him.

Breckin shrugs. "I decided to break that rule the morning I woke up gay."

I laugh. I think I like this Mormon.

Sky leans back in her seat and smiles at me. It feels good to get the approval from the only friend she seems to have here. Mr. Mulligan walks in so I lean toward Sky before he starts his lecture. "Wait for me after class?"

She smiles and nods.

When we reach her locker, it's lined with sticky notes again.

Assholes.

I wad them up and drop them on the floor, just as I always do when I pass her locker. She switches her books, then turns to face me. "You trimmed your hair," she says.

I'm not even about to admit how hard it is to find a barber open on Sunday.

"Yeah. This chick I know couldn't stop whining about it. It was really annoying."

"I like it," she says.

"Good."

She smiles at me and clutches her books to her chest. I can't stop thinking about Saturday night and how I'd give anything to be back in her room with her right now. Why the hell didn't I kiss her? I'm kissing her today, dammit. After school. Or *during* school if I can get away with it. Or right now.

"I guess we should get to class," she says, glancing past me.

"Yep," I agree. We really probably should get to class but she's not *in* my next class so I really have no urge to get to class.

She stares at me a little while longer. Long enough for me to mentally map out a plan. I know it's Monday, but I want to take her out tonight. That way I'll have to walk her to her door. Then once we get to her front door, I'm going to kiss her crazy for at least half an hour just like I should have done Saturday night.

She kicks off the locker and begins to walk away, but I grab her arm and pull her back. I push her up against the locker and she gasps while I block her in with my arms.

She's flustered again.

I reach my hand up to her face and slide it under her jaw, then run my thumb across her bottom lip. I can feel her chest heave against mine and her breaths come in quicker succession.

"I wish I had kissed you Saturday night," I whisper, staring down at her mouth. She parts her lips and I continue to run my thumb across them. "I can't stop imagining what you taste like." I press my thumb to the center of her lips and I quickly lean in and kiss her. I pull away just as fast, though, because that tease just about kills me. Her eyes are closed and I release her face and walk away.

I'm pretty sure I just became the master of willpower, because walking away from that mouth was one of the hardest things I've ever done.

"Hey, whisker biscuit," Daniel says, cutting in line to stand in front of me.

"Whisker biscuit?" I sigh and shake my head. I swear I don't know where he comes up with this shit.

"Well, you don't like it when I call you Hopeless. Or cunt nugget. Or piss flap. Or—"

"You could just call me Holder."

"Everyone else calls you Holder and I hate everyone else, so no. I can't." He takes two empty trays and hands me one. He nods in the direction of Sky's table. "So, I hope your ditching me Saturday night for cheese tits over there was worth it."

"Her name is Sky," I correct.

"Well I can't call her Sky. Everyone else calls her Sky and I hate everyone else, so . . ."

I laugh. "Well then why do you call Valerie by *her* name?"

He spins around. "Who's Valerie?" he asks, looking at me like I've lost my mind.

"*Val?* Your ex-girlfriend? Or current girlfriend. Whatever she is."

Daniel laughs. "No, man. Her name isn't Valerie, it's Tessa."
What the hell?

"I call her Val because it's short for Valium and I always tell her she needs to take that shit by the bucketful. I wasn't lying when I said she was fucking crazy."

"Do you call *anyone* by their actual name?"

He ponders my question for a second, then looks at me, confused. "Why would I want to do that?"

I give up. "I'm sitting with Sky today," I tell him. "You want to sit with us?"

Daniel shakes his head. "Nah. Val's having a good day so I better take advantage of it." He takes his change from the cafeteria cashier. "See you later, buttshark."

I'm kind of relieved he's sitting with Val. I don't know if I'm ready for Sky to get a dose of Daniel yet. I pay for my food and walk toward their table. When I reach them, it sounds like Sky is giving Breckin a recap of our weekend. Breckin sees me walk up behind her but he just winks and doesn't let her know I'm listening.

"He showed up at my house on Friday and after quite a few misunderstandings, we finally came to an understanding that we just misunderstood each other. Then we baked, I read him some smut, and he went home. He came back over Saturday night and cooked for me. Then we went to my room and . . ."

I drop my tray down beside hers and take a seat. "Keep going," I say. "I'd love to hear what we did next."

She shoots me a quick grin when she sees my tray beside hers, then she rolls her eyes and turns back to Breckin. "Then we broke the record for best first kiss in the history of first kisses without even kissing."

"Impressive," Breckin says.

"It was an excruciatingly boring weekend," I say.

Breckin shoots me a look like he wants to kick my ass for insulting Sky. He just scored major points for that one.

"Holder loves boring," Sky clarifies. "He means that in a nice way."

Breckin picks up his fork and looks back and forth between us. "Not much confuses me. But you two are an exception."

He's not the only one confused by us. I'm seriously confused by us. I've never felt this comfortable with a girl before and we aren't even dating. We haven't even kissed. Although I did give her one hell of a *non*kiss. Just thinking about it has me anxious. "You busy tonight?"

She wipes her mouth with her napkin. "Maybe," she says, smiling.

I wink at her, knowing that's her stubborn way of saying she's not busy.

"Was it the smut I let her borrow that she read to you?" Breckin asks.

"Smut?" I laugh. "I don't *think* it was smut, but I didn't catch most of the book because my mind was a little sidetracked."

Sky slaps me on the arm. "You let me read for three hours straight and you weren't even paying attention?"

I throw my arm over her shoulder and pull her to me, then kiss her on the side of the head. "I already told you I was paying attention," I whisper in her ear. "Just not to the words coming out of your mouth." I turn back to Breckin. "I did catch some of it, though. Not a bad book. I didn't think I'd ever be interested in a romance novel but I'm curious how that dude's gonna find a way out of that shit."

Breckin agrees and brings up a part of the plot. We begin talking about the book and I can't help but notice how quiet Sky is the whole time I'm talking with Breckin. I keep glancing at her but she's zoned out, just like when she zoned out in her kitchen Saturday night. After a while of her not talking or even taking a bite of her food, I become concerned that something is wrong.

"You okay?" I ask, turning my attention toward her. She doesn't even blink. I snap my fingers in front of her face. "Sky," I say a little louder. Her eyes finally jerk up to mine and she snaps out of it. "Where'd you go?" I ask, concerned.

She smiles, but looks embarrassed by the fact that she just zoned out. I reach up and cup her cheek, running my thumb reassuringly back and forth. "You have to quit checking out like that. It freaks me out a little bit."

She shrugs. "Sorry. I'm easily distracted." She smiles and pulls my hand away from her face, giving it a reassuring squeeze. "Really, I'm fine."

I look down at her hand that's now holding mine. I see the familiar half of a silver heart dangling from beneath her sleeve, so I immediately flip her hand over and twist her wrist back and forth.

She's wearing Les's bracelet.

Why the *hell* is she wearing Les's bracelet?

"Where'd you get that?" I ask her, still looking at the bracelet that sure as hell shouldn't be on her wrist right now.

She looks down at her hand and shrugs like it's not a big deal.

She just shrugs?

She shrugs like she doesn't give a shit that she just completely knocked the breath out of me. How can she be wearing this bracelet? It's Les's bracelet. The last time I saw this bracelet it was on Les's wrist.

"Where'd you get it?" I demand.

She's looking at me now like she's terrified of the person in front of her. I realize I'm holding on to her wrist with a tight grip so I release it, just as she pulls away from me.

"You think I got it from a guy?" she asks, confused.

No, I don't think it's from a *guy. Christ*. I don't think that at all. What I *think* is that she's wearing my dead sister's bracelet and she's refusing to tell me how she got it. She can't just shrug and sit here, acting like it's a coincidence, because that bracelet is handmade and there's only one other bracelet like it in the whole damn world. So unless she's Hope, then she's somehow wearing Les's bracelet and I want to know why the hell she's wearing it!

Unless she's Hope.

The truth hits me head-on and I think I'm about to be sick. *No, no, no.*

"Holder," Breckin says, shifting forward. "Ease up, man."

No, no, no. This can't be Hope's bracelet. How could she even still have it after all this time? Her words from Saturday night rush through my head.

"The only thing I have from before Karen adopted me is some jewelry, and I have no idea who it came from."

I lean forward, praying this bracelet isn't the jewelry she was referring to. "Who gave you the damn bracelet, Sky?"

She gasps, still unable to give me an answer. She can't answer me because she honestly has no idea. She's looking at me like I just crushed her and hell . . . I think I did.

I know she doesn't have a clue what's going through my mind right now, but how could I even begin to tell her? How in the hell do I explain to her that she may not know where the bracelet on her wrist came from, but I *do*? How do I tell her that bracelet came from Les? From the best friend she doesn't even remember? And how do I admit that she got that bracelet just minutes before I walked away from her? Minutes before her entire life was ripped out from under her?

I *can't* tell her. I can't tell her, because she honestly has no memory of me or Les or how she got this damn bracelet. From looking at her, I don't even think she remembers Hope. She doesn't even remember *herself*. She said Saturday night she has no memory of her life before Karen.

How can she not remember? How can anyone not remember being stolen from her own home? From her best friend?

How can she not remember *me*?

I squeeze my eyes shut and turn away from her. I press my palms against my forehead and inhale a deep breath. I have got to calm down. I'm terrifying her right now and that's the last thing I want to do. I grip the back of my neck in order to keep my hands busy so that I don't punch the table.

She's Hope. Sky is Hope and Hope is Sky and, "Shit!"

I don't mean to say it out loud, because I know I'm freaking her out. But this is as calm as I'm able to be right now. I have to get out of here. I have to figure out how the hell to explain this to her.

I stand up and rush toward the exit to the cafeteria before I do or say anything else. As soon as I'm through the doors and alone in the hallway, I collapse against the nearest locker, and pull my trembling hands to my face.

"Shit, shit, shit!"

Chapter Seventeen

Les,

I'm sorry I didn't find her sooner. I can't help but wonder if it would have made a difference. I'm so sorry.

H

Chapter Eighteen

Les,

She still has your bracelet, though. That has to mean
something to you.

H

Chapter Nineteen

Les,

I don't know what to do. It's been over six hours now and I keep trying to figure out if I should go to her house and tell her everything or if I should give it more time.

I think I'll give it more time. I need to process this.

H

Chapter Twenty

Les,

What if I call Karen and explain everything to her?
Sky seems to have a good relationship with her. Karen
could figure out what to do.

H

Chapter Twenty-one

Les,

Shit. What if Karen is the one who did it?

H

Chapter Twenty-two

Les,

What if I tell Mom? I could tell Mom and she could figure out what we need to do or if we need to call the police. She's a lawyer. I'm sure she deals with this kind of stuff all the time.

H

Chapter Twenty-three

Les,

I can't tell Mom. Mom's in intellectual property law.
She wouldn't know what to do any more than I do.

H

Chapter Twenty-four

Les,

It's almost midnight. Twelve hours I've let this continue without giving her a single explanation for what happened at lunch today. God, I hope I didn't make her cry.

H

Chapter Twenty-five

Les,

She's probably asleep right now. I'll tell her in the morning. She runs every morning so I'll just show up and run with her, then I'll tell her. We'll figure out what to do after that.

H

Chapter Twenty-six

Les,

I can't sleep.
  I can't believe I actually found her.

  H

Chapter Twenty-seven

Les,

Why do you think she calls herself Sky?

There was this thing we used to do when we were little. We only did it a few times because she was taken shortly after that. But she used to cry all the time and I hated it, so we would lie in the driveway and watch the sky and I would hold on to her finger. I remember thinking it was gross to hold a girl's hand so I would always hold her pinky, instead. Because even though I was just a kid and it was gross to hold a girl's hand, I really did want to hold her hand.

I used to tell her to think about the sky when she got sad and she always promised me she would. Now here she is. And her name is Sky.

It's three in the morning. None of this makes any sense. I'm going to sleep now.

H

Chapter Twenty-eight

Les,

Well, I ran with her. Sort of. It was more like I chased her. I couldn't bring myself to speak to her once I showed up. Then after the run we were both so exhausted we just collapsed onto the grass.

I was hoping that the incident in the cafeteria yesterday would spark some sort of memory from her. I was hoping when I showed up today that she would know exactly what upset me so much yesterday. I wanted her to tell me she remembered so I wouldn't have to be the one to tell her.

How do you tell someone something like that, Les? How do I tell her that the mother who raised her could very well be the one who stole her from us?

If I said anything, her life would change forever. And she likes her life. She likes running and reading and baking and... holy shit.

Holy shit.

It didn't make sense until just now, but the whole internet thing? Her mom not wanting her to have a phone? Karen did it. Karen fucking took her and she's doing everything she can to make sure Sky doesn't find out.

I don't know what to do. I know I can't be around

her right now. There's no way I can be around her and pretend everything is fine when it's not. But there's no way I can tell her the truth, either, because it would turn her world upside down.

I don't know what will be more painful. Staying away from her so she doesn't find out, or telling her the truth and ruining her life all over again.

H

Chapter Twenty-eight-and-a-half

Les,

It's Thursday night. I haven't spoken to her since Monday. I can't even look at her because it hurts so much. I still don't know what to do and the longer I just let this go on, the more of an asshole it makes me look. But every time I work up the nerve to talk to her I have no idea what I'd even say. I told her I'd always be honest with her and this is just something I can't be honest with her about.

I've been trying to figure out why Karen would do something like this, but there isn't a single valid excuse in the whole world that could justify someone taking a child. I've even thought about the chance that maybe Hope's dad didn't really want her, so he just gave her away. But I know that's not true because he did everything he could to find her for months.

I just can't figure it out. I don't even know if I need to. Until I barged into her life two weeks ago, she was happy. If I don't walk away now, it'll ruin all that.

Ironic, isn't it? I walked away from her thirteen

years ago and ruined her life. Now if I decide not to walk away from her, I'll ruin her life again.

Just goes to show that everything I do is hopeless. Fucking hopeless.

H

Chapter Twenty-nine

"Yo, flipdick. We on for tonight?" Daniel says, walking up to my locker.

The last thing I feel like doing tonight is going out. I know Daniel would probably get my mind off her with all the crazy shit that comes out of his mouth, but I don't really *want* to get my mind off her. I haven't spoken to her since Monday and the only thing that sounds appealing besides being with her is wallowing alone in self-pity.

"Maybe tomorrow. I don't really feel like doing anything tonight."

Daniel leans his elbow into the locker and he lowers his head, leaning toward me. "You're really being a mangina," he says. "You didn't even date the chick. Get the fuck over it and . . ." Daniel glances over my shoulder without finishing the sentence. "What the hell is your problem, powder puff?" He's speaking to someone now standing behind me. The way he says it can only mean it's Grayson. Fearing I'm about to get sucker-punched from behind, I spin around.

It's not Grayson.

Breckin is facing me and he doesn't look very pleased about it.

"Hey," I say.

"I need to talk to you," he says. I know he wants to talk about Sky and I really don't want to talk about Sky. Not to Breckin, not to Daniel, not even to Sky. No one understands anything about anything and frankly, it's nobody's business.

"Sorry, Breckin. I'm not really in the mood to talk about her."

Breckin takes a quick step forward and I take a quick step back because I wasn't expecting him to rush me like he just did. My back is against the locker and Daniel is laughing. Probably because Breckin is a good fifty pounds lighter than I am and several inches shorter and he's probably wondering why the hell I haven't laid Breckin on his ass yet. But that doesn't stop Breckin from moving in even closer and shoving his finger hard against my chest.

"I don't really give a shit what kind of mood you're in, because I'm in a pretty shitty mood myself, Holder. You aren't the one having to pick up all the shattered pieces of Sky this week. I don't know what the hell happened in the cafeteria Monday, but it was enough to show me that I don't like you. I don't like you one goddamn bit and I have no idea what Sky sees in you . . . because what you did to her? How you led her on for days and then just walked away like she was a waste of your time?" Breckin shakes his head, still fuming. He drops his eyes down to my arm. Down to the tattoo. "I feel sorry for you," he sighs. He inhales a calming breath and slowly looks back up at me. "I feel sorry for you, because people like her don't come along more than once. She deserves someone who realizes that. Someone who appreciates her. Someone who would never just . . ." he shakes his head, looking at me disappointedly. "Someone who would never crush her hope and then just walk away."

Breckin backs up a step when he's finished and Daniel gives me the look. The look that indicates he's ready to start one of his fights. Before I even have the chance to tell Daniel to refrain, he begins to lunge forward toward Breckin. I quickly step in between them and shove Daniel against the locker with my arm, keeping it pressed against his chest. "Don't," I say, holding Daniel back.

"Let him hit me," Breckin says loudly from behind me. "Or better yet, why don't you just do it, Holder? You proved to Sky on Monday what a badass you are. Have at it!"

I release Daniel and turn around to face Breckin. The last thing I want to do is hit him. Why would I hit him when everything he just said to me was the absolute truth? He's pissed at me because of how I treated Sky. He's pissed and he's protecting her and I have no idea how to tell him how much it means to me to know she has him.

I turn around and open my locker, then grab my backpack and car keys. Daniel is watching me closely, wondering why I'm not kicking Breckin's ass right now. I face Breckin again and he's eyeing me with just as much confusion as Daniel. I begin to walk away, but pause when I'm shoulder to shoulder with Breckin. "I'm glad she has you, Breckin."

He doesn't respond. I pull my backpack onto my shoulder and walk away.

Chapter Twenty-nine-and-a-half

Les,

I haven't spoken to her in two weeks. I'm still going to school, though, because I can't imagine the thought of not being able to see her every day. But I just watch her from a distance. I hate that she seems sad now.

I was hoping that my actions in the cafeteria last Monday would have left her pissed off, if even a little bit. But when I decided it was better not to allow myself back into her life, I was hoping her anger would help her get over me faster. But she doesn't seem angry. She just seems heartbroken and that crushes me.

I made a list over the weekend of the pros and cons of telling her the truth about who she is. I'll share it with you so you'll understand my decision better, because I know it doesn't make sense.

Pros to telling Sky the truth:

* Her family deserves to know what happened to her and that she's okay.
* She deserves to know what happened.

Cons to telling Sky the truth:

* The truth would ruin the life she has now.
* She never seemed happy to me when we were little, but she seems happy now. Forcing her back into a life she doesn't even remember doesn't seem like the right thing to do.
* If she found out I knew all along who she was, she would never forgive me for keeping it from her.
* I know she thinks her birthday is next week, but she still has months to go before she actually turns eighteen. If she finds out right now, the decision about what happens to her will be made for her by her father and the state. When she finds out the truth, I want her to be old enough to make her own decisions about what happens to her life.

As much as I don't want to believe Karen did this, what if she did? If the truth came out, Karen would be punished. And that probably should be listed in pros, but I just don't think her going to prison would in any way be a pro for Sky.

So you can see the cons won, which is why I've decided not to tell her the truth. Not yet, anyway. After I decided I wasn't going to tell her what happened to her as a child, I also thought about whether it was a good idea to at least try and apologize for what happened at lunch that day. I thought that somehow I could still keep the secret until she's out of high school and in the meantime, we could be together. I want to be with her again more than anything, but there are so many reasons why I shouldn't be.

Pros to being with Sky:

* I fucking miss her. I miss her rude comments, her laughter, her smile, her scowl, her cookies, her brownies, her kiss. (Even though I never really had that one. I know I'd miss it if I did.)
* She wouldn't be as heartbroken if I would just apologize. We could go back to whatever it was that we were doing and I could pretend she wasn't Hope. It would be cruel, but at least she'd be happy.

Cons to being with Sky:

* Being around her could trigger her memory. I'm not sure that I'm ready for her to remember me yet.
* Once she finds out the truth, she'll hate me for deceiving her. At least if I'm not with her, she'll be able to respect the fact that I didn't lie to her while I was allowing her to fall in love with me.
* If I spend any time with her, I know I'll slip up. I'll call her Hope or I'll say something about when we were kids or I'll talk too much about you and that could spark a memory.
* How could I ever introduce her to Mom? I'm pretty sure with as much time as Hope spent at our house, Mom would immediately recognize her.

* I'll do something to fuck it all up again. That's the only thing I seem to be consistent at in this life. Fucking things up for you and Hope.
* If I walk out of her life completely, she can go on living the contented life she's been living for the past thirteen years.
* If I stay, I'll inevitably have to tell her the truth. And no matter how much she probably needs to hear the truth; it'll turn her world upside down. I can't watch that, Les. I just can't.

So there you have it in big, bold ink. I'm not telling her the truth and I'm not letting her forgive me. She's better off without me. She's better off keeping the past in the past and keeping me at a distance.

H

Chapter Thirty

I grab the sack from the floorboard and walk to the front door, then ring the doorbell. I don't know if this is a good idea. In fact, I *know* it's not a good idea. But for whatever reason I trust him to do this for me.

The front door opens and a woman, more than likely his mother, is standing in the doorway.

"Is Breckin here?" I ask her.

She starts at the top of my head, then slowly scrolls down my entire body, stopping at my shoes. It's not the kind of scroll a guy gets from a woman who's checking him out. It's a scroll of disapproval. "Breckin isn't expecting company," she says coldly.

Okay. I didn't anticipate this obstacle.

"It's okay, Mom," I hear Breckin say as he opens the door further. "He's not here for my gay parts."

Breckin's mother scoffs, then rolls her eyes and walks away while I'm trying to hold back my laughter. Breckin is now standing in her place, scrolling over me disapprovingly just like she did. "What do you want?"

I shift my feet, feeling a little uncomfortable at how unwelcome I am at this house. "I want a couple of things," I say. "I'm here to apologize, for one. But I'm also here to ask you for a favor."

Breckin arches an eyebrow. "I told my mother you weren't here for my gay parts, Holder. So go ahead and apologize, but I'm not doing you any favors."

I laugh. I love that he can be so pissed, yet make fun of himself at the same time. That's such a Les thing to do. "Can I come in?" I ask. I feel pretty damn awkward on the porch right now and I don't really want to have this conversation standing in a doorway. Breckin steps back and opens the door farther.

"That better be an apology gift," he says, indicating the sack in my hand. He doesn't look back or invite me to follow him as he makes his way toward the hallway, so I shut the front door and glance around, then follow him. He opens the door to his bedroom and I walk in behind him. He points to a chair. "Sit there," he says firmly. He walks to his bed and takes a seat on the edge of it, facing me. I slowly take a seat in the chair and he rests his elbows on his knees and clasps his hands in front of him, looking me straight in the eyes. "I take it you'll be apologizing to Sky next? After you leave here? Because she's the one you really need to be apologizing to."

I set the sack down at my feet and lean back in the chair. "You're really protective of her, aren't you?"

Breckin shrugs indifferently. "Well, with all the assholes treating her like shit, *someone* has to watch out for her."

I purse my lips into a tight line and nod, but don't say anything right away. He stares at me for a while, more than likely attempting to figure out the motive behind my being here. I blow out a quick breath, then begin with what I came here to say.

"Listen, Breckin. I'm probably not going to make a whole lot of sense, but hear me out, okay?"

Breckin straightens up at the same time he rolls his eyes. "Please tell me you're about to explain what the hell happened in that cafeteria. We've tried to analyze your behavior no less than a dozen times, but you don't make any sense."

I shake my head. "I can't tell you what happened, Breckin. I can't. All I can tell you is that Sky means more to me than you could ever comprehend. I screwed up and it's too late to go back and make it right with her. I don't want her forgiveness because I don't deserve it. You and I both know she's better off without me. But I needed to come here and apologize to you because I know just from watching you how much you care about her. It kills me that I hurt her but I know that my hurting her indirectly hurt you, too. So, I'm sorry."

I keep my eyes trained on his. He tilts his head slightly and chews on his bottom lip while he studies me.

"Her birthday is next Saturday," I say, picking up the sack. "I got her this and I want you to give it to her. I don't want her to know it's from me. Just tell her you got it for her. I know she'll like it." I take the e-reader out of the sack and toss it to him. He catches it, then looks down at it.

He stares at it for a few minutes, then flips it over and looks at the back of it. He tosses it on the bed beside him, then clasps his hands together again, staring down at the floor. I wait for him to speak because I've said everything I came here to say.

"Can I just say one thing?" he says, lifting his gaze.

I nod. I figured he'd have way more than just *one* thing to say after all that.

"I think what pissed me off the most is the fact that I liked her with you," he says. "I liked seeing how happy she was that day. And even though it was just thirty minutes that I watched you with her at lunch before you went and flipped the fuck out," he says, waving his arm in the air, "it just seemed so *right*. You seemed right for her and she seemed right for you and . . . I don't know, Holder. You just don't make any sense. You didn't make sense when you walked away from her that day and you sure aren't making any sense right now. But I can tell you care about her. I just don't understand you. I don't understand you at all and it pisses me off because if there's one thing in the world I'm good at, it's understanding people."

I wasn't counting while he was talking, but I'm pretty sure that was more than just one thing. "Can you just trust that I really do care about her?" I say. "I want what's best for her and although it kills me that I'm not what's best for her, I want to see her happy."

Breckin smiles, then reaches beside him and picks up the e-reader. "Well, I think once I give her this awesome present I spent my life savings on, she'll forget all about Dean Holder. I'm pretty sure it'll be all about sawdust and sunshine once she dives into the books I'm about to load on here."

I smile, even though I have no idea what he means by sawdust and sunshine.

Chapter Thirty-and-a-half

Les,

Breckin is pretty cool. You would like him. I went to his house Friday night and gave him the gift I bought for Sky. We talked things out for a while and I don't think he wants to kick my ass anymore. Not that he could have. But that's what solidified my respect for him. The fact that he was so mad he wanted to fight me, even though he knew there wasn't a chance in hell he would win.

I wasn't sure how going over there would turn out, but I ended up staying until almost midnight. I've never really been into video games, but we played Modern Warfare and it was nice just letting my mind take a break for a while. Although I'm not sure how much of a break it took because Breckin made it a point to bring up how much I talked about Sky. He doesn't understand why I won't just apologize to her if I obviously like her as much as I do. Unfortunately, I can't explain it to him, so he'll never understand it. But he seems okay with that.

Neither of us thinks it's a good idea to let Sky know we hung out. I don't want her upset with Breckin, but now it feels like I'm somehow cheating on her by being friends with him. But I can assure you, Les. I wasn't there for his gay parts.

H

Chapter Thirty-one

"What do you want to do?" I ask.

"I don't care what we do," Daniel says.

"Me neither."

We're sitting in his driveway. I'm leaned back in my seat with my foot propped on his dash. He's in the same position in the driver's seat, only his hand is hanging loosely from the steering wheel and his head is resting against the headrest. He's staring out the window and he's being unusually distant.

"What's wrong with you?" I ask.

He continues to stare out the window and sighs a heavy, depressing sigh. "Broke up with Val again," he says disappointedly. "She's crazy. She's so fucking crazy."

"I thought that's why you loved her?"

"But that's also why I *don't*." He drops his leg to the floorboard and scoots his seat forward. "Let's get out of here." He cranks the car and begins backing out of the driveway.

I put my seatbelt on and slide my sunglasses off my head and over my eyes. "What do you want to do?"

"I don't care what we do," he says.

"Me neither."

"Is Breckin home?" I ask his mother, who's now eyeing Daniel from the doorway in the same way she was eyeing me last Friday night.

"Well, aren't you becoming a real regular," Breckin's mother says to me. There isn't any humor behind her voice and quite frankly, she's a little intimidating.

We stand silently for several awkward seconds and she still doesn't invite us in. Daniel leans his head toward mine. "Hold me. I'm scared."

The door widens and Breckin replaces his mother after she turns and walks away. He's now the one eyeing Daniel suspiciously. "I'm definitely not doing *you* any favors," Breckin says to him.

Daniel turns to face me, shooting me a quizzical look. "It's Friday night and you bring me to powder puff's house?" He shakes his head disappointedly. "What the hell has happened to us, man? What the hell have these bitches *done* to us?"

I look at Breckin and nudge my head sympathetically in Daniel's direction. "Girl trouble. I thought some Modern Warfare could help."

Breckin sighs, rolls his eyes, then steps aside to let us in. We make our way inside and Breckin closes the door behind us, then stops in front of Daniel. "You call me powder puff again and my new second-best friend ever in the whole wide world will kick your ass."

Daniel grins, then cuts his eyes to mine. We have one of our silent conversations where he tells me this kid isn't half bad. I smile, completely agreeing with him.

"Let me get this straight," Breckin says, trying to clarify the confession Daniel just made. "You don't even know what the girl *looked* like?"

Daniel smiles boastfully. "No clue."

"What was her name?" I ask.

He shrugs. "No clue."

Breckin sets down his game controller and turns to face Daniel. "How the hell did you end up in the maintenance closet with her?"

Daniel's face is still awash with a smug grin. He seems so proud of it, I'm shocked this is the first time he's mentioned it to me.

"Funny story, really," he says. "Last year I was never assigned a fifth-period class. It was a mistake on administration's part, but I didn't want them to know. Every day during fifth period while everyone else went to their scheduled classes, I would hide out in the janitor's closet and nap. They never cleaned that section of the hallway until after school, so no one ever went in there.

"I guess it was about six or seven months ago, right before the end of the school year, I was having one of my fifth-period naps and all of a sudden someone opens the door, slips inside, and trips over me. I couldn't see who she was because I always kept the lights out, but she landed right on top of me. We were in this really compromising position and she smelled really good and she didn't weigh very much, so I didn't mind her landing on me. I wrapped my arms around her and made no attempt to roll her off me because she felt so damn good. She was crying, though," he says, losing some of the excitement in his eyes. He leans back in his chair and continues. "I asked her what was wrong and all she said was, 'I hate them.' I asked her who she hated and she said, 'Everybody. I hate everybody.' The way she said it was just heartbreaking and I felt bad for her and her breath smelled so fucking good and I knew exactly what she meant because I hate everyone, too. So I kept my arms wrapped around her and I said, 'I hate everybody, too, Cinderella.' We were still in . . ."

"Wait, wait, wait," Breckin says, interrupting the story. "You called her Cinderella? What the hell for?"

Daniel shrugs. "We were in a janitor's closet. I didn't know her name and there were all these mops and brooms and shit and it reminded me of Cinderella, okay? Give me a break."

"But why would you even call her *anything*?" Breckin asks, not understanding Daniel's penchant for random nicknames.

Daniel rolls his eyes. "I didn't know her fucking *name*, Einstein! Now stop interrupting me, I'm just now getting to the good part." He leans forward again. "So I said to her, 'I hate everybody, too, Cinderella.' We were still in the same position and it was dark and to be honest, it was really kinda hot. You know, not knowing who she was or what she looked like. Sort of mysterious. Then she just laughs and leans forward and kisses me. Of course I kissed her back because I'd already finished my nap and we still had about fifteen minutes to kill. We kissed for the rest of the period. That's all we did. We never spoke another word and we never did more than just kiss. When the bell rang, she hopped up and walked out. I didn't even see what she looked like."

He's staring at the floor, smiling. I've honestly never seen him talk about a girl like this before. Not even Val.

"But I thought you said she was the best sex you ever had?" Breckin says, bringing us back to the point that started this whole conversation.

Daniel grins boastfully again. "She was. Turns out I wasn't hard to find after that. She showed up again a week later. The closet light was out like always and she walked in and shut the door behind her. She was crying again. She said, 'Are you in here, kid?' The way she called me kid made me think she might have been a teacher and I'd be lying if I said that didn't turn me on. Then one thing led to another and let's just say I became her Prince Charming for the rest of the hour. And *that* was the best sex I ever had."

Breckin and I both laugh.

"So who was she?" I ask.

Daniel shrugs. "I never found out. She never showed up again after that and school ended a few weeks later. Then I met Val and my life spiraled out of control." He exhales a deep rush of air, then turns to face Breckin. "Is it racist of me to not really want to hear about your gay sex?"

Breckin laughs and throws his game controller at Daniel. "Racist isn't the correct term, dipshit. Homophobic and discriminatory, yes. And understandable. I wouldn't tell you, anyway."

Daniel looks at me. "I don't even have to guess who you'll say was your best," he says. "The way Sky has you broken right now, I think it's pretty obvious."

I shake my head. "Well, you're wrong, because not only did I never have sex with her, but we never even kissed."

Daniel laughs but Breckin doesn't and neither do I, which quickly shuts Daniel up. "Please tell me you're kidding."

I shake my head.

Daniel stands up and tosses his controller onto the bed. "How the hell have you not kissed her?" he says, raising his voice. "Because the way you've been acting this month had me thinking she was the fucking love of your life."

I cock my head. "Why do you seem pissed off by this?"

He rolls his head. "Seriously?" He stalks toward me and bends forward, placing his hands on either side of my chair. "Because you're being a *pussy*. P-U-S-S-Y." He lets go of my chair and backs up. "*Jesus*, Holder. I was actually feeling sorry for you. Suck it up, man. Go to her house and fucking kiss her already and allow yourself to be happy for once."

He drops down onto the bed and grabs his controller. Breckin smiles a tight-lipped smile and shrugs. "I don't really like your friend, but he does make a good point. I still don't understand why you got so mad at her and walked away, but the only way to make it up to her is to not *stay* away." He turns back toward the TV and I'm staring at both of them, completely speechless.

They make it sound so simple. They make it sound so easy, like her whole life isn't hanging in the balance. They don't know what the fuck they're talking about.

"Take me home," I say to Daniel. I don't want to be here anymore. I walk out of Breckin's bedroom and make my way back to Daniel's car.

Chapter Thirty-two

Les,

Everyone likes to have an opinion, don't they? Daniel and Breckin have no clue what I've been through. What either of us has been through.
Fuck it. I don't even feel like telling you about it.

H

I close the notebook and stare at it. Why the hell do I even write in it? Why the hell do I bother when she's fucking *dead*? I throw the notebook across the room and it hits the wall and falls to the floor. I throw the pen at the notebook and then grab my pillow from behind my head and throw it, too.

"Dammit," I groan, frustrated. I'm pissed that Daniel thinks my life is so simple. I'm pissed that Breckin still thinks I should just apologize to her, like that would make it all okay. I'm pissed that I'm still writing to Les even though she's dead. She can't read it. She'll never read it. I'm just putting all the shit I'm living through down on paper for no reason other than the fact that there isn't a single god-damned person in the world right now that I can talk to.

I lie down, then get pissed again and punch my bed because my damn pillow is all the way across the room. I stand up and walk to the pillow, snatching it up. I look down at the notebook beneath it, spread open on the floor.

The pillow falls out of my hand.

My knees fall to the floor.

My hands clench the notebook that has flipped open to the very last page.

I frantically flip through the pages covered in Les's handwriting until I find where the words begin. As soon as I see the first words written on top of the page, my heart comes to a screeching halt.

Dear Holder,

If you're reading this, I'm so, so sor

I slam the notebook shut and throw it across the room.

She wrote me a letter?

A fucking *suicide* letter?

I can't breathe. Oh, God, I can't breathe. I pull myself up and jerk open my window, then stick my head out. I take a deep breath and it's not enough air. There isn't enough air and I can't breathe. I shut the window and run to my bedroom door. I swing it open and rush down the stairs, taking them several at a time. I pass by my mother and her eyes grow wide, seeing me in such a hurry.

"Holder, it's midnight! Where are—"

"Running!" I yell, then slam the front door behind me.

And that's what I do. I run. I run straight to Sky's house because she's the only thing in the world that can help me breathe again.

Chapter Thirty-three

These past few weeks of doing everything in my power to avoid her have taken every ounce of my strength and I can't do it anymore. I thought by staying away from her I was being strong, but not being near her is making me weaker than I've ever been. I know I shouldn't be here and I know she doesn't want me here but I have to see her. I have to hear her, I have to touch her, I have to feel her against me because that weekend I spent with her was the only time since I walked away from her thirteen years ago that I actually looked *forward*.

I've never looked forward before. I've always looked back. I think about the past way too much and I think about what I should have done and everything I did wrong and I've never once looked forward in my life. Being with her had me thinking about tomorrow and the day after that and the day after that and next year and forever. I need that right now because if I don't get to hold her one more time . . . I'm scared I'll look back again and the past will completely swallow me up.

I grab the windowsill and close my eyes. I inhale several times in an attempt to calm my pulse and the trembling going on with my hands right now.

I hate that she always leaves her window unlocked. I push it up and slide the curtains back, then climb inside. I contemplate saying something so she'll know I'm in her room, but I also don't want to scare her if she's asleep.

I turn and close the window and walk to her bed, then slowly ease myself down. She's facing the other way, so I lift the covers and scoot in beside her. Her posture immediately stiffens and she pulls her hands up to her face. I know she's awake and I know she knows it's me climbing into her bed, but the fact that it terrifies her completely breaks me.

She's scared of me. I didn't expect fear to be a reaction from her at all. Anger, yes. I'd so much rather her be angry at me right now than scared.

She's not telling me to leave yet and I don't think I could even if she asked me to. I have to feel her in my arms, so I move closer to her and slide my arm under her pillow. I wrap my other arm around her and slide my fingers into hers, then bury my face into her neck. Her scent and her skin and the feel of her heartbeat against our hands is exactly what I need, more tonight than ever before. I just need to know that I'm not alone, even if she doesn't have a clue how much allowing me to hold her is helping.

I kiss her softly on the side of her head and pull her closer. I don't deserve to be back in her bed or in her life after all I've put her through. In this moment, she's allowing me to be here. I'm not going to think about what might happen in the next few minutes. I'm not going to think about what happened in the past. I'm not looking forward *or* backward. I'm just holding her and thinking about this. Right now. Her.

She hasn't spoken in almost half an hour, but neither have I. I'm not apologizing to her, because I don't deserve her forgiveness and that's not why I'm here. I can't tell her what happened that day at lunch because I don't want her to know yet. I have no idea what to say, so I just hold her. I kiss her hair and I silently thank her for helping me breathe again.

I fold my arm up and hold her tighter. I'm trying not to fall apart right now. I'm trying so hard. She inhales a breath, then speaks to me for the first time in almost a month. "I'm so mad at you," she whispers.

I squeeze my eyes shut and press my lips desperately against her skin. "I know, Sky." I slip my hand around her to pull her closer. "I know."

Her fingers slide through mine and she squeezes my hand. All she did was squeeze my hand, but that one small gesture does more for me in this moment than I could ever give her in return. Knowing she's reassuring me, even in the slightest way, is more than I deserve from her.

I press my lips to her shoulder and kiss her softly. "I know," I whisper again as I continue kissing up her neck. She's responding to my touch and to my kiss and I want to stay here forever. I wish I could freeze time. I want to freeze the past and the future and just focus on being here in this moment with her forever.

She reaches up and runs her hand to the back of my head, pulling me against her neck even harder. She wants me here. She needs me here just as much as I need to be here and just knowing that is enough to freeze time for just a little while.

I raise up in the bed next to her and gently pull on her shoulder until she's flat on her back, looking up at me. I brush the hair away from her eyes and look down at her. I've missed her so much and I'm so scared she'll come to her senses and ask me to leave. God, I've missed her. How did I ever think walking away from her would be good for *either* of us?

"I know you're mad at me," I say, running my hand down to her neck. "I need you to be mad at me, Sky. But I think I need you to still want me here with you even more."

She continues to keep her eyes locked with mine and she nods her head slightly. I drop my forehead to hers and take her face in my hands, and she does the same to me.

"I *am* mad at you, Holder," she says. "But no matter how mad I've been, I never for one second stopped wanting you here with me."

Those words knock the breath out of me at the same time they completely fill my lungs back up with her air. She wants me here and it's the best fucking feeling in the world. "*Jesus*, Sky. I've missed you so bad." I feel like she's my lifeline and if I don't kiss her immediately, I'll die.

I dip my head and press my mouth to hers. We both inhale a deep breath the second our lips meet. She pulls me to her, welcoming me back into her life. Our mouths are pressed desperately together but our lips are completely still and we're both attempting to inhale another breath. I pull back slightly because the feel of her beneath me and having her mouth willingly pressed to mine is completely overwhelming me. In all my eighteen years, nothing has ever felt more perfect. As soon as my lips separate from hers, she looks up into my eyes and wraps her hands around my neck. She lifts up from the bed slightly, bringing her mouth back to mine. This time she kisses *me*, softly parting my lips with hers. When our tongues meet, she moans and I push her back against the mattress, kissing *her* this time.

For the next few minutes, we're completely lost in what feels like sheer perfection. Time has completely stopped, and all I'm thinking about while we kiss is how this is what saves people. Moments like these with people like her are what make all the suffering worth it. It's moments like these that keep people looking forward and I can't believe I've let them slip by for an entire month.

I know I told her that she's never really been kissed before, but until this moment I had no idea that *I* had never really been kissed before. Not like this. Every kiss, every movement, every moan, every touch of her hand against my skin. She's my saving grace. My Hope.

And I'm never walking away from her again.

* * *

I hear the door to her bedroom close, so I know she's about to walk in on me cooking breakfast for her. I still haven't explained what the hell I've done to her over the past month and I'm not sure that I can, but I'll do whatever it takes to get her to accept it without letting her forgive me. No matter what happened between us last night, I still don't deserve her forgiveness and honestly, she's not the type of girl who would put up with the shit I've put her through. If she forgave me, I feel like she would be compromising her strength. I don't want her compromising anything about herself for my sake.

I know she's standing behind me. Before everything I've done catches back up with her again, I try to explain away the fact that I've made myself at home in her kitchen again.

"I left early this morning," I say with my back still turned to her, "because I was afraid your mom would walk in and think I was trying to get you pregnant. Then when I went for my run, I passed by your house again and realized her car wasn't even home and remembered you said she does those trade days every month. So I decided to pick up some groceries because I wanted to cook you breakfast. I also almost bought groceries for lunch and dinner, but maybe we should take it one meal at a time today."

I turn around to face her and I don't know if it's because I've spent the last few weeks having to be so far away from her or what, but she's the most beautiful thing I've ever laid eyes on. I look her up and down, recognizing that this is the first time I've ever fallen in love with a piece of clothing before. What the hell is she trying to do to me?

"Happy birthday," I say casually, trying not to show her just how flustered I am looking at her in that outfit. "I really like that dress. I bought real milk, you want some?" I take a glass and pour her some milk, then slide it to her. She eyes the milk warily but I don't give her time to drink it. Seeing those lips and that mouth and . . . *shit*.

"I need to kiss you," I say, walking swiftly to her. I take her face in my hands. "Your mouth was so damn perfect last night, I'm scared I dreamt that whole thing." I expect her to resist, but she doesn't. Instead, I'm met with eager perfection when she grabs me by the shirt with both hands and kisses me back. Knowing that she still wants me after all I've put her through makes me appreciate her even more. And knowing I still have a chance with her?

That I'll still get to kiss her like this?

It's almost too much.

I separate from her and back away, smiling. "Nope. Didn't dream it."

I face the stove again so that I can stop concentrating on her mouth long enough to make her a plate of food. I have so much I need to say to her and I don't even know where or how to start. I fix our plates and walk them to the bar where she's seated.

"Are we allowed to play Dinner Quest, even though it's breakfast time?" I ask her.

She nods. "If I get the first question."

She isn't smiling. She hasn't smiled for me in over a month. I hate that I'm the reason she doesn't smile anymore.

I lay my fork down on my plate and bring my hands up, clasping them under my chin. "I was thinking about just letting you have *all* the questions," I say.

"I only need the answer to one," she says.

I sigh, knowing for a fact she needs more than just one answer. But the fact that she only wants the answer to one question leads me to believe she's about to ask me about the bracelet. And that's the one question I'm not willing to share the answer to just yet.

She leans forward in her chair and I brace myself for her question.

"How long have you been using drugs, Holder?"

I immediately look up at her, not expecting that to have been her question at all. It comes from so far out of left field that I keep my eyes locked with hers, but the randomness of the question makes me want to laugh. Maybe I should be disturbed by the fact that my behavior has given her such an absurd thought, but instead I feel nothing but relief.

I'm trying. I'm trying so hard not to laugh, but the anger in her eyes is adorable. It's adorable and beautiful and honest and I'm so *relieved*. I have to look away from her because I'm trying my damndest not to smile. She's being so serious and straightforward right now, but dammit. I can't.

My smile finally gives way and I laugh. Her eyes grow angrier, which only makes me laugh harder. "*Drugs?*" I'm trying to stop, but the more I think about how much this has affected us the entire last month, it just makes me laugh even harder. "You think I'm on *drugs?*"

Her expression doesn't change at all. She's pissed. I hold my breath in an attempt to stop the laughter until I'm able to keep a straight face. I lean forward and take her hand in mine, looking her directly in the eyes. "I'm not on drugs, Sky. I promise. I don't know why you would think that, but I swear."

"Then what the hell is wrong with you?" she snaps.

Shit. I hate the look on her face. She's hurt. Disappointed. Exhausted. I'm not sure which part of my unexplained, erratic behavior she's referring to, but I honestly have no idea how to answer that. What *is* wrong with me? What's *not* wrong with me?

"Can you be a little less vague?" I ask her.

She shrugs. "Sure. What happened to us and why are you acting like it never happened?"

Damn. That hurts. She thinks I just brushed everything that happened between us under the rug? I want to tell her everything. I want to tell her how much she means to me and how this has been one of the hardest months of my life. I want to tell her about Les and her and me, and how much it fucking hurts that she doesn't remember. How can she just forget such a significant part of her life?

Maybe Les and I weren't as significant to her as I thought. I look down at my arm. I trace the H and the O and the P and the E, wishing she remembered. But then again, if she remembered . . . she'd also know the meaning behind this tattoo. She'd know that I let her down. She'd remember that everything that's happened in her life for the last thirteen years is a direct result of me.

I look her in the eyes and answer her with the most honest answer I'll allow myself to give her. "I didn't want to let you down, Sky. I've let everyone down in my life that's ever loved me, and after that day at lunch I knew I let you down, too. So . . . I left you before you could start loving me. Otherwise, any effort to try not to disappoint you would be hopeless."

Her eyes cloud with disappointment. I know I'm being vague again, but I can't tell her. Not right now. Not until I know for sure that she'll be okay.

"Why couldn't you just say it, Holder? Why couldn't you just apologize?"

The hurt in her voice grips my heart. I look her directly in the eyes so she'll see how important it is to me that she never accepts how I treated her. "I'm not apologizing to you . . . because I don't want you to forgive me."

She immediately squeezes her eyes shut, trying to hold back tears. Nothing I can say could make her feel better about what happened between us. I release her hand and stand up, then walk to her and pick her up. I set her down on top of the bar so that we're at eye level. She may not believe the words that come out of my mouth, but I need her to feel me. I need her to see the sincerity in my eyes and the honesty in my voice so she'll know I didn't mean to hurt her. I only wanted to protect her from feeling this way, but I've only made it worse.

"Babe, I screwed up. I've screwed up more than once with you, I know that. But believe me, what happened at lunch that day wasn't jealousy or anger or anything that should ever scare you. I wish I could tell you what happened, but I can't. Someday I will, but I can't right now and I need you to accept that. Please. And I'm not apologizing to you, because I don't want you to forget what happened and you should never forgive me for it. Ever. Never make excuses for me, Sky."

She's taking in every word I'm saying and I love that about her. I lean in and kiss her, then pull back and continue saying what I need to say while she's still willing to hear me out.

"I told myself to just stay away from you and let you be mad at me, because I do have so many issues that I'm not ready to share with you yet. And I tried so hard to stay away, but I can't. I'm not strong enough to keep denying whatever this is we could have. And yesterday in the lunchroom when you were hugging Breckin and laughing with him? It felt so good to see you happy, Sky. But I wanted so bad to be the one who was making you laugh like that. It was tearing me up inside that you were thinking that I didn't care about us, or that spending that weekend with you wasn't the best weekend I've ever had in my life. Because I *do* care and it *was* the best. It was the best fucking weekend in the history of all weekends."

I run my hands down her hair to the base of her neck and brush her jawline with my thumbs. I have to take in a calming breath to say what I want to say next, because I don't want to scare her. I just need to be honest with her.

"It's killing me, Sky," I say quietly. "It's killing me because I don't want you to go another day without knowing how I feel about you.

And I'm not ready to tell you I'm in love with you, because I'm not. Not yet. But whatever this is I'm feeling—it's so much more than just *like*. It's so much more. And for the past few weeks I've been trying to figure it out. I've been trying to figure out why there isn't some other word to describe it. I want to tell you exactly how I feel but there isn't a single goddamned word in the entire dictionary that can describe this point between *liking* you and *loving* you, but I need that word. I need it because I need you to hear me say it."

I kiss her and pull back, but she's still looking at me in disbelief. I kiss her again and again, pausing after each kiss, hoping she'll respond with something. I don't care if she slaps me or kisses me back or tells me she loves me. I just want her to acknowledge everything I said. Instead, she's just staring at me and it's making me so damn nervous.

"Say something," I plead.

She continues to stare at me for a long time. I try to stay patient. She's always patient with me even though she's so quick-witted. What I wouldn't give for her to be a little more quick-witted in this moment. I need a reaction from her.

Something. Anything.

"Living," she finally whispers.

That's not what I expected to come out of her mouth, but at least it's something. I laugh and shake my head, confused about what she means. *"What?"*

"Live. If you mix the letters up in the words like and love, you get live. You can use that word."

Not only does she *get* me and not only is she smiling at me; but she just somehow gave me the one word I've been searching for since the moment I laid eyes on her in the grocery store.

I don't deserve her. I don't deserve her understanding and I sure as hell don't deserve the way she just made my heart feel. I laugh and take her in my arms, bringing my mouth to hers. "I live you, Sky," I say against her lips. "I live you so much."

And as perfect as that word sounds, as perfectly as it describes the point we're at, I know it's a lie.

I don't just live her. I *love* her. I've loved her since we were kids.

Chapter Thirty-four

Les,

*I'm not reading that letter. I'm never reading it. Ever.
And I'm done writing in this fucking notebook. So I
guess that means I'm done writing to you, too.*

H

Chapter Thirty-five

The phone rings and before I can even say hello, Daniel starts talking. "Do you and cheese tits want to come over and watch a movie with me and Val tonight?"

"I thought you broke up with Val."

"Not today," Daniel says.

"I don't know if that's a good idea." I've heard enough about Val to know that I'm not sure I feel comfortable taking Sky over there. We've only been dating two weeks.

"It *is* a good idea," Daniel argues. "My parents leave at eight. Be here at eight-oh-one."

He hangs up abruptly, so I text Sky.

Want to watch a movie with Daniel and Val tonight?

I hit send and toss my phone on the bed. I walk to my closet to inspect my shirt selection, but then I remember that I don't really have much of a shirt selection. I grab a random T-shirt and am pulling it on over my head when Sky's text sounds off.

Two conditions. (Per Karen.) I have to be home by midnight and you can't get me pregnant.

I laugh and text her back.

Considering how boring you are, I'm pretty sure you'll be home in less than an hour.

Does that mean you're still gonna try to get me pregnant, though?

Damn straight.

Laugh out loud.

She actually typed *laugh out loud*.

I really *do* lol, then I put my phone in my pocket and head to my car.

I've never really had a conversation with Val before and tonight is no exception. Sky and I are on the couch in front of the TV in Daniel's basement. Daniel and Val are in the chair and they're completely mauling each other, making me question why Daniel would even want us here in the first place if this is all they're gonna do.

Sky and I are watching them uncomfortably. It's hard to pay attention to the TV when there's actual slurping occurring.

The second Daniel's hand begins to slip up Val's shirt, I toss the remote at them, hitting Daniel in the knee. He jumps and lifts his hand to flip me off, but never breaks contact with Val's mouth. He does somehow glance at me, though, and I silently tell him to get the hell out of his basement, or get the hell out of her shirt.

He stands up and Val is now wrapped around him. They say nothing as he carries her up the stairs and to his bedroom.

"*Thank you*," Sky says, breathing a sigh of relief. "I was about to hurl."

She's curled up beside me on the couch with her head resting on my shoulder. I ease myself down into the couch so that we're more comfortable, and we both look back at the TV. But I know we aren't really paying attention to it because the energy in the room completely shifted the second Daniel and Val left. We haven't had privacy like this since we officially started dating two weeks ago.

Her hand is in mine and they're clasped together, resting on her thigh. She's not wearing the dress that completely melted me the first time I saw her in it, but she *is* wearing a dress. And I love this dress just as much as the other dress.

I wish she were wearing jeans, though. I overheard Les talking with one of her friends once when we were sixteen. They were about to go on a double date and the friend was explaining to Les the rules of "make-out" clothes. She said if Les just wanted to kiss the guy, she needed to wear jeans because the guy would be less likely to slip his hand where he shouldn't. Then she told Les if she planned to move past first base, that a skirt or a dress was the way to go. *Easy access*, she said. I remember waiting in the living room after hearing that conversation to see which outfit Les chose. She walked down the stairs in a skirt and I marched her right back up to her room and forced her to change into a pair of jeans.

I wish Sky were wearing jeans right now because my hands are starting to sweat and I know she can feel my pulse through the palm of my hand. Her dress makes me think she wants to take things a step further tonight and I absolutely can't get that out of my head. I sure as hell *want* to take the next step, but what if Sky doesn't know the rules to "make-out" clothes? What if she's wearing this dress just for the hell of it? What if she's just wearing this dress because her washing machine broke and all her jeans were dirty? What if she's wearing this dress because she didn't have time to change into jeans before I showed up at her house? What if she's wearing this dress because she went to some sort of random church today that has service on Saturdays?

I wish I knew what was going through her head right now. I rest my head against the back of the couch and swallow the huge lump in my throat before I speak. "I like your dress," I say. It comes out in more of a raspy whisper because my throat is so weak right now just thinking about her. But I think she liked the way I said it, because she tilts her head and looks up at me, then slowly drops her eyes to my mouth. Thanks to the angle we're sitting, we wouldn't even have to shift positions to kiss. Her mouth is so incredibly close, it's practically on top of mine. But neither of us is taking advantage of that. *Yet.*

"Thank you," she whispers. The sweet breath from her words crashes against my mouth, warming me from the inside out.

The tension is so thick now, I can't even inhale.

"You're welcome," I whisper back, staring at her mouth the same way she's staring at mine. We're both quiet for a moment, just silently staring. She slides her lips together and moistens them and I'm pretty sure I mutter "*holy shit*" under my breath.

She likes that she just got me all flustered because she grins. "Wanna make out?" she whispers.

Oh, hell yes.

My lips are on hers before the sentence is even completely out of her mouth. I lower my hands to her waist and pull her until she's straddling me.

Straddling me *in. Her. Dress.*

I keep my hands locked tight on her hips while her hands slowly make their way up my neck and into my hair. The way her chest is pressed against mine makes my head spin, and it feels like the only thing that could set it straight again is if I pull her even closer and kiss her even harder. So that's what I do. I slide my hands away from her hips and reach behind her and pull her closer, pressing her into me so perfectly that she moans and tugs on my hair. I keep one hand on her ass, letting it flow with the rhythm of her movements while my other hand slides up her back and into her hair. I pull her mouth deeper into mine while I straighten my posture and lean forward so that my back is no longer touching the couch and my mouth is as meshed with hers as it's gonna get. Only that just makes my head spin even worse, so we're kissing faster now and she's moaning louder and I'm gripping her hips again and moving her against me so perfectly that I'm pretty sure she's about to have a repeat of what I did to her the first night we made out.

I don't want that yet because she's wearing this dress and it's absolutely amazing and I'm not even taking advantage of it. I grip her shoulders and push her away from me, letting myself fall back against the couch.

We're both gasping for breath. We're both smiling. We're both looking at each other like this is the best night ever because it's only ten o'clock and we've got a good two hours left of this. I release her shoulders and take her face in my hands, then slowly pull her back to my mouth. I change the position of my hands to support her weight and I stand up, then lower her onto the couch. I join her, pressing one knee between her legs and the other on the couch beside her.

I'm starting to get the impression that Daniel picked out this oversized couch in the same way that girls pick out their make-out clothes. Because it's the perfect couch for this sort of thing.

I begin to kiss down her chin, down her neck and down to the area where her dress stops and her cleavage begins. I slowly glide my hand over her dress and up the length of her body until I reach her breast. I stroke my hand over the material and she hardens beneath my fingertips.

Ohmygod I fucking *love* tonight.

I groan and grab her breast a little harder and she moans, arching her back, pressing more of herself against my hand. I claim her mouth with mine and continue kissing her until we have to break for air again. I press my cheek against hers.

My lips are right next to her ear.

"Sky?" I whisper.

She inhales a quick breath. "Yeah?"

I inhale a slow one. "I live you."

She exhales. "I live *you*, Dean Holder."

I exhale.

And inhale.

And exhale.

I repeat that sentence silently in my head. *I live you, Dean Holder.* It's the first time I've heard her say Dean.

It's also the first time I've ever had my heart impaled by a word before.

I lift away from her cheek and look down at her. "Thank you."

She smiles. "For what?"

For being alive, I think to myself.

"For being you," I say out loud.

Her smile fades and I swear she looks right through my eyes and straight into my soul. "I'm good at being me," she says. "Especially when I'm with you."

I stare at her for several seconds, then I have to lower my cheek to hers again. I want to kiss her, but I keep my cheek pressed firmly against hers because I don't want her to see the tears in my eyes.

I don't want her to see how much it hurts to know she can be this close to me . . . and somehow not *remember* me.

Chapter Thirty-five-and-a-half

Dear all dead people who aren't Les, since I'm not writing letters to Les anymore,

I've loved Hope since we were kids.
  But tonight?
  Tonight I fell in love with Sky.

  H

Chapter Thirty-six

Les,

I know I said I wasn't writing to you anymore. Shut up. I'm still not writing in that notebook because I don't want to touch it, knowing that letter from you is in there. I can't read it, so I just bought a new notebook. Problem solved. Now I need to catch you up.

I've been dating Sky for a month now. She still hasn't had any recollection of me or you or all of us as kids. I keep catching myself almost slipping up, but luckily I haven't.

Remember that guy I got arrested for beating up last year? The one who was talking shit about you? Well, his brother finally said something to me today. I've been waiting for him... or anyone, really... to bring it up since the day I got back to school. It would have been fine had he just confronted me, but he didn't. He had to use Sky and Breckin and even you as a way to get back at me. He started talking shit about them to me at lunch and I swear to God, Les. I wanted to hurt him just as badly as I hurt his brother. Actually, I probably would have hurt him worse than I hurt his brother had Sky not been there.

She saw where my mind was going and she immediately pulled me out of the situation, forcing me out of the lunchroom. When we made it to my car in the parking lot I just completely broke down on her. It was like the entire past year of my life was repeatedly punching me in the gut and I just had to get it out. I told Sky everything I was feeling and for the first time since it happened... I admitted to myself and out loud that I was the one in the wrong. And I also admitted for the first time that you were in the wrong. I told Sky how pissed I was at you. How angry I've been since the second I walked in and found you lifeless in your bed. I've been so mad at you, Les, for so many things.

But the thing that pissed me off the most was the fact that you never once thought about what it would do to me when I found you. You knew I would be the one to find you and the fact that you knew that and you still killed yourself?

I hated that you did it anyway, knowing you wouldn't be the only one who died. I was so mad because you let me die, too.

Sky's right. I've got to let go of the blame. But until Sky knows the truth, I don't think I'll be able to forgive myself. I'm not even ready to forgive you.

H

Chapter Thirty-seven

I've never brought her to my house before, even though we've been dating for a month now. Hope spent a lot of time at our house when we were kids, so I'm worried my mother will recognize her and say something when she meets her. So until Sky knows the truth about her past, I don't want to risk her finding out from anyone other than me.

I don't want Sky to think I don't want her to be a part of my life by never allowing her to come to my house or meet my family, so I've taken the opportunity to bring her here tonight since I know my mother won't be home. And even though we're finally alone, kissing on my bed, I don't feel right about it. The night didn't start out well and the guilt from everything that has happened up to this point is in the forefront of my mind, even though I'd rather my mind be focused on the moment.

She's been distant all day and I should have known it was my fault somehow. After we left the art gallery where we went to support Breckin and his boyfriend, Max, she hardly spoke two words to me. I wondered if it had something to do with last night and sure enough, it had *everything* to do with last night.

After my mother's Halloween party at the law firm yesterday, where I may or may not have snuck too many drinks, I went to Sky's house and crawled through her window. Things were good and we fell asleep, only to wake up to her crying hysterically. She was crying and shaking and I've never seen anyone react to a nightmare like that.

Ever.

It scared the shit out of me. Mostly because I didn't know how to help her, but also because I really didn't know where the hell I was when I woke up next to her. I was still a little buzzed from the drinks and I had little recollection of even leaving my house and sneaking into her bedroom. It scared me to know that I was around her while I was incoherent. I was scared that I might have let something slip about her past. I held her until she stopped crying but then I left because I could still feel the effects of the alcohol and I really didn't want to say something to screw all this up.

But apparently I did, because earlier when we were downstairs, she said something about Hope. She said her name and it completely stunned me. Knocked the breath out of me. And if I wasn't trying my damndest to act like I didn't know what she was talking about, it would have knocked me to my knees.

But I let her explain herself and it turns out my fears were dead-on about being around her while I wasn't completely coherent. Apparently I mumbled Hope's name instead of Sky's, and for the entire past day she's been making herself sick about it. She's been thinking Hope was someone else entirely and the thought of her thinking I would want or need or even entertain the thought of another girl just completely breaks my heart.

So right now, I'm doing everything I can to show her that she's the only girl I think about.

Just her.

I'm kissing her, propped up on my hands and knees, attempting to avoid making her feel like I brought her here for anything other than to just spend time with her.

But she *is* wearing a dress again.

After those two hours in Daniel's basement I think we were both pretty impressed with how well my hands and her dress became acquainted. We were also pretty impressed with how well my hands and the clothing *under* her dress became acquainted.

But now, here she is, wearing a dress again. And we passed quite a few firsts on that couch two weeks ago. So much so that it pretty much only leaves one more first to pass tonight and the fact that she knows that and *I* know that and she's still wearing a dress has my mind jumbled and my heart racing.

It also didn't help matters that before we made it up here to the bedroom, we were making out on the stairs and she blurted out the fact that she was a virgin. I already knew she was a virgin, but just the fact that she was thinking about it while I was kissing her to the point that she actually blurted it out loud leads me to believe that she just wanted to warn me for when we got to that point.

And I'm thinking she's at that point, which is why she felt the need to clear the air downstairs, so she wouldn't have to say it when it actually came to that point.

To the point it's at right now.

The point at which I'm thanking the angels and the gods and the birds and the bees and sweet baby Jesus that she's wearing this dress. If there's one thing that can ease my guilt and allow me to focus solely on her for the time being, it's this dress.

"Holy shit, Sky," I say, kissing her madly. "God, you feel incredible. Thank you for wearing this dress. I really . . ." I kiss down her chin until my lips meet her neck. "I really like it. Your dress." I continue kissing her neck and she tilts her head back, allowing me easier access. I drop my hand to her thigh and run it up under her dress. When I reach the top of her thigh I desperately want to keep going. But the fact that she's allowed me there once before doesn't mean I'm allowed there right now.

But apparently I am, because she twists her body more toward mine, directing my hand to keep heading where it's heading. Her hands crawl up my back just as my hand greets the panties lining her hip. I slip my fingers underneath the lining and begin to tug at the same time she pulls on my shirt.

She begins to pull it over my head and I'm forced to move my hand away. I squeeze her thigh, not wanting to have to pull back, but I'm pretty sure I want my shirt off just as much as she wants it off.

As soon as I lift up onto my knees, away from her, she whimpers. The sound makes me smile and after my shirt is off, I bend forward and kiss the corner of her lips. I bring my hand to her face and gently stroke her hairline, watching her. I know we're about to pass the most significant first of all and I want to memorize everything about this moment. I want to remember exactly what she looks like lying beneath me. I want to remember exactly what she sounds like the moment I'm inside her. I want to remember what she tastes like and what she feels like and what she—

"Holder," she says, breathlessly.

"Sky," I say, mimicking her. I don't know what she's about to say but whatever it is, it can wait a few seconds, because I need to kiss her again. I dip my head and part her lips until our tongues meet. We kiss slowly while I memorize every inch of her mouth.

"Holder," she says again, pulling away from my mouth. She brings her hand to my cheek and looks up into my eyes. "I want to. Tonight. Right now."

Right now. She said *right now.* That's nice because I conveniently don't have any prior engagements right now. I can do right now.

"Sky . . ." I say, wanting to make sure she's not doing this just to benefit me. "We don't have to. I want you to be absolutely positive it's what you want. Okay? I don't want to rush you into anything."

She smiles and strokes her fingernails up and down my arms. "I know that. But I'm telling you I want this. I've never wanted it with anyone before, but I want it with you."

There's no doubt in my mind that I want her. I want her *right now* and she obviously wants me, too. But I can't help but feel guilty, knowing I'm still deceiving her. I haven't told her the truth about us and I feel like if she knew, she wouldn't be making this decision.

I'm about to pull away from her until she places her hand on my cheeks and lifts herself off the bed until her lips are touching mine. "This isn't me saying *yes*, Holder. This is me saying *please*."

What was it I was thinking just now? Something about waiting? *Fuck that.*

Our lips collide and I groan, pushing her back against the bed. "We're really doing this?" I ask, not really believing it myself.

"Yes." She laughs. "We're really doing this. I've never been more positive of anything in my life."

My hand resumes its position and I begin to pull down her panties.

"I just need you to promise me one thing first," she says.

I pull my hand away, thinking maybe she's about to tell me to go a little slower. "Anything."

She takes my hand and places it right back on her hip. "I want to do this," she says, firmly looking into my eyes. "But only if you promise we'll break the record for the best first time in the history of first times."

I smile. *Damn straight.* "When it's you and me, Sky . . . it'll never be anything less."

I slide my arm underneath her back and pull her up. I curl my fingers underneath the straps of her dress, then slowly slide them down her arms. She fists one of her hands through my hair, pressing her cheek to mine while my lips meet her shoulder. My fingers are still holding on to the straps of her dress.

"I'm taking it off."

She nods and I grab the loose material at her waist and begin to lift the dress over her head. Once it's completely off, I lower her back down onto the bed and she opens her eyes. I scroll over her body, running my hand down her arm and across her stomach, coming to rest on the curve of her hip. I let everything I'm seeing sink in because this is what I want to remember the most. I want to remember exactly what she looks like the second she hands over a piece of her heart.

"Holy shit, Sky," I whisper, running my hands across her skin. I bend down and kiss her softly on the stomach. "You're incredible."

I watch my hand as it glides across her body. I watch as it slides up her stomach and meets her breast. I watch my thumb disappear beneath her bra. As soon as my entire hand has slipped beneath her bra, she's locking her legs around my waist. I groan and wish at this point that I had more hands because they want to be everywhere, all at once. And I don't want there to be any material in the way of their journey.

I reach down and pull her underwear off, then remove her bra. I'm kissing her the whole time, even when I slide off the bed to remove the rest of my own clothes. I climb back onto the bed with her. Back on top of her.

As soon as I'm pressed against her I'm hit with the revelation that I've never experienced or felt anything like her in my life. This is how it should be when people pass this first. This is exactly how it should feel and it's incredible.

I reach across the bed and pull a condom out of my nightstand. We haven't stopped kissing for a single second, but I need to see her face. I need to see that she wants me to be inside her as much as I want to *be* inside her.

I grab the condom and lift up onto my knees. I open it, but before I put it on I look down at her. Her eyes are closed tightly and her eyebrows are drawn together.

"Sky?" I say. I want her to open her eyes. I just need one final look of reassurance from her, but she fails to open her eyes. I lower myself on top of her again, stroking her cheek. "Babe," I whisper. "Open your eyes."

Her lips begin to tremble and she pulls her arms up, crossing them over her eyes. "Get off me," she whispers.

My heart sinks, not knowing what I did wrong. I've done everything I could to make this right but it's obviously gone wrong somewhere and I have no idea where. I sit up on my knees and scoot away from her just as a violent sob breaks from her. She twists away from me and hugs her arms, covering herself. "*Please*," she cries.

"Sky, I stopped," I say, stroking her arm. She pushes my hand away with her own and her whole body starts to shake. Her lips are moving and she's speaking under her breath, but I can't hear what she's saying. I lean forward to try and hear what she's trying to tell me.

"Twenty-eight, twenty-nine, thirty, thirty-one . . ."

She's counting in rapid succession and crying hysterically, curling herself into a ball on my mattress.

"Sky!" I say louder, trying to get her to stop. I don't know what the hell is wrong or what I did but this isn't her and it's starting to freak me out. She's responding like I'm not even here. I try to pull her arm away from her eyes so she'll look at me, but she starts slapping my hand away, crying hysterically.

"Dammit, Sky!" I yell, frantic. I pull on her arm again but she's fighting it. I don't know what to do or why she won't snap out of this, so I scoop her up into my arms and pull her against my chest. She's still counting and crying and I think I might be on the verge of crying, too, because she's losing it and I have no idea how to help her. I rock her back and forth and brush the hair from her face, trying to get her to snap out of it, but she just continues to cry. I pull the sheet up and wrap it around us, then kiss her on the side of her head. "I'm sorry," I whisper, at a loss for what to do next.

Her eyes flick open and she looks up at me, her whole being consumed with fear. "I'm sorry, Sky," I say, still not knowing what went wrong or why she's terrified of me right now. "I'm so sorry."

I continue to rock her, still not understanding what's causing her reaction, but I've never seen eyes so terrified before and I have no fucking clue how to calm her down.

"What happened?" she cries, still looking at me with eyes full of fear.

She completely checked out and she doesn't even remember doing it?

"I don't know," I tell her, shaking my head. "You just started counting and crying and shaking and I kept trying to get you to stop, Sky. You wouldn't stop. You were terrified. What did I do? Tell me, because I'm so sorry. I am so, so sorry. What the fuck did I do?"

She shakes her head, unable to answer me. It kills me that I don't know if I did something wrong to force her so far into her own head that she lost her grasp on reality.

I squeeze my eyes shut and press my forehead to hers. "I'm so sorry. I never should have let it go that far. I don't know what the hell just happened, but you're not ready yet, okay?"

She nods, still holding on to me tightly. "So we didn't . . . we didn't have sex?" she asks timidly.

My heart sinks because I realize with those words that no matter what I try to do to protect her, there's something tearing her apart. She completely checked out like I've never experienced before and there was nothing in my power I could do to stop it. I bring my hands to her cheeks. "Where'd you go, Sky?"

She looks at me confused and shakes her head. "I'm right here. I'm listening."

"No, I mean earlier. Where'd you go? You weren't here with me because no, nothing happened. I could see on your face that something was wrong, so I didn't do it. But now you need to think long and hard about where you were inside that head of yours, because you were panicked. You were hysterical and I need to know what it was that took you there so I can make sure you never go back."

I squeeze her tight, then kiss her on the forehead. I know she probably needs to regain her bearings right now, so I stand up and pull on my jeans and T-shirt, then help her back into her dress. "I'll go get you some water. I'll be right back." I lean forward, not sure if she even wants me near her right now, but I kiss her on the lips to reassure her.

I walk out of my room and head straight down to the kitchen. As soon as my elbows meet the countertop, I bury my face in my arms and muster up every ounce of willpower in me to stop myself from breaking down. I inhale several deep breaths, exhaling even bigger ones, hoping I can stay strong for her. But seeing her that helpless and knowing there was nothing I could do to help her?

It's the most disappointed in myself I've ever been.

Chapter Thirty-eight

I'm still leaning on the counter with my head in my hands when I hear a door close upstairs. I've been down here for several minutes now and I don't want her to think I'm trying to avoid her, so I head back upstairs. I check the bedroom and bathroom, but she's not in either. I look at Les's bedroom door and pause before reaching down and turning the knob.

She's sitting on Les's bed, holding a picture. "What are you doing?" I ask her. I don't know why she's in here. I don't want to be in here and I want her to come back to my room with me.

"I was looking for the bathroom," she says quietly. "I'm sorry. I just needed a second."

I nod, since I apparently needed a second, too. I look around the room. I haven't set foot in here since the day I found the notebook. Her jeans are still in the middle of the floor, right where she left them.

"Has no one been in here? Since she . . ."

"No," I say, not wanting to hear her finish that sentence. "What would be the point of it? She's gone."

She nods, then places the picture back down on the nightstand. "Was she dating him?"

Her question throws me for a second, then I realize she must have seen a picture of Les and Grayson together. I never told her they dated. I should have told her.

I step into the bedroom for the first time in over a year. I walk to the bed and take a seat next to her. I slowly scan the room, wondering why my mom and I thought it would be a better idea to just close the door after she died, rather than get rid of her things. I guess neither of us is ready to let her go just yet.

I glance at Sky and she's still looking at the picture frame on Les's nightstand. I wrap my arm around her shoulders and pull her to me. She brings a hand to my chest and clenches my shirt in her fist.

"He broke up with her the night before she did it," I say, giving her an explanation. I don't really want to talk about it, but the only other thing left to talk about is what just happened in my bed and I know Sky more than likely needs a little more time before we bring that up.

"Do you think he's the reason why she did it? Is that why you hate him so much?"

I shake my head. "I hated him before he broke up with her. He put her through a lot of shit, Sky. And no, I don't think he's why she did it. I think maybe it was the deciding factor in a decision she had wanted to make for a long time. She had issues way before Grayson ever came into the picture. So no, I don't blame him. I never have." I grab her hand and stand up, because I honestly don't want to talk about it. I thought I could, but I can't. "Come on. I don't want to be in here anymore."

I take her hand and she stands up, then we walk toward the door. She yanks her hand free once I reach the door, so I turn around. She's staring at a picture of me and Les when we were kids.

She's smiling at the picture, but my pulse immediately quickens when I realize that she's seeing me and Les as children. She's seeing us in the exact way she used to know us. I don't want her to remember. If she were to have even the slightest recollection right now, she might start asking questions. The last thing she needs after the breakdown she just had is to find out the truth.

She squeezes her eyes shut for a few seconds and the look on her face kicks my pulse up a notch. "You okay?" I ask, attempting to pull the picture out of her hands. She immediately snatches it back and looks up at me.

It's the first sign of recognition I've seen on her face and it feels like my entire body is wilting.

I manage to take a step toward her, but she immediately takes a step back. She keeps looking at the picture, then back up to me and I just want to grab the frame and throw it across the fucking room and pull her out of here, but I have a feeling it's too late.

Her hand goes up to her mouth and she chokes back a sob. She looks up at me like she wants to say something, but she can't speak.

"Sky, no," I whisper.

"How?" she says achingly, looking back down at the picture. "There's a swing set. And a well. And . . . your cat. It got stuck in the well. Holder, I know that living room. The living room is green and the kitchen had a countertop that was way too tall for us and . . . your mother. Your mother's name is Beth." Her rush of words come to a pause and she darts her eyes back up to mine. "Holder?" she says, sucking in a breath. "Is Beth your mother's name?"

Not tonight, not tonight. God, she doesn't *need* this tonight. "Sky . . ."

She looks at me, heartbroken. She rushes past me and across the hall, into the bathroom, where she slams the door behind her. I follow after her and try to open the door but she's locked it.

"Sky, open the door. Please."

Nothing. She doesn't open the door and she says nothing.

"Baby, please. We need to talk and I can't do it from out here. Please, open the door."

Another moment passes without her opening the door. I grip the edges of the doorframe and wait. It's too late to backtrack now. All I can do is wait until she's ready to hear the truth.

The door swings open and she's looking at me, her eyes full of anger now rather than fear.

"Who's Hope?" she says, barely above a whisper.

How do I say it? How do I tell her the answer to that question, because as soon as I do I know I'll have to watch as her entire world collapses around her.

"Who the hell is Hope?" she says, much louder this time.

I can't. I can't tell her. She'll hate me and that would destroy me.

Her eyes fill with tears. "Is it me?" she asks, her voice barely audible. "Holder . . . am I Hope?"

A rush of breath escapes my lungs and I can feel the tears following. I look up to the ceiling to try to hold them back. I close my eyes and press my forehead against my arm, inhaling the breath that will encase the voice that will release the one word that will destroy her again.

"Yes."

Her eyes grow wide and she just stands there, slowly shaking her head. I can't even imagine what must be going through her head right now.

She suddenly shoves past me, out into the hallway. "Sky, wait," I yell as she descends the steps two at a time. I rush after her, trying to catch her before she leaves. As soon as she hits the bottom step, she collapses to the floor.

"Sky!" I drop to my knees and take her in my arms, but she's pushing against me. I can't let her run. She needs to know the rest of the truth before she leaves here.

"Outside," she breathes. "I just need outside. Please, Holder."

I know how it feels to need air this badly. I release my hold and look her in the eyes. "Don't run, Sky. Go outside, but please don't leave. We need to talk."

She nods and I help her stand up. She walks outside and into the front yard where she tilts her head back and stares up at the stars.

Up at the sky.

I watch her the whole time, wanting nothing more than to hold her. But I know that's the last thing she wants right now. She knows I've been lying to her and she has every right to hate me.

After a while, she finally turns and heads back inside. She brushes past me without making eye contact and she walks straight into the kitchen. She takes a bottle of water out of the fridge and opens it, downing several gulps before finally making eye contact with me.

"Take me home."

I'll get her out of the house, but I'm not taking her home.

We're at the airport now. I couldn't think of anywhere else quiet enough to take her and I refused to take her home until she asked me everything she needs to ask me. The only thing she asked me with any sincerity on the way here was why I got my tattoo. I told her the same thing I told her last time she asked me about it; only this time I think she actually understood.

"Are you ready for answers?" I ask her. We've been silently watching the stars for several minutes now. I'm just trying to give her a chance to calm down. To clear her head.

"I'm ready if you're actually planning on being honest this time," she says, anger lacing her voice.

I turn to face her and the hurt in her eyes is as prominent as the stars in the sky. I lift up onto my elbow and look down at her.

Just a while ago I was looking down at her this same way, memorizing everything about her. When we were in that moment on my bed I was looking at her with so much hope. I felt like she was mine and I was hers and that moment and feeling would last forever. But now, looking down at her . . . I feel like it's all about to end.

I lower my hand to her face and touch her. "I need to kiss you."

She shakes her head. "No," she says resolutely.

I feel like tonight is the end of us and if she doesn't let me kiss her one more time it'll kill me. "I need to kiss you," I say again. "Please, Sky. I'm scared that after I tell you what I'm about to tell you . . . I'll never get to kiss you again." I grasp her face harder and pull her closer. *"Please."*

Her eyes are desperately searching mine, possibly to see if there's any shred of truth behind my words. She doesn't say anything. She just barely nods, but it's enough. I lower my head and press my lips firmly against hers. She grasps my forearm with her hand and parts her lips, allowing me to kiss her more intimately.

We continue to kiss for several minutes, because I don't know that either of us wants to face the truth just yet. I lift up onto my knees without breaking away from her and I climb on top of her. She runs her hand through my hair and to the back of my head, where she pulls against me, urging me closer.

She begins to clench my shirt with her fists as a cry breaks free from her throat. I move my lips to her cheek and kiss her softly, then lower my mouth to her ear. "I'm so sorry," I whisper, holding on to her with my free hand. "I'm so sorry. I didn't want you to know."

She pushes me off her, then sits up. She pulls her knees to her chest and buries her face in them.

"I just want you to talk, Holder. I asked you everything I could ever ask you on the way here. I need you to answer me now so I can just go home," she says, sounding tired and exhausted. I stroke her hair and give her the answers she needs.

"I wasn't sure if you were Hope the first time I saw you. I was so used to seeing her in every single stranger our age, I had given up trying to find her a few years ago. But when I saw you at the store and looked into your eyes . . . I had a feeling you really were her. When you showed me your ID and I realized you weren't, I felt ridiculous.

It was like the wake-up call I needed to finally just let the memory of her go.

"We lived next door to you and your dad for a year. You and me and Les . . . we were all best friends. It's so hard to remember faces from that long ago, though. I thought you were Hope, but I also thought that if you really were her, I wouldn't be doubting it. I thought if I ever saw her again, I'd know for sure.

"When I left the grocery store that day, I immediately looked up the name you gave me online. I couldn't find anything about you, not even on Facebook. I searched for an hour straight and became so frustrated that I went for a run to cool down. When I rounded the corner and saw you standing in front of my house, I couldn't breathe. You were just standing there, worn out and exhausted from running and . . . *Jesus*, Sky. You were so beautiful. I still wasn't sure if you were Hope or not, but at that point it wasn't even going through my mind. I didn't care who you were; I just needed to know you.

"After spending time with you that week, I couldn't stop myself from going to your house that Friday night. I didn't show up with the intention of digging up your past or even in the hope that something would happen between us. I went to your house because I wanted you to know the real me, not the me you had heard about from everyone else. After spending more time with you that night, I couldn't think of anything else besides figuring out how I could spend more time with you. I had never met anyone who got me the way you did. I still wondered if it was possible . . . if you were her. I was especially curious after you told me you were adopted, but again, I thought maybe it was a coincidence.

"But then when I saw the bracelet . . ."

I need her to look me in the eyes for this, so I lift her chin and make her look at me.

"My heart broke, Sky. I didn't want you to be her. I wanted you to tell me you got the bracelet from your friend or that you found it or you bought it. After all the years I spent searching for you in every single face I ever looked at, I finally found you . . . and I was devastated." As soon as I say the word, I regret it. Because I know that isn't true. I was upset. I was overwhelmed. But I didn't even know the meaning of devastated. I sigh and finish my confession. "I didn't want you to be Hope. I just wanted you to be you."

She shakes her head. "But why didn't you just tell me? How hard would it have been to admit that we used to know each other? I don't understand why you've been lying about it."

God, this is so hard.

"What do you remember about your adoption?"

"Not a lot," she says, shaking her head. "I know I was in foster care after my father gave me up. I know Karen adopted me and we moved here from out of state when I was five. Other than that and a few odd memories, I don't know anything."

She's not getting it. That's not what *she* remembers at all. It's what she's been *told.* I move from my position beside her and sit directly in front of her, facing her. I grab her by the shoulders. "That's all stuff Karen told you. I want to know what *you* remember. What do *you* remember, Sky?"

She breaks eye contact with me, trying to think. When she comes up empty, she looks back up at me. "Nothing. The earliest memories I have are with Karen. The only thing I remember from before Karen was getting the bracelet, but that's only because I still have it and the memory stuck with me. I wasn't even sure who gave it to me."

I lower my lips to her forehead and kiss her, knowing the next words that come out of my mouth will be the words I know she doesn't want to hear. As if she can see how much this is hurting me, she wraps her arms around my neck and climbs onto my lap, holding me tightly. I wrap my arms around her, not quite understanding how she can even find it in herself to want to comfort me right now.

"Just say it," she whispers. "Tell me what you're wishing you didn't have to tell me."

I lower my head to hers, squeezing my eyes shut. She thinks she wants to know the truth, but she doesn't. If she could feel what it's about to do to her, she wouldn't want to know.

"Just tell me, Holder."

I sigh, then pull away from her. "The day Les gave you that bracelet, you were crying. I remember every single detail like it happened yesterday. You were sitting in your yard against your house. Les and I sat with you for a long time, but you never stopped crying. After she gave you your bracelet she walked back to our house but I couldn't. I felt bad leaving you there, because I thought you might be mad at your dad again. You were always crying because of him and it made me hate him. I don't remember anything about the guy, other than I hated his guts for making you feel like you did. I was just a kid, so I never knew what to say to you when you cried. I think that day I said something like, 'Don't worry . . .'"

"He won't live forever," she says, finishing my sentence. "I remember that day. Les giving me the bracelet and you saying he won't live forever. Those are the two things I've remembered all this time. I just didn't know it was you."

"Yeah, that's what I said to you." I take her face in my hands. "And then I did something I've regretted every single day of my life since."

"Holder," she says, shaking her head. "You didn't do anything. You just walked away."

I nod. "Exactly. I walked to my front yard even though I knew I should have sat back down in the grass beside you. I stood in my front yard and I watched you cry into your arms, when you should have been crying into mine. I just stood there . . . and I watched the car pull up to the curb. I watched the passenger window roll down and I heard someone call your name. I watched you look up at the car and wipe your eyes. You stood up and you dusted off your shorts, then you walked to the car. I watched you climb inside and I knew whatever was happening I shouldn't have just been standing there. But all I did was watch, when I should have been with you. It never would have happened if I had stayed right there with you."

She takes a deep breath. "*What* never would have happened?"

I brush my thumbs over her cheekbones and look at her with as much calmness and reassurance as I can muster, because I know she's about to need it.

"They took you. Whoever was in that car, they took you from your dad, from me, from Les. You've been missing for thirteen years, Hope."

Chapter Thirty-nine, Chapter Thirty-nine-and-a-half, Chapter Thirty-nine-and-three-quarters

She closes her eyes and lays her head on my shoulder. She tightens her grip around me, so I tighten mine in return. I wait. I wait for it to sink in. I wait for the tears. I wait for the heartbreak because I know for a fact it's coming.

We sit in silence for several minutes, but the tears never come. I begin to wonder if everything I just said to her is even registering. "Say something," I beg.

She doesn't make a sound. She doesn't even move. Her lack of reaction is starting to worry me, so I place my hand on the back of her head and lower my head closer to hers. "*Please*. Say something."

She slowly lifts her face away from my shoulder and she looks at me with dry eyes. "You called me Hope. Don't call me that. It's not my name."

I didn't even realize I did. "I'm sorry, Sky."

Her eyes grow cold and she slides off me, then stands up. "Don't call me that, either," she says.

I stand up and take both of her hands, but she pulls away and turns toward the car. I haven't really thought out what I would do or say after she finally found out the truth from me. I'm not at all prepared for whatever comes next.

"I need a chapter break," she says, continuing to walk away.

"I don't even know what that means," I say, following behind her.

Whatever she needs, it's more than just a chapter break. She needs a chapter break within a chapter break within a chapter break. I can't imagine how confused she must be right now.

She continues to walk away so I grab her arm but she immediately jerks away from me. She spins around and her eyes are wide with fear and confusion. She begins to take deep breaths like she's attempting to hold off a panic attack. I don't know what to say to her and I know she doesn't want me to touch her right now.

She takes two quick steps forward and she reaches up and grabs my face, standing on the tips of her toes. She presses her lips firmly to mine and kisses me desperately, but I can't find it in me to kiss her back. I know she's just scared and confused right now and she's doing whatever she can to not think about it.

She pulls away from my mouth when she realizes I'm not kissing her back, then she reaches up and slaps me.

What she's experiencing right now is more than likely more traumatic and more emotional than anything someone can experience in life, short of death. I try to remember that when she reaches up and slaps me again, then pushes against my chest. Panic consumes her completely and she's screaming and hitting me and the only thing I can do is spin her around and pull her against my chest. I wrap my arms around her from behind and press my lips to her ear. "Breathe," I whisper. "Calm down, Sky. I know you're confused and scared, but I'm here. I'm right here. Just breathe."

I hold her for several minutes, allowing her time to gather her thoughts. I know she has questions. I just need her mind to the point that it can handle all the answers.

"Were you ever going to tell me who I was?" she asks after she pulls away from me. "What if I never remembered? Would you have ever told me? Were you scared I would leave you and you'd never get your chance to screw me? Is that why you've been lying to me this whole time?"

The questions she just asked have all been my biggest fears. I've been so scared she wouldn't understand my reasoning for not telling her. "No. That's not how it was. That's not how it *is*. I haven't told you because I'm scared of what will happen to you. If I report it, they'll take you from Karen. They'll more than likely arrest her and send you back to live with your father until you turn eighteen. Do you want that to happen? You love Karen and you're happy here. I didn't want to mess that up for you."

She shakes her head and laughs a disheartening laugh. "First of all," she says. "They wouldn't put Karen in jail because I can guarantee you she knows nothing about this. Second, I've been eighteen since September. If my age was the reason you weren't being honest, you would have told me by now."

I look down at the ground because it's too hard to look her in the eyes.

"Sky, there's so much I still need to explain to you," I say. "Your birthday wasn't in September. Your birthday is May 7. You don't even turn eighteen for six more months. And Karen?" I walk forward and take her hands. "She has to know, Sky. She *has* to. Think about it. Who else could have done this?"

As soon as I say it, she pulls her hands from mine and steps back like I've just insulted her.

"Take me home," she says, shaking her head in disbelief. "I don't want to hear anything else. I don't want to know anything else tonight."

I grab her by the hands again and she slaps them away. "TAKE ME HOME!"

We're parked in her driveway sitting silently in her car. I made her promise me she wouldn't say anything to Karen during the drive back to her house. She says she isn't going to say anything until we talk again tomorrow, but I still don't like the thought of leaving her here in the condition she's in.

She pulls open the door, but I grab her hand. "Wait," I say. She pauses. "Will you be okay tonight?"

She sighs and falls back against the passenger seat. *"How?"* she says with a defeated voice. "How can I possibly be okay after tonight?"

I push her hair behind her ear. I don't want to leave her. I want to reassure her that I'm not walking away from her this time. "It's killing me . . . letting you go like this," I say. "I don't want to leave you alone. Can I come back in an hour?"

She shakes her head no. "I can't," she says weakly. "It's too hard being around you right now. I just need to think. I'll see you tomorrow, okay?"

I nod, then pull my hand back and place it on the steering wheel. As much as it hurts, I need to give her what she wants right now. I know she needs time to process all the things going through her mind. To be honest, I think I need time to process it, too.

Chapter Forty

Les,

She knows.
*   And I can't believe I just dropped her off at her house and left. I don't care if she doesn't want to be around me right now. There's no way in hell I can just leave her alone. I wish you were here right now because I don't know what the hell I'm doing.*

H

I shoot straight up when I hear her scream next to me on her bed. She's gasping for breath.

Another nightmare.

"What the hell are you doing here?" she says.

I glance down at my watch, then rub my eyes. I'm trying to sort out what all has been real in the past few hours and what all was a dream.

Unfortunately, it was *all* real.

I place my hand on her leg and scoot closer to her. Her eyes are terrified. "I couldn't leave you. I just needed to make sure you were okay." I slide my hand around her neck and her pulse is pounding against my palm. "Your heart. You're scared."

She's looking at me wide-eyed. Her chest is heaving and the fear rolling off her is breaking me. She brings her hand to mine and squeezes it. "Holder . . . I remember."

I immediately turn her to face me and I force her eyes up to mine. "What do you remember?" I ask, nervous for her answer.

She begins to shake her head, not wanting to say it. I need her to say it, though. I need to know what she remembers. I nod my head, silently coaxing her to continue. She takes a deep breath. "It was Karen in that car. She did it. She's the one who took me."

This is exactly what I didn't want her to feel. I hug her. "I know, babe. I know."

She clings to my shirt and I tighten my grip, but push her away as soon as her bedroom door swings open.

"Sky?" Karen says, watching us from the doorway.

Karen looks at me, trying to figure out why I'm here. She turns back to Sky. "Sky? What . . . what are you doing?"

Sky spins back around and looks me desperately in the eyes. "Get me out of here," she begs in a whisper. "Please."

I nod, then stand up and walk to her closet. I don't know where she wants to go, but I know she'll need clothes. I find a duffel bag on the top shelf, then walk it to her bed. "Throw some clothes in here. I'll get what you need out of the bathroom."

She nods and heads to her closet while I head into her bathroom to grab whatever else she might need. Karen is pleading with her not to leave. When my hands are full, I walk out of the bathroom and Karen has her hands on Sky's shoulders.

"What are you doing? What's wrong with you? You're not leaving with him."

I walk around Karen and try to remain as calm as possible for all of our sakes. "Karen, I suggest you let go of her."

Karen spins around, shocked at my words. "You are *not* taking her. If you so much as walk out of this house with her, I'm calling the police."

I don't say anything. I'm not sure if Sky wants her to know that she knows the truth, so I do my best to refrain from saying what I've wanted to say to Karen since the moment I realized she's the one responsible. I zip the duffel bag and reach for Sky's hand. "You ready?"

She nods.

"This isn't a joke!" Karen yells. "I'll call the police! You have no right to take her!"

Sky reaches into my pocket and pulls out my cell phone, then steps toward Karen. "Here," she says. "Call them."

She's testing Karen. Her wheels are churning as fast as mine and she's hoping she can prove that Karen is innocent in all of this. It makes my heart break for her, because I know Karen isn't innocent. This is only going to end badly.

Karen refuses to take the phone and Sky grabs her hand and shoves the phone into her palm. "Call them! Call the police, Mom! *Please*," she says. Sky's eyebrows draw apart and she pleads desperately, one last time. "Please," she whispers.

I can't watch Sky endure this for another second, so I grab her hand and lead her to the window, then help her climb out of it.

Chapter Forty-one

I lift my head off the pillow and immediately cover my eyes. The afternoon sun is so bright, it's painful. I pry my arm from around her and quietly lift off the bed.

I somehow managed the whole drive to Austin last night. I don't think I could have stayed awake another minute, so I pulled over at the first hotel we could find. It was daytime when we finally made it to our room, so we both took turns showering, then crashed. She's been asleep for over six hours now and I know how much she needs it.

I softly brush the hair away from her cheek and lean down and kiss it. She pulls her arm out from under the blanket and looks up at me with tired eyes. "Hey," she whispers, somehow smiling despite everything she's going through.

"Shh," I say, not wanting her to wake up just yet. "I'm about to leave for a little while to get us something to eat. I'll wake you when I get back, okay?"

She nods and closes her eyes, then rolls back over.

After we finish eating, she walks to the bed and slips on her shoes. "Where you headed?" I ask her.

She ties her shoes and stands up, wrapping her arms around my neck. "I want to go for a walk," she says. "And I want you to go with me. I'm ready to start asking questions."

I give her a quick kiss, then grab the key and head to the door. "Then let's go."

We eventually make our way to the hotel courtyard and take a seat in one of the cabanas. I pull her to me. "You want me to tell you what I remember? Or do you have specific questions?"

"Both," she says. "But I want to hear your story first."

I kiss her on the side of the head, then rest my head against hers while we stare out over the courtyard. "You have to understand how surreal this feels for me, Sky. I've thought about what happened to you every single day for the past thirteen years. And to think I've been living two miles away from you for seven of those years? I'm still having a hard time processing it myself. And now, finally having you here, telling you everything that happened . . ."

I sigh, remembering back to that day. "After the car pulled away, I went into the house and told Les that you left with someone. She kept asking me who, but I didn't know. My mother was in the kitchen, so I went and told her. She didn't really pay any attention to me. She was cooking supper and we were just kids. She had learned to tune us out. Besides, I still wasn't sure anything had happened that wasn't supposed to happen, so I didn't sound panicked or anything. She told me to just go outside and play with Les. The way she was so nonchalant about it made me think everything was okay. Being so young, I was positive adults knew everything, so I didn't say anything else about it. Les and I went outside to play and another couple of hours had passed by when your dad came outside, calling your name. As soon as I heard him call your name, I froze. I stopped in the middle of my yard and watched him standing on his porch, calling for you. It was that moment that I knew he had no idea you had left with someone. I knew I did something wrong."

"Holder," she interrupts. "You were just a little boy."

Yeah. A little boy who was old enough to know the difference between right and wrong. "Your dad walked over to our yard and asked me if I knew where you were." This is where it gets hard for me. This is the point I realized the awful mistake I had made. "Sky, you have to understand something," I say to her. "I was scared of your father. I was just a kid and knew I had just done something terribly wrong by leaving you alone. Now your police chief father is standing over me, his gun visible on his uniform. I panicked. I ran back into my house and ran straight to my bedroom and locked the door. He and my mother beat on the door for half an hour, but I was too scared to open it and admit to them that I knew what happened. My reaction worried both of them, so he immediately radioed for backup. When I heard the police cars pull up outside, I thought they were there for me. I still didn't understand what had happened to you. By the time my mother coaxed me out of the room, three hours had already passed since you left in the car."

She can feel how much this hurts me to talk about. She pulls one of her hands out of the sleeve of her shirt and places it in mine.

"I was taken to the station and questioned for hours. They wanted to know if I knew the license plate number, what kind of car took you, what the person looked like, what they said to you. Sky, I didn't know *anything*. I couldn't even remember the color of the car. All I could tell them was exactly what you were wearing, because you were the only thing I could picture in my head. Your dad was furious with me. I could hear him yelling in the hallway of the station that if I had just told someone right when it happened, they would have been able to find you. He blamed me. When a police officer blames you for losing his daughter, you tend to believe he knows what he's talking about. Les heard him yelling, too, so she thought it was all my fault. For days, she wouldn't even talk to me. Both of us were trying to understand what had happened. For almost six years we lived in this perfect world where adults are always right and bad things don't happen to good people. Then, in the span of a minute, you were taken and everything we thought we knew turned out to be this false image of life that our parents had built for us. We realized that day that even adults do horrible things. Children disappear. Best friends get taken from you and you have no idea if they're even alive anymore.

"We watched the news constantly, waiting for reports. For weeks they would show your picture on TV, asking for leads. The most recent picture they had of you was from right before your mother died, when you were only three. I remember that pissing me off, wondering how almost two years could have gone by without someone having taken a more recent picture. They would show pictures of your house and would sometimes show our house, too. Every now and then, they would mention the boy next door who saw it happen, but couldn't remember any details. I remember one night . . . the last night my mother allowed us to watch the coverage on TV . . . one of the reporters showed a panned-out image of both our houses. They mentioned the only witness, but referred to me as 'The boy who lost Hope.' It infuriated my mother so bad; she ran outside and began screaming at the reporters, yelling at them to leave us alone. To leave me alone. My dad had to drag her back inside the house.

"My parents did their best to try to make our life as normal as possible. After a couple of months, the reporters stopped showing up. The endless trips to the police station for more questioning finally stopped. Things began to slowly return to normal for everyone in the neighborhood. Everyone but Les and me. It was like all of our hope was taken right along with our Hope."

She sighs when I've finished and she's quiet for a while. "I've spent so many years hating my father for giving up on me," she says. "I can't believe she just took me from him. How could she do that? How could *anyone* do that?"

"I don't know, babe."

She sits up in the chair and looks me in the eyes. "I need to see the house," she says. "I want more memories, but I don't have any and right now it's hard. I can barely remember anything, much less him. I just want to drive by. I need to see it."

"Right now?"

"Yes. I want to go before it gets dark."

Chapter Forty-two

I should never have let her come here. As soon as we pulled up in front of the house, I could tell just looking at it wouldn't be enough for her. Sure enough, she got out of the car and demanded to see the inside of it. I tried to talk her out of it, but I can do only so much.

I'm standing outside her window, waiting. I don't want her to be in there right now, but I could clearly see that she's not having it any other way. I lean against the house and hope she hurries the hell up. It doesn't look like any of the neighbors are home, but that doesn't mean her father isn't going to drive up any second now.

I look down at the ground beneath my feet, then glance behind me at the house. This is the exact spot she was standing in when I walked away from her thirteen years ago. I close my eyes and rest my head against the house. I never expected I'd ever be back here with her again.

My eyes flash open and I stand up straight the second I hear the crash come from inside her bedroom, followed by screaming. I don't give myself time to question what the hell is going on in there. I just run.

I run through the back door and down the hall until I'm in her old bedroom with her. She's crying hysterically and throwing things across the room, so I immediately wrap my arms around her from behind to calm her down. I have no idea what the hell brought this on, but I'm at an even bigger loss how to stop it. She's frantically jerking against me, attempting to get out of my hold, but I just grip her even tighter. "Stop," I say against her ear. She's still frantic and I need her to calm down before someone hears her.

"Don't touch me!" she screams. She claws at my arms but I don't relent, even for a second. She eventually weakens and becomes defeated by whatever it is that has hold of her mind right now. She grows limp in my arms and I know I need to get her out of here, but I can't have her reacting like this once I get her outside.

I loosen my grip and turn her around to face me. She falls against my chest and sobs, grabbing fistfuls of my shirt while she tries to hold herself up. I lower my mouth to her ear.

"Sky. You need to leave. Now." I'm trying to be strong for her, but I also need her to know that being here is a very bad idea. Especially after she's just destroyed the entire room. He'll know someone was here for a fact now, so we need to leave.

I pick her up and carry her out of the bedroom. She keeps her face buried in my chest while I walk her outside and to the car. I reach into the backseat and hand her my jacket.

"Here, use that to wipe off the blood. I'm going back inside to straighten up what I can."

I watch her for a few seconds to make sure she's not about to panic again, then I shut the door and head back inside to her bedroom. I straighten up what I can, but the mirror is a hard one to cover up. I'm hoping that her father doesn't come into this room very often. If I can make it look like nothing outside this room was disturbed, it could be weeks before he even notices the mirror.

I put the blanket back on the bed and hang the curtains back up, then head back outside. When I reach the car, just the sight of her is enough to nearly bring me to my knees.

This isn't her.

She's scared. Broken. She's shaking and crying and I'm wondering for the first time if any of the decisions I've made over the last twenty-four hours have been smart ones.

I put the car in drive and pull away from the house, never wanting to see it or think about it again. I hope to hell she doesn't, either. I place my hand on the back of her head, which is tucked against her knees. I run my fingers through her hair and don't move my hand away from her the entire drive back to the hotel. I need her to know that I'm here. That no matter how she feels right now, she's not alone. If I've learned anything from losing her all those years ago or from what happened with Les, it's that I never want to let her feel alone again.

Once we're back inside the hotel room, I help her down onto the bed, then grab a wet rag and come back and inspect the cuts.

"It's just a few scratches," I say. "Nothing too deep."

I remove my shoes and climb onto the bed with her. I pull the blanket over us and rest her head against my chest while she cries.

The length of time she cries and the desperation with which she's holding on to me make me hate myself for allowing this to happen to her. I was careless last night and didn't think to keep her out of Les's room. She wouldn't be experiencing any of this now had she not seen that photo. Then she would never have gone back into that house.

She lifts her gaze to mine and her eyes are so sad. I wipe away her tears and lower my mouth to hers, kissing her softly. "I'm sorry. I should have never let you go inside."

"Holder, you didn't do anything wrong. Stop apologizing."

I shake my head. "I shouldn't have taken you there. It's too much for you to deal with after just finding everything out."

She lifts up onto her elbow. "It wasn't just being there that was too much. It was what I remembered that was too much. You have no control over the things my father did to me. Stop placing blame on yourself for everything bad that happens to the people around you."

The things he did to her? I slide my hand to the base of her neck. "What are you talking about? What things did he do to you?"

She squeezes her eyes shut and drops her head to my chest, then starts crying again. The answer she's refusing to give me right now completely rips apart my heart. "No, Sky," I whisper. "No."

I'm overcome with several different emotions at once. I've never wanted to hurt someone like I want to hurt her bastard of a father, and if she didn't need me here with her right now I'd be on my way back to his house.

I close my eyes and can't get the thought of her as a little girl out of my head. Even when I was a little boy, I could tell she was broken, and she was the first thing I ever felt the urge to protect. And now, curled up against me, crying . . . the only thing I want to do is protect her from him, but I can't. I can't protect her from all the memories that are flooding her mind right now and I'd give anything if I could.

She clenches my shirt in her fists and the sobs continue. I hold her as tightly as I can, knowing there's nothing I can do to make her pain go away, so I just hold her like I used to hold Les. I never want to let her go.

She continues to cry and I continue to hold her and I'm trying so hard to be strong for her right now but I'm breaking. Knowing what happened to her and all she's had to live through is completely unhinging me and I have no idea how she's even able to hold up at all.

After several minutes, her tears begin to soften but they never cease. She eventually lifts her face off my chest, then slides on top of me. She closes her eyes and brings her lips to mine, then she immediately tries to take off my shirt. I have no idea why she's doing this, so I flip her onto her back. "What are you doing?"

She slides her hand behind my neck and pulls my mouth back to hers. As much as I love kissing her, this just doesn't feel right. When her hands grab at my shirt again, I push them away. "Stop it," I tell her. "Why are you doing this?"

She looks at me with desperation. "Have sex with me."

What the fuck?

I immediately climb off the bed and pace the floor. I don't even know how the hell to respond to that, especially after what she just remembered about her father. "Sky, I can't do this," I say, pausing to look at her. "I don't know why you're even asking for this right now."

She crawls to the edge of the bed where I'm standing and she pulls up onto her knees, grasping at my shirt. "Please," she begs. "Please, Holder. I need this."

I step away from her, out of her grasp. "I'm not doing this, Sky. *We're* not doing this. You're in shock or something . . . I don't know. I don't even know what to say right now."

She falls back down onto the bed and begins to cry again.

Dammit. I don't know how to help her. I'm completely unprepared for this.

"*Please*," she says, looking me in the eyes. Her voice and the pain behind it is shattering me from the inside out. She drops her eyes to her hands, which are folded in her lap. "Holder . . . he's the only one that's ever done that to me." She lifts her eyes to mine again. "I need you to take that away from him. *Please*."

If I had a soul before those words, it just completely broke in half. Tears fill my eyes and I hurt for her. I hurt for her so much because I don't want her to ever have to think about that bastard again. "*Please*, Holder," she says again.

Fuck.

I don't know what to do or how to deal with all of this. If I tell her no, I'll hurt her even more. If I agree to help her by doing this; I don't know if I'll be able to forgive myself.

She's looking up at me from the bed, completely broken. Her pleading eyes are waiting for my decision. And even though neither option is one I want to choose, I just go with whatever she thinks she needs right now. If I could trade lives with her I would do it in a heartbeat, just so she'd never have to feel whatever it is she's feeling. I'll do whatever it takes to ease her pain.

Whatever it takes.

I walk back to her and sink to my knees on the floor. I scoot her to the edge of the bed, then I remove both our shirts. I pick her up and walk her to the head of the bed and lay her down gently. I lower myself on top of her, then wipe her tears away again.

"Okay," I say to her.

I know she more than likely just wants to get this over with. There's no way this moment can be what it should be. I reach to my wallet and remove a condom, then take off my pants, watching her diligently the entire time. I don't want her to panic during this like she did last night, so I watch for any signs that she's changed her mind. She's been through enough. I just want to do whatever I can to help her, and if this will help her, it's what I'll do.

I kiss her the whole time I'm taking off her clothes. I don't even try to make it romantic. I just try to think whatever thoughts about her I can think that will help me get this over with faster.

Once her clothes are off, I put on the condom and ease myself against her. "Sky," I say, praying she'll ask me to stop. I don't want it to be like this for her.

She opens her eyes and shakes her head. "No, don't think about it. Just do it, Holder."

Her voice is completely emotionless. I squeeze my eyes shut and bury my face in her neck. "I just don't know how to deal with all of this. I don't know if this is wrong or if it's what you really need. I'm scared if I do this, I'll make it even harder for you."

She wraps her arms tightly around my neck and she begins to cry again. Rather than release me, she just pulls me tighter and lifts her hips in a silent plea for me to keep going.

I kiss her on the side of her head and give her what she needs.

The moment I push into her, tears escape my eyes. She never makes a sound. She just keeps herself wrapped tightly around me and I go through the motions, trying desperately not to think about how different I wanted this to be.

I try not to think about how I feel like I'm taking advantage of her with every movement against her.

I try not to think about how doing this makes me feel like I'm no better than her father.

That thought freezes me. I'm still inside her, but I can't move. I can't do this to her for another second.

I pull away from her neck and look down at her, then roll off her completely. I sit on the edge of the bed and fist my hands in my hair.

"I can't do it," I say to her. "It feels wrong, Sky. It feels wrong because you feel so good but I'm regretting every single fucking second of it." I stand up and toss the empty condom into the trashcan, pull my clothes back on, then walk to the door, knowing I'm letting her down again.

I make my way outside and, as soon as I'm alone in the parking lot, I scream out of frustration. I pace the sidewalk for a while, trying to figure out what to do. I turn and hit the building, over and over, then fall against the brick wall and wonder how the hell I've let her end up here. How the hell did I allow it to ever get to this point? The last twenty-four hours of my life have been one huge, colossal fuck-up.

And here I am, walking away from her again. Doing what I do best. Leaving her completely alone.

Wanting to rectify at least one of my bad decisions, I immediately walk back into the hotel room. When I make it inside, she's in the bathroom, so I sit on the bed and pick up my shirt, then wrap it around my now-bleeding hand.

The bathroom door opens and she pauses midstep, just as I look up at her. Her eyes drop to my hand and she immediately rushes to me, unwrapping the shirt to inspect my hand.

"Holder, what'd you do?" she says, twisting my hand back and forth.

"I'm fine," I say, wrapping my hand back up. I stand up and look down at her, wondering how the hell she could possibly be worried about *me* right now.

"I'm so sorry," she says quietly. "I shouldn't have asked you to do that. I just needed . . ."

Jesus. *She's* apologizing to *me*? "Shut up," I say, taking her face in my hands. "You have absolutely nothing to apologize for. I didn't leave earlier because I was mad at you. I left because I was mad at myself."

She nods, then pulls away from me and walks to the bed. "It's okay," she says, lifting the covers. "I can't expect you to want me in that way right now. It was wrong and selfish and way out of line for me to ask you to do that and I'm really sorry. Let's just go to sleep, okay?" She climbs into the bed and pulls the covers over her.

I'm trying to process her words, but they aren't making any sense. I don't feel that way about what she asked me to do at all. How the hell did she ever get these crazy thoughts in her head to begin with?

"You think I'm having a hard time with this because I don't *want* you?" I walk to the bed and kneel next to her. "Sky, I'm having a hard time with this because everything that's happened to you is breaking my fucking heart and I have no idea how to help you." I climb onto the bed with her and pull her to a sitting position with me. "I want to be there for you and help you through this but every word that comes out of my mouth feels like the wrong one. Every time I touch you or kiss you, I'm afraid you don't want me to. Now you're asking me to have sex with you because you want to take that from him, and I get it. I absolutely get where you're coming from, but it doesn't make it easier to make love to you when you can't even look me in the eyes. It hurts so much because you don't deserve for it to be like this. You don't deserve this life and there isn't a fucking thing I can do to make it better for you. I want to make it better but I can't and I feel so helpless."

I take her in my arms and she wraps her legs around me, hanging on to every word I'm saying.

"And even though I stopped, I should have never even started without telling you first how much I love you. I love you so much. I don't deserve to touch you until you know for a fact that I'm touching you because I love you and for no other reason."

I press my lips to hers desperately, needing her to know that I'm speaking nothing but truth now. Every word I speak and every time I touch her, there's nothing there but honesty.

She pulls away and kisses my chin and my forehead and my cheek, then my lips again. "I love you, too," she says, proving to me that words are yet another characteristic someone can fall in love with. But I'm not falling in love with her piece by piece anymore. I'm in love with the whole girl. Every single piece of her.

"I don't know what I'd do right now if I didn't have you, Holder. I love you so much and I'm so sorry. I wanted you to be my first, and I'm sorry he took that from you."

"Don't you ever say that again," I tell her. "Don't you ever *think* that again. Your father took that first from you in an unthinkable way, but I can guarantee you that's all he took. Because you are so strong, Sky. You're amazing and funny and smart and beautiful and so full of strength and courage. What he did to you doesn't take away from any of the best parts of you. You survived him once and you'll survive him again. I know you will."

I place my palm over her heart, then pull her hand to my heart. I lower my eyes to her level, making sure she's completely in this moment with me. "Fuck all the firsts, Sky. The only thing that matters to me with you are the forevers."

She releases a breath of relief, then completely kisses the hell out of me. I grab her head and lower her back onto the bed, climbing on top of her. "I love you," I say against her lips. "I've loved you for so long but I just couldn't tell you. It didn't feel right letting you love me back when I was keeping so much from you."

She's crying again, but she's also smiling. "I don't think you could have picked a better time to tell me you loved me than tonight. I'm happy you waited."

I dip my head and kiss her. I kiss her like she deserves to be kissed. I hold her like she deserves to be held. And I'm about to make love to her like she deserves to be loved. I untie the robe she's wearing and slide my hand across her stomach. "*God*, I love you," I say to her. My hand moves from her waist, down her hip and to her thigh. I can feel her tense up, so I pull back and look down at her. "Remember . . . I'm touching you because I love you. No other reason."

She nods and closes her eyes and I recognize the nervousness seeping off her. I pull her robe closed and bring my hand to her face.

"Open your eyes," I say. She opens them and they're full of tears. "You're crying."

She just nods and smiles up at me. "It's okay. They're the good kind of tears."

I silently watch her, gauging if we should even be doing this right now. I want to show her how much I love her and I want to erase what happened between us an hour ago, because it never should have happened. I want to make it right for her. It's always been so ugly for her, but she deserves to see how beautiful it can be.

"I want to make love to you, Sky," I say, lacing our fingers together. "And I think you want it, too. But I need you to understand something first." I lower my mouth and kiss away a falling tear. "I know it's hard for you to allow yourself to feel this. You've gone so long training yourself to block the feelings and emotions out any time someone touches you. But I want you to know that what your father physically did to you isn't what hurt you as a little girl. It's what he did to your faith in him that broke your heart. You suffered through one of the worst things a child can go through at the hands of your hero . . . the person you idolized . . . and I can't even begin to imagine what that must have felt like. But remember that the things he did to you are in *no way* related to the two of us when we're together like this. When I touch you, I'm touching you because I want to make you happy. When I kiss you, I'm kissing you because you have the most incredible mouth I've ever seen and you know I can't not kiss it. And when I make love to you—I'm doing exactly that. I'm making love to you because I'm in love with you. The negative feeling you've been associating with physical touch your whole life doesn't apply to me. It doesn't apply to *us*. I'm touching you because I'm in love with you and for no other reason." I kiss her softly. "I love you."

She kisses me harder than she's ever kissed me, pulling me down to the bed with her. We continue to kiss and she continues to allow me to explore every single part of her with my mouth and my hands. When I ready myself against her after putting another condom on, I look down at her and she's finally looking up at me with a serene expression. The love in her eyes right now can't be mistaken, but I still want to hear her say it.

"Tell me you love me."

She tightens her grip around me, looking me hard in the eyes. "I love you, Holder. *So* much," she says firmly. "And just so you know . . . so did Hope."

As soon as the words leave her mouth, I'm completely consumed by a sense of peace. For the first time since the second she was taken from me, I finally know what forgiveness feels like. "I wish you could feel what that just did to me." I claim her mouth with mine at the same time she completely consumes my heart.

Chapter Forty-three

When I turn my phone on, I'm flooded with texts. Several from Breckin, several from my mother. There are missed calls from Sky's phone, so I can only assume they're from Karen. I don't listen to any of the voicemails, though. I know everyone's just worried about us, especially Karen. I'm still not sure how what she did fits into the picture, but I find it hard to believe that what she did was done from a place of evil.

Sky rustles in the bed, rolling over. I look down at her and lean forward to kiss her but she turns her face away and I kiss her cheek, instead.

"Morning breath," she mumbles, sliding off the bed. She heads for the shower and I check the time. Check-out is in an hour, so I decide to gather our things.

After I've got most of our things packed, she walks out of the bathroom. "What are you doing?" she asks.

I glance at her. "We can't stay here forever, Sky. We need to figure out what you want to do."

She rushes toward me. "But . . . but I don't know yet. I don't even have anywhere to go."

Her voice is full of panic, so I walk to her in order to ease her mind. "You have me, Sky. Calm down. We can go back to my house and figure this out. Besides, we're both still in school. We can't just stop going and we definitely can't live in a hotel forever."

"One more day," she says. "Please, let's just stay one more day, then we'll go. I need to try to figure this out and in order to do that, I need to go there one more time."

I don't know how she can possibly think going back to that house is in any way a good idea. There's absolutely nothing she needs from there. "No way. I'm not putting you through that again. You're not going back."

"I need to, Holder," she says pleadingly. "I swear I won't get out of the car this time. I swear. But I need to see the house again before we go. I remembered so much while I was there. I just want a few more memories before you take me back and I have to decide what to do."

Jesus, she's relentless. I pace the floor, not knowing how I can get it through her head that she can't do this.

"Please," she says again.

Ugh! I can't say no to that voice.

"Fine," I groan. "I told you I would do whatever it was you felt you needed to do. But I'm not hanging all of those clothes back up."

She laughs and rushes to me, throwing her arms around my neck. "You're the best, most understanding boyfriend in the whole wide world."

I hug her back and sigh. "No, I'm not. I'm the most *whipped* boyfriend in the whole wide world."

We're sitting in my car across the street from her old house and I'm gripping the steering wheel so hard I'm afraid I might break it. Her father just pulled up into his driveway, and as mad and outraged as I've been in the past, I've never had the urge to actually kill someone until now. Just seeing him makes my stomach turn and my blood boil. I lift my hand to the ignition, knowing nothing good can come of this if I don't drive away right now.

"Don't leave," she says, pulling my hand away from the ignition. "I need to see what he looks like."

I sigh and fall back against the seat. She needs to hurry up and get what she needs because this is bad. This is bad, bad, bad.

"Oh, my God," she whispers. I turn to her, wanting to know what made her just say that. "It's nothing," she says. "He just looks . . . familiar. I haven't had an image of him in my head at all but if I was to see him walking down the street, I would know him."

We watch as he ends a conversation on his cell phone and walks to the mailbox.

"Have you had enough?" I ask her. "Because I can't stay here another second without jumping out of this car and beating his ass."

"Almost," she says, leaning across the seat to get a better look. I don't understand why she would even want to see him. I don't understand how she's not jumping out of this car in order to rip his balls off, because that's the only urge I have right now.

After her father finally disappears inside his house, I turn and look at her.

"Now?"

She nods. "Yeah, we can go now."

I place my hand on the ignition and crank the car, then watch in horror as she swings open the door and rushes out of the car.

What the fuck?

I turn the car off and swing open my door, running after her. I chase her all the way across the front yard and halfway up the porch steps. I wrap my arms around her and lift her up, then turn back to the car. She's trying to fight me and kick me and I'm doing everything I can to get her as far away from the house as I can so he doesn't hear her.

"What the hell do you think you're *doing*?" I say through clenched teeth.

"Let go of me right now, Holder, or I'll scream! I swear to God, I'll scream!"

I let go of her and spin her around to face me. I grip her shoulders tightly and try to shake some goddamned sense into her.

"Don't *do* this, Sky. You don't need to face him again, not after what he's done. I want you to give yourself more time."

She looks at me and begins to shake her head. "I have to know if he's doing this to anyone else. I need to know if he has more kids. I can't just let it go, knowing what he's capable of. I have to see him. I have to talk to him. I need to know that he's not that man anymore before I can allow myself to get back in that car and just drive away."

I take her face in my hands and try to reason with her. "Don't do this. Not yet. We can make a few phone calls. We'll find out whatever we can online about him first. Please, Sky." I turn her toward the car and she sighs. She finally relents and begins walking toward the car with me.

"Is there a problem here?"

We both spin around at the sound of his voice. He's standing at the base of the porch steps, eyeing me carefully. If I wasn't having to physically prevent Sky from falling to the ground right now, I'd be rushing him.

"Young lady, is this man hurting you?"

She grows limp in my arms the second he speaks to her directly. I pull her against my chest. "Let's go," I whisper. I turn her toward the car. I need to get her away from him. I just need to get her to the car.

"Don't move!" he yells.

Sky freezes at the sound of his voice, but I'm still trying to urge her toward the car.

"Turn around!"

I can't force Sky forward at this point and there really isn't a way out of this situation. I begin to turn her around with me and keep my arm wrapped around her. She looks into my eyes and there's more terror in them than I ever imagined a single person could feel.

"Play it off," I whisper in her ear. "He might not recognize you."

She nods and we both face her father now. I'm not concerned with the fact that he may recognize me. Other than the day Hope went missing, he never spoke to me. I'm just hoping to hell he doesn't recognize her, but I know he will. A parent would recognize his own child, no matter how long it's been.

He's making his way toward us, and the closer he gets, the more I see the recognition in his eyes. He knows her.

Shit.

He pauses when he's several feet from us and tries to look her in the eyes, but she presses herself against me and looks down at the ground.

"*Princess?*" he says.

She begins to slide out of my arms and I look down at her. Her eyes have rolled back into her head and she's falling. I keep a tight grip on her and ease her to the ground completely so that I can get a better grip on her. I need to get her out of here right now.

I slide my hands under her arms and try to pull her up. Her father comes closer and grabs her hands to help me.

"Don't you fucking touch her!" I scream. He immediately backs away, looking at me in shock.

I look back down at her and grab her head, trying to bring her back to consciousness.

"Baby, open your eyes. Please."

Her eyelids flutter open and she looks up at me. "It's okay," I reassure her. "You just passed out. I need you to stand up. We need to leave." I pull her to her feet and steady her against me. I give her a second to regain her strength. Her father is right in front of her now.

"It *is* you," he says staring at her. He looks at me, then back to Sky. "Hope? Do you remember me?" His eyes are full of tears.

"Let's go," I say to her, attempting to pull her with me. She has to know how much I'm trying to refrain from attacking him right now. We. Need. To. Leave.

She resists my pull as her father takes another step toward her, so I pull her a step away from him.

"Do you?" he says again. "Hope, do you remember me?"

Sky's whole body grows tense. "How could I *forget* you?" she spits.

He sucks in a breath. "It's you," he says, fidgeting his hand down at his side. "You're alive. You're okay." He pulls out his radio, but I take a step forward and knock it out of his hand before he can report it.

"I wouldn't let anyone know she's here if I were you," I say. "I doubt you would want the fact that you're a fucking pervert to be front-page news."

The blood drains from his face. *"What?"* He looks back at Sky and shakes his head. "Hope, whoever took you . . . they lied to you. They told you things about me that weren't true." He takes another step forward and I have to pull her back again. "Who took you, Hope? Who was it?"

She begins to shake her head back and forth. "I remember everything you did to me," she says, taking a confident step toward him. "And if you just give me what I'm here for, I swear I'll walk away and you'll never hear from me again."

He's shaking his head, not wanting to believe that she remembers. He watches her for a minute. I know he's just as caught off guard as we are.

"What is it you want?" he asks her.

"Answers," Sky says. "And I want anything you have that belonged to my mother."

Sky reaches down to my hand, which is wrapped around her waist, and she squeezes it. She's scared.

Her father glances at me, then back to Sky. "We can talk inside," he says quietly. He looks around the neighborhood nervously, making sure there aren't any witnesses. The fact that he's even looking for witnesses lights up a huge caution sign. There's no telling what this man is capable of.

"Leave your gun," I demand.

He pauses, then removes his gun from his holster. He lays it on the porch.

"Both of them," I say.

He reaches down and removes the extra gun from his leg, laying it on the porch right before he walks into his house. I spin Sky around to face me before we walk through the door.

"I'm staying right here with the door open. I don't trust him. Don't go any farther than the living room."

She nods and I give her a quick kiss, then watch her turn and step into the living room. She walks to the couch and takes a seat, eyeing him guardedly the entire time.

He raises his eyes to hers. "Before you say anything," he says. "You need to know that I loved you and I've regretted what I did every second of my life."

"I want to know why you did it," she says.

He leans back in his seat and rubs his hands over his eyes. "I don't know," he says. "After your mother died, I started drinking heavily again. It wasn't until a year later that I got so drunk one night that I woke up the next morning and knew I had done something terrible. I was hoping it was just a horrible dream, but when I went to wake you up that morning you were . . . different. You weren't the same happy little girl you used to be. Overnight, you somehow became someone who was terrified of me. I hated myself. I'm not even sure what I did to you because I was too drunk to remember. But I knew it was something awful and I am so, so sorry. It never happened again and I did everything I could to make it up to you. I bought you presents all the time and gave you whatever you wanted. I didn't want you to remember that night."

She grips her knees and I can tell by the way she's struggling for breath that she's doing everything she can to remain calm.

"It was night . . . after night . . . after night," she says. I immediately rush to the couch and kneel next to her. I wrap my arm around her back and grip her arm so that she stays put. "I was scared to go to bed and scared to wake up and scared to take a bath and scared to speak to you. I wasn't a little girl afraid of monsters in her closet or under her bed. I was terrified of the monster that was supposed to love me! You were supposed to be *protecting* me from the people like you!"

The pain in her voice is heart-wrenching. I want her out of here. I don't want her to have to hear him speak.

"Do you have any other children?" she asks.

He drops his head and presses a palm to his forehead, but fails to answer her. "*Do* you?" she screams.

He shakes his head. "No. I never remarried after your mother."

"Am I the only one you did this to?"

He keeps his eyes trained to the floor, avoiding her question.

"You owe me the truth," she says, her voice quiet now. "Did you do this to anyone else before you did it to me?"

There's a long silence. He's staring at the floor, unable to admit the truth. She's staring at him, waiting for him to give her what she came here for.

After a long silence, she begins to stand up. I grasp her arm but she looks me in the eyes and shakes her head. "It's okay," she says. I don't want to let her go, but I have to allow her to handle this the way she wants to handle it.

She walks to him and kneels in front of him. "I was sick," she says. "My mother and I . . . we were in my bed and you came home from work. She had been up with me all night and she was tired, so you told her to go get some rest."

He's looking her in the eyes like a regretful father. I don't know how.

"You held me that night like a father is supposed to hold his daughter. And you sang to me. I remember you used to sing a song to me about your ray of hope. Before my mother died . . . before you had to deal with that heartache . . . you didn't always do those things to me, did you?"

He shakes his head and touches her face.

I have the urge to rip his hand off, just like all the urges I've had to rip Grayson's hand off. Only this time I don't want to stop at his hand. I want to rip his head off and his balls off and . . .

"No, Hope," he says to her. "I loved you so much. I still do. I loved you and your mother more than life itself, but when she died . . . the best parts of me died right along with her."

"I'm sorry you had to go through that," she says with little emotion. "I know you loved her. I remember. But knowing that doesn't make it any easier to find it in my heart to forgive you for what you did. I don't know why whatever is inside of you is so different from what's inside other people . . . to the point that you would allow yourself to do what you did to me. But despite the things you did to me, I know you love me. And as hard as it is to admit . . . I once loved you, too. I loved all the good parts of you."

She stands up and steps back. "I know you aren't all bad. I *know* that. But if you love me like you say you do . . . if you loved my mother at *all* . . . then you'll do whatever you can to help me heal. You owe me that much. All I want is for you to be honest so I can leave here with some semblance of peace. That's all I'm here for, okay? I just want peace."

Her father is crying now. She walks back to me and I can honestly say I'm amazed by her right now. I'm amazed by her resolve. Her strength. Her courage. I slide my hand down her arm until I find her pinky, and I hold it. She wraps her pinky tightly around mine in return.

Her father sighs heavily, then looks back up at her. "When I first started drinking . . . it was only once. I did something to my little sister . . . but it was only one time. It was years before I met your mother."

She exhales a breath. "What about *after* me? Have you done it to anyone else since I was taken?" It's obvious he has by the guilt that consumes his features. "Who?" she asks. "How many?"

He shakes his head slightly. "There was just one more. I stopped drinking a few years ago and haven't touched anyone since. I swear. There were only three and they were at the lowest points of my life. When I'm sober, I'm able to control my urges. That's why I don't drink anymore."

"Who was she?" Sky asks.

He nudges his head to the right, toward the house next door.

Toward the house I used to live in.

The house I lived in with Les.

I don't hear another word after that.

Chapter Forty-four

One would think that finding my sister's body was the worst thing that's ever happened to me.

It wasn't. The worst thing that ever happened to me came later that night, when I had to tell my mother her daughter was dead.

I remember pulling Les onto my lap, doing everything I could to make sense of what was happening. I tried to make sense of why she wasn't responding. Why she wasn't breathing or talking or laughing. It just didn't make sense that someone could be here one minute, then the very next minute they're not. They're just . . . *not*.

I don't know how long I held her. It could have been seconds. It could have been minutes. Hell, I was so out of it that it could have been hours. I just know that I was still holding her when the front door slammed shut downstairs.

I remember panicking, knowing what was about to happen. I was about to have to walk downstairs and look my mother in the eyes. I was about to have to tell her that her daughter was dead.

I don't know how I did it. I don't know how I let go of Les long enough to stand up. I don't know how I found the strength to even stand. When I made it to the top of the stairs, she and Brian were removing their jackets. He took hers and turned around to hang it on the coatrack. She glanced up at me and smiled, but then she stopped smiling.

I began to walk down the stairs toward her. My body was so weak, I was taking them slowly. One at a time. Watching her the whole way.

I don't know if she had mother's intuition or if she could just tell by the look on my face what had happened, but she started to shake her head and back away from me.

I started to cry and she started to panic and she continued to back away from me until her back met the front door. Brian was looking back and forth between us, not understanding at all what was going on.

She turned around and gripped the doorframe, pressing her cheek against the door while she squeezed her eyes shut. It was like she was trying to shut me out. If she shut me out, she wouldn't have to face the truth.

Her body was racked with grief and she was crying so hard, there wasn't even a sound coming out of her mouth. I remember reaching the bottom step, watching her from where I was standing. Watching as she gave the word devastated a whole new meaning. I truly believed, at that point, that the word devastated should be reserved for mothers.

I no longer believe that.

The word devastated should be reserved for brothers, too.

"Les," I whisper, turning away from Sky and her father. "Oh, God, no." I press my head against the doorframe and grip the back of my neck with both hands. I begin to cry so hard that I'm not even able to make a sound. My chest hurts and my throat hurts, but my heart has just been completely obliterated.

Sky comes up behind me. She wraps her arms around me and tries to comfort me in whatever way she can, but I can't feel it. I can't feel her and I can't feel the devastation anymore because all I feel is this overwhelming amount of hatred and rage. I'm trying to refrain from lunging at him but I don't think I have enough self-control. I wrap my arm around Sky and pull her against me, hoping her presence can help calm me, but it doesn't. The only thing that could calm me would be knowing the man behind me is no longer breathing.

He's the reason. He's the reason for *all* of it.

He's why Les isn't here anymore. He's what broke Hope. He's the reason my mother knows the meaning of devastation. This bastard is who stole my sister's strength away from her, and I want him dead. But I want to be the one to do it.

I remove my arm from around Sky and push her away from me. I turn to face her father, but she steps between us, facing me with pleading eyes, pushing against my chest. She knows what I want to do to him and she's trying to push me out the door. I shove her out of the way because I don't know what I'm capable of right now and I don't want her to get hurt.

I begin to step toward him, but he reaches behind the couch, then quickly turns and holds up a gun. I honestly wouldn't even care that he's holding a gun, but my protective instinct kicks in when I think about Sky, so I pause. He pulls the radio to his mouth with his free hand, keeping his gun trained on me the entire time he speaks into it.

"Officer down at thirty-five twenty-two Oak Street."

His words immediately register in my head and I realize what he's about to do.

No.

No, no, no.

Not in front of Sky.

He turns his gun on himself, then looks at her. "I'm so sorry, Princess," he whispers.

I close my eyes and reach for her the second he fires the gun at himself. I cover her eyes and she begins to scream hysterically. She pulls my hand from her eyes, right when he falls to the floor, causing her to scream even louder.

I clamp my hand over her mouth and immediately pull her out the front door. She's too hysterical to carry right now, so I just drag her behind me.

The only thing running through my head at this point is how we need to get into the car. We need to get the hell out of here before anyone finds out we were ever here. Because if anyone finds out we were here, Sky's world will never be the same.

When I reach the car I keep my hand clamped to her mouth and I press her back against her door, looking her hard in the eyes. "Stop," I tell her. "I need you to stop screaming. Right now."

She nods vigorously, wide-eyed. "Do you hear that?" I say, trying to get her to understand the ramifications of what could happen if we don't leave right now. "Those are sirens, Sky. They'll be here in less than a minute. I'm removing my hand and I need you to get in the car and be as calm as you can because we need to get out of here."

She nods again so I remove my hand and quickly shove her into the car. I rush around to the driver's side and climb in, then crank the car and pull away. She leans forward in the seat and drops her head between her knees. She keeps saying, "No, no, no" under her breath, all the way back to the hotel.

Chapter Forty-five

Once we're back inside our hotel room, I walk her to the bed. She's having one of her moments where she's completely zoned out and I don't do anything to bring her out of it. It's probably best if she stays like this for a while.

I pull off my shirt, which is now covered in blood. I remove my socks and shoes and jeans and toss them all aside. I walk to where Sky is still standing and I remove her jacket. There's blood all over her and I'm trying to hurry so I can get her in the shower and wash it off. She finally turns to face me with a blank expression. I lay her jacket across the chair next to us, then lift her shirt over her head.

I reach down to the button on her jeans and undo it, then begin to lower them. When I reach her feet, she just stands still. I look up at her. "I need you to step out of them, babe."

She looks down at me and places her hands on my shoulders while I pull the jeans off her, one foot at a time. I feel her reach to my hair and brush her fingers through it. I toss her jeans aside and look back up at her. She's shaking her head looking down at her hands, which are now moving frantically over her stomach. She's smearing her father's blood all over her stomach, attempting to wipe it off. She's gasping for breath, trying to scream, but nothing's coming out. I stand up and immediately pick her up, rushing her to the shower. I need to get this off her before she completely loses control.

I set her down in the shower and turn on the water. Once it's warm, I close the shower curtain and pull her wrists away from her stomach. I wrap her arms around me and pull her against my chest, then turn her to where she's standing under the stream of water.

As soon as the water splashes her face, she gasps and the clarity begins to return to her eyes.

I grab the soap and a washcloth, and rub them under the water, then turn and begin wiping the blood off her face.

"Shh," I whisper, staring her in the eyes. "I'm getting it off you, okay?"

She squeezes her eyes shut and I diligently wash away every speck of blood from her face. When she's finally clean, I reach behind her in order to remove her ponytail holder.

"Look at me, Sky," I say. She opens her eyes and I rest my hand reassuringly on her shoulder. "I'm going to take off your bra now, okay? I need to wash your hair and I don't want to get anything on it."

Her eyes grow wide with my words and she pulls her arms through the straps of her bra, then frantically rips it over her head.

"Get it out," she says quickly, referring to the blood in her hair. "Just get it *off* me."

I take her wrists again and wrap her arms around me. "I'll get it. Hold on to me and try to relax. I'll do it."

I pour the shampoo into my hands and bring it to her hair. I have to wash it several times before the water finally runs clean. Once I'm finished washing her, I begin to wash my own hair. I get what I can but without being able to see myself, I don't know if I've washed away everything. I don't want to ask her to help me do this, but I have to make sure it's all gone. "Sky, I need you to make sure I got it all, okay? I need you to wipe away anything I missed."

She nods and takes the washcloth out of my hands. She eyes my hair and my back and my shoulders, then finally rubs the washcloth over my ear.

She pulls the washcloth away from me and looks down at it, running it under the stream of water.

"It's all gone," she whispers.

I take the washcloth and toss it onto the edge of the tub.

It's all gone, I repeat in my head.

I wrap my arms around her and close my eyes. I can feel it building. The questions. The memories. All the times I held Les at night while she cried and I had no idea what he'd done to her. No idea what she'd been through.

I hate him. I fucking hate that he got away with it for so long. He got away with what he did to Sky, to his sister, to Les. And the worst part is, he's not alive anymore for me to even be able to kill him.

Sky looks up at me and her eyes are full of sympathy. For a second I don't understand it, but then I realize I'm crying . . . and that she's just as sad for me as I am for her. Her shoulders begin to shake and a sob breaks free. She slaps her hand over her mouth and squeezes her eyes shut.

I pull her against my chest and kiss the side of her head.

"Holder, I'm so sorry," she cries. "Oh, my God, I'm so sorry."

I tighten my grip around her and press my cheek to the top of her head. I close my eyes and I cry. I cry for her. I cry for Les. I cry for myself.

She curls her arms up behind my shoulders, gripping me tightly, then she presses her lips against my neck. "I'm so sorry," she says quietly. "He never would have touched her if I . . ."

I grab her by the arms and push her away from me so that I can look her in the eyes. "Don't you dare say that." I grab her face with both hands. "I don't ever want you to apologize for a single thing that man did. Do you hear me? It's not your fault, Sky. Swear to me you will never let a thought like that consume you ever again."

She nods. "I swear."

I continue to maintain eye contact with her, needing to know that she's telling me the truth. This girl has done nothing that warrants an apology and I never want her thinking like that again.

She throws her arms around my neck, tears falling from both of us now. We hold each other tightly. Desperately. She kisses my neck repeatedly, wanting to reassure me in the only way she knows how.

I lower my lips to her shoulder and kiss her in return. She holds me tighter and I let her. I let her hold me as tight as she possibly can. I continue to kiss her neck and she continues to kiss mine, both of us working our way toward each other's mouth. Before I reach her lips, I pull back and look into her eyes. She looks into mine and for once in my life, I can honestly say I've found the only other person in this world who understands my guilt. The only person who understands my pain. The only person who accepts that it's who I am.

I used to think the best part of me died with Les, but the best part of me is standing right here in front of me.

In one swift movement, I crash my lips to hers and grip her by the hair. I push her against the shower wall and kiss her with so much conviction, I know she could never for a second doubt how much I love her. I slide my hands down her thighs and lift her up until she wraps her legs around my waist.

I press myself against her and continue kissing her, wanting to feel *her*, rather than the pain that's trying to take over. I want nothing but to be a part of her right now and let everything else in our lives just fade away.

"Tell me this is okay," I say as I pull away from her mouth and search her eyes. "Tell me it's okay to want to be inside you right now . . . because after everything we've been through today, it feels wrong to need you like I do."

She throws her arms around my neck and grasps my hair, pulling my mouth back to hers, showing me that she needs this just as much as I do. I groan and pull her away from the shower wall, then walk her out of the bathroom and into the bedroom. I drop her down onto the bed, then grab her panties and pull them down her legs. I crash against her mouth and pull off my boxers, which are now soaking wet. All I can think about is how much I need to be inside her right now. I pull apart from her long enough to get a condom on, then I grab her hips and pull her to the edge of the bed. I lift her leg to my side and slide my other arm underneath her shoulder.

She looks up at me and I look down at her. I grip her leg and her shoulder and keep my eyes trained on hers, then push into her. The second I'm inside her, it doesn't feel like enough. I press my lips to hers and try to search for whatever it is that's missing from the moment. I move in and out of her, more and more frantic with each thrust, trying desperately to reach a feeling that I don't even know exists. She relaxes her body against mine, following my movements, allowing me to be in control.

But I don't want that right now.

That's what's wrong with me.

My mind is so exhausted and so tired and my heart hurts so much right now. I just need her to help me figure out how to stop trying to be the hero for once.

I pull away from her and she looks up at me, never questioning why I've drastically slowed against her. She just brings her hands to my face and gently runs her fingers over my eyes and my lips and cheeks. I turn my mouth toward the inside of her palm and I kiss it, then drop down on top of her, stopping completely. I keep my gaze locked with hers and I pull her to me, then lift her up as I stand. I'm still inside her and she's wrapped around me, so I turn my back to the bed and slide down to the floor. I lean forward and kiss her bottom lip softly, then her whole mouth.

I bring a hand to her cheek and drop the other to her hip. I begin to move beneath her, slowly guiding her with my hand, wanting her to just take control. I need her to want to comfort me the same way that I always want to comfort her.

"You know how I feel about you," I whisper, staring into her eyes. "You know how much I love you. You know I would do whatever I could to take away your pain, right?"

She nods, never pulling her gaze from mine, even for a second.

"I need that from you so fucking bad right now, Sky. I need to know you love me like that."

Her expression grows soft and her eyes fill with compassion. She laces our hands together and places them over our hearts. She strokes her thumb against my hand and lifts up slightly, then slowly glides back down me again.

The incredible sensation that rushes through my body causes my head to collapse against the mattress behind me. I groan, unable to keep my eyes open.

"Open your eyes," she whispers, still moving against me. "I want you to watch me."

I lift my head and watch her. It's the easiest thing I've ever been asked to do, because she's fucking beautiful right now.

"Don't look away again," she says, lifting herself up. When she slides back onto my lap, I can barely keep my head up. Especially when that moan escapes her lips and she squeezes my hands even harder.

"The first time you kissed me?" she says. "That moment when your lips touched mine? You stole a piece of my heart that night."

You stole a piece of mine, too.

"The first time you told me you lived me because you weren't ready to tell me you loved me yet? Those words stole another piece of my heart."

But I did love you. I loved you so much.

I open my hand and press it flat against her heart. "The night I found out I was Hope? I told you I wanted to be alone in my room. When I woke up and saw you in my bed I wanted to cry, Holder. I wanted to cry because I needed you there with me so bad. I knew in that moment that I was in love with you. I was in love with the way you loved me. When you wrapped your arms around me and held me, I knew that no matter what happened with my life, you were my home. You stole the biggest piece of my heart that night."

I didn't steal it. You gave it to me.

She lowers her mouth to mine and I drop my head back against the mattress and let her kiss me. "Keep them open," she whispers, pulling away from my lips. I do what she says and somehow open my eyes again, looking directly into hers. "I want you to keep them open . . . because I need you to watch me give you the very last piece of my heart."

This moment. Right now. It's almost worth every ounce of pain I've ever had to endure.

I tighten my grip on her hands and lean into her, but I don't kiss her. We get as close as we possibly can and we keep our eyes open until the very last second. Until she completely consumes me and I completely consume her and I have no idea where my love ends and hers begins.

As soon as I begin to tremble and moan beneath her, my head falls against the mattress and she allows me to close my eyes this time. She continues to move on top of me until I'm completely and utterly still.

I give my heart a second to calm down, then I lift my head and look at her. I remove my hands from hers and I slide them through her hair to the back of her head. My lips connect with hers and I kiss her, pushing her off me and onto the floor beneath me. I slide my hand between us and flatten my palm against her stomach, then slowly lower my hand until I find the exact spot that makes my favorite sound escape her mouth. I drink in every single moan and breath that passes her lips. And I let her keep her eyes closed, but I keep mine open and watch her steal the very last piece of *my* heart.

Chapter Forty-six

Les,

I have so much I want to say, but I don't even know how to begin.

Everything with Sky couldn't have turned out better. She's back home with Karen now where she belongs.

I knew Karen wouldn't have harmed Sky. I could tell just from the little time I spent with them that Karen loved her as much as I did. It turns out, I was right. Karen took Sky from her father because Karen knew what he was doing to her. Karen was his sister... Sky's aunt. And she had been through every single thing that Sky went through. She took her because she couldn't just sit back and allow it to continue to happen. Now that Sky knows the whole truth, she's decided to stay with Karen. Karen risked her entire life for that girl. She risked her entire future and I could never thank her enough.

I said this to Sky and I'll say it to you. The only thing I wish Karen would have done differently is, I wish she could have taken you, too.

I didn't know, Les. I had no idea what he was doing to you and I'm so sorry.

*I'll tell you more tomorrow, but tonight I just
needed to tell you that I love you.*

H

Chapter Forty-seven

Happy Halloween. Sure hope you decide to wear something sexy for once.

I hit send and set the phone on my nightstand, then climb out of bed. I didn't leave Sky's house until after four o'clock this morning, then I came home and wrote Les a note before I crawled into bed. It's been days of little sleep and high emotion.

I walk to the closet and grab a T-shirt, then pull it on over my head. My phone sounds off so I walk to it and pick it up to read her text.

Hi, Holder. It's Karen. Still haven't returned Sky's phone to her, but I'll relay the message. Or not.

Oh, shit. I laugh and text Karen back.

lol . . . sorry about that. But while I'm texting you, how is she today?

I wait for her response, which doesn't take long.

She's okay. She's been through a lot and I know it'll take time. But she's the bravest girl I know, so I have complete faith in her.

I smile and text her back.

Yeah. She kind of reminds me of her mother.

She texts back a heart. I set my phone on the bed and sit down beside it. I pick it back up and scroll through it, finding my father's number.

Hey, Dad. Miss you. I'm thinking about bringing my girlfriend to visit during Thanksgiving break. I want you to meet her. Tell Pamela I promise to stay off her couch.

I hit send, but I know the text wasn't enough, so I text him one more time.

And I'm sorry. I'm really sorry.

I set the phone down and look across the room to the notebook still lying on the floor where I threw it. The one that contains the majority of my notes to Les.

I still don't want to read it, but I feel like I owe it to her. I stand up and walk to it. I bend over and pick it up at the same time I lower myself to the floor. I lean against the wall and pull my knees up, then open the notebook and flip to the back of it.

Chapter Forty-seven-and-a-half

Dear Holder,

If you're reading this, I'm so, so sorry. Because if you're reading this, then I know what I did to you.

But I really hope you never find this letter. I'm hoping whoever finds this notebook doesn't see much use for it and throws it out, because I don't want to break your heart. But I have so much I need to say to you that I'll never be able to tell you face to face, so I'm doing it here, instead.

I'm going to start with what happened when we were kids. With Hope.

I know how much you blamed yourself for walking away from her. But you need to realize that you weren't the only one, Holder. I walked away from her, too. And you were doing what any other child in that situation would do. You were trusting that the adults in her life were doing what was right for her. How could you have anticipated what was going to happen when she walked to that car? You couldn't have, so just stop thinking you could have done something differently. You couldn't have and frankly, you shouldn't have. Hope climbing into that car was the best thing that ever happened to her.

A few weeks after she was taken, her father asked me if I wanted to help him make some flyers. Of course I wanted to help him. I would have done anything that would have helped bring Hope back to us.

When I walked into his house, I could feel something wasn't right. He walked me to her bedroom. He told me the materials for the flyers were in Hope's room. Then he shut the door behind us and completely shattered my life.

It went on for years after that. It went on until the day I couldn't bear it anymore and finally told Mom.

She immediately went to the police. That same day I was interviewed by a therapist and my confession was documented. I was only nine or ten years old, so I don't remember a lot about it. I just remember that weeks went by and Mom and Dad had to go to the police station several times. The whole time all of this was going on, Hope's father never once returned home.

I found out later he had been arrested. An investigation was completed and it was even taken to court. I remember the day Mom came home and told me we were moving. Dad couldn't leave his job and she refused to keep us in Austin, so she moved us. I don't know if you know this, but they tried to work it out. Dad tried to find a job that could support us in our new town, but he never did. I think they eventually realized that it was easier being apart. Maybe they both blamed each other for what happened to me.

Now that I look back on all the therapy Mom had me undergo, I hate that she didn't see the need for her to see a therapist, too. I always wondered if their marriage could have been saved if they had talked to someone about it. But then again, I've been in therapy for years and it obviously didn't save me. I wish it did, and maybe it could have if I knew how to apply it. It did help me get through for several years, but it couldn't save me from myself every time I had to close my eyes at night. And as much as Mom tried to save me, she couldn't do it, either. I wasn't looking to be saved.

I just wanted to be let go.

I found out several years later that Hope's father never had to pay for what he did to me. For what he did to Hope. He was extremely manipulative and made it seem like I was blaming him for Hope's disappearance and this was my way of getting back at him. The entire community rallied behind him. They couldn't believe someone would accuse a man of such a cruel act after having his daughter ripped out from under him.

So he got away with it. He was free to do whatever he wanted and I felt like I was locked in hell for eternity.

Mom didn't want you to find out what happened to me. She was afraid of what it would do to you. We both saw how much you blamed yourself for what happened to Hope and she didn't want to see you hurt any more.

I didn't want to see that, either.

Now comes the most difficult part of this letter. This is so hard for me to say, because I've held so much guilt over it. Every day that I saw the pain in your eyes, I knew that if I just confessed to you what I'm about to tell you, it would have relieved you of so much agony.

But I couldn't. I couldn't find a way to tell you that Hope was alive. That she was okay and that Mom and I saw her once, about three years ago.

I was fourteen and we were eating at a restaurant, just Mom and me. I was taking a drink when I looked up and saw her walking through the door.

I turned to Mom and I know I had to be as pale as a ghost, because she reached across the table and grabbed my hand.

"Lesslie, what's wrong, sweetie?"

I couldn't talk. All I could do was stare at Hope. Mom turned around and the second she laid eyes on her, she knew it was her. We were both stunned silent.

The waitress led them to a table right next to ours. Mom and I were both just sitting there, staring at her. Hope glanced at me when she took her seat, then looked away like she didn't even recognize me. It broke my heart that she didn't recognize me. I think I started crying at that point. I was just so emotionally overwhelmed and I didn't know what to do. I fingered the bracelet on my wrist and whispered her name, just to see if she would hear me and turn around again.

She didn't hear me, but the woman who was with her did. She darted her head in our direction with sheer panic in her eyes. It confused me. It confused Mom.

The woman looked at Hope. "I think I left the stove on," she said, standing up. "We need to leave." Hope looked confused, but she stood up, too. Her mother ushered her toward the exit to the restaurant. That's when Mom stood up and rushed after them. I did, too.

When we were all outside, the woman rushed Hope

to the car, then immediately shut her door. Mom and I walked up behind her and as soon as the woman turned around and faced Mom, tears welled in her eyes.

"Please," the woman begged. She didn't say anything after that. Mom stared at her for a while without saying anything in return. I just stood there, trying to understand what was happening.

"Why did you take her?" Mom finally asked her.

The woman began to cry and she kept shaking her head. "Please," she cried. "She can't go back to him. Please don't do that to her. Please, please, please."

My mother nodded. She stepped forward and placed a reassuring hand on the woman's shoulder. "Don't worry," Mom said. "Don't worry." Mom glanced at me and tears filled her eyes, then she glanced back to the woman. "I would do whatever it took to keep my daughter safe, too."

The woman looked at Mom in confusion. I know she didn't understand exactly just how much Mom knew, but she understood Mom's honesty. She tilted her head and exhaled. "Thank you," she said, backing away from us. "Thank you." She opened her door and climbed into her car, then they drove away.

I don't know where she lives. We never found out the woman's name and we never found out the name Hope goes by now. I also stopped wearing the bracelet after that day because I knew in my heart that she didn't need to be found. But I needed you to know, Holder. I just need you to know that she's alive and she's okay and you walking away from her that day was the best thing you could have done for her.

As far as me, well... I'm a lost cause. I've spent the last eight or so years existing in this constant nightmare and I'm just tired. The therapy and medication help numb the pain, but it's the numbness I don't want to endure, Holder. That's why I plan to do what I need to do, and that's what led to your reading this letter. I'm tired and exhausted and sick of living a life that I don't really want to live anymore. I'm tired of pretending to be happy for you, because I'm not happy. Every single time I smile, I feel like I'm lying to you, but I don't know how to live any other way. And I know when I do it, it'll break your heart. I know it'll devastate Mom and Dad. And I know that you'll hate me.

But knowing all of that can't change my mind. I've lost the ability to care anymore, so it's hard to empathize with what you'll experience after I'm gone. I don't remember what it's like to care enough about life that the thought of death could destroy me. So I need you to know that I'm sorry, but I can't help it.

I've been let down by this life one too many times and quite frankly, I'm tired of losing hope.

I love you more than you know.

Les

P.S. I hope you never allow yourself to believe I went through with it because you failed me in some way. All those nights you held me and just let me cry... you have no idea how many times you've already saved me.

Chapter Forty-eight

I drop the notebook onto the floor.

And I cry.

Chapter Forty-nine

I walk into my mother's office and she's on the phone. She looks up as I shut her door behind me. I walk to her desk and pull the receiver from her ear and hang it up.

"You *know*?" I ask her. "You know about what that bastard did to Les?" I wipe my eyes with the back of my hand, just as she stands up and her own eyes fill with tears. "You know what he did to Hope? And you know that Hope is alive and that she's fine? You know everything?"

My mother is shaking her head and fear is filling her eyes. She can't tell if I'm mad or if I've lost it or if I'm about to flip out.

"Holder . . ." she says. "We couldn't tell you. I knew what it would do to you if you knew something like that happened to your sister."

I collapse into a chair, unable to stand up for another second. She walks around the desk and kneels in front of me. "I'm so sorry, Holder. Please don't hate me. I'm so sorry."

She's crying, looking at me with so much regret and apology. I immediately find the strength to stand back up and I pull her up with me. "God, no," I say to her, throwing my arms around her neck. "Mom, I'm so glad you know. I'm so relieved Les had you through all of that. And Hope?" I push her away from me and look her in the eyes. "She's *Sky*, Mom. Hope is Sky and Sky is okay and I love her. I love her so much and I had no idea how to tell you because I was so scared you would recognize her."

Her eyes grow wide and she backs away from me, falling back into her chair. "Your girlfriend? Your girlfriend is Hope?"

I nod, knowing none of this is making any sense to her. "Remember when I met Sky at the store a few months ago? I recognized her. I thought she was Hope, but then I thought maybe she wasn't. Then I fucking fell in love with her, Mom. I can't even begin to tell you the shit we've been through this week." I'm talking faster than she can probably comprehend. I sit in the chair across from her and pull it closer to her, then lean forward and take her by the hands. "She's okay. I'm okay. I'm *more* than okay. And I know you did your best for Les, Mom. I hope you know that, too. You did everything you could, but sometimes even all the love in the world from mothers and brothers isn't enough to help pull someone out of their nightmare. We just need to accept that things are what they are, and all the guilt and regret in the world can't change that."

She begins to sob. I wrap my arms around her and I hold her.

Chapter Forty-nine-and-a-half

Sky and I took the last two days of the week off school. We figured we already missed three days, what's two more? Besides, Karen wanted to keep a close eye on Sky all week. She's concerned about how everything is affecting her.

I agreed to give Sky space for a few days, but what Karen doesn't realize is that Sky's window still sees regular traffic in the middle of the night. All from me.

I've spent the last few days in deep discussions with Mom. She wanted to know everything I knew about Les and Hope and of course she wanted to know what happened last weekend in Austin. Then she wanted to know all about my relationship with Sky, so I brought her up to date. Then she said she wanted to meet her.

So here we are. Sky just walked through the front door and my mom has her arms around her. She started crying almost immediately, which in turn made Sky tear up a little. Now they're standing in the foyer and my mother won't let go of her.

"I don't want to interrupt this homecoming," I say. "But if you don't let her go, Mom, you might scare her away."

My mother laughs and sniffles, pulling away from Sky. "You're so beautiful," she says, smiling at Sky. She turns to me. "She's beautiful, Holder."

I shrug. "Yeah, she's okay."

Sky laughs and hits me on the arm. "Remember? The insults are only funny in text form."

I grab her and pull her to me. "You're not beautiful, Sky," I whisper in her ear. "You're incredible."

She wraps her arms around me in return. "You're not so bad, yourself," she says.

My mother takes her by the hand and pulls her away from me and into the living room, then she begins to bombard her with questions. I appreciate it, though, because she doesn't ask her questions about her situation or her past. She just asks normal questions about what she wants to major in when she goes to college and *where* she's planning to go to college. I leave them both in the living room to continue their conversation while I walk to the garage and grab a few boxes. Mom and I have talked about clearing out Les's room before. Now that I have Sky here, I think I'll actually be able to do it.

I walk back to the living room and hand them each a box. "Come on," I say, heading toward the stairs. "We've got a room to clean."

We spend the rest of the afternoon cleaning out Les's room. We box her pictures and anything that meant something to her in one box, then we put all her clothes in boxes to take to Goodwill. I take both notebooks and I wrap them in the pair of jeans that have been on the floor for over a year and I place it all in a box. A box I keep.

After the room is finished, my mother and Sky head downstairs. I stack the boxes in the hallway, then turn to shut the door. Before I close it completely, I look to her bed. I don't watch her die again. I watch her smile.

Chapter Forty-nine-and-three-quarters

"I thought she said she wasn't going this weekend," I say to Sky as we walk through her front door.

"I begged her to go. She's been stuck to me like glue for days now and I told her if she didn't go do her flea market thing, I'd run away."

We make our way to Sky's bedroom and I close the door behind us. "So does that mean I can get you pregnant tonight?"

She turns around and faces me, then shrugs. "I guess we could practice," she says, smiling.

And we do. We practice at least three different times before midnight.

We're lying on her bed, tangled together beneath her sheet. She's holding up our hands, which are clasped between us, and she's staring at them. "I remember, you know," she says softly.

I tilt my head until it meets hers on the pillow. "You remember what?"

She pulls her fingers away, then she wraps her pinky around mine. "This," she whispers. "I remember the first time you held my hand like this. And I remember everything you said to me that night."

I close my eyes and inhale a deep breath.

"Not long after Karen brought me here, she asked me to forget my old name and all the bad that went along with it. So I thought about you . . . and I told her I wanted to be called Sky."

She lifts up onto her elbow and looks down at me. "You were always there, you know. Even when I couldn't remember . . . you were always there."

I push her hair behind her ear and kiss her, then pull back. "I love you so much, Sky."

"I love you, too, Holder."

I pull my arm out from under her and roll her onto her back, looking down at her. "Will you do me a favor?"

She nods.

"From now on, I want you to call me Dean."

Final Chapter

Les,

It's been a while. I came across these letters today after needing boxes to pack for college. I also came across the pair of jeans that sat in your bedroom floor for over a year. I just threw them in the hamper for you. You're welcome.

So... yeah. College. Me. Me going to college. Pretty cool, huh?

It's still about a month away before I go, but Sky has already been there for a couple of months. She had all her credits from being homeschooled, so right after high school graduation she left to get a head start on me.

She's so competitive.

But I'm not worried, because I plan on surpassing her once I get there. I have this elaborate evil plan all mapped out. Every time I catch her studying or doing homework, I'll just whisper something sexy in her ear or flash my dimples. Then she'll get all flustered and sidetracked and she'll fall behind on her schoolwork and she'll fail her classes and I'll get my degree first and victory will be mine!

Or I'll just let her win. I sort of like letting her win sometimes.

I miss her like crazy, but we'll be in the same town again in less than a month.

A town with no parents.

A town with no curfews.

And if I have anything to do with it, she'll have a closetful of nothing but dresses.

Shit. Now that I look at it, I think we both might end up failing.

A lot has happened since I last wrote to you, but then again nothing has happened. Compared to the first few months following my return from living with Dad in Austin, the rest of the year has been pretty tame. Once Sky found out the truth, Karen eased up on the technology restrictions. I got her an iPhone for her real birthday and she has a laptop now, so we get to see each other every night through Skype.

I love Skype. A lot. Just sayin'.

Mom and Dad are good. Dad didn't put two and two together when he met Sky, which I didn't really think he would to begin with. He never really spent a lot of time around her when we were kids because he worked so much. He does love her, though. And Mom? Good lord, Les. Mom can't get enough of her. It kind of weirds me out how close they've become, but it's also good. It's good for Mom. I think having Sky as part of the family now has helped relieve some of the grief she still feels from your death.

And yes, we all still feel it. Everyone who loved you still feels it. And while I don't really relive your death anymore, I still miss you like hell. I miss you so much. Especially when something happens that I know you would think was funny. I catch myself laughing and then all of a sudden I realize I'm the only one laughing and it hits me that I was expecting you to laugh, too. I miss your laugh.

I could go on and on about all the things I miss about you to the point that I start to feel sorry for myself again. But I've learned over the past year what it really means to be able to miss someone. In order to miss someone, that means you were privileged enough to have them in your life to begin with.

And while seventeen years doesn't seem like near enough time to have spent with you over the course of a lifetime, it's still seventeen more years than the people that never knew you at all. So if I look at it that way... I'm pretty damn lucky.

I'm the luckiest brother ever in the whole wide world.

I'm gonna go live my life now, Les. A life I'm actually able to look forward to, and I honestly thought I'd never be able to say that. Then again, I honestly thought I'd always be hopeless, but I find hope every single day.

And sometimes I find her at night, too... on Skype.

I love you.

Dean

Acknowledgments

First and foremost, a huge thank-you to Griffin Peterson for gracing the cover of *Losing Hope*. Your kindness and humbleness are much appreciated by me, as well as the readers.

Also, I would once again like to acknowledge all bloggers for your endless support. Without you, these books would not be possible.

During the process of writing both *Hopeless* and *Losing Hope*, I never expected the type of support and feedback I have received from readers. So many of you have shared your stories with me and have taken the time to let me know how these books helped you overcome your own struggles and "chapter breaks." For that, I thank each and every one of you who have reached out to me. It's why I continue to write . . . because you continue to support me.

For Stephanie and Craig.
Fist bump.

Finding
Cinderella

Prologue

"You got a tattoo?"

It's the third time I've asked Holder the same question, but I just don't believe it. It's out of character for him. Especially since I'm not the one who encouraged it.

"Jesus, Daniel," he groans on the other end of the line. "Stop. And stop asking me why."

"It's just a weird thing to tattoo on yourself. *Hopeless*. It's a very depressing term. But still, I'm impressed."

"I gotta go. I'll call you later this week."

I sigh into the phone. "God, this sucks, man. The only good thing about this entire school since you moved is fifth period."

"What's fifth period?" Holder asks.

"Nothing. They forgot to assign me a class, so I hide out in this maintenance closet every day for an hour."

Holder laughs. I realize as I'm listening to it that it's the first time I've heard him laugh since Les died two months ago. Maybe moving to Austin will actually be good for him.

The bell rings and I hold the phone with my shoulder and fold up my jacket, then drop it to the floor of the maintenance closet. I flip off the light. "I'll talk to you later. Nap time."

"Later," Holder says.

I end the call and set my alarm for fifty minutes later, then place my phone on the counter. I lower myself to the floor and lie down. I close my eyes and think about how much this year sucks. I hate that

Holder is going through what he's having to go through and there isn't a damn thing I can do about it. No one that close to me has ever died, much less someone as close as one of my sisters. A *twin* sister to be exact.

I don't even try to offer him advice, but I think he likes that. I think he needs me to just continue being myself, because God knows everyone else in this whole damn school has no clue how to act around him. If they weren't all such stupid assholes he'd probably still be here and school wouldn't suck half as bad as it does.

But it does suck. Everyone in this place sucks and I hate them all. I hate everybody but Holder and they're the reason he isn't here anymore.

I stretch my legs out in front of me and cross my ankles, then fold my arm over my eyes. At least I have fifth period.

Fifth period is nice.

• • •

My eyes flick open and I groan when something lands on me. I hear the sound of the door slam shut.

What the hell?

I place my hands on whatever just fell on me and begin to roll it off me when my hands graze a head full of soft hair.

It's a human?

A girl?

A chick just fell on me. In the maintenance closet. And she's crying.

"Who the hell are you?" I ask cautiously. Whoever she is, she tries to push off me but we both seem to be taking turns moving in the same direction. I lift up and try to roll her to my side but our heads crash together.

"Shit," she says.

I fall back onto my makeshift pillow and grab my forehead. "Sorry," I mumble.

Neither one of us moves this time. I can hear her sniffling, trying not to cry. I can't see two inches in front of me because the light is still out but I suddenly don't mind that she's still on top of me because she smells incredible.

"I think I'm lost," she says. "I thought I was walking into the bathroom."

I shake my head, even though I know she can't see it. "Not a bathroom," I say. "But why are you crying? Did you hurt yourself when you fell?"

I feel her whole body sigh on top of me. Even though I have no idea who she is or what she looks like, I can feel the sadness in her and it makes me a little sad in return. I'm not sure how it happens, but my arms go around her and her cheek falls against my chest. In the course of five seconds we go from extremely awkward to kind of comfortable, like we do this all the time.

It's weird and normal and hot and sad and strange and I don't really want to let go. It feels kind of euphoric, like we're in some sort of fairytale. Like she's Tinkerbell and I'm Peter Pan.

No, wait. I don't want to be Peter Pan.

Maybe she can be like Cinderella and I'll be her Prince Charming.

Yeah, I like that fantasy better. Cinderella's hot when she's all poor and sweaty and slaving over the stove. She also looks good in her ball gown. It also doesn't hurt that we're meeting in a broom closet. Very fitting.

I feel her pull a hand up to her face, more than likely wiping away a tear. "I hate them," she says softly.

"Who?"

"Everybody," she says. "I hate everybody."

I close my eyes and lift my hand, then run it down her hair, doing my best to comfort her. *Finally, someone who actually gets it.* I'm not sure why she hates everybody but I have a feeling she's got a pretty valid reason.

"I hate everybody too, Cinderella."

She laughs softly, probably confused as to why I just referred to her as Cinderella, but at least it's not more tears. Her laugh is intoxicating and I try to think of how I can get her to do it again. I'm trying to think of something funny to say when she lifts her face off my chest and I feel her scoot forward. Before I know it, I feel lips on mine and I'm not sure if I should shove her away or roll on top of her. I begin to lift my hands to her face, but she pulls back just as quick as she kissed me.

"Sorry," she says. "I should go." She places her palms beside me on the floor and starts to lift up, but I grab her face and pull her back down on top of me.

"No," I say. I bring her mouth back to mine and I kiss her. I keep our lips pressed firmly together as I lower her to my side. I pull her against me so that her head is resting on my jacket. Her breath tastes like Starburst and it makes me want to keep kissing her until I can identify every single flavor.

Her hand touches my arm and she gives it a tight squeeze just as my tongue slips inside her mouth. That would be strawberry on the tip of her tongue.

She keeps her hand on my arm, periodically moving it to the back of my head, then returning it to my arm. I keep my hand on her waist, never once moving it to touch any other part of her. The only thing we explore is each other's mouths. We kiss without making another sound. We kiss until the alarm sounds on my phone. Despite the noise, neither of us stops kissing. We don't even hesitate. We kiss for another solid minute until the bell rings in the hallway outside and suddenly lockers are slamming shut and people are talking and everything about our moment is stolen from us by all the inconvenient external factors of school.

I still my lips against hers, then slowly pull back.

"I have to get to class," she whispers.

I nod, even though she can't see me. "Me, too," I reply.

She begins to scoot out from beneath me. When I roll onto my back, I feel her move closer to me. Her mouth briefly meets mine one more time, then she pulls away and stands up. The second she opens the door, the light from the hallway pours in and I squeeze my eyes shut, throwing my arm over my face.

I hear the door shut behind her and by the time I adjust to the brightness, the light is gone again.

I sigh heavily. I also remain on the floor until my physical reaction to her subsides. I don't know who the hell she was or why the hell she ended up here, but I hope to God she comes back. I need a whole hell of a lot more of that.

• • •

She didn't come back the next day. Or the day after that. In fact, today marks exactly a week since she literally fell into my arms, and I've convinced myself that maybe that whole day was a dream. I did stay up most of the night before watching zombie movies with Chunk, but even though I was going on two hours of sleep, I don't know that I would have been able to imagine that. My fantasies aren't that fun.

Whether she comes back or not, I still don't have a fifth period and until someone calls me out on it, I'll keep hiding out in here. I actually slept way too much last night, so I'm not tired. I pull my phone out to text Holder when the door to the closet begins to open.

"Are you in here, kid?" I hear her whisper.

My heart immediately picks up pace and I can't tell if it's that she came back or if it's because the light is on and I'm not really sure I want to see what she looks like when she opens this door.

"I'm here," I say.

The door is still barely cracked. She slips a hand inside and slides it around the wall until she finds the light, then she flicks it off. The door opens and she slips into the room, then quickly shuts it behind her.

"Can I hide with you?" she asks. Her voice sounds a little different than last time. It sounds happier.

"You're not crying today," I say.

I feel her make her way over to me. She grazes my leg and can feel that I'm seated on a countertop, so she feels around me until she finds a clear spot. She pushes herself up beside me and takes a seat next to me.

"I'm not sad today," she says, her voice much closer this time.

"Good." It's quiet for several seconds, but it's nice. I'm not sure why she came back or why it took her a week, but I'm glad she's here.

"Why were you in here last week?" she asks. "And why are you in here now?"

"Schedule mishap. I was never assigned a fifth period, so I hide out and hope administration doesn't notice."

She laughs. "Smart."

"Yep."

It's quiet again for a minute or so. Our hands are gripping the edge of the counter and every time she swings her legs, her fingers barely touch mine. I eventually just move my hand on top of hers and pull it onto my lap. It seems odd to just grab her hand like this, but we pretty much made out for fifteen minutes straight last week so holding hands is actually reversing a base.

She slides her fingers between mine and our palms meet, then

I fold my fingers over hers. "This is nice," she says. "I've never held anyone's hand before."

I freeze.

How the hell old is she?

"You're not in junior high, are you?"

"*God* no. I've just never held anyone's hand before. The guys I've been with seem to forget this part. But it's nice. I like it."

"Yeah," I agree. "It is nice."

"Wait," she says. "*You* aren't in junior high, are you?"

"No. Not yet," I say.

She swings her leg out to the side and kicks me, then we both laugh.

"This is kind of weird, isn't it?" she asks.

"Elaborate. Lots of things could be considered weird, so I'm not sure what you're referring to."

I feel her shoulders shrug. "I don't know. This. Us. Kissing and talking and holding hands and we don't even know what the other looks like."

"I'm really good looking," I say.

She laughs.

"I'm serious. If you could see me right now, you'd be on your knees begging me to be your boyfriend so you could flaunt me around the school."

"Highly unlikely," she says. "I don't do boyfriends. Overrated."

"If you don't hold hands and you don't do boyfriends, then what *do* you do?"

She sighs. "Pretty much everything else. I've got quite a reputation, you know. In fact, it's possible the two of us may have had sex before and we don't even realize it."

"Not possible. You'd remember me."

She laughs again and as much as I'm having fun talking to her, that laugh makes me want to drag her to the floor with me and do nothing but kiss her again.

"Are you actually good looking?" she asks skeptically.

"Terribly good looking," I reply.

"Let me guess. Dark hair, brown eyes, great abs, white teeth, Abercrombie & Fitch."

"Close," I say. "*Light* brown hair, correct on the eyes, abs, and teeth, but American Eagle Outfitters all the way."

"Impressive," she says.

"My turn," I say. "Thick blonde hair, big blue eyes, an adorable little white dress with a matching hat, royal blue skin, and you're about two feet tall."

She laughs loudly. "You have a thing for Smurfette?"

"A guy can dream."

The sound of her laughter actually makes my heart hurt. It hurts because I really want to know who this chick is but I know once I find out, I more than likely won't want her like I want her right now.

She inhales a breath and then the room becomes quiet. So quiet, it's almost uncomfortable.

"I'm not coming back in here after today," she says softly.

I squeeze her hand, surprised by the sadness I feel at that confession.

"I'm moving. Not right away, but soon. This summer. I just think it'd be silly if I came back here, because eventually we'll have to turn on the light or we'll slip up and say our names and I just don't think I want to know who you are."

I graze my thumb over her hand. "Why'd you come back today, then?"

She exhales a delicate breath. "I wanted to thank you."

"For what? Kissing you? That's all I did."

"Yeah," she says, matter-of-fact. "Exactly. For kissing me. For *just* kissing me. Do you know how long it's been since a guy has actually *just* kissed me? After I left last week I tried to remember, but I couldn't. Every time a guy has ever kissed me, he's always been in such a hurry to move on to what comes after the kisses that I don't think anyone has ever taken the time to give me an honest to God, genuine kiss before."

I shake my head. "That's really depressing," I say. "But don't give me too much credit. I've been known to want to rush past that part in the past. I just didn't really care to rush past it last week because you're a pretty phenomenal kisser."

"Yeah," she says confidently. "I know. Imagine what making love to me could feel like."

I swallow the sudden lump in my throat. "Believe me, I have. For about seven days straight now."

Her legs stop swinging next to me. I don't know if I just made her uncomfortable with that comment.

"You know what else is sad?" she asks. "No one's ever made love to me before."

This conversation is headed in a weird direction. I can already tell.

"You're young. Plenty of time for that. Virginity is actually a turn-on, so you have nothing to worry about."

She laughs, but it's a sad laugh this time.

Weird how I can already differentiate her laughs.

"I am *so* not a virgin," she says. "That's why it's sad. I'm pretty skilled in the sex department, but looking back . . . I've never loved any of them. None of them have ever loved me, either. Sometimes I wonder if sex with someone who actually loves you is different. Better."

I think about her question and realize that I don't have an answer. I've never loved anyone, either. "Good question," I say. "It's kind of sad that we've both had sex, multiple times it sounds like, but neither of us has ever loved anyone we've done it with. Says a lot about our characters, don't you think?"

"Yeah," she says quietly. "Sure does. A lot of sad truth."

It's quiet for a while and I still have hold of her hand. I can't stop thinking about the fact that no one's ever held her hand before. It makes me wonder if I've ever held the hands of any of the girls I've had sex with. Not that there have been a ton, but enough that I should be able to recall holding one of their hands.

"I might be one of those guys," I ashamedly admit. "I don't know if I've ever held a girl's hand before."

"You're holding mine," she says.

I nod slowly. "So I am."

A few more beats of silence pass before she speaks again.

"What if I leave here in forty-five minutes and never hold another guy's hand again? What if I go through life like I am right now? What if guys continue to take me for granted and I do nothing to change it and I'll have lots of sex, but never know what it's like to make love?"

"So don't do that. Find you a good guy and tie him down and make love to him every night."

She groans. "That terrifies me. As curious as I am about the difference between making love and having sex, my stance on relationships makes it impossible to find out."

I think about her comment for a while. It's weird, because she sounds a little like the female version of me. I'm not sure I'm as opposed to relationships as she is, but I've definitely never told a girl I loved her and I really hope that doesn't happen for a hell of a long time.

"You're really never coming back?" I ask.

"I'm really not coming back," she says.

I let go of her hand and press my palms onto the cabinet, then jump down. I move and stand in front of her, then place my hands on either side of her. "Let's solve our dilemma right now."

She leans back. "Which dilemma?"

I move my hands and place them on her hips, then pull her to me. "We have a good forty-five minutes to work with. I'm pretty sure I could make love to you in forty-five minutes. We can see what it's like and if it's even worth going through relationships in the future. That way when you leave here, you won't worry about never knowing what it's like."

She laughs nervously, then leans toward me again. "How do you make love to someone you aren't in love with?"

I lean forward until my mouth is next to her ear. "We pretend."

I can hear the breath catch in her lungs. She turns her face slightly toward mine and I feel her lips graze my cheek. "What if we're bad actors?" she whispers.

I close my eyes, because the possibility that I might actually be making love to this chick in a matter of minutes is almost too much to take in.

"You should audition for me," she says. "If you're convincing then I just might agree to this absurd idea of yours."

"Deal," I say.

I take a step back and remove my shirt, then lay it on the floor. I grab my jacket off the counter and unfold it, then lay it on the floor as well. I turn back to the counter, then scoop her up. She locks herself around me, burying her head in my neck.

"Where's your shirt?" she asks, running her hands across my shoulder. I lower her to the floor, onto her back. I ease myself to her side and pull her against me.

"You're lying on it," I respond.

"Oh," she says. "That was considerate of you."

I bring my hand up to her cheek. "That's what people do when they're this in love."

I feel her smile. "How in love are we?"

"All the way," I say.

"Why? What is it about me you love so much?"

"Your laugh," I say immediately, not sure how much of that is actually made up. "I love your humor. I also love the way you tuck your hair behind your ears when you're reading. And I love how you hate to talk on the phone almost as much as I do. I really love that you leave me those little notes all the time in your adorable handwriting. And I love that you love my dog so much, because he really likes you. I also love taking showers with you. Those are always fun."

I slide my hand from her cheek to the nape of her neck. I ease my mouth forward and rest my lips against hers.

"Wow," she says against my mouth. "You're really convincing."

I smile and pull away. "Stop breaking character," I tease. "Now it's your turn. What do you love about me?"

"I do love your dog," she says. "He's a great dog. I also love how you open doors for me even though I'm supposed to want to open doors for myself. I love that you don't try to pretend you like old black and white movies like everyone else does, because they bore the hell out of me. I also love it when I'm at your house and every time your parents turn the other way, you steal little kisses from me. My favorite part about you though is when I catch you staring at me. I love that you don't look away and you stare unapologetically, like you aren't ashamed that you can't stop watching me. It's all you want to do because you think I'm the most amazing thing you've ever laid eyes on. I love how much you love me."

"You're absolutely right," I whisper. "I love staring at you."

I kiss her mouth, then trail kisses across her cheek and up her jawline. I press my lips against her ear and even though I know we're pretending, my mouth runs dry at the thought of the words about to pass my lips. I hesitate, almost deciding against it. But an even bigger part of me wants to say it. A huge part of me wishes I could mean it and a small part of me thinks I probably could.

I run my hands up and through her hair. "I love you," I whisper.

The next breath she draws in is a deep one. My heart is hammering against my chest and I'm quiet, waiting on her next move. I have no idea what comes next. Then again, neither does she.

Her hands move from my shoulders and slowly make their way up to my neck. She tilts her head until her mouth is flush against my ear. "I love you more," she whispers. I can feel the smile on her lips and I wonder if it matches the smile on my face. I don't know why I'm suddenly enjoying this so much, but I am.

"You're so beautiful," I whisper, moving my lips closer to her mouth. "So damn beautiful. And every single one of those guys who somehow passed this up is a complete fool."

She closes the gap between our lips and I kiss her, but this time the kiss seems so much more intimate. For a brief moment, I actually feel like I really do love all those things about her and she really does love all those things about me. We're kissing and touching and pulling the rest of our clothes off in such a hurry, it feels as if we're on a timer.

I guess we technically are.

I pull my wallet out of the pocket of my jeans and grab a condom, then ease myself back against her.

"You can change your mind," I whisper, hoping to hell she doesn't.

"So can you," she says.

I laugh.

She laughs.

Then we both shut the hell up and spend the rest of the hour proving exactly how much we love each other.

• • •

I'm on my knees now, quietly gathering our clothes. After I slip my shirt over my head, I pull her up and help her with her own shirt. I stand up and pull on my jeans, then help her to her feet. I rest my chin on top of her head and pull her against me, recognizing the perfect fit.

"I could turn on the light before you leave," I say. "Aren't you a little curious to see the face of the guy you're madly in love with?"

She shakes her head against my chest with her laugh. "It'll ruin everything," she says. Her words are muffled by my shirt, so she lifts her head away from my chest and tilts her face up to mine. "Let's not ruin it. Once we find out who the other is, we'll find something we don't like. Maybe *lots* of things we don't like. Right now it's perfect. We can always have this perfect memory of that one time we loved somebody."

I kiss her again, but it doesn't last long because the bell rings. She doesn't release her hold from around my waist. She just presses her head against my chest again and squeezes me tighter. "I need to go," she says.

I close my eyes and nod. "I know."

I'm surprised by just how much I don't want her to go, knowing I'll never see her again. I almost beg her to stay, but I also know she's right. It only feels perfect because we're *pretending* it's perfect.

She begins to pull away from me, so I lift my hands to her cheeks one last time. "I love you, babe. Wait for me after school, okay? In our usual spot."

"You know I'll be there," she says. "And I love you, too." She stands on her tiptoes and presses her lips to mine—hard and desperate and sad. She pulls away and makes her way to the door. As soon as she begins to open it, I walk swiftly to her and push the door shut with my hand. I press my chest against her back and I lower my mouth to her ear.

"I wish it could be real," I whisper. I put my hand on the doorknob and open it, then turn my head when she slips out the door.

I sigh and run my hands through my hair. I think I need a few minutes before I can leave this room. I'm not sure I want to forget the way she smells just yet. In fact, I stand here in the dark and try my hardest to commit every single thing about her to my memory, since that's the only place I'll ever see her again.

Chapter One

"Oh, my *God*!" I say, frustrated. "Lighten up." I crank the car just as Val climbs inside and slams her door in a huff, then pushes herself back against the seat.

As soon as she's inside the car, the overwhelming amount of perfume she has on begins to suffocate me. I crack the window, but just enough so that she won't think I'm insulting her. She knows how much perfume bothers me, especially when chicks smell like they bathe in it, but she never seems to care what I think, because she continues to douse it on by the gallon.

"You're so immature, Daniel," she mutters. She flips the visor down and pulls her lipstick from her purse, then begins to reapply it. "I'm beginning to wonder if you'll *ever* change."

Change?

What the hell is *that* supposed to mean?

"Why would I change?" I ask, cocking my head out of curiosity.

She sighs and drops her lipstick back into her purse, smacks her lips together, then turns toward me. "So you're telling me you're happy with the way you act?"

What?

With the way *I* act? Is she really commenting on the way *I* act? The same girl I've seen curse at waitresses for something as simple as too much ice in her glass is seriously commenting on the way *I* act?

I've been seeing her off and on for months now and I haven't had a single clue that she was hoping I would eventually change. Hoping I'd become someone I'm not.

Come to think of it, I keep getting back together with her, thinking *she'll* be the one to change. To be *nice* for once. In reality, people are who they are and they'll never really change. So why the hell are Val and I even wasting our time on this exhausting relationship if we don't even really like who the other is?

"I didn't think so," she says smugly, incorrectly assuming my silence was admission that I'm not happy with how I act. In actuality, my silence was the moment of clarity I've needed since the day I met her.

I remain silent until we pull into her driveway. I leave the car running, indicating that I have no plans on going inside with her tonight.

"You're leaving?" she asks.

I nod and stare out the driver's side window. I don't want to look at her, because I'm a guy and she's hot and I know if I look at her, then my moment of clarity regarding our relationship will become foggy and I'll end up inside her house, making up with her on her bed like I always do.

"You aren't the one who gets to be mad, Daniel. You acted ridiculous tonight. And in front of my parents, no less! How do you expect them to ever approve of you if you act the way you do?"

I have to exhale a slow, calming breath so that I don't raise my voice like she's doing right now. "How do I act, Val? Because I was myself at dinner tonight, just like I'm myself every other minute of the day."

"Exactly!" she says. "There's a time and a place for your stupid nicknames and immature antics and dinner with my parents isn't the time *or* the place!"

I rub my hands over my face out of frustration, then I turn and look at her. "This is me," I say, gesturing toward myself. "If you don't like all of me, then we've got serious issues, Val. I'm not changing and honestly, it wouldn't be fair of me to ask you to change, either. I would never ask you to pretend to be something you're not, which is exactly what you're asking of me right now. I'm *not* changing, I'll *never* change and I would really like it if you would get the hell out of my car right now because your perfume is making me fucking nauseous."

Her eyes narrow and she grabs her purse off the console and pulls it toward her. "Oh, that's nice, Daniel. Insult my perfume to get back at me. See what I mean? You're the epitome of immature." She opens the car door and unbuckles her seatbelt.

"Well at least I'm not asking you to *change* your perfume," I say mockingly.

She shakes her head. "I can't do this anymore," she says, getting out of the car. "We're done, Daniel. For good this time."

"Thank *God*," I say loud enough for her to hear me. She slams her door and marches toward her house. I roll down her window to air out the perfume and I back out of the driveway.

Where the hell is Holder? If I don't get to complain to someone about her, I'll fucking scream.

• • •

I climb into Sky's window and she's sitting on the floor, rummaging through pictures. She looks up and smiles as I make my way into her room. "Hey, Daniel," she says.

"Hey, Cheese Tits," I say as I drop down onto her bed. "Where's your hopeless boyfriend?"

She nudges her head toward her bedroom door. "They're in the kitchen making ice cream. You want some?"

"Nah," I say. "I'm too heartbroken to eat anything right now."

"Val having a bad day?"

"Val's having a bad *life*," I say. "And after tonight I've finally realized I don't want to be a part of it."

She raises her eyebrows. "Oh, yeah? Sounds serious this time."

I shrug. "We broke up an hour ago. And who's *they*?"

She shoots me a confused look, so I clarify my question. "You said *they* were in the kitchen making ice cream. Who's *they*?"

Sky opens her mouth to answer me when her bedroom door swings open and Holder walks in with two bowls of ice cream in his hands. A girl is following behind him with her own bowl of ice cream and a spoon hanging out of her mouth. She pulls the spoon from her lips and kicks the bedroom door shut with her foot, then turns toward the bed and stops when she sees me.

She looks vaguely familiar, but I can't place her. Which is odd because she's cute as hell and I feel like I should probably know her name or remember where I've seen her, but I don't.

She walks to the bed and sits down on the opposite end of it, eyeing me the whole time. She dips her spoon into her ice cream, then puts the spoon back in her mouth.

I can't stop staring at that spoon. I think I love that spoon.

"What are you doing here?" Holder asks. I regretfully take my eyes off the Ice Cream Girl and watch as he takes a seat on the floor next to Sky and picks up a few of the pictures.

"I'm done with her, Holder," I say, stretching my legs out in front of me on the bed. "For good. She's fucking crazy."

"But I thought that's why you loved her," he says mockingly.

I roll my eyes. "Thanks for the insight, Dr. Shitmitten."

Sky takes one of the pictures out of Holder's hands. "I think he's actually serious this time," she says to him. "No more Val." Sky tries to look sad for my sake, but I know she's relieved. Val never really fit in with the two of them. Now that I think about it, she never really fit in with me, either.

Holder looks up at me curiously. "Done for good? Really?" He sounds oddly impressed.

"Yeah, *really*, really."

"Who's Val?" Ice Cream Girl asks. "Or better yet, who are *you*?"

"Oh, my bad," Sky interrupts. She points back and forth between Ice Cream Girl and me. "Six, this is Dean's best friend, Daniel. Daniel, this is my best friend, Six."

I'll never get used to hearing Sky call him Dean, but her introduction gives me an excuse to look over at that spoon again. Six pulls it out of her mouth and points it at me. "Nice to meet you, Daniel," she says.

How in the hell can I steal that spoon before she leaves?

"Why does your name sound familiar?" I ask her.

She shrugs. "I dunno. Maybe because six is a fairly common number? Either that or you've heard of what a raging whore I am."

I laugh. I don't know why, though, because her comment really wasn't funny. It was actually a little disturbing. "No, that's not it," I say, still confused as to why her name sounds so familiar. I don't think Sky has ever mentioned her in front of me before.

"The party last year," Holder says, forcing me to look at him again. I'm pretty sure I roll my eyes when I have to look away from her, but I don't mean to. I'd just much rather stare at her than at Holder. "Remember?" he says. "It was the week I got back from Austin and a few days before I met Sky. The night Grayson pummeled you on the floor for saying you took Sky's virginity?"

"Oh, you mean the night you pulled me off of him before I even got the chance to kick his ass?" It still irritates me just thinking about it. I could have had him if Holder hadn't stepped in.

"Yeah," Holder confirms. "Jaxon mentioned something that night about Sky and Six, but I didn't know who they were at the time. I think that's where you heard her name."

"Wait, wait, wait," Sky says, waving her hands in the air and looking at me like I'm crazy. "What do you mean Grayson pummeled you because you said you took my *virginity*? What the *hell*, Daniel?"

Holder puts a reassuring hand on Sky's lower back. "It's cool, babe. He just said it to piss Grayson off because I was about to kick the idiot's ass for the way he was talking about you."

Sky is shaking her head, still confused. "But you didn't even know me. You just said it was a few days before you met me, so why would you be pissed that Grayson was talking shit about me?"

I stare at Holder, too, waiting for his answer. I never thought about it then, but that is odd that he was pissed over Grayson's comments when he didn't even know Sky at the time.

"I didn't like how he was talking about you," he says, leaning in to kiss Sky on the side of the head. "It made me think he probably talked about Les the same way and it pissed me off."

Shit. Of course he would think that. Now I *really* wish he had let me kick Grayson's ass that night.

"That's sweet, Holder," Six says. "You were protecting her before you even knew her."

Holder laughs. "Oh, you don't know the half of it, Six."

Sky looks up at him and they smile at each other, almost like they have some sort of secret, then they both turn their attention back to the pictures on the floor in front of them.

"What are those?" I ask, inquiring about the pictures they're looking through.

"For the yearbook," Six says, answering me. She sets the bowl of ice cream on the bed beside her, then pulls her feet up and sits cross-legged. "Apparently we're supposed to submit pictures of ourselves as kids for the senior page, so Sky is going through the pics Karen gave her."

"You go to the same school as us?" I ask, referring to the fact that she included herself in the explanation of the assignment. I know we go to a huge school, but I have a feeling I would remember her, especially if she's Sky's best friend.

"I haven't been to that school since junior year," she says. "But I'll be there once Monday rolls around." She says it like she's not at all looking forward to it.

I can't help but smile at her reply, though. I wouldn't mind having to see this girl on a recurring basis. "So does that mean you'll be joining our lunchroom alliance?" I lean forward and grab the bowl of ice cream she didn't finish. I pull it to me and take a bite.

She watches me as I close my lips around the spoon and pull it out of my mouth. She scrunches up her nose, staring at the spoon. "I could have herpes, you know," she says.

I grin at her and wink. "You somehow just made herpes sound appealing."

She laughs, but her bowl is suddenly ripped from my hands by Holder and he's pulling me off the bed. My feet hit the floor and he shoves me toward the window. "Go home, Daniel," he says, releasing his grip on my shirt as he lowers himself back to the floor next to Sky.

"What the *hell*, man?" I yell.

Seriously, though. *What the hell?*

"She's Sky's best friend," he says, waving a hand in Six's direction. "You're not allowed to flirt with her. If the two of you mess around it'll just cause tension and make things weird and I don't want that. Now leave and don't come back until you can be around her without having the perverted thoughts I know are going through your head right now."

For the first time in my life, I think I'm actually speechless. Perhaps I should nod and agree with him, but the idiot just made the biggest mistake he could possibly make.

"Shit, Holder," I groan, running my palms down my face. "Why the hell did you have to go and *do* that? You just made her off-limits, man." I begin to make my way back out the window. Once I'm outside, I stick my head back through and look at him. "You should have told me I should date her, then I more than likely wouldn't have been interested. But you had to go and make her forbidden, didn't you?"

"Gee, Daniel," Six says, unenthusiastically. "Glad to know you think of me as a human being and not a challenge." She looks at Holder as she stands up from the bed. "And I didn't realize I had a fifth overprotective brother," she says, making her way toward the window. "I'll see you guys later. I probably need to go rummage through my own pictures before Monday, anyway."

Holder glances back at me as I step aside and allow Six to climb out the window. He doesn't say anything, but the look he gives me is a silent warning that Six is completely off-limits to me. I raise my hands in defense, then pull the window shut after Six is outside. She walks a few feet to the house next door and begins to climb through that window.

"Do you take shortcuts through windows all the time, or do you happen to live in that house?" I ask, walking toward her. Once she's inside, she spins around and leans her head out. "This would be *my* window," she says. "And don't even think about following me inside. This window has been out of commission for almost a year and I have no plans to reopen for business."

She tucks her shoulder-length blonde hair behind her ears and I take a step back, hoping a little distance will allow my heart to stop attacking the walls of my chest. But now all I want to do is figure out a way to recommission her window.

"You really have four older brothers?"

She nods. I hate the fact that she has four older brothers, but only because it presents four more reasons why I shouldn't date her. Add that to Holder making her off-limits and I know she's the only thing I'll be able to think about now.

Thanks, Holder. Thanks a lot.

She rests her chin in her hands and stares at me. It's dark outside, but the moon overhead is casting a light right on her face and she looks like a fucking angel. I don't even know if people should use the words *fucking* and *angel* in the same thought structure, but *shit*. She really looks like a fucking angel with her blonde hair and big eyes. I'm not even sure what color her eyes are because it's dark and I didn't really pay attention when we were in Sky's bedroom, but whatever color they are, it's my new favorite color.

"You're very charismatic," she says.

Jesus. Her voice completely slays me. "Thanks. You're pretty cute yourself."

"I didn't say you were cute, Daniel. I said you were charismatic. There's a difference."

"Not much of one," I say. "You like Italian?"

She frowns and pulls back a few inches like I just insulted her. "Why would you ask me that?"

Her reaction confuses me. I have no idea how that comment could have offended her. "Uh, have you never been asked out on a date before?"

The scowl disappears from her face and she leans forward again. "Oh. You mean food. I'm sort of tired of Italian food, actually. Just got back from a seven-month exchange there. If you're asking me out on a date, I'd rather have sushi."

"I've never had sushi," I admit, trying to process the fact that I'm pretty sure she just agreed to go out on a date with me.

"When?"

This was way too easy. I figured she'd put up a fight and make me beg a little like Val always does. I love that she isn't playing games. She's straightforward and I like that about her already.

"I can't take you tonight," I say. "I had my heart completely broken about an hour ago by a psychotic bitch and I need a little more time to recover from that relationship. How about tomorrow night?"

"Tomorrow is Sunday," she says.

"Do you have an issue with Sundays?"

"Not really, I guess. It just seems odd to go on a first date on a Sunday night. Meet me here at seven o'clock, then."

"I'll meet you at your front door," I say. "And you might not want to tell Sky where you're going unless you want to see me get my ass kicked."

"What's to tell?" she says sarcastically. "It's not like we're going on a random Sunday night date or anything."

I smile and back away, slowly heading backward to my car. "It was nice to meet you, Six."

She places her hand on her window to pull it down. "Likewise. I think."

I laugh, then turn to head toward my car. I'm almost to the door when she calls my name. I spin back around and she's leaning out her window.

"I'm sorry about your broken heart," she whispers loudly. She ducks back into her bedroom and the window closes.

What broken heart? I'm pretty sure this is the first time my heart has actually felt any form of relief since the moment I started dating Val.

Chapter Two

"Does this look okay?" I ask Chunk when I make it into the kitchen. She turns and looks me up and down, then shrugs.

"I guess. Where ya going?"

I step in front of one of the mirrors lining the hallway and check my hair again. "A date."

She groans, then turns back around to the table in front of her. "You've never cared before what you look like. You better not be proposing to her. I'll divorce this family before I allow you to make her my sister."

My mother walks past me and pats me on the shoulder. "You look great, honey. I wouldn't wear those shoes, though."

I look down at my shoes. "Why? What's wrong with my shoes?"

She opens a cabinet, takes out a pan, then turns to face me. Her eyes fall to my shoes again. "They're too bright." She turns and walks to the stove. "Shoes should never be neon."

"They're yellow. Not neon."

"*Neon* yellow," Chunk says.

"Not saying I think they're ugly," my mother says. "I just know Val, and Val is more than likely going to hate your shoes."

I walk to the kitchen counter and grab my keys, then put my cell phone in my pocket. "I don't give a shit what Val thinks."

My mother turns and looks at me curiously. "Well you're asking your thirteen-year-old sister if you look good enough for your date, so I think you kind of *do* care what Val thinks."

"I'm not going out with Val. I broke up with Val. I have a new date tonight."

Chunk's arms go up in the air and she looks up to the ceiling. "Thank the *Lord*!" she proclaims loudly.

My mother laughs and nods. "Yes. Thank the Lord," she says, relieved. She turns back toward the stove and I can't stop looking back and forth between the both of them.

"What? Neither of you like Val?" I know Val is a bitch, but my family seemed to like her. Especially my mom. I honestly thought she'd be upset we broke up.

"I hate Val," Chunk says.

"God, me, too," my mother groans.

"Me three," my father says, walking past me.

None of them are looking at me, but they're all responding like this has been a previously discussed topic.

"You mean all of you hated Val?"

My father turns to face me. "Your mother and I are masters at reverse psychology, Danny-boy. Don't act so surprised."

Chunk raises her hand in the air toward my father. "Me, too, Dad. I reverse psychologized him, too."

My dad reaches over and high-fives Chunk's hand. "Well played, Chunk."

I lean against the frame of the door and stare at them. "You guys were just pretending to like Val? What the hell for?"

My dad sits at the table and picks up a newspaper. "Children are naturally inclined to make choices that will displease their parents. If we had told you how we really felt about Val, you probably would have ended up marrying her just to spite us. Which is why we pretended to love her."

Assholes. All three of them. "You're never meeting another one of my girlfriends again."

My father chuckles, but doesn't seem at all disappointed.

"Who is she?" Chunk asks. "The girl you're actually making an effort for."

"None of your damn business," I reply. "Now that I know how this family works, I'm never bringing her around any of you."

I turn to head out the door and my mother calls after me. "Well if it helps, we already love her, Daniel! She's a sweetheart!"

"And beautiful," my dad says. "She's a keeper!"

I shake my head. "Y'all suck."

• • •

"You're late," Six says when she appears at her front door. She walks out of her house with her back to me, inserting her key in the lock.

"You don't want me to meet your parents?" I ask, wondering why she's locking her door this early in the evening. She turns around and faces me.

"They're old. They ate dinner like ten hours ago and went to bed at seven."

Blue. Her eyes are blue.

Holy shit, she's cute. Her hair is lighter than I thought it was last night in Sky's room. Her skin is flawless. It's like she's the same girl from last night, only now she's in HD. And I was right. She really does look like a fucking angel.

She steps out of the way and I shut the screen door, still unable to take my eyes off her. "I actually got here early," I say, finally replying to her first comment. "Holder was dropping Sky off at her house and I swear it took them half an hour to say their good-byes. I had to wait until the coast was clear."

She slides her house key into her back pocket and nods. "Ready?"

I eye her up and down. "Did you forget your purse?"

She shakes her head. "Nope. I hate purses." She pats her back pocket. "All I need is my house key. I didn't bother bringing money since this date was your idea. You're paying, right?"

Whoa.

Back up.

Let's assess the last thirty seconds, shall we?

She hates purses. That means she didn't bring makeup. Which means she won't constantly be reapplying that shit like Val does. It also means she's not hiding a gallon of perfume anywhere on her person. And it also means she had no plans at all to offer to pay for her half of dinner, which seems a little old-fashioned, but for some reason I like it.

"I love that you don't carry a purse," I say.

"I love that you don't carry one, either," she says with a laugh.

"I do. It's in my car," I say, nudging my head toward my car.

She laughs again and begins walking toward the porch steps. I do the same until I see Sky standing just inside her room with her window wide open. I immediately grab Six by her shoulders and pull her until both of our backs are flat against the front door. "You can see Sky's window from the front yard. She'll see us."

Six glances up at me. "You're really taking this *off-limits* order seriously," she says in a hushed voice.

"I *have* to," I whisper. "Holder doesn't kid around when he forbids me to date people."

She arches a curious eyebrow. "Does Holder usually dictate who you can and can't date?"

"No. You're actually the first."

"Then how do you know he'll actually get mad over it?"

I shrug. "I don't, really. But the thought of hiding it from him just seems sort of fun. Is it not a little bit exciting for you, hiding this date from Sky?"

"Yeah," she says with a shrug. "I guess it is."

Our backs are still pressed against the door and for some reason, we're still whispering. It's not like Sky could hear us from here, but again, the whispering makes it more fun. And I really like the sound of Six's voice when she whispers.

"How do you propose we get out of this situation, Six?"

"Well," she says, pondering my question for a moment. "Normally when I'm attempting a risky, clandestine, secret date and I need to escape my house undetected, I ask myself, 'What would MacGyver do?'"

Oh, my god, this chick just mentioned MacGyver?

Hell.

Yes.

I break my eyes away from hers long enough to hide the fact that I think I just fell for her and also to assess our escape route. I glance at the swing on the porch, then look back at Six when I'm sure the cheesy grin is gone from my face.

"I think MacGyver would take your porch swing and build an invisible force field out of grass and matches. Then he would attach a jet engine to it and fly it out of here undetected. Unfortunately I'm all out of matches."

"Hmmm," she says, squinting her eyes like she's coming up with some brilliant plan. "That's an unfortunate inconvenience." She glances toward my car parked in her driveway, then back up to me. "We could just crawl to your car so she doesn't see us."

And a brilliant plan it would be if it didn't involve a girl getting dirty. I've learned in my six months of on-again off-again with Val that girls like to stay clean.

"You'll get dirt on your hands," I warn her. "I don't think you can walk into a fancy sushi restaurant with dirty hands and jeans."

She looks down at her jeans, then back up to me. "I know this great Bar-B-Q restaurant we could go to, instead. The floor is covered in discarded peanut shells. One time I saw this really fat guy eating at a booth and he wasn't even wearing a shirt."

I smile at the same time I fall a little harder for her. "Sounds perfect."

We both drop to our hands and knees and crawl our way off her porch. She's giggling, and the sound of it makes me laugh. "Shh," I whisper when we reach the bottom of the steps. We crawl across the yard in a hurry, both of us glancing toward Sky's house every few feet. Once we reach the car, I reach up to my door handle. "Crawl through the driver's side," I say to her. "She'll be less likely to see you."

I open the door for her and she crawls into the front seat. Once she's inside the car, I climb in after her and slide into my seat. We're both crouched down, which is pointless if you think about it. If Sky were to look out her bedroom window, she'd see my car parked in Six's driveway. It wouldn't matter if she saw our heads or not.

Six wipes the dirt from her hands onto the legs of her jeans and it completely turns me on. She turns her head to face me and I'm still staring at the dirt smeared across the thighs of her jeans. I somehow tear my gaze away and look her in the eyes.

"You'll have to disguise your car next time you come over," she says. "This is way too risky."

I like her comment a little too much.

"Confident there'll be a next time already?" I ask, smirking at her. "The date just started."

"Good point," she says with a shrug. "I might hate you by the end of the date."

"Or I might hate *you*," I say.

"Impossible." She props her foot up on the dash. "I'm unhateable."

"Unhateable isn't even a real word."

She peers over her shoulder into the backseat, then faces forward again with a scowl. "Why does it smell like you had a harem of whores in here?" She pulls her shirt up over her nose to cover up the smell.

"Does it still smell like perfume?" I don't even smell it anymore. It's probably seeped into my pores and I'm now immune to it.

She nods. "It's awful," she says, her voice muffled by her shirt. "Roll down a window." She makes a fake spitting sound like she's trying to get the taste of it out of her mouth and it makes me laugh.

I crank the car, then put it in reverse and begin to back out.

"The wind will mess up your hair if I roll down the windows. You didn't bring a purse, which means you didn't bring a brush, which means you won't be able to fix your hair when we get to the restaurant."

She reaches to her door and presses the button to roll down her window. "I'm already dirty and I'd rather have messy hair than smell like a harem," she says. She rolls the window down completely, then motions for me to roll mine down as well, so I do.

I put the car in drive and press on the gas. The car immediately fills with wind and fresh air and her hair begins flying around in all directions, but she just relaxes into the seat.

"Much better," she says, grinning at me. She closes her eyes while inhaling a deep breath of the fresh air.

I try to pay attention to the road, but she makes it pretty damn hard.

•   •   •

"What are your brothers' names?" I ask her. "Are they numbers, too?"

"Zachary, Michael, Aaron, and Evan. I'm ten years younger than the youngest."

"Were you an accident?"

She nods. "The best kind. My mother was forty-two when she had me, but they were excited when I came out a girl."

"I'm glad you came out a girl."

She laughs. "Me, too."

"Why'd they name you Six if you were actually the fifth child?"

"Six isn't my name," she says. "Full name is Seven Marie Jacobs, but I got mad at them for moving me to Texas when I was fourteen so I started calling myself Six to piss them off. They didn't really care, but I was stubborn and refused to give up. Now everyone calls me Six but them."

I love that she gave herself a nickname. My kind of girl.

"Question still applies," I say. "Why did they name you *Seven* if you were actually the fifth child?"

"No reason, really. My dad just liked the number."

I nod, then take a bite of food, eyeing her carefully. I'm waiting for that moment. The one that always comes with girls, where the pedestal you place them on in the beginning gets kicked out from under them. It's usually the moment they start talking about ex-boyfriends or mention how many kids they want or they do something really annoying, like apply lipstick in the middle of dinner.

I've been waiting patiently for Six's flaws to stand out, but so far I can't find any. Granted, we've only interacted with each other for a collective three or four hours now, so hers may just be buried deeper than other people's.

"So you're a middle child?" she asks. "Do you suffer from middle-child syndrome?"

I shake my head. "Probably about as much as you suffer from fifth-child syndrome. Besides, Hannah is four years older than me and Chunk is five years younger, so we have a nice spread."

She chokes on her drink with her laugh. "Chunk? You call your little sister Chunk?"

"We all call her Chunk. She was a fat baby."

"You have nicknames for everyone," she says. "You call Sky

Cheese Tits. You call Holder *Hopeless.* What do you call me when I'm not around?"

"If I give people nicknames, I do it to their faces," I point out. "And I haven't figured yours out yet." I lean back in my seat and wonder myself why I haven't given her one yet. The nicknames I give people are usually pretty instant.

"Is it a bad thing you haven't nicknamed me yet?"

I shrug. "Not really. I'm just still trying to figure you out is all. You're kind of contradictory."

She arches an eyebrow. "I'm contradictory? In what ways?"

"All of them. You're cute as hell, but you don't give a shit what you look like. You look sweet, but I have a feeling you're just the right mix of good and evil. You seem really easygoing, like you aren't the type to play games with guys, but you're kind of a flirt. And I'm not judging at all by this next observation, but I'm aware of your reputation, yet you don't seem like the type who needs a guy's attention to stroke your self-esteem."

Her expression is tight as she takes in everything I've just said. She reaches to her glass and takes a sip without breaking her stare. She finishes her drink, but holds the glass against her lips while she thinks. She eventually lowers it back to the table and looks down at her plate, picking up her fork.

"I'm not like that anymore," she says softly, avoiding my gaze.

"Like what?" I hate the sadness in her voice now. Why do I always say stupid shit?

"I'm not how I used to be."

Way to go, Daniel. Dumbass.

"Well, I didn't know you back then, so all I can do is judge the girl sitting in front of me right now. And so far, she's been a pretty damn cool date."

The smile spreads back to her lips. "That's good," she says, looking back up at me. "I wasn't sure what type of date I'd be, considering this is the first one I've ever been on."

"No need to stroke my ego," I say. "I can handle the fact that I'm not the first guy to ever express an interest in you."

"I'm serious," she says. "I've never been on a real date before. Guys tend to skip this whole part with me so they can just get to what they really want me for."

My smile disappears. I can tell by the look on her face she's being completely serious. I lean forward and look her hard in the eyes. "Those guys were all fucktards."

She laughs, but I don't.

"I'm serious, Six. Those guys all need a good kick to the clit, because dinner talk is by far the best part of you."

When the sentence leaves my mouth, the smile leaves her face. She looks at me like no one's ever given her a genuine compliment before. It pisses me off.

"How do you know this is the best part of me?" she asks, somehow finding that teasing, flirtatious tone in her voice again. "You haven't had the pleasure of kissing me yet. I'm pretty sure that's the best part of me, because I'm a phenomenal kisser."

Jesus Christ. I don't know if that was an invitation, but I want to send her my RSVP right this second. "I have no doubt being kissed by you would be fantastic, but if I had to choose, I'd take dinner talk over a kiss any day."

She narrows her eyes. "I call bullshit," she says with a challenging glare. "There's no way any guy would pick dinner talk over a good make-out session."

I attempt to return her challenging look, but she makes a good point.

"Okay," I admit. "Maybe you're right. But if I had my way, I'd pick kissing you *during* dinner talk. Get the best of both worlds."

She nods her head, impressed. "You're good," she says, leaning back in her seat. She folds her arms over her chest. "Where'd you learn those smooth moves?"

I wipe my mouth with my napkin, then set it on top of my plate. I lift my elbows until they're resting on the back of the booth and I smile at her. "I don't have smooth moves. I'm just charismatic, remember?"

Her mouth curls up into a grin and she shakes her head like she knows she's in trouble. Her eyes are smiling at me and I realize I've never felt like this before with any other girl. Not that I have it in my head that we're about to fall in love or we're soulmates or some shit like that. I've just never been around a girl where being myself was actually a good thing. With Val, I was always trying my hardest not to piss her off. With past girlfriends, I always found myself holding back from all the shit I really wanted to say. I've always felt like being myself with a girl wasn't necessarily a positive, because I'll be the first to admit, I can be a little over the top.

It's different with Six, though. Not only does she get my sense of humor and my personality, but I feel like she encourages it. I feel like the real me is what she likes the most and every time she laughs or smiles at the perfect moment, I want to fist bump her.

"You're staring at me," she says, breaking me out of my thoughts.

"So I am," I say, not bothering to look away.

She stares right back at me, but her demeanor and expression grow competitive as she narrows her eyes and leans forward. She's silently challenging me to a staring contest.

"No blinking," she says, confirming my thoughts.

"Or laughing," I say.

And it's on. We silently stare at each other for so long, my eyes begin to water and my grip tightens on the table. I try my hardest to keep my eyes locked on hers but they want to stare at every inch of her. I want to stare at her mouth and those full, pink lips and that soft, silky blonde hair. Not to mention her smile. I could stare at her smile all day.

In fact, I'm staring at it right now so I'm pretty sure that means I just lost the staring contest.

"I win," she says, right before she takes another drink of her water.

"I want to kiss you," I say bluntly. I'm a little shocked I said it, but not really. I'm pretty impatient and I really want to kiss her and I usually say whatever I'm thinking, so . . .

"Right now?" she asks, looking at me like I'm insane. She sets her glass back down on the table.

I nod. "Yep. Right now. I want to kiss you over dinner talk so I can have the best of both worlds."

"But I just ate onions," she says.

"So did I."

She's working her jaw back and forth, actually contemplating an answer. "Okay," she says with a shrug. "Why not?"

As soon as she gives me permission, I glance down at the table between us, wondering what the best way to do this would be. I could go sit with her on her side of the booth, but that might be invading her personal space too much. I reach in front of me and push my glass out of the way, then scoot hers to the left.

"Come here," I say, placing my hands on top of the table as I lean toward her. She must have thought I was kidding by the way her eyes dart nervously around us, taking in the fact that we're about to experience our first kiss in public.

"Daniel, this is awkward," she says. "Do you really want our first kiss to be in the middle of a restaurant?"

I nod. "So what if it's awkward? We'll have a do-over later. People put way too much stock in first kisses, anyway."

She tentatively places her palms facedown on the table, then pushes herself up and slowly leans in toward me. "Okay, then," she says, following her words up with a sigh. "But it would be so much better if you waited until the end of our date when you walk me to my front door and it'll be dark and we could be really nervous and you could accidentally touch my boob. That's how first kisses are supposed to be."

I laugh at her comment. We still aren't close enough for me to kiss her yet, but we're getting there. I lean forward a little more, but her eyes leave mine and focus on the table behind me.

"Daniel, there's a woman in the booth behind you changing her baby's diaper on the table. You're about to kiss me and the last thing I'll see before your lips touch mine is a woman wiping her infant's ass."

"Six. Look at me." She brings her eyes back to mine and we're finally close enough that I could reach her mouth. "Ignore the diaper," I command. "And ignore the two men in the booth to our left who are swigging their beer and watching us like I'm about to bend you over this table."

Her eyes dart to the left, so I catch her chin in my hand and force her attention back to me. "Ignore it all. I want to kiss you and I want you to want me to kiss you and I don't really feel like waiting until I walk you to your porch tonight because I've never really wanted to kiss someone this much before."

Her eyes drop to my mouth and I watch as everything around us disappears from her field of vision. Her tongue slips out of her mouth and glides nervously across her lips before it disappears again. I slide my hand from her chin to the nape of her neck and I pull her forward until our lips meet.

And holy shit, do they meet. Our mouths meld together like they used to be in love and they're just now seeing each other for the first time in years. My stomach feels like it's in the middle of a damn rave and my brain is trying to remember how to do this. It's like I suddenly forgot how to kiss, even though it's only been a day since I broke up with Val. I'm pretty sure I kissed Val yesterday, but for some reason my brain is acting like this is all new and it's telling me I should be parting my lips or teasing her tongue, but the signals just aren't making it to my mouth yet. Or my mouth is just ignoring me because it's been paralyzed by the soft warmth pressed against it.

I don't know what it is, but I've never held a girl's lips between mine for this long without breathing or moving or taking the kiss as far as I can possibly take it.

I inhale, even though I haven't taken a breath in almost a minute. I loosen my grip on the back of Six's head and begin to slowly pull my lips from hers. I open my eyes and hers are still closed. Her lips haven't moved and she's taking in shallow, quiet breaths as I remain poised close to her face, watching her.

I don't know if she expected more of a kiss. I don't know if she's ever had a peck last more than a minute before. I don't know what she's thinking, but I love the look on her face.

"Don't open your eyes," I whisper, still staring at her. "Give me ten more seconds to stare, because you look absolutely beautiful right now."

She tucks her bottom lip in with her teeth to hide her smile, but she doesn't move. My hand is still on the back of her head and I'm silently counting down from ten when I hear the waitress pause at our table.

"Y'all ready for your ticket?"

I hold up a finger, asking the waitress to give me a second. Well, five seconds to be exact. Six never moves a muscle, even after hearing the waitress speak. I count down silently until my ten seconds are up, then Six slowly opens her eyes and looks up at me.

I back away from her, putting several inches of space between us. I keep my eyes locked with hers. "Yes, please," I say, giving the waitress her answer. I hear her tear off the ticket and slap it down on the table. Six smiles, then begins laughing. She backs away from me and falls back down in her booth.

I breathe and it feels like the air is all brand new.

I slowly take my seat in the booth again, watching her laugh. She scoots the ticket toward me. "Your treat," she says.

I reach into my pocket and pull out my wallet, then lay cash down on top of the ticket. I stand up and reach out for Six's hand. She looks at it and smiles, then takes it. When she stands, I wrap my arm around her shoulder and pull her against me.

"Are you going to tell me how awesome that kiss was or are you going to ignore it?"

She shakes her head and laughs at me. "That wasn't even a real kiss," she says. "You didn't even try to put your tongue in my mouth."

I push open the doors to walk outside, but step aside and let her out first.

"I didn't have to put my tongue in your mouth," I say. "My kisses are that intense. I don't even really have to do anything. The only reason I pulled back was that I was sure we were about to experience a classic 'When Harry met Sally' moment."

She laughs again.

God, I love that she thinks I'm funny.

I open the passenger door for her and she pauses before climbing inside. She looks up at me. "You realize that classic scene is Sally proving a point about how easy it is for women to fake orgasms, right?"

God, I love that I think she's funny.

"Do I have to take you home yet?" I ask.

"Depends on what you have in mind next."

"Nothing really," I admit. "I just don't want to take you home yet. We could go to the park next to my house. They have a jungle gym."

She grins. "Let's do it," she says, holding up a tight fist in front of her.

I naturally bring my fist up and bump hers. She hops into the car and I shut her door, dumbfounded over the fact that she just fist bumped me.

The girl just fist bumped me and it was probably the hottest thing I've ever seen.

I walk to my side of the car and open the door, then take a seat. Before I crank the car I turn to look at her. "Are you really a guy?"

She raises an eyebrow, then pulls the collar of her shirt out and takes a quick glance down at her chest. "Nope. Pretty damn girl," she says.

"Are you dating someone?"

She shakes her head.

"Are you leaving the country tomorrow?"

"Nope," she says, her face obviously confused by my line of questions.

"What's your deal, then?"

"What do you mean?"

"Everyone has something and I can't figure yours out. You know, that one thing about themselves that's eventually a deal-breaker." I crank the car and begin to back out. "I want to know what yours is right now. My heart can't take another second of these tiny little things you do that drive me completely insane."

Her smile changes. It grows from a genuine smile to a guarded one. "We all have deal breakers, Daniel. Some of us just hope we can keep them hidden forever."

She rolls down her window again and the noise makes it impossible to continue the conversation. I'm almost positive the overwhelming scent of perfume is gone, so I'm curious if her need for the noise is why she rolled down the window this time.

• • •

"Do you bring all your dates here?" she asks.

I think about her question for a minute before answering. "Pretty much," I finally say after silently tallying the ends of all my dates. "I did take this chick out once in eleventh grade, but I took her home during the middle of the date because she got a stomach virus. I think she's the only one I never brought here."

She digs her heels into the dirt and comes to a stop in the swing. I'm standing behind her, so she turns around and looks up at me. "Seriously? You've brought all but one girl here?"

I shrug. Then nod. "Yeah. But none of them has ever wanted to literally *play* before. We usually just make out."

We've been here half an hour and already she's made me watch her on the monkey bars, push her on the merry-go-round and now I've been pushing her while she's been swinging for the last ten minutes. I'm not complaining, though. It's nice. Really nice.

"Have you ever had sex out here?" she asks.

I'm not sure how to take her bluntness. I've never really met anyone who asks the same straightforward questions I would, so I'm beginning to feel a little sympathetic to the people I put on the spot like this. I glance around the park until I see the makeshift wooden castle. I point to it. "You see the castle?"

She turns her head to look at the castle. "You had sex in there?"

I drop my arm and slide both my hands into the back pockets of my jeans. "Yep."

She stands and begins to walk in that direction.

"What are you doing?" I ask her. I'm not sure why she's heading toward the castle, but I'm almost positive it's not because she's weird and wants to have sex in the same spot I had sex with Val two weeks ago.

Does she?

God I hope not.

"I want to see where you had sex," she says, matter-of-fact. "Come show me."

This girl confuses the hell out of me. What's strange is how much I freaking love it. I begin jogging until I catch up with her. We walk until we reach the castle. She looks at me expectantly, so I point to the doorway. "Right in there," I say.

She walks to the doorway and peeks inside. She looks around for a minute, then pulls back out. "Looks really uncomfortable," she says.

"It was."

She smiles. "If I tell you something will you promise not to judge me?"

I roll my eyes. "It's human nature to judge."

She inhales a breath, then releases it. "I've had sex with six different people."

"At once?" I say.

She shoves my arm. "Stop. I'm trying to be honest with you here. I'm only eighteen and I lost my virginity when I was sixteen. Plus, I haven't had sex in about a year, so if you add it up, that's six people in just a little over fifteen months. That's like a whole new person every two and a half months. Only sluts do that."

"Why have you not had sex in over a year?"

She rolls her eyes and begins to walk past me. I follow her. When she reaches the swings, she takes her seat again. I sit in the swing beside her and twist my body until I'm facing her, but she faces forward.

"Why have you not had sex in over a year?" I say again. "You didn't like any of the boys you met in Italy?"

I can't see her face, but her body language reveals that this could be that *one thing*. The thing that changes it all for me.

"There was this one boy in Italy," she says softly. "But I don't want to talk about him. And yes, he's why I haven't had sex in over a year." She looks back at me. "Look, I know my reputation precedes me and I don't know if that's why you brought me here or what you expect to happen at the end of this date, but I'm not that girl anymore."

I lift my legs until my swing spins forward again. "The only thing I was hoping for at the end of this date was a kiss on your front porch," I say. "And maybe an accidental boob grab."

She doesn't laugh. I suddenly hate that I brought her here.

"Six, I didn't bring you here expecting anything. Yes, I've brought girls here in the past but that's only because I live across the street and I come here a lot. And yes, maybe I brought all those other girls here to have a little privacy while we made out, but that's only because I more than likely just wanted them to shut up and kiss me because they were getting on my everlasting nerves. But I only brought you here because I wasn't ready to take you home yet. I don't even really want to make out with you because I like talking to you too much."

I close my eyes, wishing I hadn't just said all that. I know girls like guys who play the uninterested asshole part. I'm usually pretty good at playing that part, but not with Six. Maybe because I usually am an uninterested asshole, but with her I'm as interested and curious and hopeful as I can possibly be.

"Which house is yours?" she asks.

I point across the street. "That one," I say, pointing to the one with the living room light on.

"Really?" she asks, sounding genuinely interested. "Is your family home?"

I nod. "Yeah, but you aren't meeting them. They're evil liars and I already told them I was never bringing you home to meet them."

I can feel her turn and look at me. "You told them you were never bringing me to meet them? So you already mentioned me?"

I meet her gaze. "Yes. I might have mentioned you."

She smiles. "Which one is your bedroom?"

"First window on the left side of the house. Chunk's bedroom is the window on the right. The one with the light on."

She stands up again. "Is your window unlocked? I want to see what your bedroom looks like."

Jesus, she's nosey.

"I don't want you to see my bedroom. I'm unprepared. It's messy."

She begins walking toward the street. "I'm going anyway."

I lean my head back and groan, then stand up and follow her toward the house.

"You're a piece of work," I say as we reach my window. She presses her palms against the glass and pushes up. The window doesn't budge, so I push her aside and open it for her. "I've never snuck into my own bedroom before," I admit. "I've snuck *out* before, but never in."

She begins to lift herself up over the ledge, so I grab her by the waist and assist her. She throws her leg over the edge of it and slips inside. I climb in behind her, then walk to the dresser and turn on my lamp. I make a scan of the room to ensure there isn't anything I don't want her to see. I kick a pair of underwear under the bed.

"I saw those," she whispers. She walks to my bed and presses her palms into the mattress, then straightens back up. She scans the room slowly, taking in everything about me. It feels weird, like I'm being exposed.

"I like your room," she says.

"It's a room."

She disagrees with a shake of her head. "No, it's more than that. This is where you live. This is where you sleep. This is where you feel the most privacy in your whole entire life. This is more than just a room."

"It doesn't feel very private right now," I say, watching as she skims her hand across every surface of my room. She turns and looks at me, then faces me full-on.

"What's the one thing in this room that tells the biggest secret about you?"

"I'm not telling you that."

She tilts her head. "So I'm right. You have secrets."

"I never said I didn't."

"Give me one," she asks. "Just one."

I'll give them all to her if she keeps looking at me like this. She's so damn adorable. I walk slowly toward her and she swallows a gulp of air. I stop when I'm several inches from her, then I nod my head down toward my mattress. "I've never kissed a girl on this bed," I whisper.

She looks down at my mattress, then back up to me. "I hope you really don't expect me to believe you've never made out with a girl in your room before."

"I didn't say that. I stated I had never kissed a girl on this particular bed. I was being honest, because it's a brand-new mattress. I just got it last week."

I can see the change in her eyes. The heavy rise and fall of her chest. She likes that I'm so close to her and she likes that I'm insinuating I want to kiss her on my bed.

Her eyes fall to the bed. "Are you saying you want to kiss me on your bed?"

I lean in closer until my lips are right next to her ear. "Are you saying you would let me?"

She sucks in a soft rush of air and I love that we're both feeling this. I want to kiss her on my bed so damn bad. I want it more than I even wanted the damn bed. Hell, I don't even care if it's on the bed. I just want to kiss her. I don't care where it is. I'll kiss her anywhere she'll allow me to kiss her.

I close the small gap between our bodies by resting my hands on her hips and pulling her to me. Her hands fly up to my forearms and she gasps. I dig my fingers into her hips and rest my cheek against hers. My mouth is still grazing her ear as I close my eyes, enjoying the feel of this.

I love the way she smells. I love the way she feels. And even though I haven't really given her an honest to God kiss yet, I already love the way she kisses.

"Daniel," she whispers. My name crashes against my shoulder when it rushes out of her mouth. "Will you take me home now?"

I wince at her words, immediately wondering what I just did wrong. I remain still for several long seconds, waiting until the feel of her against me no longer has me completely paralyzed.

"You didn't do anything wrong," she says, immediately easing the doubt building inside me. "I just think I should go home."

Her voice is soft and sweet and I suddenly hate every single guy in her past who has ever failed to get to know this side of her.

I don't release her immediately. I turn my head slightly until my forehead is touching the side of her head. "Did you love him?" I ask, allowing my brilliant brain to completely ruin this moment between us.

"Who?"

"The guy in Italy," I clarify. "The one who hurt you. Did you love him?"

Her forehead meets my shoulder and the way she fails to respond to that question reveals her answer, but it also fills me with so many more questions. I want to ask her if she still loves him. If she's still with him. If they still talk.

I don't say anything, though, because I have a feeling she wouldn't be here with me right now if any of that were the case. I bring my hand up to the back of her head and I press my lips into her hair. "Let's get you home," I whisper.

• • •

"Thanks for buying me dinner," she says when we reach her front door.

"You didn't really give me a choice. You left your house without a penny and then you shoved the bill in my face."

She laughs as she unlocks her front door, but doesn't open it yet. She turns back around and lifts her eyes, looking at me through lashes so long and thick, I have to refrain from reaching out and touching them.

Kissing her at dinner was definitely spontaneous, but I was sure it would make this moment a breeze.

It isn't.

If anything, I feel even more pressure to kiss her because it's already happened once tonight. And the fact that it's already happened and I know how damn good it feels makes me want it even more, but now I'm scared I've built it up too much.

I begin to lean in toward her when her lips part.

"Are you gonna use tongue this time?" she whispers.

I squeeze my eyes shut and take a step back, completely thrown off by her comment. I rub my palms down my face and groan.

"Dammit, Six. I was already feeling inadequate. Now you've just put expectations on it."

She's smiling when I look at her again. "Oh, there are definitely expectations," she says teasingly. "I expect this to be the most mind-blowing thing I've ever experienced, so you better deliver."

I sigh, wondering if the moment can possibly be recovered. I doubt it. "I'm not kissing you now."

She nods her head. "Yes you are."

I fold my arms over my chest. "No. I'm not. You just gave me performance anxiety."

She takes a step toward me and slides her hands between my folded arms, pushing against them until they unlock. "Daniel Wesley, you owe me a do-over since you made me kiss you in a crowded restaurant next to a dirty diaper."

"It wasn't crowded," I interject.

She glares at me. "Put your hands on my face and push me against this wall and slip me some tongue! Now!"

Before she can laugh at herself, my hands are casing her face and her back is pressed against the wall of her house and my lips are on hers. It happens so fast, it catches her off guard and she gasps, which causes her lips to part farther than she probably meant for them to. As soon as I caress the tip of her tongue with mine, she's clenching my shirt in two tight fists, pulling me closer. I tilt my head and take the kiss deeper, wanting to give her all the feels she can possibly get from a kiss and I want her to have them all at once.

My mouth isn't having a problem remembering what to do this time. What it's having a problem with is remembering how to slow down. Her hands are now in my hair and if she moans into my damn mouth one more time I'm afraid I might carry her to the backseat of my car and try to cheapen this date.

I can't do that. I can't, I can't, I can't. I like this girl too much already and I'll be damned if this isn't our first date and she already has me thinking about the next one. I brace my hands on the wall behind her head and I force myself to push off of her.

We're both panting. Gasping for breath. I'm breathing heavier than any kiss has ever made me breathe before. Her eyes are closed and I absolutely love how she doesn't immediately open them when I'm finished kissing her. I like that she seems to want to savor the way I make her feel, just like I want to savor her.

"Daniel," she whispers.

I groan and drop my forehead to hers, touching her cheek with my hand. "You make me love my name so damn much."

She opens her eyes and I pull back, looking down on her, still stroking her cheek. She's looking at me the same way I'm looking at her. Like we can't believe our luck.

"You better not turn out to be an asshole," she says quietly.

"And you better be done with that guy in Italy," I reply.

She nods. "I am," she says, although her eyes seem to tell a different story. I try not to read into it because whatever it is, it doesn't matter now. She's here with me. And she's happy about that. I can tell.

"You better not take back the girl who broke your heart last night," she adds.

I shake my head. "Never. Not after this. Not after you."

She seems relieved by my answer.

"This is scary," she whispers. "I've never had a boyfriend before. I don't know how this works. Do people become exclusive this fast? Are we supposed to pretend we're not that interested for a few more dates?"

Oh, dear God.

I've never been turned on by a girl laying claim to me before. I usually run in the other direction. She's obliterating every single thing I thought I knew about myself with every new sentence that passes those lips.

"I have no interest in faking disinterest," I say. "If you want to call yourself my girlfriend half as much as I wish you would, then it would save me a whole lot of begging. Because I was literally about to drop to my knees and beg you."

She squints her eyes playfully. "No begging. It screams desperation."

"You make me desperate," I say, pressing my lips to hers again. I choose to keep this kiss simple, even though I want to grab her face again and hold her against the wall. I pull away from her and we stare at each other. We stare at each other for so long I begin to worry that she's put some kind of spell on me, because I've never wanted to just stare at a girl like I want to stare at her. Just looking at her causes my heart to burn and my chest to constrict and I'm sort of freaking out that I barely know her at all and we've just made ourselves exclusive.

"Are you a witch?" I ask.

Her laugh returns and I suddenly don't care if she's a witch. If this is some kind of spell she's put on me, I hope it never breaks.

"I have no idea who you even are and now you're my damn girlfriend. What the hell have you done to me?"

She holds her palms up defensively. "Hey, don't blame me. I've gone eighteen years swearing off boyfriends and then you show up out of the blue with your vulgar mouth and terribly awkward first kisses and now look at me. I'm a hypocrite."

"I don't even know your phone number," I say.

"I don't even know your birthday," she says.

"You're the worst girlfriend I've ever had."

She laughs and I kiss her again. I notice I have to kiss her every time she laughs and she laughs a lot. Which means I have to kiss her a lot. God, I hope she doesn't laugh in front of Sky or Holder, because it's going to be so damn hard not to kiss her.

"You better not tell Sky about us," I say. "I don't want Holder to know yet."

"What about school? I enroll tomorrow. You don't think it'll be obvious when we interact?"

"We'll pretend we hate each other. It could be fun."

She tilts her face up and finds my mouth again, giving me a light peck. "But how do you plan on keeping your hands off me?"

I slide my other hand to her waist. "I won't keep my hands off you. I'll just touch you when they aren't looking."

"This is gonna be so much fun," she whispers.

I smile and pull her against me again. "Damn right it is." I dip my head and kiss her one last time. I release her, then reach behind her and turn the doorknob, pushing open her front door. "See you tomorrow."

She backs up two steps until she's in her doorway. "See you tomorrow."

She begins to turn and head into her house, but I grab her wrist and pull her back out. I wrap an arm around her lower back and lean in until my lips touch hers. "I forgot to accidentally touch your boob."

I catch her laugh with my mouth and graze her breast with the palm of my hand, then I immediately pull away from her. "Oops. Sorry."

She's covering her laugh with her hand as she backs into her house. She closes the door and I immediately fall to my knees, then onto my back. I stare straight up at the roof of her porch, wondering what in the hell just happened to my heart.

The door slowly reopens and she looks down at me, sprawled across her front porch like an idiot.

"I just needed a minute to recover," I say, smiling up at her. I'm not even excusing the fact that I'm shamelessly affected by her. She winks, then begins to close the door.

"Six, wait," I say, pushing myself up. She opens the door again and I reach up and grab the doorframe, then lean in toward her. "I know I just broke up with someone last night, but I need you to know you aren't a rebound. You know that, right?"

She nods. "I know," she says confidently. "Neither are you."

With that, she steps back into her house and closes her door.

Christ.

Motherfucking angel.

Chapter Three

"Let's go!" I tell Chunk for the fifth time.

She grabs her backpack and groans, then stands up and pushes her chair in. "What's your freakin' deal, Daniel? You're never in a hurry to get to school." She downs the rest of her orange juice. I'm standing at the door where I've been standing for five minutes, ready to leave. I hold open the front door and follow her outside.

Once we're in the car I don't even wait for her to shut her door before I'm putting it in reverse.

"Seriously, why are you in such a hurry?" she asks.

"I'm not in a hurry," I say defensively. "You were just being really slow."

The last thing she needs to know is how utterly pathetic I am. So pathetic I've been awake for two hours now, waiting until we could leave. I probably won't even see Six until lunch if we don't have classes together, so I really don't know why I'm in a hurry.

I didn't think about that. I hope we *do* have classes together.

"How was your date last night?" Chunk asks as she puts on her seatbelt.

"Good," I say.

"Did you kiss her?"

"Yep."

"Do you like her?"

"Yep."

"What's her name?"

"Six."

"No, really. What's her name?"

"*Six.*"

"No, not whatever nickname you gave her. What does everyone else call her?"

I roll my head and look at her. "Six. They call her Six."

Chunk scrunches up her nose. "Weird."

"It fits her."

"Do you love her?"

"Nope."

"Do you want to?"

"Ye—"

Whoa.

Hold up.

Do I want to?

I don't know. Maybe. Yes? Shit. I don't know. How screwed up is it that I broke up with a girl two days ago and I'm already contemplating the possibility of loving someone else?

Well, technically, I don't think I really loved Val. I sort of thought I did on occasion, but I think if a person is really, truly in love then it has to be unconditional. How I felt about Val was definitely not unconditional. I had conditions for every single feeling I had about her. Hell, the only reason I ever asked her out in the first place is that for about fifteen seconds, I thought she was Cinderella.

After that experience in the closet last year, that mystery girl was all I could think about. I looked for her everywhere, even though I had no idea what she looked like. I was pretty sure she had blonde hair, but it was dark, so I could have been wrong. I listened to every single girl's voice I walked past to see if they sounded like her. The problem was, they *all* sounded like her. It's hard to memorize a voice when you don't have a face to back it up with, so I would always find small things that reminded me of her in every girl I spoke to.

With Val, I actually convinced myself she was Cinderella. I was walking past her in the hallway one afternoon on my way to history class. I'd seen her in the past but never paid much attention because she seemed a little high-maintenance for me. I accidentally bumped her shoulder when I passed her because my head was turned and I was talking to someone else. She called out after me, "Watch it, kid."

I froze in my tracks. I was too scared to turn around because hearing her use the term "kid" had me convinced I was about to come face to face with the girl from the closet. When I finally gained the courage to turn around, I was floored by how hot she was. I always hoped if I ever found out who Cinderella was that I'd be attracted to her. But Val was way hotter than how I'd been fantasizing.

I walked back up to her and made her repeat what she said. She looked shocked, but she repeated it anyway. When the words fell from her mouth again, I immediately leaned forward and kissed her. As soon as I kissed her I knew she wasn't Cinderella. Her mouth was different. Not *bad* different, just different. When I pulled back after realizing it wasn't her, I was a little annoyed with myself for not just letting it go. I was never going to find out who the girl was, so there was no point in dwelling on it. Plus, Val really was hot. I forced myself to ask her out that day and thus began "the relationship."

"You just passed my school," Chunk says.

I slam on the brakes when I realize she's right. I kick the car into reverse and back up, then pull over to let her out. She looks out the passenger window and sighs.

"Daniel, we're so early there isn't even anyone else here yet."

I lean forward and look out her window, scanning the school. "Not true," I say, pointing to someone pulling into a parking spot. "There's someone."

She shakes her head. "That's the maintenance guy. I beat the freaking maintenance guy to school." She opens her door and steps out, then turns and leans into the car before shutting her door. "Do I need to plan for you to be here to pick me up an hour early, too? Is your brain stuck in eastern time today?"

I ignore her comment and she shuts the door, then I hit the gas and drive toward my school.

· · ·

I don't know what kind of car she drives, so I pull into my usual spot and wait. There are a few other cars here, including Sky and Holder's, but I know they're at the track running like they do every morning.

I can't believe I don't know what kind of car she drives. I also still don't know her phone number. Or her birthday. Or her favorite color or what she wants to be when she's older or why the hell she chose Italy for her foreign exchange or what her parents' names are or what kind of food she eats.

My palms begin to sweat, so I wipe them on my jeans, then grip my steering wheel. What if she's really annoying around other people? What if she's a junkie? What if . . .

"Hey."

Her voice breaks me out of my near-panic attack. It also calms me the hell down because as soon as I see her sliding into the front seat of my car, my unjustified fears are replaced by pure relief.

"Hey."

She shuts her door and pulls her leg up, turning to face me in the car. She smells so good. She doesn't smell like perfume at all. She just smells good. Kind of fruity.

"Have you had your panic attack yet?" she asks.

Confusion clouds my face. I don't have time to answer her before she begins talking again.

"I had one this morning," she says, looking at everything else around us, unable to make eye contact with me. "I just keep thinking we're idiots. Like maybe this connection we think we have is all in our heads and we didn't really have as much fun as we thought we did last night. I don't even know you, Daniel. I don't know your birthday, your middle name, Chunk's real name, if you have any pets, what your major will be in college. I know it's not like we made this huge commitment or got married or had sex, but you have to understand that I have never thought the idea of having a boyfriend was even remotely appealing and maybe I still don't think it's all that appealing, but . . ."

She finally looks at me and makes eye contact. "But you're so funny and this entire past year has been the worst year of my life and for some reason when I'm with you it feels good. Even though I hardly know you, the parts of you I do know I really, really like." She leans her head into the headrest and sighs. "And you're cute. Really cute. I like staring at you."

I turn in my seat and mirror her position by resting my head against my own headrest. "Are you finished?"

She nods.

"I had my panic attack right before you got in the car just now. But when you opened your door and I heard your voice, it went away. I think I'm good now."

She smiles. "That's good."

I smile back at her and we both just stare at each other for several seconds. I want to kiss her, but I also kind of like just staring at her. I would hold her hand, but she's running her fingers up and down the seam of the passenger seat and I like watching her do that.

"I should go inside and register for classes now," she says.

"Make sure you get second lunch."

She nods. "I can't wait to pretend I hate you today."

"I can't wait to pretend I hate you more."

I can tell she's about to turn, so I lean forward and slip my hand behind her neck, then pull her to me. I kiss her good morning, hello and good-bye all at once. When I pull back, I glance over her shoulder and see Sky and Holder making their way off the track and toward the parking lot.

"Shit!" I push her head down between us. "They're coming this way."

"Crap," she whispers.

She begins humming the theme to *Mission Impossible* and I start laughing. I start to crouch down with her, but if they reach my car they'll see us whether our heads are down or not.

"I'll get out of the car so they don't come over here."

"Good idea," she says, her voice muffled by her arms. "I think you just gave me whiplash."

I lean over and kiss the back of her head. "Sorry. I'll see you later. Lock my doors when you get out."

I open the car door just as Holder begins to head in my direction. I start walking their way to intercept them. "Good run?" I ask when I reach them.

They both nod, out of breath. "I need my change of clothes," Sky says to Holder, pointing to her car. "Want me to grab yours?" Holder nods and she heads in that direction. Holder's eyes move from hers over to mine.

"Why are you here so early?" he asks. He doesn't ask it like he's accusing me of anything. He's probably just making small talk, but I already feel defensive.

"Chunk had to be at school early," I say.

He nods and grabs the hem of his shirt, then wipes sweat off his forehead. "You still coming tonight?"

I think about his question. I think really hard, but I'm drawing a blank about what could be going on tonight that I would need to go to.

"Daniel, do you even know what the hell I'm talking about?"

I shake my head. "No idea," I admit.

"Dinner at Sky's house. Karen invited you and Val? They're having a big welcome-back thing for Sky's best friend."

That gets my attention. "Yeah, of course I'll be there. Not bringing Val, though. We broke up, remember?"

"Yeah, but dinner is still ten hours away. You might love her again by then."

Sky walks up and hands Holder his bag. "Daniel, have you seen Six?"

"No," I immediately blurt out.

Sky glances toward the school, not having noticed the defensiveness in my immediate response. "She must be registering for classes inside." She turns to Holder. "I'm gonna go find her." She reaches up and kisses him on the cheek, but Holder's eyes remain on mine.

They're narrowed.

This isn't good.

Sky walks away and I begin to walk right behind her, toward the school. Holder's hand lands on my shoulder when I pass him, so I pause. I turn around, but it takes me a few seconds to look him in the eyes. When I do, he doesn't look happy.

"Daniel?"

I raise an eyebrow to match his expression. "Holder?"

"What are you up to?"

"I do not know what you are talking about," I reply innocently.

"You do know what I am talking about because when you are lying, you do not use contractions when you speak."

I ponder his observation for a few seconds. *Is that true?*

Shit. It's true.

I breathe out a heavy breath and do my best to look like I'm giving him a confession. "Fine," I say, kicking at the dirt beneath my feet. "I had sex with Val just now. In my car. I didn't want you to know because you and Sky seemed excited that we broke up."

Tension releases from Holder's shoulders and he shakes his head. "Dude, I could care less who you date. You know that." He begins walking toward the school, so I follow suit. "Unless it's Six," he adds. "You aren't allowed to date Six."

I keep walking forward, even though that comment makes me want to freeze. "I have no desire to date Six," I say. "She's not really that cute, anyway."

He stops in his tracks and spins around to face me. He holds up a finger like he's about to lecture me. "You're not allowed to talk shit about her, either."

Christ. Hiding our relationship from him may be more exhausting than it is fun. "No loving her, no hating her, no screwing her, no dating her. Got it. Anything else you want to add?"

He thinks for a second, then lowers his arm. "Nope. That covers it. See you at lunch." He turns and walks inside. I glance back to the parking lot in time to see Six sneaking out of my car. She gives me a quick wave. I wave back, then turn and head inside.

• • •

I walk my tray toward the table and internally rejoice when I see the only available spot is right next to Six. She glances at me as I walk up and her eyes smile, but only briefly. I set my tray down across from Holder and find my way into the current conversation. Everyone is discussing the dinner at Sky's house tonight, but I've had dinner there before. Karen doesn't know what real food is. She's vegan, so I normally turn down meals at their house. Not tonight, though.

"Will there be meat?" I ask.

Sky nods. "Yeah. Jack's actually cooking, so the food should be good. I also baked a chocolate cake."

I reach across the table for the salt, even though I don't need it. It gives me an excuse to lean in ridiculously close to Six.

"So, Six. How do you like your classes?" I ask casually.

She shrugs. "They're okay."

"Let me see your schedule."

She narrows her eyes like I'm doing something wrong. I give her a look to let her know she has nothing to worry about. Even if I wasn't into her, I'm not an asshole. I'd still be making conversation with her.

"It sucks we don't have any classes together," Sky says. "Who do you have for history?"

Six pulls her schedule out of her pocket and hands it to me. I open it and make a quick scan of the classes, but none are the same as mine. "Carson for history," I say, replying to Sky's question. I hand Six back her schedule and give her a look to let her know we don't have any classes together. She looks bummed, but says nothing.

"Can you speak Italian very well?" Breckin asks Six.

"Not well at all. I speak better Spanish than I do Italian. I chose Italy because I had enough funding and I'd rather have spent half a year there than in Mexico."

"Good choice," Breckin says. "The men are hotter in Italy."

Six nods. "Yes they are," she says appreciatively.

I immediately lose my appetite and drop my fork onto my plate. It makes a loud clanking noise, so naturally everyone turns to look at me. It's quiet and awkward and everyone is still staring, so I say the first thing on my mind. "Italian men are too hairy."

Sky and Breckin laugh, but Six purses her lips together and looks back down at her plate.

God, I suck at this.

Luckily, Val walks up and takes everyone's attention off me.

Wait. Did I just say luckily? Because Val walking up is *not* a good thing.

"Can I talk to you?" she says, glaring down at me.

"Do I have a choice?"

"Hallway," she says, spinning on her heels. She heads toward the exit to the cafeteria.

"Do us all a favor and go see what Val wants," Sky says. "If you don't meet her out there she'll come back to the table."

"*Please*," Breckin mutters.

I'm watching all their reactions and I don't know if they've always reacted this way when it comes to Val or if I'm only recognizing it for the first time because I finally have clarity.

"Why is everyone referring to Tessa Maynard as *Val?*" Six asks, confused.

Breckin points over his shoulder in the direction Val walked off in. "Tessa is Val. Val is Tessa. Daniel can't seem to call anyone by their actual name, if you haven't noticed."

I watch as Six inhales a slow breath, then looks directly at me. She looks really disgusted. "Your girlfriend is Tessa Maynard? You have sex with Tessa Maynard?"

"*Ex*-girlfriend and *had* sex," I clarify. "And yes. Probably coincided with the same time you were falling in love with a hairy Italian."

Six's eyes narrow, then she quickly looks away. I instantly feel bad for what I said, but I was only kidding. Sort of. We're *supposed* to be mean to each other. I can't tell if I really hurt her feelings or if she's just a really good actress.

I sigh, then stand up and head toward the cafeteria doors in a hurry so I can get back to the table and somehow make sure Six really isn't pissed at me.

I make it out to the hallway and Val is standing right outside the cafeteria doors. "I'll take you back under one condition," she says.

I'm curious what the condition is, but it doesn't really matter at this point.

"Not interested."

Her mouth literally drops open. It's not even that cute a mouth now that I'm looking at it. I don't know how I fell for it all those other times.

"I'm serious, Daniel," she says firmly. "If you screw up one more time, I'm done."

I let my head fall backward until I'm looking up at the ceiling. "Jesus, Tessa," I say. She's not really worthy of my nicknames anymore. I look her in the eyes again. "I don't want you to take me back. I don't want to date you. I don't even want to make out with you. You're mean."

She scoffs, but stands frozen. "Are you serious?" she says, dumbfounded.

"Serious. Positive. Convinced. Enlightened. Take your pick."

She throws her hands up in the air and spins around, then walks back into the cafeteria. I walk to the doors and open them. Six is staring at me from our table, so I make a quick glance around at the rest of the group. No one is paying attention, so I motion for her to come out into the hallway. She takes a quick drink of her water, then stands, making up an excuse to the rest of the table. I step out of view while she makes her way to the exit. When the doors open I immediately grab her by the wrist and pull her until we reach the lockers. I push her against them and crash my mouth to hers. Her hands immediately fly up to my hair and we rush our kisses like we might get caught.

And we really might.

After a good solid minute, she pushes lightly against my chest, so I pull away from her.

"Are you mad?" I ask her, almost blurting out the question between heavy breaths.

"No," she says, shaking her head. "Why would I be mad?"

"Because Val is Tessa and you obviously don't like Tessa very much and because I had a jealous moment and called Italian men hairy."

She laughs. "We're acting, Daniel. I was actually a little impressed. And kind of turned on when you got jealous. But highly *un*impressed with the fact that Val is Tessa. I can't believe you had sex with Tessa Maynard."

"I can't believe you had sex with pretty much everyone else," I reply teasingly.

She grins. "You're a jerk."

"You're a slut."

"Will you be at my dinner tonight?" she asks.

"That's a really dumb question."

A smile spreads slowly across her face and it's so damn sexy I have to kiss her again.

"I should get back," she whispers when I pull away.

"Yes, you should. So should I."

"You first. I'm supposed to be in the administration office clearing up an issue with my schedule."

"Okay," I say. "I'll go first, but I'll miss you until you get back to the table."

"Don't make me puke," she says.

"I bet you're adorable when you puke. I bet your actual puke is even adorable. It's probably bubble-gum pink."

"You're seriously disgusting." She laughs and reaches up to kiss me again. She pushes against my chest, then slips out from between me and the locker. She puts both of her hands on my back and pushes me toward the cafeteria doors. "Act natural."

I turn and wink at her, then walk back through the doors. I casually make my way back to the table and take a seat.

"Where's Six?" Breckin asks.

I shrug. "How should I know? I was busy making out with Val in the hallway."

Sky shakes her head and lays her fork down. "I just lost my appetite, Daniel. Thanks."

"You'll have your appetite back by dinner tonight," I say.

Sky shakes her head. "Not with you and Val there. You'll probably be sucking face next to my food. If you drool on my chocolate cake you aren't getting any."

"Sorry, Cheese Tits," I say. "But Val won't be at your dinner tonight. I'll be there, though."

"I bet you will," Breckin says under his breath.

I glance over at him and he looks at me challengingly.

"What'd you just mumble, Powder Puff?" He absolutely hates it when I call him Powder Puff, but he should know I only give nicknames to the people I like. I think he does know that, though, because he doesn't really give me too much shit about it.

"I said I bet you will," he repeats louder this time. He turns to Sky, who is seated right next to him. "Six, right?"

Sky nods. "Six or six-thirty."

"I'll be there at six," Breckin says. He looks back at me and smirks. "I bet you'll be there at six, too, right, Daniel? You like six? Is six good for you?"

He's on to us. Fucker.

"Six is perfect," I say, holding his stare. "My absolute favorite time of day."

He smiles knowingly, but I'm not worried. I have a feeling he's going to have just as much fun with this as I am.

"All cleared up?" Sky asks Six when she returns to the table. Six nods and takes her seat. Her hand brushes across my outer thigh when she adjusts herself. I press my knee against hers and we both pick our forks up at the same time and take a bite of food.

Having her here just inches from me and not being allowed to touch her is complete torture. I'm beginning to think I'd rather just lean over and kiss her and take Holder's ass beating than have to pretend I don't want her.

Since the moment she disappeared into her house last night I've felt more restless than I've ever felt before. I've been fidgeting all day. I can't stop tapping my fingers and shaking my leg. It feels like I want to scratch at my skin when she's not around, like I'm coming down from a high.

That's exactly what this feels like. Like she's a drug I've become immediately addicted to, but I have none in supply. The only thing that satiates the craving is her laugh. Or her smile or her kiss or the feel of her pressed against me.

God, it's so hard not to touch her. So hard.

She begins laughing loudly at something Sky said and the craving becomes almost intolerable because of the intense need I have to catch that sound with my mouth.

I drop my fork onto my plate and lower my head into my hands and groan. "Stop laughing," I say quietly.

She's obviously laughing too loud to hear me, so I turn toward her and say it again. "Six. Stop laughing. Please."

Her jaw clamps shut and she turns to look at me. "Excuse me?"

About that same time, Holder kicks the shit out of my knee. I scoot back and immediately pull my leg up and rub the spot he kicked. "What the hell, man?"

Holder looks at me like I'm clueless. "What the hell is wrong with you? I told you not to be mean to her."

Ha. He thinks I'm being mean? If he only knew how nice I want to be to her right now.

"You don't like my laugh?" Six says. I can tell in her voice she knows how much I like her laugh, but she's enjoying the fact that Holder is clueless to what her laugh does to me.

"No," I grumble, scooting back toward the table.

She laughs again and the sound of it causes me to wince.

"Are you always this grumpy?" she asks. "Do you want me to go get your girlfriend and bring her back to the table so she can put you in a better mood?"

"No!" Sky and Breckin yell in unison.

I look at Six. "You think my girlfriend could put me in a better mood?"

She grins. "I think your *girlfriend* is a pathetic idiot for agreeing to date you."

I shake my head. "My girlfriend makes incredibly wise decisions. I can't wait until tonight when I get to show her just how smart she was when she decided to lay claim to me."

"I thought you said she wasn't coming to dinner," Sky says, disappointed.

Six's hand slips under the table and she begins to gently rub at the spot on my knee that Holder just finished kicking.

"Jesus Christ," I mutter, leaning forward. I put my elbows on the table and run my hands up and down my face, attempting to appear unaffected by the fact that it feels like Six just crawled her way inside my chest and is wrapping herself around my heart.

"Is lunch over yet?" I say to no one in particular. "I need to get out of here."

Holder looks at his phone. "Five more minutes." He looks back up at me. "Are you sick, Daniel? You're not being yourself today. It's starting to freak me out a little bit."

Six's hand is still on my knee. I casually lower my hand and slide it under the table, then place it over hers. She flips her hand over and I lace our fingers together and squeeze her hand.

"I know," I say to Holder. "I'm just having a weird day. Girlfriends. They have that effect on you."

He's still looking at me suspiciously. "You seriously need to make up your mind when it comes to her. It's past the point that any of us feel sorry for you, because now it's just irritating."

"Doesn't help that she used to be a slut," Six says.

"Six!" Sky says with a laugh. "That was so mean."

Six shrugs. "It's true. Daniel's girlfriend used to be a big, fat slut. I heard she had sex with six different guys in just over a year."

"Don't talk about my girlfriend that way," I say. "Who gives a shit what she did in the past? I sure as hell don't."

Six squeezes my hand, then pulls hers away and brings her hand back up to the table. "Sorry," she says. "That wasn't nice. If it helps, I heard she's a good kisser."

I grin. "*Phenomenal* kisser."

The bell rings and everyone picks up their trays. I notice Six isn't in any hurry, so I take my time as well. Sky kisses Holder on the cheek, then walks off with Breckin toward the exit. Holder picks up both their trays and lifts his eyes to mine. "I'll see you tonight," he says. "And I hope to hell the real Daniel shows up, because you aren't making a whole lot of sense today."

"I know," I say, pointing briefly at my head. "She's got me all screwed up in here, man. All screwed up. I'm losing my mind."

Holder shakes his head. "That right there is exactly what I'm talking about. You seem more affected by Val today than you ever have. It's just weird." He walks off, still looking confused. I feel sort of bad for lying to him, but it's his own fault. He shouldn't try to tell me who I can date, then I wouldn't have to hide it from him.

"That was fun," Six says quietly. She begins to pick up her tray, but I intercept it. I take a step toward her and look her hard in the eyes.

"Don't you ever insult my girlfriend again. You hear me?"

She tightens her lips to hide her smile. "Noted."

"I want to walk you to your locker. Wait for me."

Her smile becomes harder for her to hide as she nods her head. I take both of our trays and place them on the tray pile, then walk back to the table. I glance around us and don't really see anyone paying attention, so I quickly lean in and kiss her briefly on the lips, then pull away.

"Daniel Wesley, you're gonna get caught," she says with a grin. She turns and begins walking toward the exit, so I discreetly place a hand on her lower back and walk next to her.

"God, I hope so," I say. "If I have to sit through another lunch like that, I'll lose my shit and you'll end up on your back on top of the table."

She laughs. "What a way with words you have."

We exit the cafeteria and I walk her to her locker. It's on the opposite hall from mine, which couldn't be more inconvenient. We don't have a single class together and I won't even see her in the hall-way while we're at school. I know I haven't even been dating her for an entire day, but I already miss her.

"Can I come over before dinner?" I ask her.

She shakes her head. "No, I'll be helping Karen and Sky prep. I'm going over there right after school."

"What about after dinner?"

She shakes her head again while she switches her books. "Sky crawls through my window every night. You can't be in my room."

"I thought your window was out of commission."

"Only to people with penises."

I laugh. "What if I told you I didn't have a penis?"

She glances at me. "I would probably rejoice. My experiences with people who have penises never end well."

I shake my head. "That's not something my penis wants to hear you say. He has a very sensitive ego."

She smiles and shuts her locker, then leans against it. "Well, maybe you should go home after school and stroke his ego a little bit until he feels better."

I cock an eyebrow. "You just made a masturbation joke."

She nods. "So I did."

"I have the coolest girlfriend in the world."

She nods again. "So you do."

"I'll see you at dinner."

"So you will," she says.

"Can we sneak off and make out while everyone's eating?"

She squints her eyes as if she's actually contemplating it. "Don't know. We'll play it by ear."

I nod and lean my shoulder against the locker next to hers. We're just a few inches apart and we're staring at each other again. I love how she looks at me like she actually enjoys staring at me.

"Give me your phone number," I say.

"As long as you aren't planning to text me pics of your ego stroking after school."

I clutch at my heart. "Dammit, Six. I love every single word that comes out of your mouth."

"Cock," she says dryly.

She's evil.

"Except that word," I say. "I don't love cock."

She laughs and opens her locker again. She takes out a pen, then turns and grabs my hand. She writes her phone number down, then puts the pen back in her locker. "I'll see you tonight, Daniel." She begins backing away. All I can do is nod, because I'm pretty sure her voice just hardcore made out with my ears. She turns and disappears down the hallway just as something appears in my line of sight.

I look to the eyes that are now glaring at me.

"What do you want, Powder Puff?" I ask him, pushing off the locker.

"You like her?"

"Who?" I ask, playing dumb. I don't know why I'm trying to play dumb. We both know who he's referring to.

"I think it's adorable," he says. "She likes you, too. I can tell."

"Really?"

"You're too easy. And yes, I don't know how, but I can tell she likes you. Y'all are cute. Why are you hiding it? Or better yet, who are you hiding it from?"

"Holder. He says I can't date her." I begin walking toward class and Breckin falls into step with me.

"Why not? Because you're an asshole?"

I stop and look at him. "I'm an asshole?"

Breckin nods. "Yeah. I thought you knew that."

I laugh, then start walking again. "He thinks it'll screw everything up since we're all best friends."

"He's right. It will."

I stop walking again. "Who's to say things won't work out with me and Six?"

"Didn't you just meet her? Like two days ago?"

"Doesn't matter," I say defensively. "She's different. I have a good feeling about her."

Breckin studies me for a moment, then he smiles. "This should be fun. I'll see you tonight." He turns and walks in the opposite direction, but he stops and faces me again. "Call me Powder Puff again and your secret is out."

"Okay, Powder Puff."

He laughs and points at me. "See? Such an *ass*hole."

He spins and heads toward his class. I pull my phone out of my pocket and open up Val's contact information. I hit delete, then add Six's number into my phone. I'll wait until I make it to my classroom before I text her.

Don't want to seem desperate.

Chapter Four

Me: Pretend you're going to the bathroom or something.

I place my phone back down on the table and begin eating again. I've been here almost an hour and Six and I have barely had a chance to talk. I don't know if I'll even need Breckin to out us, because I'm about to lose my patience and do it myself.

I know everyone's curious about her trip to Italy, but she seems uncomfortable talking about it. Her answers are short and clipped and I hate that I'm the only one who seems to notice how much she doesn't want to bring up Italy. I also like that I'm the only one who notices, because it proves that whatever connection I feel with her is more than likely genuine. I feel like I know her better than anyone else here. Maybe even better than Sky knows her.

Although it's absurd to feel that way, since I still don't even know her birthday.

Six: There's only one bathroom in the hallway. Even if I were to go there it would be obvious if you got up and followed me.

I read her text and groan out loud.

"Everything okay?" Jack asks. He's seated next to me at the table, which is fine any other time but I really wanted Six to be in his chair. I nod, then put my phone facedown on the table.

"Irritating girlfriend drama," I say.

He nods and turns back to Holder, continuing with their conversation. Six is involved in a discussion with Sky and Karen. Breckin ended up not being able to come, which was probably a good thing. Not sure I could have handled the fact that he knows.

Right now it's just me and my impatience having a silent war at the dinner table.

"That reminds me," Six says loudly. "I bought you all presents. I forgot." She scoots back from the table. "They're at my house. I'll be right back." She stands and takes two steps before turning back toward us. "Daniel? They're kind of heavy. Mind giving me a hand?"

Don't act too excited, Daniel.

I sigh heavily. "I guess," I say as I scoot back from the table. I look at Holder and roll my eyes, then follow Six outside. Neither of us says a word while we make our way to the side of the house. She reaches her window, then turns around.

"I lied," she says. Her eyes are worried, which causes me to worry. "About what?"

She shakes her head. "I didn't buy anyone presents. I just can't take another second of all the questions, and then seeing you across the table and knowing how much I just wish it could be the two of us is making this whole dinner really irritating. But now I don't have presents. How do I go back in there without presents?"

I try not to laugh, but I love that she's been just as irritated as I've been. I was starting to worry I might have a few issues.

"We could just stay out here and never go back inside."

"We could," she says in agreement. "But they'd eventually come look for us. Not to mention it would be rude, since Jack and Karen went through all this trouble to cook for me and oh, my God, what if it's true, Daniel?"

I don't know if it's me or if she's just really difficult to keep up with, but I have no idea what she's talking about. "What if what's true?"

She exhales a quick breath. "What if our feelings are just reverse psychology? What if Holder had told you to date me Saturday night? You might not have been interested in me after that. What if the only reason we like each other so much is that it's forbidden? What if the second they all find out the truth, we can't stand each other?"

I hate that the worry in her voice sounds genuine, because that means she actually believes the shit she's saying right now.

"You think there's a chance I only like you because I'm not supposed to like you?"

She nods.

I grab her hand and yank her back toward the front of the house.

"Daniel, I don't have presents!"

I ignore her and walk her up the front steps, open the door, and march her straight into the kitchen.

"Hey!" I yell. Everyone turns around and looks at us. I glance at Six and her eyes are wide. I inhale a deep breath, then turn back to the table. Specifically to Holder.

"She fist bumped me," I say, pointing at Six. "It's not my fault. She hates purses and she fist bumped me, then she made me push her on the damn merry-go-round. After that, she demanded to see where I had sex in the park, then she forced me to sneak into my own bedroom. She's weird and half the time I can't keep up with her, but she thinks I'm funny as hell. And Chunk asked me this morning if I wanted to love her someday, and I realized I've never hoped I could love someone more than I want to love her. So every single one of you who has an issue with us dating is going to have to get over it because . . ." I pause and turn toward Six. "Because you fist bumped me and I could care less who knows we're together. I'm not going anywhere and I don't want to go anywhere so stop thinking I'm into you because I'm not supposed to be into you." I lift my hands and tilt her face toward mine. "I'm into you because you're awesome. And because you let me accidentally touch your boob."

She's smiling wider than I've ever seen her smile. "Daniel Wesley, where'd you learn those smooth moves?"

"Not moves, Six. Charisma."

She throws her arms around my neck and kisses me. I wait for the moment Holder yanks me away from her, but that moment doesn't come. We kiss for a solid thirty seconds before people begin clearing their throats. When Six pulls away from me, she's still smiling.

"Does it feel different now that they know?" I ask her. "Because it actually feels better to me."

She shoves my chest. "Stop! Stop saying things that make me grin like an idiot. My face has been hurting since the second I met you."

I pull her to me and hug her, then suddenly become aware that we're still standing in Sky's kitchen and everyone is still staring at us. I hesitantly turn and look at Holder to gauge his level of anger. He's never actually hit me before, but I've seen what he can do and I sure as hell don't want to experience it.

When my eyes meet his, he's . . . smiling. He's actually smiling.

Sky has a napkin to her eyes and she's wiping tears away.

Karen and Jack are both smiling.

It's weird.

Too weird.

"Do you guys talk to my parents?" I ask cautiously. "Did they teach you their dirty reverse psychology tricks?"

Karen is the first to speak. "Sit down, you two. Your food is getting cold."

I kiss Six on the forehead, then take my seat back at the table. I keep glancing at Holder, but he doesn't look upset at all. He actually looks a little impressed.

"Where the hell is my present?" Jack asks Six.

She clears her throat. "I decided to wait until Christmas." She picks up her glass and brings it to her lips, then glances at me. I smile at her.

Everyone else resumes whatever conversations were going on before my interruption. It's like no one is even that shocked. They act like it's completely normal. Like it's a natural thing . . . me and Six.

And I totally get it, because it is. Whatever we have is good, and even though I still don't know her birthday, I know this is right. And based on the look on her face right now, so does she.

• • •

"I really like this one," I say, looking at the picture in my hands. I'm leaning against the wall, sitting on the floor in Sky's bedroom. Six is passing around pictures she took in Italy to Sky, Holder, and me.

"Which pic are you looking at?" she says. She's lying next to me on the floor. I look down at her and flip the photo over so she can see it. She shakes her head with a quick roll of her eyes. "You only like that one because my cleavage looks great."

I immediately turn the photo back around. She's right. It does look great. But that's not at all why I liked it at first. She looks happy in this one. Peaceful.

"I took that picture the day I got to Italy," she says. "You can keep it."

"Thank you. I wasn't planning on giving it back to you, anyway."

"Consider it an anniversary present," she says.

I immediately look down at the time on my phone. "Oh. Wow. It really is our anniversary." I readjust myself until I'm leaning over her. "I almost forgot. I'm the worst boyfriend ever. I can't believe you haven't dumped me yet."

She grins. "That's okay. You can remember the next one." She slips her hand to the back of my neck and pulls me forward until our lips meet.

"Anniversary?" Sky says, confused. "Exactly how long have the two of you been dating?"

I pull away from Six and sit back up against the wall. "Precisely twenty-four hours."

An awkward silence follows, then of course Holder fills it. "Am I the only one who has a bad feeling about this?"

"I think it's great," Sky says. "I've never seen Six so . . . nice? Happy? Spoken for? It's a good look for her."

Six sits up and wraps her arms around my neck, then pulls me to the floor with her. "That's because I've never met anyone as vulgar and inappropriate and horrible at first kisses as Daniel." She pulls my mouth to hers and kisses me while she laughs at herself.

This is a first. A kiss and a laugh at the same time? I think I might be in heaven.

"Six has a bedroom, too, you know," Holder says.

Six stops laughing. *And* she stops kissing me.

Holder is about to be put on my shit list.

"Six doesn't allow penises in her bedroom," I reply to him while still staring down at her.

Six moves her mouth to my ear. "As long as you don't expect me to stroke his ego tonight, I kind of want to kiss you on my bed."

I didn't know people could move as fast as I'm moving right now. This has to be some sort of record, because my hands are under her back and knees and I'm scooping her up in my arms before her sentence even completely registers. She throws her arms around my neck and squeals as I head straight for Sky's window. I put her down gently, but then practically shove her outside. I begin to follow right behind her without even telling Sky or Holder good-bye.

"They are so strange together," I hear Sky say right before I'm out the window.

"Yeah," Holder says in agreement. "But also oddly . . . *right.*"

I pause.

Did Holder just compliment my relationship with Six? I don't know why I always want his approval so much, but hearing him say that fills me with this weird sense of pride. I turn around and take a step back to the window and lean inside. "I heard that."

He looks at the window and sees me leaning inside, so he rolls his eyes. "Go away," he says with a laugh.

"No. We're having a moment."

He cocks an eyebrow, but doesn't respond.

"You're my best friend, Holder."

Sky shakes her head and laughs, but Holder is still looking at me like I've lost my mind.

"For real," I say. "You're my best friend and I love you. I'm not ashamed to admit that I love a guy. I love you, Holder. Daniel Wesley loves Dean Holder. Always and forever."

"Daniel, go make out with your girlfriend," he says, waving me off.

I shake my head. "Not until you tell me you love me, too."

His head falls back against Sky's headboard. "I fucking love you, now GO AWAY!"

I grin. "I love you more."

He picks up a pillow and tosses it at the window. "Get the hell out of here, dipshit. "

I smile and back away from the window.

"You two are so strange together," Sky says to him.

I pull the window shut, then turn around to find Six. She's already in her bedroom, leaning out her window with her chin in her hands. She's grinning.

"Daniel and Holder, sittin' in a tree," she says in a singsong voice.

I walk toward her and improvise the next line of the song. "But then Daniel climbs down," I finish the rest of the sentence in a hurry, "and goes to Six's window and climbs inside her bedroom and throws her on the bed and kisses her until he can't take any more and has to go home and stroke his ego."

She's laughing and backing into her bedroom to make room for me to climb inside.

Once I'm inside, I look around and observe her room. I finally understand what she meant when she said my bedroom was more than just a room. This is like a secret glimpse into who Six really is. I feel like I could study this room and everything in it and find out everything I ever need to know about her.

Unfortunately, she's standing at the foot of her bed and she looks a little bit nervous and way more beautiful than I deserve, and I can't take my eyes off of her long enough to even study her bedroom.

I can't help but smile at her. I can already tell this is about to be the best anniversary I've ever had. The lights are off, so the mood is already perfect for making out. It's quiet, though. So quiet I can hear her breaths increase with each deliberately slow step I take toward her.

Shit. Maybe those are *my* breaths. I can't tell, because every inch closer I get requires an extra intake of air.

When I reach her, she's looking up at me with an odd mixture of peaceful anticipation. I want to push her onto the bed right now and climb on top of her and kiss the hell out of her.

I could do that, but why do the one thing she's expecting me to do?

I lean in slowly. Very slowly . . . until my mouth is so close to her neck she more than likely can't even tell if I'm touching her skin or not. "I have three questions I need to ask you before we do this," I say quietly, but very seriously. I pull back just far enough to see her gulp softly.

"Before we do what?" she asks hesitantly.

I lift a hand to the back of her head, then pull back from her neck and position my lips close to hers. "Before we do what we both want to do. Before I lean in one more inch. And before you part your lips for me just enough for me to steal a taste. Before I put my hands on your hips and back you up until you have nowhere to go but onto your bed."

I can feel her breath teasing my lips and it's so tempting I have to force myself to lean in to her ear again so I'm not so close to her mouth. "Before I slowly lower myself on top of you and our hands become curious and brave. Before my fingers slip under the hem of your shirt. Before my hand begins to explore its way up your stomach, and I discover I've never touched skin as soft as yours."

She gasps, then exhales a shaky breath and it's almost as sexy as the fist bump.

It may even be sexier.

"Before I finally get to touch your boob on *purpose*."

She laughs at that one, but her laugh is cut short when I press my thumb to the center of her lips.

"Before your breaths pick up pace and our bodies are aching because everything we're feeling is just making us want more and more and more of each other. Until I'm afraid I'll beg you not to ask me to slow down. So instead, I regrettably tear my mouth from yours and force myself away from your bed and you lift up unto your elbows and look at me, disappointed, because you kind of wished I would have kept going, but at the same time you're relieved I didn't, because you know you would have given in. So instead of giving in, we just stare. We watch each other silently as my heart rate begins to slow down and your breaths are easier to catch and the insatiable need is still there, but our minds are clearer now that I'm not pressed against you anymore. I turn around and walk to your window and leave without even saying good-bye, because we both know if either of us speaks . . . it'll be the collective demise of our willpower and we'll cave. We'll cave so hard."

I move my hand to her cheek. She whimpers and looks like she's about to collapse onto the bed, so I wrap my other arm around her lower back and pull her against me.

"So yeah . . . three questions first."

I let go of her and immediately turn around two seconds before I hear her fall onto her bed. I walk straight to the desk chair and take a seat, for two reasons. One, I want her to think I mean business and that everything I just said to her didn't affect me like it did her. And two, because I want her more than I've ever wanted anything and my knees were about to give out on me if I didn't sit down.

"Question number one," I say, watching her from across her room. She's lying on her back with her eyes closed and I hate that I'm not watching her up close right now. "When's your birthday?"

"October . . ." She clears her throat, obviously still recovering. "Thirty-first. Halloween."

How could the date of a birthday make me fall even harder for her? I have no idea, but it somehow does.

"Question number two. What's your favorite food?"

"Homemade mashed potatoes."

Never would have guessed that one. Glad I asked.

"Question number three," I say. "It's a big one. Are you ready?"

She nods, but keeps her eyes closed.

"What's the one thing in this room that tells the biggest secret about you?"

As soon as the question leaves my mouth, she's completely still. Her exaggerated breaths come to a halt. She remains motionless for almost a whole minute before she slowly pushes herself up until she's seated on the edge of the bed, facing me. "It has to be something inside this room?"

I nod slowly.

She lifts her hand and touches a finger to her heart, pointing at it. "This," she whispers. "My biggest secret is right in here."

Her eyes are moist and sad and somehow with that answer, the air instantly changes between us. In a dangerous way. A terrifying way. Because it feels like her air just became *my* air and I suddenly want to take in fewer breaths in order to ensure she never runs out.

I stand up and walk to the bed. Her eyes follow me closely until I'm directly in front of her. "Stand up."

She stands slowly.

I weave both hands through the locks of her hair until I'm holding the back of her head. I stare at her until my heart can't take anymore, then I press my lips to hers. I've lost count of how many times I've kissed her over the past day. Every time I kiss her, the feeling I get is like nothing I've ever experienced. The closest I've ever come to feeling this way is the day I was pretending to be in love with the girl in the closet. But even that day, the day I thought would surpass every day after it, doesn't come close to this.

Her mouth is warm and inviting and everything it always is when I kiss her, but it's also so much more. The fact that I have this reaction to her after one day scares the living shit out of me.

One day.

I've been doing this with her for one day and I have no idea what's happening. I don't know if it's a full moon or if I have a tumor wrapped around my heart or if she really is a witch. Whatever it is still doesn't explain how this kind of thing can exist between two people this ridiculously fast . . . and actually last.

I feel like deep down my heart knows she's too good to be true. My mind and my whole body know she's too good to be true, so I kiss her harder, hoping to convince myself that this is real. It's not some fairy tale. It's not an hour of make-believe.

This is reality, but even in our imperfect reality, people don't fall for each other like this. They don't develop feelings like this for someone they barely know.

The only thing my entire thought process is proving to me right now is how much I need to grab her tight and hang on, because wherever she goes, I want to go, too. And right now, she's going backward, down onto the bed. I'm easing myself on top of her in the same way I just told her this would happen. And we're kissing, just like I said we would, only this time it may just be a little more frantic and needy and holy *shit*.

Her skin.

It really is the softest skin I've ever touched.

I move my hand from her waist and inch my fingers underneath the hem of her shirt, then slowly begin to work my way to her stomach.

She pushes my hand away.

"Daniel."

She immediately lifts up and I immediately lift off her. She's breathing so heavily I catch myself holding my own breath, scared I'm hogging too much of her air.

She looks both regretful and embarrassed that she suddenly asked me to stop. I lift my hand and stroke her cheek reassuringly.

My eyes scroll over her features, taking in her nervous demeanor. She's afraid of what might happen between us. I can see on her face and in the way she's looking at me that she's just as scared as I am. Whatever this is between us, neither one of us was searching for it. Neither one of us knew it even existed. Neither one of us is even remotely prepared for it, but I know we both want it. She wants this to work with me as much as I want it to work with her and seeing the look in her eyes right now makes me believe that it will. I've never believed in anything like I believe in the possibility of the two of us.

I can tell by the way she's looking at me that if I tried to kiss her again, she'd let me. It's almost as if she's torn between the girl she used to be and the girl she is now and she's afraid if I try to kiss her again, she'll cave.

And I'm afraid if I don't get up and walk away, I'll let her.

We don't even have to speak. She doesn't even have to ask me to leave, because I know that's what I need to do. I nod, silently answering the question I don't want her to have to ask. I begin to ease off her bed and a silent *thank you* flashes in her eyes. I stand up, back away from her and climb out her window without a word. I walk a few feet until I reach the edge of her house, then I lean against it and slide down to the ground.

I lean my head back and close my eyes, attempting to figure out where I went right in my life to deserve her.

"What the hell are you doing?" Holder asks. I look up and he's halfway out Sky's window. Once he makes it all the way out, he turns and pulls her window shut.

"Recovering," I say. "I just needed a minute."

He walks toward me and takes a seat on the ground across from me, then leans against Sky's house. He pulls his legs up and rests his elbows on his knees.

"You're already leaving?" I ask him. "It's not even nine o'clock yet."

He reaches down to the ground and rips up a few blades of grass, then spins them between his fingers. "Got kicked out for the night. Karen walked in and my hand was up Sky's shirt. She didn't like that too much."

I laugh.

"So," he says, glancing back up at me. "You and Six, huh?"

Despite my effort not to smile, I do it anyway. I smile pathetically and nod. "I don't know what it is about her, Holder. I . . . she just . . . yeah."

"I know what you mean," he says quietly, looking back down at the grass between his fingers.

Neither one of us says anything else for several moments until he drops the blades of grass and wipes his hands on his jeans, preparing to stand up. "Well . . . I'm glad we had this talk, Daniel, but the fact that we already professed our mutual love for each other tonight is leaving me a little overwhelmed. I'll see you tomorrow." He stands up and begins walking toward his car.

"I love you, Holder!" I yell after him. "Best friends forever!"

He keeps walking forward, but lifts his hand in the air and flips me off.

It's almost as cool as a fist bump.

Chapter Five

"You're wrong," she says.

We're standing in my kitchen. Her back is pressed against the counter and I'm standing in front of her with my arms on either side of her. I catch her lips with mine and shut her up. It doesn't last long because she pushes my face away.

"I'm serious," she whispers. "I don't think they like me."

I bring a hand up and wrap it around the nape of her neck and look her directly in the eyes. "They like you. I promise."

"No we don't," my dad says as he makes his way into the kitchen. "We can't stand her. In fact, we hope you never bring her back." He refills his cup with ice, then walks back to the living room.

Six's eyes follow him as he exits the room, then she looks back up at me, wide-eyed.

"See?" I say with a smile. "They love you."

She points toward the living room. "But he just . . ."

My father's voice cuts her off when he walks back into the kitchen. "Kidding, Six," he says, laughing. "Inside joke. We actually like you a lot. I tried to give Danny-boy Grandma Wesley's ring earlier, but he says it's still too soon to make you a Wesley."

Six laughs at the same time she breathes a sigh of relief. "Yeah, maybe so. It's only been a month. I think we should wait at least two more weeks before we talk proposals."

My dad walks farther into the kitchen and leans against the counter across from us. I feel a little awkward standing so close to Six now, so I move next to her and lean against the bar.

"Did you come back in here so you could think of things to say that would embarrass me?" I ask. I know that's why he's standing here. I can see the glimmer in his eyes.

He takes a drink of his tea. He scrunches his nose up. "Nah," he says. "I would never do that, Danny-boy. I'm not the type of dad who would tell his son's girlfriend how he talks about her incessantly. I would also never tell my son's girlfriend that I'm proud of her for not having sex with him yet."

Holy shit. I groan and slap myself in the forehead. I should have known better than to bring her here.

"You talk to him about the fact that we haven't had sex?" Six says, completely embarrassed.

My father shakes his head. "No, he doesn't have to. I know because every night he comes home he goes straight to his bedroom and takes a thirty-minute shower. I was eighteen once."

Six covers her face with her hands. "Oh, my God." She peeks through her hands at my dad. "I guess I know who Daniel gets his personality from."

My father nods. "Tell me about it. His mother is terribly inappropriate."

Right on cue, my mother and Chunk walk through the front door with dinner. I glare at my father, then walk toward my mother and grab the pizza boxes out of her hands. She sets her purse down, walks over to Six, and gives her a quick hug.

"I'm sorry I didn't cook for you. Busy day today," she says.

"It's fine," Six replies. "Nothing like inappropriate conversation over pizza."

I watch as my mother spins around and eyes my father. "Dennis? What have you been up to?"

He shrugs. "Just telling Danny-boy how I would never embarrass him in front of Six."

My mother laughs. "Well, as long as you aren't embarrassing him, then. I'd hate for Six to find out about his lengthy showers every night."

I slap the table. "Mom! Jesus Christ!"

My dad winks at her. "Already covered that one."

Six walks to the table, shaking her head. "Your parents actually make you seem like a gentleman." She takes a seat at the table and I sit in the chair next to her.

"I'm so sorry," I whisper to her. She looks at me and smiles.

"Are you kidding me? I *love* this."

"Why would long showers embarrass you?" Chunk says to me, taking a seat across from Six. "I would think wanting to be clean is a good thing." She picks up a slice of pizza and begins to take a bite, but then her eyes squeeze shut and she drops the pizza onto her plate. By the look on her face, the meaning behind the long showers has just hit her. "Oh, gross. *Gross!*" she says, shaking her head.

Six begins to laugh and I rest my forehead against my hand, convinced this is more than likely the most uncomfortable, embarrassing five minutes of my life. "I hate all of you. Every last one of you." I quickly look at Six. "Except you, babe. I don't hate you."

She smiles and wipes her mouth with a napkin. "I know exactly what you mean. I hate everybody, too."

As soon as the words fall from her mouth, she looks away like she didn't just punch me in the gut, rip out my intestines, and stomp them into the ground.

I hate everybody too, Cinderella.

The words I said that day in the closet are screaming loudly inside my head.

There's no way.

There's no way I wouldn't have noticed she was Cinderella.

I bring my hands to my face and close my eyes, trying hard to remember something about that day. Her voice, her kiss, her smell. The way we seemed to connect almost instantly.

Her *laugh*.

"Are you okay?" Six asks quietly. No one else can tell something major is going on with me right now, but she notices. She notices because we're in sync. She notices because we have this unspoken connection. We've had it since the second I laid eyes on her in Sky's bedroom.

We've had it since the second she fell on top of me in the maintenance closet.

"No," I say, bringing my hands down. "I'm not okay." I grip the edge of the table, then slowly turn to face her.

Soft hair.

Amazing mouth.

Phenomenal kisser.

My mouth is dry, so I reach to my cup and down a huge gulp of water. I slam my cup back down on the table, then turn and face her. I'm trying not to smile, but this whole thing is slightly overwhelming. Realizing that the girl from my past that I wished I could know is the same girl from my present that I'm thankful to have is practically one of the best moments of my life. I want to tell Six, I want to tell Chunk, I want to tell my parents. I want to scream it from the rooftops and print it in all the papers.

Cinderella is Six! Six is Cinderella!

"Daniel. You're scaring me," she says, watching as my face grows paler and my heart pounds faster.

I look at her. *Really* look at her this time.

"You want to know why I haven't given you a nickname yet?"

She looks confused that this is what I decide to say in the middle of my silent freak-out. She nods cautiously. I place one hand on the back of her chair and one hand on the table in front of her, then lean in toward her.

"Because I already gave you one, Cinderella."

I pull back slightly and watch her face closely, waiting on the realization she's about to have. The flashback. The clarity. She's about to wonder how the hell she failed to realize it, too.

Her eyes slowly move up my face until they meet mine. "No," she says, shaking her head.

I nod slowly. "Yes."

She's still shaking her head. "No," she says again with more certainty. "Daniel there's no way it could . . ."

I don't let her finish. I grab her face and kiss her harder than I've ever kissed her. I don't give a shit that we're seated at a dinner table. I don't care that Chunk is groaning. I don't care that my mom is clearing her throat. I keep kissing her until she begins to back away from me.

She's pushing on my chest, so I pull away from her just in time to see the regret wash over her entire face. I focus on her eyes long enough to see them squeeze shut as she stands to leave the kitchen. I watch her rush away long enough to see her stifle a sob by slapping her hand over her mouth. I remain in my seat until the front door slams shut and I realize she's gone.

I'm immediately out of my seat. I rush out the front door and run straight to her car, which is now backing out of my driveway. I slam my fist against her hood as I rush to catch up to her window. She's not looking at me. She's wiping tears away, trying her hardest not to look out the window I'm banging on.

"Six!" I yell, repeatedly banging on her window with my fist. I see her hand reach down to put the car in drive. I don't even think. I sprint to the front of the car and slap my hands down on the hood, standing directly in front of it so she can't take off. I'm watching her do everything she can to avoid looking at me.

"Roll down your window," I yell.

She doesn't move. She continues to cry as she focuses on everything other than what's right in front of her.

Me.

I slap the hood of the car again until she finally brings her eyes up to meet mine. Seeing her heartache confuses the hell out of me. I couldn't have been happier finding out she was Cinderella, yet she seems embarrassed as hell that I realized it.

"Please," I say, wincing from the ache that just reached my chest. I hate seeing her upset and I really hate that this is why she's upset.

She puts the car in park, then reaches a hand to her door and lowers the driver's side window. I'm not so sure she still won't drive away if I move out from in front of her car. I carefully and very slowly begin to make my way toward her window, the whole time keeping an eye on her hand to ensure she doesn't put the car back into drive.

When I reach her window, I bend my knees and lower myself until I'm face to face with her. "Do I even need to ask?"

She looks up at the roof and leans her head against the headrest. "Daniel," she whispers through her tears. "You wouldn't understand."

She's right.

She's absolutely right.

"Are you embarrassed?" I ask her. "Because we had sex?"

She squeezes her eyes shut, giving away the fact that she thinks I'm judging her. I immediately reach a hand through her window and pull her gaze back to mine. "Don't you dare be embarrassed by that. Ever. Do you know how much that meant to me? Do you know how many times I've thought about you? I was there. I made that choice right along with you, so please don't think for a second that I would ever judge you for what happened between us."

She begins to cry even harder. I want her to get out of the car. I need to hold her because I can't see her this upset and not do whatever I can to take it away.

"Daniel, I'm sorry," she says through her sobs. "This was a mistake. This was a huge mistake." Her hand reaches down to the gearshift and I'm already reaching into the car, trying to stop her.

"No. No, Six," I plead. She puts the car in drive and reaches to the door, then places her finger on the window button.

I make one last attempt to lean in and kiss her before the window begins to rise on me. "Six, *please*," I say, shocked at the sadness and desperation in my own voice. She continues to raise the window until I'm completely out of it and it's all the way up. I press my palms to her window and slap the glass, but she drives away.

There's nothing left for me to do but watch the back of the car as it disappears down the street.

What the hell was that?

I pull my hands through my hair and look up at the sky, confused as to what just happened.

That wasn't her.

I hate that she had the complete opposite reaction from me when she found out who I was.

I hate that she's embarrassed about that day, like she just wants to forget it. Like she wants to forget *me*.

I hate it because I've done everything I possibly can to commit that day to my memory, like no one or nothing else I've ever experienced.

She can't do this. She can't just push me away like this without an explanation.

Chapter Six

I couldn't give my parents an explanation when I went back inside to grab my keys. They were apologetic, thinking they did something wrong. They felt bad about their jokes, but I didn't even have it in me to reassure them that they weren't the problem. I couldn't reassure them, because I don't even know what the problem is.

I'll be damned if I don't find out tonight, though. Right now.

I put my car in park and turn off the engine, relieved to see her car parked in her driveway. I get out of my car and shut my door, then head to her front door. Before I make it to her front porch, I detour to the side of the house. I know with the shape she left my house in a few minutes ago, there's no way she would have walked through her front door. She would have taken the window.

I reach her bedroom and the window is shut, as well as the curtains. The room is dark, but I know she's inside. Knocking won't do me any good, so I don't even bother. I push the window up, then slide the curtains to the side.

"Six," I say firmly. "I'm respecting your window rule, but it's really hard right now. We need to talk."

Nothing. She says nothing. I know she's in her room, though. I can hear her crying, but barely.

"I'm going to the park. I want you to meet me there, okay?"

Several silent moments pass before she responds.

"Daniel, go home. Please." Her voice is soft and weak, but the message behind that sad, angelic voice is like a stab to my heart. I back away from the window, then kick the side of the house out of frustration. Or anger. Or sadness or . . . *shit*. All of it.

I lean back into her window and grip the frame. "Meet me at the goddamned park, Six!" I say loudly. My voice is angry. *I'm* angry. She's pissing me the hell off. "We don't do this kind of thing. You don't play these games. You owe me a fucking explanation."

I push away from her window and turn to walk back to my car. I make it five feet before my palms are running down my face and I'm wishing I could punch the actual air in front of me. I stop walking and pause for several moments while I search for patience. It's in here somewhere.

I walk back to her window and hate that she's crying much louder now, even though she's trying to stifle the sounds with her pillow.

"Listen, babe," I say quietly. "I'm sorry I said goddamned. And fucking. I shouldn't cuss when I'm upset, but . . ." I inhale a deep breath. "But *dammit*, Six. *Please. Please* just meet me at the park. If you aren't there in half an hour, I'm done. I had enough of this bullshit with Val and I'm not putting myself through it again."

I turn to leave and make it all the way to my car this time before pausing and kicking at the ground. I walk back to her window again. "I didn't mean it just now when I said I'd be done if you didn't show up. If you don't show up to the park, I'll still want to be with you. I'll just be sad that you didn't show up. Because we show up, Six. It's what we do. It's me and you, babe."

I wait for a reply for a lot longer than I even need to. She never responds, so I go back to my car and climb inside, then head to the park and hope she shows up.

• • •

Twenty-seven minutes pass before her car finally pulls into a parking spot.

I'm not surprised she showed up. I knew she would. Her reaction was uncharacteristic of her and I know she just needed time to let everything soak in.

I watch her as she slowly makes her way toward me, never once looking up at me. She keeps her eyes trained to the ground the whole time until she passes me. She sinks into the swing next to me and grabs the chains, then leans her head against her arm. I wait for her to speak first, knowing she more than likely won't.

She doesn't.

I run my hands up the chain rope until they're even with my head, then I lean into my arm and mirror her position. We're both staring quietly into the dark night in front of us.

"After you left that day," I say. "I wasn't sure of what you wanted me to do. I wondered if you thought about me, too, and if you had changed your mind. If maybe you wanted me to try and find you."

I tilt my head and look at her. Her blonde hair is tucked behind her ears and her eyes are closed. Even with her eyes closed I can see the pain in her features.

"For days I wondered if that's what you wanted me to do. I waited and waited for you to come back, but you never did. I know we both said we would be better off not knowing who the other was, but honestly, you were all I could think about. I wanted you to come back so fucking bad that I spent every single fifth period in that damn closet for the rest of the semester. The last day of school was the absolute worst. When the bell rang and I had to walk out of that closet for the last time, it absolutely sucked. So much. I felt like an idiot for being so consumed by the thought of you. When I met Val, I forced myself to go forward with her because it helped to not think about that damn closet so much."

I twist the swing until I'm facing her. "I like you, Six. A lot. And I know this sounds all kinds of jacked up and crazy, but pretending to make love to you that day was the closest I've ever been to actually loving someone until now."

I turn my swing to face forward again, then I stand up. I walk to her and kneel down on both knees in front of her, then wrap my arms around her waist. I look up at her and see the pain flash across her face when I touch her. "Six. Don't let what happened between us become a negative thing. *Please.* Because that day was one of the best days of my life. Actually, it was *the* best day of my life."

She lifts her head away from her arm and opens her eyes, then looks directly at me. Tears are streaming down her face. It breaks my damn heart.

"Daniel," she whispers through her tears. She squeezes her eyes shut and turns her head like she can't even look at me. "I got pregnant."

Chapter Seven

Sometimes when I'm almost asleep, I'll hear something that pulls me right back into a state of high alert. I'll listen closely, wondering if I actually heard a sound or if it's just my imagination playing tricks on me. I'll hold my breath and be really still, and I'll just listen quietly.

I'm quiet.

I'm still.

I'm holding my breath.

I'm listening.

I'm concentrating really hard while my head rests on her thighs. I don't know when I lowered it here, but my hands are still gripping her waist. I'm trying to figure out if those words are going to hit me and completely knock my heart around like a punching bag all over again, or if it was just my imagination.

God, I hope it was my imagination.

A tear hits my cheek that just fell straight from her eyes.

"I didn't find out until I was already in Italy," she says, her voice coated and laced with sorrow and shame. "I'm so sorry."

In my head, I'm counting backward. Counting the days and the weeks and the months and trying to make sense of what she's saying, because she's obviously not pregnant now. My mind is still churning, crunching numbers, erasing errors, crunching more numbers.

She was in Italy for almost seven months.

Seven months there, three months before she left and one month since she returned.

That's almost a year.

My mind hurts. Everything hurts.

"I didn't know what to do," she says. "I couldn't raise him by myself. I was already eighteen when I found out, so . . ."

I immediately lift up and look at her face. *"Him?"* I ask, shaking my head. "How do you know . . ." I close my eyes and blow out a steady breath, then release my grip on her waist. I stand up and turn around, then pace back and forth, absorbing everything that's happening.

"Six," I say, shaking my head. "I don't . . . are you saying . . ." I pause, then turn and face her. "Are you telling me you had a fucking *baby*? That *we* had a baby?"

She's crying again. Sobbing, even. Hell, I don't know if she ever even stopped. She nods like it's painful to do.

"I didn't know what to do, Daniel. I was so scared."

She stands up and walks toward me, then places her hands delicately on my cheeks. "I didn't know who you were, so I didn't know how to tell you. If I knew your name or what you looked like I never would have made that decision without you."

I bring my hands up to hers, and I pull them away from my face. "Don't," I say as I feel the resentment building within me. I'm trying so hard to hold it back. To understand. To let it all soak in.

I just can't.

"How could you not tell me? It's not like you found a puppy, Six. This is . . ." I shake my head, still not getting it. "You had a *baby*. And you didn't even bother telling me!"

She grasps my shirt in her fists, shaking her head, wanting me to see her side of things. "Daniel, that's what I'm trying to tell you! What was I supposed to do? Did you expect me to plaster flyers all over the school asking for information on who knocked me up in the maintenance closet?"

I look her directly in the eyes. "Yes," I say in a low voice.

She takes a step back, so I take a step forward. "*Yes*, Six! That's *exactly* what I would have expected you to do. You should have plastered it all over the hallways, aired it on the radio, taken an ad out in the motherfucking newspaper! You get pregnant with my kid and you worry about your *reputation*? Are you *kidding* me?"

My hand covers my cheek a second after she slaps me.

The pain in her eyes can't even come close to matching the pain in my heart, so I don't feel bad for saying what I said. Even when she begins to cry harder than I knew people were capable of crying.

She rushes back to her car.

I let her go.

I walk back to the swing and I sit.

Fucking life.

Motherfucking life.

Daniel: Where are you?

Holder: Just left Sky's house. Almost home. What's up?

Daniel: I'll be there in five.

Holder: Everything okay?

Daniel: Nope.

Five minutes later Holder is standing on his curb waiting for me. I pull onto the side of the street and he opens the passenger door, then climbs inside. I put my car in park and prop my foot on the dash, then look out my window.

I'm surprised at how pissed I am. I'm even surprised at how sad I am. I don't know how to separate everything I'm feeling in order to get a grip on the core of what's upsetting me the most. Right now I can't tell if it's the fact that I didn't have a say in whatever decision she made or if it's because she was even put into that situation to have to make that kind of decision to begin with.

I'm pissed I wasn't there to help her. I'm pissed I was careless enough to make a girl go through something like that.

I'm sad because . . . *hell*. I'm sad that I'm so mad at her. I'm sad I have to know something this overwhelming and there isn't a damn thing I can do about it now, even if I wanted to. I'm sad because I'm sitting here in a parked car and I'm about to have a breakdown in front of my best friend and I really don't want to do that but it's too late.

I punch the steering wheel the second I begin to cry. I punch it several times, over and over, until the car begins to close in on me and I need to get the hell out of it. I open the door and climb out, then turn around and kick my tire. I kick it over and over until my foot starts to go numb, then I collapse against the hood onto my elbows. I press my forehead against the cold metal of the car and focus on burying this anger.

It's not her fault.

It's not her fault.

It's not her fault.

When I'm finally calm enough to return to the car, Holder is sitting quietly in the passenger seat, watching me closely.

"You want to talk about it?" he asks.

I shake my head. "Nope."

He nods. He's probably relieved I don't want to talk about it.

"What do you want to do?" he asks.

I wrap my fingers around the steering wheel, then crank the car. "I don't care what we do."

"Me neither."

I put the car in drive.

"We could go to Breckin's house and let you get your aggression out on a video game," he suggests.

I nod, then begin to drive toward Breckin's house. "You better not fucking tell him I cried."

Chapter Eight

"You look like hell," Holder says, leaning against the locker next to mine. "Did you even sleep last night?"

I shake my head. Of course I didn't. How the hell could I have slept? I knew she wasn't sleeping, so there's no way in hell I could have.

"You gonna tell me what happened?" he asks. I shut my locker, but keep my hand on it as I look down at the floor and slowly inhale.

"No. I know I usually tell you everything, but not this, Holder."

He taps the locker next to him a couple of times with his fist, then he pushes off of it. "Six isn't telling Sky anything, either. Not sure what happened, but . . ." He looks at me until I make eye contact with him. "I like you with her. Get it worked out, Daniel."

He walks away and I close my locker. I wait next to it for a few minutes more than necessary because my next class is down the hallway where Six's locker is. I haven't seen her since she left the park last night and I'm not sure I really want to see her. I'm not sure about anything. I have so many questions, but just thinking about having to ask her any of them makes my chest hurt so bad I can't fucking breathe.

After the final bell rings, I decide to walk to my next class. I debated staying home from school altogether, but I figured it would be worse just sitting in my room thinking about it all day. I'd rather be preoccupied for as long as I can today because I know as soon as school is out I need to confront her.

Or maybe I'm supposed to confront her right now, because as soon as I round the corner, my eyes land on her.

I come to a quiet stop and watch her. She's the only one in the hallway. She's standing still, facing her locker. I want to walk away before she sees me, but I can't stop watching her. Her whole demeanor is heartbroken and I want so bad to rush over to her and wrap my arms around her but . . . I can't. I want to scream at her and hug her and kiss her and blame her for every single jumbled-up emotion I've spent the last day trying to process.

I sigh heavily and she turns to look at me. I'm far enough away that I can't hear her crying, but close enough I can see the tears. Neither one of us moves. We just stare. Several moments pass and I can see she's hoping I say something to her.

I clear my throat and begin walking toward her. The closer I get, the louder her soft cry becomes. I get about five feet away, then I pause. The closer I get to her, the harder it is to breathe.

"Is he . . ." I close my eyes and pass a calming breath, then open them again and try my hardest to finish my sentence with dry eyes. "When you talked about the boy who broke your heart in Italy . . . you were referring to him, weren't you? The baby?"

I can barely see the nod of her head when she confirms my thoughts. I squeeze my eyes shut and tilt my head back.

I didn't know hearts could literally ache like this. It hurts so much I want to reach inside and rip it out of my chest so I'll never feel this again.

I can't do this. Not right here. We can't stand in the hallway of a high school and have this discussion.

I turn around before I open my eyes so I don't have to see the look on her face again. I walk straight to my classroom and open the door, then walk inside without looking back at her.

Chapter Nine

I don't know why I'm still here. I don't want to be here and I'm pretty sure I'll leave in half an hour. I just can't leave before then because I'm scared of what she might think if I don't show up to lunch. I could text her and tell her I'll talk to her later, but I'm not even sure I feel like sending her a text yet. There's still so much I have to process, I'd rather just ignore it all until I find the strength to sort through everything.

I walk through the cafeteria doors and head straight to our table. There's no way I can eat lunch so I don't even bother getting food. Breckin is sitting in my usual spot next to Six, but that's probably a good thing. Not so sure I could sit by her right now, anyway.

Her eyes are focused on the textbook in front of her. She's not crying anymore. I take a seat across from her and I know she knows I just sat down, but her eyes never move. Sky and Holder are deep in conversation with Breckin, so I watch them, trying to find a spot to jump in.

I can't though, because I'm completely unable to pay attention. I keep stealing glances at her to make sure she isn't crying or to see if she's looking at me. She never does either of those things.

"You're not eating?" Breckin says, catching my attention.

I shake my head. "Not hungry."

"You need to eat something," Holder says. "And a nap might do you some good, too. Maybe you should go home."

I nod, but don't say anything.

"If you do go home, you should take Six with you," Sky says. "You both look like you could use a nap."

I don't even respond to that with a nod. My eyes fall back to Six just in time to see a tear land on a page in front of her. She quickly swipes it away with her hand and flips the page over.

Fuck if that just didn't make me feel like complete shit.

I continue to watch her and tears continue to fall onto the pages, one by one. Her hand is always quick to wipe them away before anyone notices and she always flips to a new page before she can even possibly have read the last one.

"Get up, Breckin," I say. He looks at me blankly, but doesn't make an effort to move. "I want your seat. Get up."

He finally realizes what I'm saying, so he quickly stands up. I stand and walk around the table. I sit down beside her and when I do, she brings her arms onto the table. She folds them and buries her head into the crease in her elbow. I watch as her shoulders begin to shake and dammit if I can allow her to keep feeling this way. I wrap an arm around her and lower my forehead to the side of her head and I close my eyes. I don't say anything. I don't do anything. I just hold her while she cries into her arms.

"Daniel," I hear her say through her muffled tears. She lifts her head and looks up at me. "Daniel, I'm so sorry. I'm so, so sorry." Her tears become sobs and her sobs become too much. It's too fucking much.

I pull her to my chest. "Shh," I say into her hair. "Don't. Don't apologize."

Her body becomes limp against mine and everyone in the cafeteria is beginning to stare at us. I want to hold her and tell her how sorry I am for allowing her to walk away last night, but she needs privacy. I wrap my arm tighter around her, then scoop her legs up into my other arm. I pull her against me, then stand up and carry her out into the hallway. I keep walking until I round the corner and find our room. She's still crying against my chest, wrapped tightly around me. I open the door to the maintenance closet, then I close it behind us. I back up to the door and slide down until I meet the floor, still holding her in my arms.

"Six," I say, lowering my mouth to her ear. "I want you to try to stop crying, because I have so much I want to say to you."

I feel her nod against my chest and I remain quiet, waiting on her to calm down. Several minutes pass before she's finally quiet enough for me to continue.

"First of all, I am so sorry for letting you walk away last night, but I don't want you to think for one second it was because I was judging your choices. Okay? I'm not about to put myself in your shoes and tell you that you made a bad choice, because I wasn't there and I have no clue how hard that must have been for you."

I adjust her and straighten out my legs so she's forced to sit up and look at me. I pull one of her legs to the other side of me until she's facing me. "I'm just sad, okay? That's all this is. I'm allowed to be sad about this and I need you to let me be sad because this is a whole hell of a lot to process in a day."

She pulls her lips into a thin line and she nods while I wipe away her tears with both my thumbs. "I have so many questions, Six. And I know you'll answer them when you're ready, but I can wait. If you need me to give you time I can."

She shakes her head. "Daniel. He's your son. I'll answer any question you ask me. I just don't know if you want to hear the answers because . . ." She squeezes her eyes shut to hold back more tears. "Because I think I made the wrong choice and it's too late. It's too late to go back now."

She's crying hard again, so I wrap my arms around her and hug her.

"If I knew he was yours or that I would eventually find you I would have never done it, Daniel. I would have never given him up.

But I did and now you're here and it's too late because I don't know where he is and I'm sorry. God, I'm so sorry."

I shake my head, wishing she would stop. It's hurting me more to see her upset with herself than anything else about this whole situation.

"Listen to me, Six." I pull back and look her in the eyes, holding her face firmly between my hands. "You made a choice for *him*. Not for yourself. Not for me. You did what was best for him and I will never be able to thank you enough for that. And please don't think this changes how I feel about you. If anything, it just lets me know that I'm not crazy. For the past month I've been thinking my feelings for you couldn't be real because there are so many of them and they're so much. *Too* much sometimes. I constantly have to bite my tongue when I'm around you because all I've been wanting to do lately is tell you how much I love you. But it's only been a month since we met and the only other time I've said those words out loud to a girl was over a year ago. Right here on this floor. And you wouldn't believe how real I wanted that moment to be for us, Six. I know I didn't know you but my *God*, I wished I did. And now that I do know you . . . *really* know you . . . I know it's real. I love you. And knowing what we shared last year and now knowing what you had to go through and how it's made you exactly who you are right now . . . it just blows my mind. It blows my mind that I get to love you."

I feel her hands wiping tears from my cheeks when I lean in to kiss her. I pull her against me and she pulls me against her and I have no plans to ever let her go. I kiss her until her hands move up to my face and she pulls her lips from mine. Our foreheads meet and she's still crying, but her tears are different now. I feel like they're tears of relief rather than tears of worry.

"I'm so happy it's you," she says, keeping her hands locked on my face. "I'm so happy it was you."

I pull her against me and hold her. I hold her for so long that the bell rings and the hallway fills and empties and another bell rings and we're still sitting here together, holding on to each other when the silence in the hallway returns. I'm periodically pressing kisses into her hair, stroking her back, kissing her forehead.

"He looked like you," she says quietly. Her hand is lightly trailing up and down my arm and her cheek is pressed against my chest. "He had your brown eyes and he was kind of bald, but I could tell he was going to have brown hair. And he had your mouth. You have a great mouth."

I rub my hand up her back and kiss the top of her head. "He's got it made," I say. "Looks just like his daddy, hopefully acts like his mommy, and he'll have a nice Italian accent. Kid won't have any problems in life."

She laughs and hearing that sound immediately brings tears to my eyes again. I squeeze her tight against me, rest my cheek against the top of her head, and sigh.

"It's probably for the best that it all happened like it did," I say. "If we had decided to keep him I would have ruined him with some stupid nickname. I probably would have called him Salty Balls or some shit like that. I'm not cut out to be a dad yet, obviously."

She shakes her head. "You'd be a great dad. And one of these days, Salty Balls will be the perfect nickname for one of our kids. Just not yet."

Now I'm the one laughing. "What if we have all girls?"

She shrugs. "Even better."

I smile and keep her held close against me. After last night and being apart from her, knowing how much she was hurting, I know I'll never want to feel that way again. I never want *her* to feel that way again.

"You know what I just realized?" she says. "We've already had sex. I've been kind of bummed because if I had sex with you, it would have made you the seventh person I've ever had sex with and that's a lot. But you'll still be the sixth, because I was already counting you and I didn't even know it."

"I like six," I say. "That's a good number to be. It's actually my favorite number."

"Don't get too excited now that you know we've already had sex," she says. "I'm still making you wait."

"I'll wear you down soon enough," I tease.

I bring one of my hands up to her head and I hold it while I lean forward and kiss her softly on the lips. I stay close to her mouth and make a confession. "I haven't brought this up because we haven't been together that long and I didn't want to scare you off. But now that I know we have a kid together, it makes it less embarrassing."

"Oh, no. What is it?" she asks nervously.

"We graduate in less than a month. I know you and Sky and Holder were planning on going to the same college in Dallas after the summer. I had already applied to a college in Austin, but after I met you I might have applied to Dallas, too. You know . . . in case things worked out with us. I didn't like the thought of being five hours apart."

She tilts her head and looks up at me. "When did you apply?"

I shrug like it's not a big deal. "The night Sky had that dinner for you."

She sits up and looks at me. "That was twenty-four hours after we went out for the first time. You applied to my college after knowing me for one day?"

I nod. "Yeah, but technically I knew you for a whole year. If you look at it that way, it's way less creepy."

She smiles at my logic. "Well? Did you get accepted?"

I nod. "I might have already made living arrangements with Holder, too."

She grins and it's probably the most I've ever loved a smile. "Daniel? This is serious. This thing with us. It's pretty intense, huh?"

I nod. "Yeah. I think we might really be in love this time. No more pretending."

She nods. "Things are so serious now, I think it's time I introduced you to all my brothers."

I stop nodding and start shaking my head back and forth. "I may be exaggerating. I don't love you *that* much."

She laughs. "No, you love me. You love me so much, Daniel. You've loved me since the second I let you accidentally touch my boob."

"No, I think I've loved you since you forced me to stick my tongue in your mouth."

She shakes her head. "No, you've loved me since I let you kiss me in a crowded restaurant next to a dirty diaper."

"Nope. I've loved you since you walked through Sky's bedroom door with that spoon in your mouth."

"Actually, you've loved me since the first time you told me you loved me a year ago. Right here in this room."

I shake my head. "I've loved you since the moment you fell on top of me and said you hated everybody."

She stops smiling. "I've loved you since the moment you said you hated everybody, too."

"I used to hate everybody," I say. "Until I met you."

"I told you I was unhateable." She grins.

"And I told you unhateable isn't even a real word."

Her eyes focus on mine and she takes both my hands, then laces her fingers through them. We stare at each other like we've done so many times before, but this time I feel it in every single part of me. I feel *her* in every part of me and the feeling is new and heavy and intense. I realize in this moment that we just became so much more together than we could ever possibly be alone.

"I love you, Daniel Wesley," she whispers.

"I love you Seven Marie Six Cinderella Jacobs."

She laughs. "Thank you for not turning out to be an asshole."

"Thank you for never asking me to change." I lean forward and kiss the smile that just spread across her lips as I silently thank the universe for sending her back to me.

My fucking angel.

Epilogue

"What in the world is wrong with you, Daniel?" Chunk says, slapping her pen down on the table.

I pause the drumming of my fingers against the wooden table-top. "Nothing." I didn't realize my nervousness was so obvious. Especially to a thirteen-year-old.

"Something's wrong with you," she says. She pushes her homework aside and folds her arms across the table, leaning forward. "Did you break up with Six?"

I shake my head. "No."

"She break up with you?"

"*Hell* no," I say defensively.

"Get in trouble at school?"

I shake my head and look down at the time on my phone. Ten more minutes and I'll leave. I just need ten more minutes.

"You get her pregnant?" Chunk asks.

My eyes dart up to hers and my pulse increases. I technically can't answer that with a no, because . . . well.

"Oh, my god," Chunk says. "You got her pregnant? Daniel! Mom and Dad are gonna *kill* you!"

She pushes away from the table just as my mother walks into the kitchen. Chunk's hands go up to her mouth in disbelief and she's shaking her head, still staring at me. She doesn't know my mother is behind her now. "Daniel, are you stupid? I'm only thirteen, but even *I* know what safe sex is. Christ, I can't believe you got her *pregnant*!"

I'm shaking my head, too flustered to tell her Six isn't pregnant.

My mother is frozen, staring at me with wide eyes. She covers her mouth with her hand at the same moment my father walks into the kitchen. Chunk hears him and spins around.

"What's wrong?" my father asks. "You all look like you've seen a ghost."

Before I have the chance to defend myself or dismiss the words that just came out of Chunk's mouth, my mother turns to face my father. She points at me.

"He got her pregnant," she whispers disbelievingly. "Your son got his girlfriend pregnant."

My father stares silently at my mother. I know I should be standing up right now—denying everything before they all get too worked up, but everything they're saying is technically true.

I *did* get Six pregnant.

However, that was over a year ago and none of them know about that, nor do they *need* to know about it. But Six sure as hell isn't pregnant right now. I know that for a fact. We've been dating for over three months, and I'm sure it'll be at least three more months before she allows me to break that bread.

I don't like that analogy. Doesn't even make sense.

Jump that fence?

Nah, that's not sexy enough.

Cross that finish line?

Nope. It'll be more like a starting *line.*

Tap that ass?

Meh. Too tacky.

Poke that potato?

"Daniel?" my father asks, pulling my gaze to his. He doesn't look happy, but he also doesn't look angry. Which is weird, since he's just been told he'll likely be a grandfather, and he's only forty-five. He's looking at me like he's confused. "How can Six be pregnant?" he asks, shaking his head. "Every time you're with her you still come home and take those embarrassingly long showers."

I swear to God. Why do these people continue to bring that up?

I look over at Chunk and shake my head. "Six isn't pregnant," I tell all of them. "Chunk just has an overactive imagination."

A collective sigh comes from the three of them. My mother slaps her hand to her heart and releases a quick "Oh dear good lord, Jesus Christ, holy shit, thank *god!*" She blows out a calming breath after her slew of blasphemy.

Chunk rolls her eyes when she realizes I'm telling the truth. She takes her seat across from me and pulls her homework back in front of her. "Well, if she's not pregnant then what in the heck are you so nervous about?"

Oh yeah. This little distraction almost helped me forget everything that's about to happen. As soon as the night's plans invade my mind again, I have to inhale slowly through my nose to remind my lungs they need air.

"What is it, Danny boy?" my father asks. "She break up with you?"

I drop my head into my hands, frustrated at how damn nosey they all are.

"No," I groan. "She didn't break up with me. I also didn't break up with her. She's not pregnant, we aren't having sex, and I didn't get in trouble at school!" I'm standing now, pacing back and forth. The three of them are watching me practically have a meltdown. I finally turn and face them with my hands planted firmly on my hips. "I'm just freaking out a little bit, okay? I'm supposed to be at her house right now, because she wants me to meet her brothers. *All* of them. Like *right now*."

My father looks amused, and it kind of pisses me off.

"How many brothers does she have?" my mother asks. Her voice is soothing, like she's about to give me the pep talk I'm desperately in need of.

"Four. And they're all older than she is."

My mother's mouth presses into a thin line as she gently nods her head. "Oh, boy," she says in a whisper. "You're screwed, Daniel." She turns around and walks into the kitchen. I'm stuck in the same position, wondering where her words of advice went.

My father is nodding his head, still with that annoying smile plastered on his face. "I really don't like Six," he says. "I'm starting to hate her, actually. Three months now, and she's *still* holding firm to that trophy?"

"Stop, Dad," I say immediately. "You are *not* allowed to talk about my sex life. And you're especially not allowed to use shitty analogies to reference the fact that Six is making me wait."

He holds his palms up defensively. "Sorry." He laughs. "Besides, I forget that your sister isn't an adult sometimes." He pats Chunk on her shoulder. "Sorry, Chunk. I'll never mention in front of you again how your brother's girlfriend won't allow him to kill that mockingbird." He pulls out a chair and sits at the table. Chunk and I groan at the same time.

"Dad," she says. "You just ruined my favorite book with that comparison. Thanks a lot."

He winks at her before turning to face me again. "You'll be fine, Danny boy. Just don't be yourself at all, and they'll have no choice but to love you."

I grab my jacket off the back of the chair and pull it on as I exit the kitchen. "You all still suck," I mumble as I walk out the front door.

•   •   •

I don't remember walking into her house. I don't remember anything I said as I was being introduced to any of them. I don't even remember how I made it to my seat, but here I am—being stared down across the kitchen table by four of the most intimidating men I've ever met. I was hoping we were going to make it through the meal with everyone stuffing his face and no one addressing me directly.

That didn't even last a whole bite.

One of them just asked what my plans are after graduation, but I'm not sure which one he is. He's the one who looks the most like Six because he's the only blond, but he's also the largest of the four. His hands make his fork look like a toothpick.

I look down at my hands and frown, because they make my fork look like a spatula. I set my fork down on the table before they notice how tiny they all make my hands look.

Six taps my leg under the table, reminding me to speak. I gently clear my throat. "I'm not sure."

My voice sounds like a damn child's, compared to the four of their voices. I've never even thought about my voice or how it might sound to an outsider until this moment. I've never really thought about how my hands might make a fork look until now, either. I've also never really thought about breaking up with Six before, but . . . *nah*. I don't care how scary they are or how much they hate me. There's no way in hell I'm breaking up with Six.

"Well, are you at least going to college?" Evan asks.

I know Evan's name. He's the one closest in age to Six. He's also the only one who smiled at me when he introduced himself, so I made sure to remember him. That way, if the other three decide to jump me, I can scream Evan's name for help, since he'd be the only one likely to defend me.

"I am going to college," I say with a nod. *Finally. A question I can answer.* "I'm attending the same one Six will be at."

Evan nods his head slowly, digesting that response with a bite of food.

"What if the two of you aren't dating after graduation?" the big one says.

"Aaron, shut up," Six says with a roll of her eyes. She squeezes my leg under the table. "Stop antagonizing him."

Aaron's eyes are still locked with mine. "Do you think I'm antagonizing you?" he asks coolly. "I just thought we were having polite conversation."

I swallow the lump in my throat and shake my head. "You're fine," I say. "I get it. I have two sisters. Granted, one of them is older than me but I still give the douchebags she brings home a hard time. And don't even get me started on Chunk. The first guy she brings home doesn't stand a chance. I already hate him, and the kid probably doesn't even know she exists yet."

The brother directly across from me smiles a little bit. It might be my imagination, but I know for a fact he's not frowning anymore.

"Chunk?" Aaron asks. "Six said you give nicknames to people. That's what you call your little sister?"

I nod.

"What do you call Six?" the brother across from me says. I'm pretty sure his name is Michael. I have a fifty-fifty chance of being right, considering the brother on the end could also be named Michael. It's either that or Zachary.

Six bumps my leg again, and I realize I haven't answered him. "Cinderella," I blurt out.

They're all staring at me now, waiting for an explanation for that one. I don't think I want to give them one. How do you tell four brothers that you call their little sister Cinderella because you had random hot sex with her in the maintenance closet of a school?

"Why do you call her that?" Aaron asks. He turns toward the brother at the end. "Zach, didn't you used to have a turtle named Cinderella?"

Zach. Zach is the quietest one.

He shakes his head. "Ariel," he says, correcting Aaron. "I had a thing for the little mermaid."

The one I can now assume is Michael, based on the process of elimination, says, "You didn't answer the question. Why do you call her Cinderella?"

Six laughs under her breath, and I know she finds this extremely amusing, even though I sort of wish I would choke to death on a turkey bone so I could be put out of my misery.

"I call her Cinderella because the first time I laid eyes on her, I thought she was so beautiful she couldn't be real. Girls like her were reserved for fairy tales and fantasies."

I'm proud of my own answer. Didn't know I could bullshit under pressure like this.

The quiet one straightens up in his seat. *Zach.* "So you're saying you fantasize about our little sister?"

What the . . .

"Jesus, Zach!" Six yells. "Stop it! All four of you, stop it! You're just interrogating him to amuse yourselves."

All four of them begin to laugh. Evan winks at me, and they all begin eating again.

I'm still not brave enough to pick up my fork in front of them.

"We're just messing with you," Zach says with a laugh. "We never get to do this, because you're the first guy Six has ever let us meet."

I turn and look at Six. I didn't know this little fact, and I think I kind of love it. "Am I, really?" I ask her. "You've never introduced anyone to your brothers before?"

Six smiles and gives her head a small shake. "Why would I?" she says. "No other guy has ever deserved to meet them."

I immediately pull her to me, and I give her a loud smack on the lips. "Dammit, I love you, girl," I say, finding the confidence to finally pick up my fork again. It looks like a fork now rather than a spatula.

I dig in to the food and take a huge bite.

All four of her brothers are quietly staring back at me.

All four are smiling.

•   •   •

I fall onto Sky's bed with a huge sigh, landing on my back next to Holder, who is propped up against the headboard.

"I see you survived the meeting of the brothers," he says, looking down at me.

"Barely," I say. "But I think I won them over in the end."

"How'd you manage that?" Sky asks. She's sitting on the other side of Holder, messing with her phone.

"I gave them all nicknames. They found me highly amusing."

Holder laughs. "Only you, Daniel."

"Where's Six?" Sky asks me.

"She didn't feel like coming over." I pull myself up to a standing position. "I just wanted to let Holder know I'm still alive. I'm gonna head back over there."

Before I walk back to her bedroom window, I see a frown form on Sky's face. I don't like it, because she never frowns. She's one of the happiest people I've ever met.

Come to think of it, I also didn't like the fact that Six didn't want to come over here tonight. It was weird, because she didn't feel like it last night, either.

It hits me that something is up between the two of them.

"What's wrong, Cheese Tits?"

Her eyes shoot up to mine and she forces a smile. "Nothing."

I take a step back toward the bed. "I call bullshit," I say. "When's the last time you spoke to my girl?"

She glances down at her phone again and shrugs. Holder sees what I've noticed, and he puts an arm around her.

"Hey," he says reassuringly. "What's wrong, babe?" He pulls her in close to him and kisses her on the side of the head, just as a tear falls from her eyes. She quickly pulls her hand up to wipe it away, but Holder notices. He sits up straighter and turns to face her at the same time I take a seat back down on the bed.

"Sky, what's wrong?" he says, urging her to look up at him.

She shrugs it off, shaking her head. "It's probably nothing," she says. "I'm sure she's just tired or something."

"Who's tired?" I ask her. "Six?"

She nods.

Her assumption confuses me, because Six isn't tired. She seemed fine tonight.

"It's just that she hasn't been over here in the three days we've been out for Christmas break," Sky says. "She also hasn't texted or called me back. I think she's mad at me, but I have no idea what I did."

I immediately stand up. "Well, we have to fix this," I say, somewhat panicked. "She can't be mad at you. Y'all aren't allowed to fight." I begin pacing the room. Holder is watching me with those narrowed, intimidating eyes of his.

"Daniel, calm down. They're girls. Girls argue sometimes."

I shake my head, refusing to accept it. I'm pacing again. "Not Sky and Six. They aren't like all the other girls, Holder. You know that. They don't fight. They *can't* fight. We're supposed to go to college together. They're supposed to be roommates." I turn and face him, coming to a pause. "We're a team, man. Me and Six and you and Sky. Me and you. Six and Sky. They can't break up. I won't let it happen." I'm already heading to the window. Sky is pleading with me not to make a big deal out of it, but it's too late for that. I'm climbing in Six's bedroom window and my heart is racing, and there's no way I can let them keep this up for another day.

Six is lying on her bed, staring up at the ceiling. She doesn't turn to look at me when I enter her room. "What's the matter?" I ask her.

"Nothing," she says immediately.

Bullshit.

I kneel down on the bed and move toward her until I'm on top of her, looking down at her face. "Bullshit."

She turns away from me, so I grab her chin and make her look at me again. "Why are you mad at Sky?"

She shakes her head, and I can see in her eyes that she isn't mad at Sky. "I'm not mad at her," she says, sounding offended. I want to feel relieved, but something is still bothering her.

She looks worried. Scared, even. I feel like an asshole for not recognizing it earlier, but she *was* more quiet than usual during dinner.

And last night. She was really quiet last night.

Shit. Maybe she's mad at *me.*

"I'm sorry," I tell her. She looks up at me, confused.

"For what?"

I shrug. "I don't know. For whatever I did. Sometimes I do or say really stupid shit, and I don't even realize I'm doing it until I hurt someone's feelings. So if that's what's wrong, I'm sorry." I lower my head and kiss her. "I'm really, really sorry."

She pushes against my chest, and I sit back on my knees. She pulls herself to a seated position in front of me. "You didn't do anything wrong, Daniel. You're perfect."

I love that answer, but hate that I still don't know what's upsetting her.

"It's just that . . ." Her voice grows quiet, and she looks down at her lap. "If I tell you something . . . you swear you'll never ever tell Holder?"

I immediately nod my head. As much as I'll always be there for Holder, there's no way in hell I'd ever break Six's trust. "I swear."

Her eyes meet mine, and she's silently telling me I better be serious, because whatever she's about to tell me is a big deal.

I don't like this look in her eyes. Luckily, she scoots off the bed and walks to her desk. She picks up her laptop and brings it back to the bed with her. "I want to show you something." She opens the laptop and pulls up a minimized screen before turning it to face me. "And please never bring this up again, Daniel."

I pull the laptop in front of me and begin reading.

Words like *missing child* and *reward* and dates and statements and pictures are all flooding my eyes. I'm shaking my head, because the words on the screen don't make any sense when they're referring to the picture of the little girl who looks just like Sky.

"What is this, Six?" I ask.

She pulls the laptop back out of my hands. "I'm not sure," she says. "I left my computer here while I was in Italy. I just noticed a few days ago that this was in my search history from several months ago. I don't know what to do, Daniel," she says, looking down at the screen. "It's her. This is Sky. I would ask her about it, but I think if she knew about it, she would have said something to me."

I'm still trying to process what I just saw on the computer and all the words coming out of Six's mouth.

"What if it was Karen who used my computer? Or Holder? Or someone else entirely? I don't know for sure that Sky was the one looking this up, and I'm scared if I say anything to her, I'll be bringing up something she doesn't even want to know."

I don't even hesitate. I grab the laptop and stand up. "Six? This isn't something you keep to yourself. If you don't tell her now, nothing will ever be the same between the two of you, because you'll feel too guilty to talk to her." I grab her hand. "Come on. Let's just rip off the Band-Aid."

Her eyes are wide and scared, but I don't care. She can't keep something like this bottled up. And if this little girl really is Sky, she has every right to know.

We stand up but before we head to the window, I pull Six in for a tight hug. I kiss her on top of the head and tell her it'll be fine. "It might not even have anything to do with her," I say. "It could just be a coincidence."

• • •

We're standing at the foot of Sky's bed, watching her. Holder has the laptop and Sky's hand is covering her mouth. They're both staring wide-eyed at the screen.

They're both quiet.

"I'm sorry," Six says. "I don't know what it is or who was looking it up . . . but I didn't know how to tell you. I also didn't know how *not* to tell you."

Sky finally pulls her eyes away from the computer, but they don't fall on Six. They slide up to Holder's face. He looks at her calmly and expels a deep breath, then gently closes the laptop.

Their reactions are way too weird. I expected a little crying. A little bit of yelling, maybe. Perhaps a few flying objects I'd have to duck from.

Holder pushes the laptop back toward Six. "We don't need to see it," he says. "She already knows."

Six gasps, and I grab her hand. Sky stands up at the same time Holder does. She walks toward us and places her hands on Six's shoulders, looking at her calmly. "I would have told you, Six," she says. "But if this ever gets out . . . it's not me that would be affected. It's Karen. That's the only reason I haven't told you."

Six's eyes are wide and hurt, but I can tell she's also trying to be understanding. "So it was Karen?" Six whispers, backing away from Sky.

Sky nods her head. "Everything you read about my childhood was true," she says. She looks at Holder for permission to continue. He nods, but looks at me and shoots me that look. The look that tells me that whatever I'm about to hear will never leave this room.

"Karen did what she had to do because my father was a monster," Sky says. Tears fill her eyes and Holder steps up behind her and places his hands on her shoulders. He kisses the top of her head, pulling her back against his chest. "I found out everything after Holder told me. While you were in Italy."

I look over at Holder. "How did *you* know?"

He regards me silently for a few seconds. He looks as if he regrets not telling me, but I don't blame him. It's not my business. "I recognized her. Me and Les . . . we used to live next door to them before we moved here. We were all friends. I was there when it happened."

Six and I both begin to pace the room. It's too much to take in. I'm not sure I even want to know something like this about them. That's a lot of pressure . . . having this kind of knowledge in my head. I don't like that they know I know this now. I liked how things were yesterday. I liked how easy it was, before all this new information was planted in my head. Now I have to bury it and pretend it's not there, but it's so huge. It's too much for Sky and Holder to have to trust us with this kind of thing.

"I got Six pregnant!" I blurt out, feeling somewhat relieved that I'm giving them a secret, too. "Last year. She was the girl in the closet," I say to Holder. I told him about her once before, so I know he'll know what I'm referring to. "We had sex without even knowing what the other looked like. She got pregnant and found out when she was in Italy. She didn't know who I was and she was scared, so she gave our son up for adoption and . . . *yeah*," I say, pausing to face all of them. I drop my hands to my hips and take a calming breath. "We had a baby."

They're all facing me now. Six is looking at me like I'm suddenly not perfect anymore. "Daniel?" she whispers. "What the hell?"

She's mad at me. She's hurt that I would just blurt out the biggest secret she's ever had in her entire life.

I walk to her and place my hands on her shoulders. "I had to make the score even. We had to tell them. We know this really huge thing about them and unless they know *our* really huge thing, it wouldn't be even between us. Things would be weird."

I don't know if I'm making any sense to her.

"Six?" Sky whispers. "Is that true?"

Six pulls away from me and looks down. She nods, ashamed.

"Why didn't you tell me?"

Six looks back up at Sky. "Why didn't you tell me your name isn't even *Sky*?" Six says in defense.

Sky nods her head slowly, understanding that she can't really blame Six and Six can't really blame her. We're all even now. We stand quietly, each of us absorbing everything that's been revealed.

"Let's spit on it," I say. I hold my palm up and spit into my hand. "None of this will ever leave the room." I hold my hand out between the four of them and urge them to do the same.

"I'm not swapping spit with you," Sky says with a disgusted look on her face.

Six lifts her eyes to meet mine. "Me, neither," she says, crinkling up her nose.

I shake my head in confusion. "It's *spit*," I say. "You don't have a problem sticking your tongue in my mouth, but you won't touch a little spit with your hand?"

She winces. "That's different."

Holder steps forward and holds up his pinky. I laugh at him. "Really, Holder? You want us to *pinky* swear?"

He glares at me. "I'd like you to know there is nothing wrong with holding pinkies," he says defensively. "Now wipe the spit off your hand like a man and hold my damn pinky."

I can't believe I'm about to pinky swear. What are we, five?

I do what he asks and wipe my hand on my jeans, then we all step toward him. We wrap our pinkies together, and we all look each other in the eyes. No one says a word, because we don't have to. We all know that no matter what happens, everything we've learned about each other tonight will never leave this room.

Once we all release our pinkies, we step back and observe the moment silently. After several minutes of awkwardness, I turn to Six.

"Want to go make out at the park?"

She nods and expels a breath of relief. "Yep."

Thank God.

I turn to Holder and Sky. "We all still on for dinner at my house tomorrow night?"

Holder nods. "Sure. As long as you tell your dad he's not allowed to bring up anything embarrassing."

Has Holder not learned anything from watching me?

"He's my dad, Holder. If I tell him that, he'd take it as a dare."

Holder laughs. I step forward and pull him and Sky both in for a hug. I reach my arm behind me and grab Six, pulling her in with us. "Best friends forever," I tell them. "I love y'all so damn much."

They all groan and pull away from me. "Go make out with your girlfriend, Daniel," Holder says.

I wink at Six and push her toward the window.

I know it won't be tonight, but I'm still curious how long it'll be before she finally lets me pop her cork.

Nope. Still not sexy enough.

Smash her burger?

Oh God, no.

Plant my flower in her garden?

What the hell, Daniel?

Make love to her?

Yeah. That's it. That's the one.

●　●　●

The end.

My Cinderella Story

Two years ago I was living in a mobile home with my husband and three sons, and working at a job that paid $9 per hour. I was happy with what I had been given, but it was not exactly the life I had envisioned for my family or myself.

Since childhood, I dreamed of being a writer, but for thirty-one years I made excuse after excuse as to why I couldn't be one:

> *"I have no spare time."*
> *"My writing isn't good enough."*
> *"I'll never get published."*
> *"I'm too busy writing excuses to write a novel."*

In reality, the only reason I was not pursuing my dream was because I thought dreams were just that . . . *dreams*. Intangible. Unrealistic. Childish.

I've always been a realist, never looking at the glass half empty *or* half full. I'm the type of person who is just thankful to have a glass at *all*. That was exactly how I viewed my life two years ago. I never allowed myself to be ungrateful or wish for more.

My husband and I both come from low-income families, and we did our best to make ends meet and put ourselves through college. I took out student loans and we both worked full-time, trading days off so we didn't have to pay for child care. I received a Bachelor of Social Work from Texas A&M University–Commerce in December 2005, two months before giving birth to our third child.

After a few years of our moving around from rent-house to rent-house and my working as a social worker, my parents helped us buy a three-bedroom, two-bath singlewide mobile home that was barely more than one thousand square feet. I felt blessed to have three healthy children, a wonderful, supportive husband, and a roof over our heads.

As happy as I was, I felt like something was missing. That childhood dream of writing a book kept resurfacing and I kept pushing it back down with more excuses.

Then in October 2011, after watching one of my own children follow one of his dreams, I began to entertain the thought that maybe dreams *are* tangible.

My middle child, who was eight years old at the time, wanted to audition for the local community theater. I was thrilled at his bravery, but when he actually got the part, I was forced to face reality. There was no way I could work eleven-hour days and take him to rehearsals five evenings a week. My husband was working as a long-haul truck driver at the time and was home only a few days each month, so I was essentially a single mother. However, my children's happiness has always been my priority, and I was not about to let my son down. I received help from a friend who dropped him off at my work after school so we could make it to his rehearsals, while my mother watched my other two children.

For the next two months, I sat in the audience for three hours each evening watching rehearsals. I watched my son on stage and was filled with pride at seeing him pursue his passion at such a young age. Those moments prompted me to think about my own childhood passions and how much I dreamed of becoming a writer. When I was younger, I wrote during every free moment and on any surface I could find. My mother would enthusiastically read my "Mystery Bob" stories that I penned from crayon on scraps of paper stapled together. I continued to write for fun throughout high school and even pursued journalism my first year in college. However, after I married my high school sweetheart and had our first son by the age of twenty, my childhood dream began to fade as the responsibilities of real life set in. As much as I wanted to be a writer, it seemed impossible. Instead, I held on to my self-doubt and insecurities for ten years, allowing responsibility after responsibility to become my crutch.

As I sat in the audience of my son's rehearsals, I saw something in him that had long been dormant in myself—*creative passion*.

While it was a remarkable moment to see my son pursuing his dream, it was also a rude awakening. I was doing my children a disservice by setting the example that it's okay to put yourself last . . . to put your own desires on the back burner while you take care of everyone else. I made a promise to myself that night that I would start writing again, even if it was only for my own enjoyment. After coming to this realization, I began to find inspiration and motivation from other areas.

One of my biggest motivators came from an Avett Brothers concert I attended with my sister. It was one of the best experiences of my life, not because we were in the front row, but because of a few powerful seconds during their song "Head Full of Doubt, Road Full of Promise." I had heard these lyrics sung many times before, yet the meaning had never resonated with me until that very moment.

"Decide what to be, and go be it."

The sentence was simple and straightforward; yet it left a profound impression on me. For days, the words continued to repeat in my head until they finally sunk in: if I wanted to be a writer, there was no reason I couldn't *"go be it."* I pulled out my laptop at one of the play rehearsals, and I wrote the very first line to *Slammed*:

"Kel and I load the last two boxes into the U-Haul."

It was the first sentence to the book that would change my life.

At the time, I was writing the book only for myself, but my mother was a huge supporter of my writing. After all, she still had the riveting "Mystery Bob" stories I'd written in crayon. Even though I knew her opinion would be biased, I let her read what I had completed. She loved it, as any good mother would, and began pestering me for the next chapters.

I also allowed my boss and both of my sisters to read the first several chapters and they, too, asked for more. The fact that they wanted more of the story gave me the inspiration to continue. I enjoyed it so much that I wrote at every opportunity. I would put my children to bed at night, write until well after midnight and then have to be at work at seven o'clock the next morning. By the end of December, I had traded so much sleep in favor of writing that I had a complete manuscript. I also had three children who were now very adept at working a microwave.

When I reached those two final words, *The End*, I felt like I had just achieved my childhood dream, despite not having a real book, a publisher, or even an audience.

After word spread that I had written a book, friends and family began requesting to read it. I couldn't afford to have paperbacks printed, so I researched and found Amazon's Kindle Direct Publishing program. After days of more research and attempting to learn everything I could about self-publishing, I uploaded my book to Amazon.

I had no expectations. I never even tried to get the book traditionally published, because in my mind I had already achieved my dream of writing the book. I didn't think there was a chance that people who didn't know me would ever read it.

The opposite happened. Hundreds of people, complete strangers, started to order my book. I began receiving requests for a sequel from those readers and, since I enjoyed writing the first book so much, I was more than thrilled to deliver a sequel. I released *Point of Retreat* in February 2012. Soon after, I began receiving royalty payments. Everything was happening so fast, I held on to every moment, afraid it would all end overnight. Since the sales weren't guaranteed, I refused to accept the possibility that things could improve from there. I was waiting for the excitement, positive reviews, and requests for more books to come to an end, because it was all too good to be true.

But it didn't end. Every day brought new readers until the books eventually hit the *New York Times* Best Sellers List. Publishers took notice of the rapid success of both books and, after signing up with a literary agent, I accepted a publishing offer from Atria Books.

My life became so busy that I had to quit my job in order to focus on writing full-time. I was worried there wouldn't be enough money in it to support my family, but with the release of my third book, *Hopeless*, in December 2012, I was finally convinced that this was now my career. *Hopeless* went on to hit #1 on the *New York Times* Best Sellers List and was Amazon's best selling self-published e-book of 2013, and their sixteenth bestselling e-book overall of 2013.

We moved out of our mobile home less than ten months ago and now live in a lake house that we never thought could be ours. Each morning I wake up and I'm consumed with disbelief that this is now our life. We've been able to pay off all our debt and create college funds for our boys. We've also donated to several charities as a way to give back for all the incredible things that have happened to us.

In the past two years, I have gone from a mother who refused to believe that a childhood fantasy could become a reality, to a writer with five books that have all become *New York Times* Best Sellers, a free novella, and two more novels to be published this year.

Each of those books is tangible proof that if you have the courage to make them happen, dreams are very real and attainable. All you have to do is find what inspires you, which can be something as simple as a song lyric or a child's smile on stage. Then you have to make the long, brave effort, which can be as daunting as sitting down at a computer, facing a blank page, and not giving up until you reach the finish line.

Despite all the great experiences and accomplishments that have come after it, I still consider my proudest moment to be the first time I typed the words *The End*.

For that was my beginning.

Colleen Hoover

About the Author

Colleen Hoover is the #1 *Sunday Times* bestselling author of more than twenty-three novels, including *It Ends with Us*, *All Your Perfects*, *Ugly Love* and *Verity*. Colleen lives in Texas with her husband and their three boys.

For more information, please visit colleenhoover.com.

Discover more from
COLLEEN HOOVER

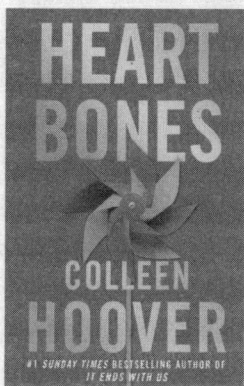